Praise for
Finding Alice

"Kudos aplenty for Melody Carlson's latest, *Finding Alice*. We tumble down the dark hole with Alice and hope against hope that the voices she sorts through on her otherworld journey will take her at last to a peaceful place. All the while we wonder: How do we make sense of the sometimes competing voices that bombard us each day, voices of news and neighborhood, charity and church? Is that person a friend or foe? How will we know? And most important, will we find the one voice we're meant to listen to before someone like Alice's friend Amelia threatens and turns us away? This is a compelling story filled with insights not only about mental illness but about what passes for normal in a sometimes crazy world. I kept reading, knowing that in finding Melody Carlson's Alice safe at last, I'd be finding a part of myself."

—JANE KIRKPATRICK, a licensed clinical social worker and best-
selling author of *A Name of Her Own* and *Every Fixed Star*

"*Finding Alice* is a journey to one of the most unusual places I've ever been. Melody addresses the complex issues of mental illness with wisdom and compassion, painting a subtle portrait of healing grace. I believed every word."

—LISA SAMSON, author of *The Church Ladies*
and *Women's Intuition*

"*Finding Alice* takes us down the rabbit hole of mental illness and gives us a looking-glass view of the pain of schizophrenia mixed lovingly into the grace and mercy of God's love. Melody Carlson's style is mature and bitingly funny, and her gift for connecting our heart to the character's plight also connects us to the complicated human condition and our need for one another."

—PATRICIA HICKMAN, best-selling author of *Fallen Angels* and *Sandpebbles*

"Melody has crafted a superb story that takes readers into Alice's mind and world. I was captured from the first page and filled with a deep sense of hope by the last page. This book will bring insight and courage to anyone who has an Alice in their life."

—ROBIN JONES GUNN, best-selling author of the Glenbrooke series and the Sisterchick novels

"*Finding Alice* offers the riveting journey of a young woman teetering on the edge of reality. Melody Carlson skillfully creates Alice's schizophrenic world and then brings this endearing character to a place of genuine hope. I laughed and cried and cared deeply for Alice. Thank you, Melody, for an enlightened and compassionate story!"

—LESLIE GOULD, author of *Garden of Dreams*

"The Christian community has not often known what to do with the very real and deeply complex issue of mental illness. In *Finding Alice*, Melody Carlson confronts it in an insightful and creative way, providing clues to its nature and treatment and reminding us that Hope lives even in the dark worlds of such illnesses."

—JO KADLECEK, author of *Fear: A Spiritual Navigation*

finding
ALICE

finding
ALICE

To Debbe—

MELODY
CARLSON

Enjoyed
Seeing You...
Melody Carlson

WaterBrook
PRESS

FINDING ALICE
PUBLISHED BY WATERBROOK PRESS
12265 Oracle Blvd., Suite 200
Colorado Springs, Colorado 80921
A division of Random House, Inc.

ISBN 1-57856-773-4

Library of Congress Cataloging-in-Publication Data
Carlson, Melody.
   Finding Alice : a novel / Melody Carlson.—1st ed.
     p. cm.
   ISBN 1-57856-773-4
  1. Women college students—Fiction. 2. Schizophrenics—Fiction. I. Title.
   PS3553.A73257F56 2003
   813'.54—dc21

                          2003014018

Printed in the United States of America
2005

10 9 8 7 6 5 4

Dedicated with love to Gabriel Douglas Carlson,
one of the bravest men I know.
Without your help and expertise, this book would not exist.
Thank you for sharing your life and experience with me.

chapter ONE

Down the Rabbit Hole

I'm not sure how it all started or even why. I was simply walking through my life, minding my own business, when someone pulled the earth out from under me. And I began to fall, down, down, down. Yet I don't think I even realized I was falling, at least not in the beginning. It felt more like a curious adventure. Not so unlike another Alice I once knew.

I still remember that rainy day back in the fifth grade when my mother caught me reading *Alice's Adventures in Wonderland*. It was during spring break, and I was bored silly and had decided to snoop around our musty attic while my mother went to the store. I discovered this book, along with a few others, packed neatly into an olive drab metal footlocker that appeared to have survived some ancient war. I'm guessing it had belonged to my grandfather who served in the Pacific during World War II. My mother's maiden name was written in a childish script inside the book cover, so I assumed this book must've belonged to her at one time—another lifetime ago. Although I felt certain she would never admit as much, not to me anyway. I also suspected this was *not* a book that our fundamentalist church would approve, since it was neither historical nor biographical and definitely not biblical. I could imagine Miss Finley, my teacher at the conservative Christian school, raising her eyebrows in dismay to see her star pupil resorting to such "worldly trash," as I'm sure she would have called it. But I was drawn to it anyway.

For one thing, the odd looking young heroine's name was the same as my own. Plus we both had curly blond hair, only hers was much longer and cut bluntly across the ends, similar to a broom, I remember thinking. And I'll admit that the story seemed a bit strange as I first started reading, unlike anything I'd ever seen before, but I was quickly pulled in and had just reached the part where the Duchess throws her howling baby (really a pig) at a confused Alice when my mother walked in and startled me.

"What are you doing up here, Alice?"

"Reading." I closed the book and placed it facedown in my lap.

My mother stepped closer with a worried expression drawing her brows together in a way that creased her forehead. "Oh, dear, you're not reading *that*, are you?"

"It's good, Mom. Did you read it when you were a girl?"

"Well…" She shook her head, flustered I'm sure because she didn't want to lie—that would be a sin—but she didn't want to admit it either.

"I like it."

Mom moved a step closer. "They say the author was on drugs when he wrote it," she announced in a flat voice.

I frowned. Even in my sheltered little world, I knew that drugs were bad. "How do you know he was on drugs?"

"Everyone knows that." Then she held out her hand for the book.

Feeling cheated and wondering what would become of poor Alice, I relinquished my prize. It wasn't until I was seventeen, when I was finally allowed to attend public school, that I finished reading that book as well as its sequel, *Through the Looking Glass.* But the stories, although intriguing, had lost some of their magic by then. Somehow they just didn't seem quite the same. Or maybe it was me. I read them again for an English literature project just last year. My theory was that a secret code was contained within the rhythmic text, and I did manage to unwind something or other, or so I thought at the time. Although my professor told me I was "stretching things a bit." I think those were his exact words too. Of course, he didn't seem to have much imagination either.

But back to falling down my rabbit hole. Back to when my own strange "adventures in wonderland" began. So there I was just starting my senior year of college, maintaining a fairly decent GPA, dating someone I thought I loved, and basically keeping my life on track. But the next thing I knew I was getting locked in the hospital by an old coot in a stained lab coat.

Now, other than my grandmother, I never really knew anyone who'd been labeled *crazy* before. And I never really knew her that well. She's mostly a vague childhood memory that has faded over the years. The only times I ever actually saw the poor woman were at various mental institutions, and that was between her brief escapades when she'd managed to live on the city streets until someone tracked her down and brought her back to "the home," which was anything but. However, the few times I did go to visit her with my mother, who was always edgy and nervous and never stayed longer than thirty minutes, my grandmother was so drugged up that she didn't recognize either of us anyway.

To this day I despise the smell in those institutions—a mixture of overcooked green beans, stale urine, and Lysol disinfectant that combine to emit an odor reminiscent of something dead and rotting. As a child I assumed it was probably the stench of the unlucky residents confined there. But despite the putrid smell, something about those places did engage my childish curiosity, and I stared unashamedly, in fascination, at the variety of people sitting around on sagging sofas or in molded plastic chairs or stainless steel wheelchairs, many of them with their heads hanging limply, discarded marionettes with their strings cut.

"Alice," my mother would hiss at me as she clutched the handle of her purse tighter, *"don't stare!"*

But I did anyway. And I thought to myself, No wonder these people are here. Why, it's plain to see that they're all flipping mad. But I never, never in a thousand years dreamed I would find myself residing in a place like that someday. But as it turns out, I've been wrong about a number of things.

chapter TWO

Drink Me

So here I am, several weeks into my fall term at Portland State. It's my senior year, and I am lugging my stuff up the stairs to my new studio apartment on the edge of campus. It's raining sheets of bullet-size drops outside, which doesn't help the hideous cold I've been fighting all week. I cough and hack as I dig through my backpack until I locate my precious Robitussin, which I guzzle straight from the bottle as if it's labeled "drink me," like the bottle for that other Alice. But this helps to numb my aching throat as well as to dull my senses. Anyway, this is what I tell myself as I replace the childproof lid and survey my dismal new surroundings. The apartment is small and dark, with only one window, and it smells as if the last tenant smoked heavily.

Not for the first time today, I wonder why on earth I am doing this. I know I never would've left the security of my dorm room if I hadn't planned to share this particular space with my boyfriend, Shay Reynolds. Naturally, I haven't divulged this information to my mom since I know she'll freak. Not that we talk much, but I figured I should let her know about my change of address. This is especially important due to the fact that she's still helping with my college expenses since my dad's Social Security doesn't quite cover everything. But in the case of my mom, ignorance really is bliss.

Anyway, I had decided, with Shay's loving encouragement, that since this was my senior year, it was about time for me to experience a little freedom, a little autonomy, maybe even a little fun. Besides, with graduation not too far off, I knew I could get a job if my mom eventually found out and pulled the plug on me.

Then, less than a week after I'd paid my nonrefundable deposit and signed the six-month lease, Shay decided to break up with me. I guess I should've suspected something when he informed me that he didn't want to sign the lease since his credit rating was in the toilet. For a "smarter than average girl," I can be awfully gullible.

"It's not you," he kindly assured me just a few days ago. As if that's not the oldest line in the book. Then he pushed a lock of sandy hair off his forehead and tossed me one of his famous smiles. "It's me, Alice. I'm just not ready for that kind of commitment yet. I hope you can understand."

"Understand?" I echoed meekly, although I wanted to cry out, *Why are you doing this to me?* "No, I guess not. It's probably for the best."

He patted me on the back. "You're so cool, Alice. I really hope we can keep being friends."

I nodded and said, "Sure," then turned away in time to escape being seen with two streams of tears running down my face. I don't like to cry in public. But I did cry myself to sleep for the next two nights. Last night I didn't cry. But I didn't sleep either. I just kept replaying every single scene of our relationship through my head.

Shay and I had been together for nearly a year, and I guess I really thought it would last forever. Besides Tommy Randall back in fifth grade, I suppose this was my first real boyfriend, and I felt as if someone had punched me and drained the very breath of life out of me.

But I suppose that's being overly melodramatic. Anyway, I'm sure that's what my mom would say. Naturally, I've never told her anything about Shay. Why would I? I knew she would not approve of my dating a boy who didn't go to church, not to mention "fornicating" with him, which is how I'm sure she and her church friends would refer to the idea of the two of us sharing accommodations, regardless of whether it's true. But by the same token, she would have little compassion for my aching heart now. I'm sure she would say that it's my own fault and God's way of chastising me for my folly. *Folly* is a word that is liberally volleyed around at Salvation Center. Naturally, they have an entire vocabulary that members are required to know. I used to think the word *folly* was simply their attempt at levity when discussing sin issues. Not that they think sin is funny. No, not on your life! But I try not to think about those things anymore.

Of course, I realize my relationship with Shay had its flaws. It's not that I'm stupid or blind even. I was well aware that Shay took me too much for granted. And it always bothered me when his gaze casually wandered off to check out other girls. But even so, it was a low blow to be dumped for a freshman who giggles like a thirteen-year-old. Her name is Kiki, of all things, and she reminds me of Britney Spears. I saw them holding hands and laughing near the soccer fields close to campus. I was on my way to class but couldn't bear to sit through the French Revolution. I try to quit thinking about Shay. Why torture myself?

I attempt to distract myself from him as I pry open a cardboard box, but I am interrupted by a neighbor who has wandered into my apartment. I assume I've left the door ajar and am not terribly surprised by this woman's appearance since people tend to come and go as they please back at the dorm. I figure she's simply being friendly. I smile at her and say "hey" as I stoop over the box, struggling to remove a heavy stack of English lit books. Did I ever finish unpacking that box? Come to think of it, I'm not sure I ever unpacked much of anything that fall.

"You should scoot your bed up against that wall over there, away from the door and the window," she instructs me with a serene confidence that catches my attention. She sounds like a veteran helping the new kid learn the ropes. For a moment I question this kind of interference. But something about her soothing voice with its soft Southern drawl sounds quite comforting to me, and in some ways familiar, like I've known her all along. And so I am not bothered by this, and for whatever reason, her advice makes sense.

So, without questioning my new friend, I obediently drag my futon over to the windowless wall and away from the door. And to my surprise it *does* feel safer there. And feeling secure seems important today, especially in light of how empty I've felt since Shay dumped me. She nods her approval, wanders around my tiny apartment, and then disappears. Strange, she didn't even introduce herself. Oh well, I figure. She'll turn up again, or I'll run into her in the elevator or the laundry room.

Now, exhausted from being sick and then moving (unexpectedly by myself with no help from my now *ex*-boyfriend), not to mention it's midterm week, I swig down another gulp of cough syrup and finally collapse onto my thoughtfully relocated bed and sleep surprisingly soundly. When I awake, in the middle of the night, I am frightened by something, or maybe it's just a bad dream or even my new surroundings. But that's when she speaks to me again.

"You'll be okay, Alice," she says in that same honey-coated voice. I sleepily realize that it reminds me of my mom's Aunt Miriam back in North Carolina. "Don't worry. I'll take good care of you."

Even so, my heart pounds as I fumble to find the light switch on the wall, but I quickly discover that the light bulb is missing. So I peer into the darkness until I think I can see her standing by the window, like a dimly lit shadow. She leans against the wall with her arms folded neatly across her chest.

"Who *are* you?" I ask, blinking in surprise. Now I'm certain that I closed and locked my door. But then I wonder if perhaps I am still asleep and just dreaming this whole thing. It seems very surreal.

"I'm Amelia. I'm here to help."

"Help?" I shake my head sharply.

She nods. "I've been sent."

"Sent?"

Now, even though I was raised in a fairly conservative—what some people call an overly religious—home, I really believe I left all that far behind me long ago. Or so I like to think. And yet—like a flash from my fundamentalist past—it occurs to me that this Amelia chick might actually be an angel sent down from God. I vaguely recall talk about guardian angels from my childhood. I'm sure it was my mom who told me of such beings, most likely trying to coax me back to sleep after some terrible nightmare. I had plenty as a child. Traumatized, I usually hotfooted it to my parents' bedroom and tugged on my mom's pillow, wishing that I'd be invited to sleep with them. But Mom would take my hand and walk me back to my bed. Then she would kneel down and pray with me, asking God to take my demons away, and I'm sure she must've mentioned something about a special angel who would watch over me while I slept.

But I had completely forgotten all about such things until this night when I meet Amelia. And for whatever reason I begin to think that Amelia might possibly be my guardian angel. I know it sounds strange. But sometimes life is like that. Now, does this change the way I perceive God? Not much, at least not yet. I still view God—if there truly is a God, and I'm not convinced—as a distant and often angry father who mostly does not want to be bothered. Not unlike my own father before he passed away shortly after I started college. Maybe he's up there still reading his newspaper and sent Amelia in his place to help me out.

Anyway, my eyes adjust to the lack of light as I study this new apparition now seated on a box marked "shoes and stuff," and I'm thinking she doesn't look much like an angel. If anything, Amelia resembles a has-been country singer with her big brown hairdo and red gingham blouse tucked into too tight jeans and her outfit complete with pointed-toe cowboy boots—sort of like Loretta Lynn back in the seventies. I know this because of an album cover in my parents' dusty old record collection. For some reason they kept all their vinyl LPs in an apple crate in a closet under the stairway even long after the FM stereo had been removed from our house. I think my dad believed that all music was sinful back then. But I discovered that the records were an odd mix of country and pop and gospel, although I felt fairly certain that the religious titles reigned supreme since they were always stacked proudly in front, as if to conceal the more shameful titles lurking in the back.

Sometimes my dad punished me for coloring on the table or some such childish act of indiscretion or rebellion, and I was sent to the stairway closet to "consider the gravity of my transgressions." He thought the darkness would impress me with the significance of "walking in the light." But as soon as my dad's footsteps faded away, I would pull the cord on the overhead light bulb and then entertain myself by thumbing through the stack of funky old albums. I studied the faces of singers from the sixties and seventies, and in time they became familiar, like old friends to me. I suppose I must've spent a fair amount of time in that closet. But Loretta Lynn was always my favorite. Her smile seemed so genuine and warm. And I thought she probably gave good hugs.

I glance back over to where Amelia was sitting and discover she's not there anymore. But this does not strike me as odd. In fact, I quickly accept that she's just like that. She comes and goes at will. Not unlike my old roommate Chelsea. But I must give it to Amelia; she's right there when I need her. She wanders in and out but always seems to show up when I need support or comfort. So, I tell myself, even if Amelia doesn't exactly *look* like an angel, her voice is kind and comforting, just like you expect an angel's to be. And for the most part she seems dependable enough. Not to mention thoughtful and helpful, and since I enjoy her companionship, I take to listening to her.

"Alice," she warns me after a few days, "you need to be more careful. There are people out there who want to hurt you. Don't let your guard down. You need to be on the lookout for them."

"What people?" I ask. "Here in the building? Where?"

She narrows her eyes. "Just you watch out, honey."

It sounds crazy, but I take Amelia at her word, and I begin watching out. And sure enough, she is absolutely right. I do begin to notice people out there who like to follow me around, people who talk meanly about me and even threaten me with bodily harm. It doesn't take long before I realize they may want to kill me too. At first I think it's only my ex-boyfriend, Shay. I see him everywhere, lurking in the shadows, ducking down an alley, and always, always watching me with those dark, sinister eyes. His little girlfriend, Kiki, sneaks along with him, whispering what a terrible person I am and how Shay should have broken up with me long ago. Soon I realize that he sneaks into my apartment at night sometimes and says mean, hateful things to me. But it's not long before I realize there are others, too. The man down the hall. A woman in my psychology class. The teenager who works at the corner market.

Amelia shows me ways to protect myself. First I stack the boxes (the ones I haven't unpacked) like a fortress wall, all around my bed. It makes me feel safer, more secure. And then I use all my pushpins from my bulletin board to hang my unzipped sleeping bag over my only window to keep people from looking through the flimsy miniblinds that anyone can see do absolutely no good to protect me from prying eyes. It doesn't matter that my studio is on the second floor because I know someone, especially someone as athletic as Shay, can easily scale that brick wall if he really wants. I am certain he might be inclined to just hang there on the ledge, to peer in and watch me.

I continue going to classes at first. But I keep a constant, vigilant watch, always looking over my shoulder. And following Amelia's sage advice, I begin to layer on articles of clothing, just in case I need to make a quick getaway. They keep me warm and secure and help me disguise myself from the growing number of people after me.

One morning on the way to class I run into Chelsea, my old roommate from the dorm. "How are you doing in your new place?" she asks in what I'm sure she hopes is an innocent sounding voice. Amelia has warned me to trust no one, especially those who used to be my closest friends.

"Why?" I study her with open suspicion. Has Shay sent her to spy on me? Has he asked her to check on my whereabouts? Is she his new girlfriend?

She acts like she doesn't understand my question. "I just wondered how it was going is all."

"Everything's cool," I snap, glancing past her to see if that's Shay hiding behind the maple tree in front of the library.

"Are you okay, Alice?" I sense her penetrating gaze, as if she's trying to strip away something, to see beneath the layers of my protective clothing to the hidden places inside me.

"I'm fine." I turn and hurry away. But somehow I know she's following me. I run a zigzag path, just to throw her off, before I return to my apartment. I don't go to classes for the rest of that day. Or the next.

"Chelsea is telling everyone that you're crazy," Amelia informs me later that week. "You can't trust her anymore."

"I know," I reply. "Shay probably set her up."

"He wants to hurt you, Alice. Shay thinks you know too much."

I want to escape everyone and everything that has to do with

chapter THREE

The Golden Key

As a child, I always wanted to be special. Not as in "special" like Mikey Randall, the boy who had to be "specially" tutored at SCCS (Salvation Christian Center School). But I wanted to be noticed, to be somebody that mattered. I used to fantasize about it, imagining myself as someone famous or smart or beautiful—or even better, all three. Of course, I knew this was "sinful thinking" since most of the congregation at Salvation Center thrived upon a sense of "pious humility" both in spirit and in appearances, and any form of self-promotion or personal importance was highly frowned upon.

I still remember the Sunday when Mrs. Price wore a bright red dress to church, with shoulder pads and everything. Scandalous! Oh, I don't think anyone actually said anything—if they did it was whispered between the pews. But the scathing glances that poor woman got. Being about ten years old and a secret admirer of fashion, I thought she looked absolutely lovely and wished my mother had the nerve to dress like that.

That was probably about the same era that I secretly imagined myself starring in a film. Not that I'd ever been inside a theater.

Movies were strictly prohibited by our church, as was television. Hollywood was considered the devil's domain, and no self-respecting Christian would be caught dead watching anything so worldly and carnal.

When I was in seventh grade and still attending SCCS, I sneaked into a movie with Jenny Lund, my most rebellious and adventuresome friend. I can't even recall the title now, and I was so nervous at being discovered that it was hard to concentrate fully, but I do remember it starred Meg Ryan, and I thought she was wonderful. And I saw nothing inherently evil or even sensational about the movie. Not like I'd expected anyway. I suppose it was a bit of a letdown. Although the damage was done, and I was hooked on Hollywood.

Unfortunately the opportunities for sneaking out were few and far between, and by ninth grade Jenny was kicked out of SCCS for smoking, and her parents left the church in shame. Naturally I was forbidden to associate with her. But how I envied her freedom. And by my junior year in this rigid school, I thought I was about to suffocate.

"I cannot do this anymore," I finally told my mom. Mrs. Pike had reprimanded me that afternoon for wearing *colorless* lip gloss. "If I have to stay at SCCS for one more day, I will do something very regrettable."

"What do you mean?" My mother looked horrified.

"Whatever it takes to get kicked out," I said with false confidence. "And I'll make it bad enough to ensure they never let me back in."

Somehow she believed me, and afraid I'm sure of public humiliation, she managed to convince my father to allow me this liberty. Of course, it came with a severe warning—any trouble and I would be doing homeschool. Now there's a threat with some teeth to it. Also, I was expected to keep my grades up. But looking back, I think my dad was secretly relieved to save the tuition money, and it wasn't long before my little brother was released from his bondage too.

Anyway, I didn't disappoint them. Being the odd duck, misfit, nerdy new girl in high school, I managed to maintain a perfect GPA right up until graduation. I could've been a candidate for valedictorian except that my previous ten years spent in an unaccredited private church school made me ineligible. I still remember my disappointment when the guidance counselor informed me. I thought my day had finally come to feel special, standing before Warren High School and delivering a speech worthy of my honor. My consolation prize was the offer of a state scholarship. And I suppose that made me feel special, but it didn't feel nearly as spectacular as being valedictorian or, say, a star of stage or screen.

Not that I necessarily think I have any great theatrical skills. But during my last three years at college, I made up for lost time by seeing a couple of hundred movies. I think I've become something of a film expert in the process. Shay was a movie buff too and would get so stoked whenever I saw a really good flick for the first time. Being an impoverished student, I lived on a miserly budget, so most of these films have been watched on videos or late night TV. But I really prefer the theater experience with the sticky crushed-velvet seats and smell of stale popcorn.

Still, I must admit to having felt a bit guilty about this "carnal and forbidden" activity at first, but before long I realized it was simply a necessary facet of my education. I had lived in a cultural vacuum for so long that I was somewhat out of touch with reality. Not that

Hollywood is reality. Maybe that's why I like it so much. Maybe I want to escape from all this reality. And I can admit that I sometimes overly connect with the main characters. After seeing *Gone With the Wind* for the first time, I went around talking like Scarlett O'Hara for three days. I guess it just made me feel special. "With God as my witness, I will never go hungry again!" I was actually pretty good.

And perhaps this need to feel special makes it even easier to believe I've finally been chosen. Although I'm not exactly sure what it is I've been chosen for. Or even who I've been chosen by, but I'm beginning to suspect it might be God. As I recall, it was Amelia who implied this to start with, but as days go by, it seems quite plausible. More and more I begin to believe that God is for real and that he is actually speaking to me personally. I know he is preparing me for something quite *big* and important. For the first time I really do feel special.

It's as if I've been given a golden key that will open any door set before me.

Not long after receiving this revelation, I begin to read my old Bible. I am actually quite surprised to discover that I still have it and that I can find it. But this morning I wake up before sunrise, and I head straight for a Nike shoebox that must be left over from my brother Aaron's big feet since he's the only one in our family who's ever worn a size thirteen and has since the eighth grade. My mother insisted I bring this shoebox full of useless books to college with me, but for three years I managed to shelve the dog-eared shoebox and nearly forget it.

But today I get up and am energized. It's as if the air is charged with power and light, and I believe I am having a true revelation. I am amazed at how I tumble out of bed and head straight for that box, almost like I have radar in my fingertips. I open the orange box to discover the Bible on top of some other religious books that my mother assumed I couldn't live without. I rub my hand over the smooth-grained cowhide cover and breathe it in. It smells just like Sunday school. I open it to find the pages soft and feathery—almost edible. This Bible was presented to me in third grade, and I remember how proud I was to stand at the front of the church with the other third graders. Our whole class filed by, one by one, with solemn maturity, except for Timothy Bevins, who wet himself and had to be excused, as we soberly received "God's Word" from Pastor John.

Naturally, I hadn't read the Bible for years, not since I quit going to church with my parents shortly after my high school graduation. My second form of open rebellion. My father didn't react as strongly as I'd expected, but then I think perhaps he, like me, was beginning to question some things as well. My mother was beside herself. I'm sure she checked the sky on a regular basis to see if a lightning bolt was aimed toward our house. I know that she and her church friends prayed for me daily, probably with sackcloth and ashes, which is not an exaggeration.

It was such a relief to leave Warren and escape the heavy oppression of Salvation Center. I've become quite an expert at reasons for not going home. Other than my father's funeral and my brother's graduation from high school, I've managed to keep a safe distance from my old world. I always take a few summer classes and work summer jobs just to avoid it. Even now, I find myself somewhat amazed and slightly frightened that I am actually handling this old Bible again and without being forced to. But the pull is so strong.

So I open it up, on this golden morning of revelation, allowing the pages to fall as they will, like waves when Moses parted the Red Sea. I know I'm in the Old Testament, the book of Jeremiah. And I know from years of Sunday school and church that this man is a prophet. But I don't remember much more than that. Sheltered by my walls of boxes, and with my window shrouded against the rising sun, I begin to read.

I quickly discover that this is unlike any reading I've ever done. Suddenly everything is crystal clear. *Inspired.* The meaning seems plain to me, incredibly obvious—as if God is speaking to me personally. As if he's standing before me and holding out the golden key of complete and perfect knowledge. He is giving me the secret of understanding it all.

I begin to record all my profound thoughts in my computer word-processing program. I sit there for hours and hours, just writing line after line of the prophet's true meaning and how it relates to the state of the world at present. There's so much that has to do with the Middle East and our lifestyle in America and many symbols of water, fire, destruction, and rebirth. I write page after page, creating new documents as needed, and a whole new file system to contain them—all safely stored in my computer under a secret name with a secret code that only I can access.

During the days to come, this writing becomes my obsession. It is my calling. I no longer attend classes. I have no need to further my education. I now hold the key to all knowledge, to all that is important. God is giving me the answers, and I intend to write them all down. I am certain that my words will be published someday, probably within the month, and then everyone on the planet will know the real truth. And they will also know that I am special—*chosen*. I imagine myself being interviewed on the *Today* show.

But one morning my computer suddenly freezes up, right in the middle of what feels like a very powerful and prophetic sentence. I am completely flabbergasted. How could God allow this to happen? But then I realize that *someone else* is intruding—someone evil who wants to thwart my work. Although I don't think I am online, I know without doubt that the enemy has hacked his way into my computer for the purpose of stealing my thoughts—my genius inspirations. I immediately shut down my computer and unplug it from the wall.

With my divine knowledge I am suddenly cognizant that it's through my computer that they are tracking me now, watching my every move, and plotting to destroy me. I can hear them whispering through my computer. Shay has led them to me, and his voice is the loudest. But they whisper horrifying threats and obscenities, using words I've never even heard and don't fully understand. A secret language perhaps for those who conspire to steal my prophetic translations. They are clearly planning to destroy me—to shut me up for good.

First I put my computer tower behind a stack of boxes, but I can still feel the eyes of the evil screen watching me, recording everything I do, every move I make—perhaps even reading my mind. As if on cue, Amelia wanders in and suggests I dispose of it entirely, but it's my idea to throw it out the window. I feel very clever for thinking of this. I open my window and make sure no one is below, then simply drop the monitor and watch in fascination as it shatters into a hundred pieces all over the wet sidewalk.

Unfortunately that doesn't completely solve my problem. While

I don't fear being watched—not so much anyway—the voices and insidious threats continue to pour from the computer's main box. Amelia reminds me that the computer's brain still dwells in the tower and that it has already been reading my mind, perhaps transmitting misleading messages, and ultimately trying to control me.

So, using a screwdriver and hammer, I open up the box and destroy its interior parts. It doesn't occur to me that it took nearly a year's worth of budgeting from my dad's Social Security benefits for me to pay off this computer. Money is irrelevant now. I put all these broken components into a large cardboard box and tape it up securely. This will show them!

From now on I will write my prophecy and spiritual interpretations only onto yellow legal tablets, and these will remain safely zipped in my backpack. I vow to myself and God to keep my backpack with me always, even when I sleep, which is becoming less and less. However, this lack of rest does not trouble me much. Sleep, like money or education or even food, is completely irrelevant in the larger realm of great spiritual awakenings.

I'm not sure how much time actually passes during my revelation era, maybe a couple of weeks, but sometimes people stop by to check on me. Mostly, like when it is Chelsea, and later on Shay, I don't bother to answer or even open the door. But I do open the door to Mr. Scoggins, since he manages the apartments and is very insistent in his knocking.

"You know anything about that smashed-up piece of junk down on the sidewalk?" he asks me with a furrowed brow.

I keep my door open about six inches, my foot planted firmly against it as I tell him, "I most certainly do not." Lying is also irrelevant.

"Well, someone thought it might've come from your apartment." His voice oozes with suspicion, accusation, threat, and innuendo, and I suddenly wish that I'd never opened the door.

"That's impossible." I slowly close the door a few more inches.

"Everything okay in there?"

"Sure."

He nods to his left. "Your neighbor thinks something's not right with you. Says things aren't normal in there. You better be straight with me, girl. Something wrong?"

"Nothing's wrong!" I close the door completely now and gasp for breath. That was a close one. My pulse pounds like a jackhammer against my temples, and it seems as if something inside of me, like a blood vessel or possibly an aneurysm, is about to burst. My body feels as if I've just run uphill for several miles.

"It's Linda," suggests Amelia in her calm voice as she emerges from the bathroom.

I consider the middle-aged Asian woman who brought over some homemade bran muffins shortly after I moved in. "But she seemed nice."

"It's all an act. She's really spying on you."

"But what about the muffins?" I suddenly recall how, despite my concerns over food tainting, I went ahead and ate them.

"That's part of the problem, Alice. Her food is inside you now."

Even though it's been a couple of weeks since the muffins, I dash straight to the bathroom and gag myself with my finger, making myself throw up.

"That's better," says Amelia. "You must be very, very careful about what you put inside your body."

So I look at the food in my refrigerator, what little there is since I haven't been to the store in days, and I am certain that Linda has sneaked over here during the few times I've been out. I suspect she has poisoned all my food. Upon closer inspection I can see tiny pinpricks where she has surely injected each item with poison.

"That's right," confirms Amelia. "They paid her to spy on you, as well as to poison your food. It's a slow acting sort of toxin, related to lead. It builds up in your system, but it's impossible to trace its origins."

Already I feel sick. My eyesight is blurry, and my fingers are swollen. I can tell that the poison is taking effect. I find an oven mitt, and using it to protect my hand, I carefully empty the contents of my fridge and cupboard into a trash container. I'm about to take it downstairs to the rubbish bin when Amelia stops me.

"You might run into Linda out there," she warns.

"That's right." I set the garbage just inside my door and leave it there. But after a few days it begins to stink like the compost pile my mom used to keep by her garden, and the putrid smell is penetrating through my skin. And so I decide to sneak the offensive trash container out into the hallway.

It's the first time I've opened my door since the manager stopped by. I peer up and down the vacant hallway to be sure no one's watching me, especially Linda. Then I carry the garbage out, uncertain where I should leave it so that it doesn't look like it came from my apartment. But that's when I hear voices coming up the stairwell. I pause to listen for a moment. Then, convinced they are talking about me, plotting a way to get inside my apartment and steal my notebooks, I abandon the noxious garbage right there in the middle of the hallway.

I rush back into my apartment and close and deadbolt my door. I wait and wait for them to come, expecting them to pound down my door and demand that I hand over my secret journals. But they must suspect I am ready for them, for they never show up. Tonight I shove a dresser in front of the door and finally fall asleep. For a few hours anyway.

You'd think that my lack of food would make me ravenous. But I honestly don't feel a bit hungry. It seems that food is unnecessary. In fact, the mere thought of actually ingesting anything nauseates me. I can't imagine putting something solid into my mouth and chewing, swallowing. And although I used to adore Burger King Whoppers, the mere idea of eating any animal products—especially animal flesh—makes my skin literally crawl. It makes me want to vomit. It becomes my firm conviction that the only safe thing for me to consume now is hot tea.

So Amelia and I have regular tea parties these days. Since I'm already Alice, I pretend that she is the Mad Hatter. But then I examine a teabag one day and am shocked to discover that even these have been tampered with. I immediately throw them all away and furiously scrub my hands with soap and water. Now I will drink only boiled water and only while it is hot—scalding hot. These are the sacrifices you make when you're on a mission.

chapter FOUR

The Pool of Tears

I'm still not sure how my mother found out about me. But I am stunned when Mr. Scoggins unlocks my door and lets her enter. With a lot of huffing and puffing and a string of profanity from Mr. Scoggins, the two of them manage to shove and push until they finally budge the dresser from its post. Terrified, I hide under the covers on my bed, the safest place, although I'm certain that my enemy has won this battle. And yet at the same time I am strangely relieved. I think I am just tired. In my exhaustion I am ready for the spies to storm in, bash me over the head, and steal my precious journals. I think I just want it to be over and done with.

But I look up to realize it is only my mom with Mr. Scoggins's scowling face right behind her. They are peering over my wall of boxes, and my mom looks confused. She's wearing her dark plaid wool dress with the covered buttons down the front, the same one she's had since I was in grade school. But her hair seems even grayer than before. She grayed prematurely right after my father died, making her appear much older than her actual forty-two years. Naturally, she believes it is sinful to color hair. I can see she is saying something to me—her lips are moving—but the words are floating around like butterflies, and they can't seem to land in my head. I stare at her blankly, and consequently her face looks pulled and strained. She could be my mother, but she might be an impostor sent by the spies.

"Alice!" Her cries penetrate. *"Are you all right?"*

Wordlessly, I look at her, and I think that this woman is my mother. But at the same time I'm not absolutely sure. Suddenly I am worried that this is all just a very clever trick. I glance around to see if Amelia is anywhere nearby, but I don't see her. Have they already come and taken her away?

"Alice?"

I pull my faded denim comforter up to my chin now, shrinking down into my bed as if it might swallow me whole. How I wish that it could. Disappearing sounds so appealing just now.

"What's wrong?" This mother-type woman comes closer now, and I peer up at her with unveiled suspicion. Who is this impostor? And yet something about the crinkly lines that fan out at the edges of her watery blue eyes entices me to believe that she might possibly be my mother after all.

"Mom?" I take in a breath, like breaking the surface from under water. It seems like years since I've uttered a word. "Is that you?"

"Of course it's me. I've been trying to call you for days, Alice, but you never answer your cell phone. I've left dozens of messages. Don't you ever check your voice mail anymore?"

"I, uh, don't have it… My phone's gone."

"Where is it?"

"I don't know." This is partially true. I threw it in a garbage can by the bookstore several weeks ago. I knew they were listening, using it to read my thoughts, to get into my head. But it's true that I have absolutely no idea where it might be right now. Perhaps in a dump-site on the east side of the river—who can know?

Mom steps around to the opening in my wall of boxes and kneels down, studying me carefully. "You don't look well, Alice."

"My neighbor is poisoning me," I whisper with urgency. Maybe my mom can help me.

"*What?*" She stands now and glares at Mr. Scoggins. "What on earth is going on here?"

He shrugs. Then with his index finger pointing to his head, he makes a slow circling motion.

"What do you mean?" My mom turns back and peers at me more closely this time. And that's when I see it—the same expression she used around Grandma. It's a mixture of frustration and fear and, I think, embarrassment.

"I'm *not* crazy, Mom." I sit up in bed now, determined to make her understand my predicament. "They've been spying on me. Linda is working for them. Amelia said that they want to hurt me."

"Who's Amelia?"

"She's my…" I glance over at Mr. Scoggins, who stares at me with what seems to be some sickening sort of fascination. I lower my voice. "*You know,* Mom. She's my guardian angel. She tells me things."

For a moment she almost appears to believe me. I stand up now, hoping to make her see the truth. I take a step toward her, but my legs wobble beneath me. I grab on to a box to help me stand.

I see the tears fill her eyes and then stream down her smooth cheeks. "Oh, Alice, *look* at you! You're nothing but skin and bones."

I nod. "See. *That's* what I'm telling you. Linda is poisoning me so she can steal my notes. I have all the answers, Mom. Really, you've got to believe me. I have the *golden key*."

I notice Mr. Scoggins shaking his head as he moves toward the door. "Stupid kids and their drugs these days," he mutters. "What a waste."

Mom's brow creases. "Are you on drugs, Alice?"

"No." I sigh. It feels as if my legs are made of shoestrings, and thanks to the poison in my body, my vision is getting blurry again. I sink back down to the bed and bury my head in my hands. "It's useless."

"You're coming home with me right now, Alice."

I don't argue with her. I just pick up my backpack and follow. She holds on to me as we slowly walk down the stairs, and then she guides me to the car. I feel as if I am about a hundred years old—or maybe two.

Yet it is oddly comforting to slump into the front seat of her old Taurus. She's been driving the same car for more than ten years now. I can still smell the familiar mixture of Aaron's old dirty basketball sneakers and Ralph's canine odor, even though Aaron's off at college, and our old dog was put to sleep last summer. But it's not such a bad aroma, familiar and even comforting.

My mom talks as she drives. But I can't make her words line up right in my head. It's like a crossword puzzle all mixed up. Or maybe she's actually praying for me to get better. Maybe this is her secret prayer language. Yes, that seems more likely. But just like the Cheshire cat speaking backward, it makes no sense to me.

Now I am sorry that I mentioned the golden key to her, but at least I didn't tell her that I am the chosen one. I know she won't get that. Not yet anyway. And maybe this is meant to be my secret. At least for the time being. For I still believe that all things will be revealed in due time. I keep reaching down and feeling for my backpack, making sure that my journals are still with me and safe.

I see my mom's lips continuing to move as she expertly guides her car down the freeway. It feels as if we are flying in a jet, and I am scared by the motion. I see trees and signs flashing by me, and for a moment I am certain that I'm being swooped away to some secret location where I will be completely deprogrammed and my journals decoded, and I will most certainly be destroyed. But then I think, No, that's just my mom driving her old Taurus. She's taking me home, and everything will be okay now.

Maybe it's this sense of false relief that first makes me begin to cry. But once I start crying, I am unable to stop. I know it's upsetting my mother, but the tears just keep pouring down, like rivers from my eyes. I am fairly certain that all this fluid will soon fill the inside of the Taurus. I imagine us trapped in a lukewarm pool of salt water, unable to breathe, finally drowning in here. But even so I cannot make myself stop.

chapter FIVE

Off with Her Head!

I should've known, especially after my uncontrollable flood of tears, that Mom would cart me straight to her church. I start to say something when I notice she's turning left toward town instead of right toward home, but it's too late. I never get the chance.

"Don't worry, honey," she attempts to assure me, using her church voice now. "God is in control. He's going to help you through this trial."

"I know that God is in control, Mom. God is the one who's been doing all this and showing me these things."

She frowns and looks slightly confused but continues driving down Oak Street with determination, straight toward Salvation Center. Then, instead of parking in the back graveled lot as she would do under normal circumstances, she pulls her old Taurus right up to the front door and turns off the engine and looks at me. In a firm voice, she says, "Don't worry. Pastor John will know exactly what to do, Alice."

"I don't want to see Pastor John," I complain. I feel like I am about six years old and going to see the dentist.

"You need to, Alice. He can help us."

As much as I want to resist, to simply leap from the car and run for my life, I submit to her. I am too tired to do anything else. Like a lamb to the slaughter, I allow my mother to lead me into the brown boxy building that used to be an auto parts shop. We stand like timid shadows in the small, dark foyer that still emits the faint odor of old motor oil. I glance around, expecting that everything should look familiar since nothing has changed here for years, and yet it all feels strange and foreign to me. Evil even. I believe I am being taken straight to hell, and Pastor John is the devil himself. I tell myself this is crazy and absurd, but I don't believe me. I look around for Amelia, but she doesn't seem to be here just now.

My heart pounds furiously as we sit on the frumpy plaid couch and wait. The receptionist, Mary Cates, has gone to "speak to the pastor." It is several years before she finally returns with a smile that is either sympathetic or gloating. I can't be sure. "He'll see you both now."

I am seated in a folding chair, and I can feel the chill of the icy metal seeping through my jeans. I think I'm beginning to shiver, but I try desperately to listen as my mother whispers to Pastor John. But once again her words get all mixed up, turning themselves inside out and sideways, and I am baffled that Pastor John can understand a single thing she has said. But he nods from time to time, causing the loose skin in his neck to wobble like a turkey. In fact, I'm thinking he truly does resemble a turkey with his beaklike nose and thick glasses. *Wobble-gobble-wobble-gobble.* These sounds run in circles through my head, almost like a song, and I giggle. Suddenly I notice that Pastor John and my mom are no longer talking, but instead they are both looking at me with curious expressions. And I am thinking that I may have actually said those words aloud. It's plain to see that they both think I'm bonkers, or worse. Although I am certain I'm the sanest one in this room at the moment. Not to mention the *chosen one.*

Now Pastor John begins speaking to me, but his words are coming out backward too—it sounds a bit like when you play a tape in reverse. I wonder if he knows how ridiculous he sounds. And that's when I start laughing. I can tell he's getting quite irritated at me now, especially when I can't seem to stop. He doesn't look like a turkey now so much as a scolding parent.

Suddenly I know he is the Queen of Hearts—they look quite similar with their big, puffy red faces. I remember how the queen cornered Alice and shrieked, "Off with your head!" And I honestly believe this is what the "good" pastor is saying to me right now. And although I should probably be frightened, for some reason this strikes me as totally hilarious. I know I am embarrassing my mom, but I can't help it. Everything just seems so funny right now. Am I hysterical? Or maybe I'm simply experiencing some sort of reverse reaction from having shed so many tears earlier. How am I supposed to know? It's too hard to think about.

"I'm sorry," I finally manage to say, gasping slightly. I am really trying to make myself sober up. I can tell by their faces that this is a very serious situation. Indeed.

Pastor John clears his throat. "That's better. Now, tell me what's going on with you, Alice."

I shrug, a little surprised that I can actually understand him now, but then it occurs to me that it must be God interpreting for me.

"Come on, now, Alice. What seems to be the trouble?"

"I'd tell you, but you wouldn't get it."

He smiles, but I suspect that it's a fake smile. Although I'm not certain, since I'm not certain of much of anything at the moment. "Oh, you'd be surprised what an old guy like me can understand."

For one moment I actually feel myself starting to trust him. It's as if I want to trust someone and have someone understand my mission. Why not him? My mother certainly seems to think he's God's gift to her church.

"Well." I take a deep breath. "God has been telling me things… important things…and I've been writing them all down."

"What does God tell you, Alice?" Pastor John leans back in his chair and folds his hands as if he's really listening. But suddenly his superior smile makes everything crystal clear to me. I know that this man cannot be trusted. He is clearly the enemy. Then suddenly the words all come to me, like an inspiration.

"You are like King Zedekiah," I say with the authority of the one given the golden key.

"Who?" He sits forward now, adjusting his thick glasses.

"The prophet Jeremiah warned King Zedekiah that God was going to use his own weapons against him and his kingdom—to destroy them. And that's what God is going to do to you, Pastor John."

My mother gasps, but I keep my gaze directly forward and continue to speak. "God is going to demolish both you and your church …by fire."

Pastor John scoots back his chair with a loud screech, then rises to his feet. "If you will both excuse me for a few minutes." He moves toward the door, glancing toward me. "Stay right here, both of you. I will be back in a just a few minutes."

He is barely out the door when my mother turns to me and grabs me by the arm. "What on earth are you saying?" Her eyes are wide and filled with real fear.

"The truth."

"The truth? You actually believe that God is going to burn this place down, Alice? And everybody in it? Including Pastor John?"

"*Especially* Pastor John."

She sighs and shakes her head. Her shoulders crumple forward as if her muscles have all gone slack. "Oh, Alice."

Pastor John returns just then with his reinforcements in tow. Before I know what is happening, I am surrounded by four men and one woman, and they're all putting their hands on me—even my mother—and they are praying, loudly and with vigor. Their words and their breath come down on me like the heated stench of a garbage pit. I try desperately not to breathe. I am certain the air in this tiny room will poison me.

"We cast you out, O demon spirits," cries Pastor John in his low, theatrical voice that he usually reserves for sermons. "In the powerful name of Jesus, we bind you and cast you out into the fiery pit of hell."

"That's right, you false prophet spirits," chimes in Deacon Bolder. "You have no right to inhabit this child. In the name of Jesus we rebuke you and send you crawling back to wherever it is that you slithered from. Satan, Prince of Lies, you are not welcome here. Depart from her!"

I hear other voices praying too, but it's not long until they all blur together in a mind-splitting cacophony. Everyone presses in so close that I can recognize them by their smells. The mothballs from Pastor John's wool jacket mix with the body odor from Deacon Bolder's work shirt, and even the familiar almond aroma of my mother's Jergens hand lotion makes me want to gag. I cannot breathe, and my head is going to burst, or perhaps I am simply having a heart attack. Then everything just goes hazy, smoky, then dark, like the screen fading at the end of the movie.

When I awake I am at home, stretched out on the old tweed couch in the living room with the harvest colored afghan spread over me. I can tell it's dark outside, and I have no idea how long I've slept. But it's clear that I haven't escaped the praying fanatics yet, because sitting directly across from me, in my dad's old leatherette recliner, is Mary Cates. Her plump arms remind me of pink water balloons as they rise and fall to her soft snoring.

"How are you feeling, Alice?"

I slowly rise to a seated position and turn to see Mrs. Knoll looking at me with her arms folded neatly across her front. She's sitting in the old wooden rocker that's been passed down on my dad's side of the family for three generations. She's partially hidden by the shadows, which makes her angular face look even more menacing than usual. Mrs. Knoll is a childless widow who's in charge of the women's ministry at Salvation Center, a formidable woman who supposedly served as an army nurse long, long ago. As a child I used to imagine that she'd murdered her husband since there seemed to be some sort of mystery attached to his untimely death. But tonight she is the one who looks like a ghost.

I hear my mom calling from the kitchen. "Is Alice awake?"

"Yes," answers Mrs. Knoll, and Mary Cates suddenly snorts loudly, then sits up straighter in her chair.

"Time to pray again?" asks Mary with bleary eyes.

"She needs to eat first." My mom emerges from the kitchen with a bowl of something that's steaming, and I desperately hope that it's not chicken noodle soup, her regular standby for whatever ails you. The mere thought of eating a chicken's flesh makes me want to hurl.

Mom sits down next to me and tries to give me the bowl, but I can't force my hands to take it. With some relief, I see that it's only oatmeal, but even so, I am afraid. I know there is milk on it, and the idea of ingesting milk is grotesque. I do not want to put that cow secretion into my mouth.

"Come on, Alice." My mom holds the spoon to my lips. "Just a bite or two, please?"

I shake my head.

"It's them demons," mutters Mary. "They're trying to starve her—want to drive her right out of her own malnourished body."

I sigh and look down at the familiar white bowl trimmed in blue cornflowers. Suddenly I wish that I could take at least one bite, if only to show them. Either that or spin my head around a few times, but that doesn't seem likely.

"Demons are trying to destroy you, Alice," says Mrs. Knoll in a voice that sounds as if it's coming at me in surround sound straight from the depths of hell. "They don't want you to eat. They want you to suffer and die."

I try to swallow, but my throat feels like sandpaper. I look at my mother and notice her eyes, once again, are filled with tears. I know I must take a bite…for her. Even if it kills me, and it probably will.

"Okay, Mom, just one bite." I close my eyes and open my mouth and wait. I taste the metal of the spoon on my tongue, and I feel the warm lumpy texture of the oatmeal in my mouth. But it's the smelly taste of cow's milk that gets to me, and I begin to gag. I can't help it. The stuff just shoots out of me like an explosion—all over my mother's face and plaid woolen dress.

"It's them demons," says Mary in a matter-of-fact voice.

"I'm sorry, Mom."

She dabs at her face and dress with a paper napkin. "It's okay, Alice; it's not your fault."

"You're right, dear," agrees Mary. "It's them demons making her act this way. They've taken over her body and soul. She's helpless to fight them."

"Not entirely," says Mrs. Knoll. "Alice has something to do with this."

Then Mrs. Knoll slowly stands and walks over to me. She peers down at me with her dark, narrowed eyes. "What did you do to invite this evil into your heart, Alice? What sin have you partaken in that's opened you up to this wickedness?"

I don't answer her but simply look down at the orange and yellow stripes of the afghan, sticking my fingers through the holes like I did when I was little. I don't want to talk to these women. More than anything I wish these churchwomen would vanish and just leave me alone.

"You must've done something," continues Mrs. Knoll. "Satan doesn't come into our hearts uninvited, you know. You got to give him some kind of leeway. You open the door and say 'come on in.'

Is there some hidden sin in your life, Alice? Something you need to confess to us?"

I still don't look up, but I can sense her face close to mine, and I can smell her breath just as sour as a nasty old dishrag. She peers down at me now, looking as if she can actually see into my soul. Suddenly I am not entirely sure that she can't. And why shouldn't she? After all, she is part of the church leadership, the church that God is going to destroy.

It becomes perfectly clear to me. Mrs. Knoll is in cahoots with Pastor John. They're the ones behind this whole thing. The real enemies. I am absolutely certain that they are the ones who hired my neighbor to spy on me, told her to poison me. *They want my journals. They're jealous that God didn't choose them to receive the golden key.*

"Where's my backpack, Mom?" I ask suddenly.

"In your room."

"You hiding something sinful in your backpack?" continues Mrs. Knoll. "Some drugs maybe? Or pornography? Tools of witchcraft?"

"Oh, Mrs. Knoll!" My mother looks scandalized. "Alice is a *good* girl."

"No one is *good*, Susan!" snaps Mrs. Knoll. "Don't be deceived by sin's folly. We are all evil by nature. It's only when we repent of our evil that we can be saved by the blood. But I can sense that Alice has fallen from grace. She's not under God's protection anymore. She has made herself an enemy of God. That's why she's demonized now. Plagued with demons. Why, I can feel it in my very spirit."

"We can't help you, Alice," Mary agrees. "Not unless you're willing to be helped."

I suspect they're playing good cop–bad cop now. I simply sit and watch, like a first offender in the squad interrogation room.

"That's right, honey." My mother nods. "We can pray for you, but you have to cooperate with us if we're going to get the demons out."

I just look at her without speaking. I am confused, and I wonder where I am and who these women really are. I long for Amelia to come and explain what is going on—she's the only real friend I have left—but she seems to have vanished completely. I don't understand what's happening.

My mother reaches out and takes my hand. "Trust me, Alice. We only want to help you."

I look into her eyes and realize she is not really a stranger. She's my mother, and I'm thinking maybe she's right. Maybe they are all right. Perhaps I am demonized. It's obvious that something is terribly wrong. I certainly feel like I'm stuck in some sort of hell. I finally shrug. "I don't know what to do."

"You just need to agree with us when we pray for you, honey." My mom places her other hand on my shoulder. "Are you ready?"

"I guess so."

"You've got to *want* them to be gone, Alice." Mrs. Knoll's voice is stern and fierce.

All I can think is that I want her to be gone and how maybe she'll leave sooner if I play along.

They've barely begun to pray when I feel myself growing blurry and sleepy again. Maybe it's due to lack of food, but Mrs. Knoll insists it's those demons at work in me.

After what seems like hours, the two churchwomen grow weary and finally leave. I remain on the couch with my mom sitting in the recliner across from me, as though keeping some sort of a vigil. There is a small comfort in her presence. I sleep off and on, and each time I wake up, she is still there, and so I think it is safe to sleep some more. Sometimes I wake to hear her praying again. But not like the church ladies, none of that "binding and loosing" talk. This time she's praying simply, as if she's really talking to God. I am a bit stunned by this kind of prayer. She sounds earnest and childlike.

"I don't understand what's going on with Alice," she says quietly. "But I believe you have her in your hands, O Lord. I believe you will take care of her. Please show me what to do. Help us through this thing."

I sit up then and tell her that I'd like to try to eat again. "Maybe some juice," I suggest.

"There's some apple juice."

I nod. "Yes, that might be good."

I drink most of the apple juice, and by morning I am able to eat a small bowl of thin cream of wheat, with milk. That is something.

"I've called Dr. Thornton," my mother announces as she clears the breakfast dishes.

The name sounds familiar, but I can't quite place it. "Who's that?"

"He used to treat your grandmother—"

"A psychiatrist?"

"He's an experienced doctor, Alice—"

"He must be about a hundred and two by now."

"He's probably close to retirement age."

"So you really think I'm crazy? I thought demons were my problem."

"I don't know *what* to think anymore. But I've been praying about this, and it seems the right thing to do."

I sigh and slump down into the straight-backed kitchen chair. I'm not sure which is worse, having people thinking I'm demonized or crazy. Maybe I am both.

"The appointment's at ten." She frowns at me now. "Do you think you could clean up a little? Take a shower? Wash your hair maybe?"

I nod, then slowly trudge up to my old room. I am eager to check on my backpack and make sure that my journals haven't been removed or tampered with. However, I can tell that someone has gone through my things. I suspect it's Mrs. Knoll, probably searching for drugs. But fortunately my journals are still there. Of course, it occurs to me, they could've been copied or photographed by now.

When my mother comes up to get me, I am still sitting on the floor. I haven't showered, but I have layered on several items of clothing from my backpack.

"Are you ready?"

"I guess."

"Is that what you're wearing?"

I looked down and shrug. "Why not?"

She shakes her head. "You look like some sort of refugee."

I slowly stand and look at her. "Yeah? Well, maybe that's what I am."

My mother speaks in a forced calm voice as she drives her Taurus down a country road. It's as if she's afraid to say anything that might upset or disturb me. I realize that this is the exact same tone she used to use around her mother. But I am getting seriously aggravated by it, and even more and more nervous and agitated. It's as if all my nerve endings are exposed on the surface of my skin now, raw and sensitive. Most of all I feel really frightened. And when my mother turns into the same gated road that we always took when we went to visit my grandma, I seriously begin to freak. The sign above the gate reads Forest Hills.

"You're taking me to the nut house!" I scream and grab for the door handle. "The same place you brought Grandma. Why are you bringing me here?"

"It's just for an evaluation, Alice."

"No!" I shriek, trying to open the door only to find that it's locked. "You're going to leave me here!"

She stops the car now and turns to look at me. "I promise you, Alice, I am *not* going to leave you here. Not unless you decide you want to stay, that is. I swear to you, this is just an evaluation. Dr. Thornton's office is here. Have I ever lied to you about anything?"

I shake my head, but I am not completely certain.

"You can trust me, Alice. I'm your mother. I would never do anything to hurt you. I *love* you."

I want to believe her. I want to believe *somebody.* But somehow I know this is all just a trick. Part of the big plan to get my journals, to silence and ultimately destroy me. As she drives down the blacktop road toward the big beige building, I hear Amelia whispering from the backseat. It's the first time she's made an appearance since my mom showed up and whisked me away.

I glance over my shoulder and see Amelia sitting there with one leg crossed over her knee, swinging a cowboy boot in a cocky sort of way. She's not wearing her seat belt, and this amuses me.

Amelia leans forward and points through her palm at my mother. "She slipped something into your cream of wheat, Alice," she whispers into my ear. "Some sort of mind-controlling substance. I think Pastor John must've given it to her yesterday. Or perhaps Mrs. Knoll."

I slump down into my seat and clutch my backpack to my chest. How do you fight something like this? Where do you turn when it seems even your own mother has betrayed you? How do you resist this sort of thing? Why not just give up and give in to it? Well, I try to console myself, at least Amelia is back.

chapter SIX

The Golden Scissors

At some point, I imagined God with a pair of golden scissors, neatly snipping my life into two separate sections. One life I call "BC" (before crazy); the other one is simply "now." But it's not until I hear Dr. Thornton say that hideous word that I begin to differentiate between the two separate lifetimes. Even then I am not entirely convinced. The convincing will take time.

"Do you *know* what schizophrenia is?" he asks me in a voice that reminds me of a grade-school teacher. We are seated in his wood-paneled office, dimly lit and somber, as if the room itself is warning me that all is not well in here. The sun sinks low into the sky, and I am terribly worried that my mother isn't coming back to get me. I fidget with the stack of papers that I have promised to read.

"Schizophrenia." I pronounce the word as if it's my turn in a spelling bee, as if I'm about to articulate each letter correctly, although I doubt I can. Still, I don't want to appear stupid. It seems I've spent the entire day trying hard not to appear stupid or crazy. "Doesn't it mean you have a split mind?" I venture carefully. "Or is that like a multiple personality disorder?"

"I can see you're a smart young woman, Alice, and I want to speak candidly with you now." He leans forward, and the bald spot on the top of his head glimmers from his desk lamp. He is a small man but intense and, I suspect, powerful. At least in this God-forsaken place where everyone seems to jump whenever he walks by.

I nod in agreement, as if I'm his colleague and not some crazy misfit that he'd just as soon lock up.

"The word *schizophrenia* does mean 'split-mind' in Greek, but that's not what this illness is about. This is an illness of the brain. You might call it an impairment or chemical imbalance, but for whatever reason the brain is unable to differentiate between what is real and what is not. It experiences hallucinations that can be very deceptive. These hallucinations can come in audible or visual forms. Some people even experience what seems like an assault on their entire sensory system. They smell aromas that don't exist. Like smoke for instance. It's as if the brain's ability to send messages is completely scrambled. Does this make any sense to you?"

I press my lips together and nod without speaking. As much as I hate to admit it, some of what he's saying *does* make sense. But then how would I know since I'm the one who's supposedly crazy here? Besides, I am fairly tired and discouraged right now. It's been a long day filled with all sorts of tests. I've been poked and prodded and quizzed and examined. During my "questionings," I lied again and again. Particularly in response to the inquiries about hearing voices or seeing faces that don't exist. I mean how would I know if they exist or not? I'm the one who's supposed to be bonkers. How can I be expected to discern what's real and what's not? If I'm nuts, that is. I'm still not convinced that Dr. Thornton hasn't been sent by Pastor John and my other enemies. How to tell if you're crazy or not? Aren't we all a little crazy?

I guess I must've let my guard down there for a moment and possibly even said some of those thoughts out loud, because I am now being lectured on how they don't use the words *crazy, nuts,* or *bonkers* here.

"Okay." I shrug now, getting weary of the game that never ends.

"It's an illness," he tells me again, as if being told that you are sick is encouraging.

"So, how'd I catch it?" I ask in a flippant voice.

"It's not contagious, Alice. But it is hereditary."

"Grandma." It's not a question as much as an answer.

He nods. "You know that she was diagnosed as schizophrenic-paranoid?"

"Paranoid? As in thinking that people were trying to get her?"

He nods again. "Do you experience that too, Alice?"

"No," I answer quickly, probably too quickly. I look down at the papers in my lap and pretend to be quite interested. Then in a quiet voice I ask the dreaded question. "When can my mom take me home?"

"As soon as we finish."

I'm not sure whether I can trust him, but I wait while he writes something on one of those little white pads that doctors like to use. "I am prescribing an antipsychotic. It should help you to think more clearly."

I don't tell him that I *have* been thinking quite clearly. Too clearly, I'm afraid. Or that I am able to interpret the ancient Scriptures, discern God's deepest mysteries, and even write prophetic inspirations. Somehow I don't think he'd appreciate this sort of clarity.

He tears off the sheet. "This is for clozapine. My nurse will give you some samples to tide you over until your mother can get to the drugstore. It's fairly mild with some side effects like dry mouth, sleepiness, and rapid heartbeat. Just read the paper in the sample box; it's all there. You need to avoid caffeine and nicotine, as well as alcohol and any other drugs, of course. However, I am pleased to see that your blood test shows you are clean of drugs, Alice. Good for you."

Clean of drugs until now, I'm thinking. Until I start taking his little prescription. But what makes his particular brand of drugs so good? Still, I keep these questions to myself. Or at least I think I do. I can never be sure what's going through my mind and coming out of my mouth these days. I take his little white notepaper and nod as if everything is perfectly fine. I just want out of here. But I'm thinking, You can't make me take your stupid pills. It could be more of the poison they've been slipping into my food.

"It's natural for you to want to resist the meds." He peers over his half-glasses at me, and now I am worried he can actually read my mind because I am certain I didn't just say that.

I hold up the paper and force a smile to my lips. "Don't worry. I'll take these. I want to get well."

"You need to understand that the only reason I'm not keeping you here at Forest Hills today is because your mother has promised to oversee your recovery at home. She has assured me that you will take your meds. But it's your choice, Alice. If you refuse, you will find yourself right back here with us. Not that that's a bad option. This is, after all, a place of healing." He smiles now, and I suddenly remember, word for word, a poem from the Alice book.

How doth the little crocodile
Improve his shining tail,
And pour the waters of the Nile
On every golden scale!

How cheerfully he seems to grin,
How neatly spread his claws,
And welcome little fishes in
With gently smiling jaws!

I hold tightly to Dr. Thornton's little white slip of paper and assure him once more that I do want to get better as I carefully back up toward the door.

"That's the key," he tells me as he pats my back.

No, I'm thinking, that is not *the* key. Not the golden key. Still, I am cornered. What are my choices anyway? As I walk back toward the reception area, I wonder again if Dr. Thornton is in cahoots with Pastor John and Mrs. Knoll. Perhaps even my mother is involved. Who can you trust? Who can you trust?

Trust Jesus.

I turn around to see who said that. I know it's not Amelia, although the voice is somewhat comforting. And it's nothing like Pastor John's voice or any of the church people. There's obviously no one in the hallway, but then it's nothing new to hear voices that have no bodies attached. But it's not like those other voices, the vicious ones that threaten to destroy me. I'm sure that I just imagined it.

Nurse Kelly already has the clozapine samples ready for me when I reach the reception area. She is smiling, just as she did earlier when she talked me into eating a green salad and a small bowl of peaches in the cafeteria. She told me she's a vegetarian and can understand my aversion to meats. She's a pretty woman, early thirties I'd guess, but not the showy type. She has nice white teeth and dark hair that's smoothed back into a neat ponytail. For some reason I don't think she's part of this particular conspiracy. But then how can I be sure?

"Make sure you take these with food." She gently squeezes my arm. "You could use a little more weight on you, Alice."

Despite her kindness, I'm still not convinced they're going to let me leave. I walk quickly to the waiting area. I expect to find it empty and deserted, the front door locked. But there's my mother, reading what looks like a well-worn magazine. She stands quickly and walks my way.

"Everything okay, dear?"

"Just peachy."

She smiles a stiff smile and picks up her handbag and coat. I cling to my backpack as I tentatively head toward the front exit, still expecting someone to run up and stop me. I remember seeing a fairly burly looking orderly earlier today as I was waiting in the hallway for a blood test. He had to hold down an agitated man while a nurse injected the poor guy with what I'm sure was some sort of sedative. I felt sorry for the man but must also admit to feeling slightly relieved when his screaming finally came to a halt. I didn't allow myself to look at him again after that. Not only because it seemed disrespectful, but also because I felt truly scared deep inside my soul. It seems so wrong to treat another human being this way.

"Did you get the samples?" she asks as I open the door and bolt out into the cool evening air.

I turn and hand the packets to her. "Here, you might as well keep them since you're supposed to be managing my meds." I am sorry to hear my sarcastic tone. I tell myself that it's not my mother's fault, that she's not the enemy. But how can I be sure?

As she drives home in the semidarkness, I contrive an elaborate scheme that I will use to make her believe I am taking my pills. I imagine how I will "take them with food" as Nurse Kelly recommended, but somehow I will adhere them to the roof of my mouth, and then when my mother's not looking, I will slip them into my napkin or a pocket or something. I'm not sure if it's my idea or Amelia's, but it makes perfect sense to me.

My mother is talking about my brother, Aaron, now, telling me how well he's doing in football, how fortunate he was to get that full scholarship to the junior college. I nod and act as if I'm listening, as if everything is still perfectly normal, as if I still care about anyone or anything other than my messed-up little life.

But I'm still pondering Dr. Thornton's words about schizophrenia and how it's an illness that can be managed, if not cured. And I'll admit that a small part of me actually wants to believe him, but that seems to be the BC part of me, the part that has been neatly sliced off and tossed away. Mostly I remember Grandma...how she sat in a chair with a blank stare and didn't even recognize her own daughter. Do I want to end up like her? Locked up and doped up and totally useless? I don't think so. No, I'm certain there must be another way out of this mess. Somehow my "messed-up" brain will figure it out. I'll show them!

chapter SEVEN

The Tiny Door

It seems there is a tiny door that I must walk through. It is called "normal." But I am not. As a result I cannot fit through this door. And yet *they* keep telling me I must go through it. *They* being my mom, the doctor, and the medical profession in general—at least according to the literature that Dr. Thornton gave me to read. Now at times some of this actually makes sense, and then at other times it all sounds absolutely ridiculous. I wonder where they get this stuff. I wonder who invented "normal" in the first place. And I question whether or not it really exists. Or if it exists, perhaps it's not for me. Because I am certain this is a door I will never be able to squeeze through.

Now the other *they* have been curiously silent these past couple of days. I'm not sure if it's because I'm in my family home, in familiar territory, and *they* don't feel quite comfortable here. Or perhaps, other than Amelia, they simply haven't located me yet. I never did send my change-of-address card. Just the same, one can never be too sure. They may be waiting on my porch right now.

But back to the tiny door, the one I'm expected to force myself through. As I recall, the only way the other Alice could fit through her tiny door was to take the pills that made her get very, very small. I guess that is what Dr. Thornton's pills are supposed to do for me. Make me very, very small. Or, in a word, *normal.* But what if I don't care to be normal or even very small for that matter? Shouldn't I have a choice in these things? It is, after all, my life. Or rather it used to be. Sometimes I wonder who's really running things here. And did I only imagine that God was speaking to me, that he gave me the golden key and all the answers? It seemed so real at the time, and at times still does, despite what everyone else keeps telling me. And I worry that these "normal" pills will undo something important and powerful. Yet at the same time I'm not so sure.

Anyway, I just don't know who I can believe anymore. So naturally I balk at taking these suspicious pills. Not only that, but according to the manufacturer, these pills can have some pretty frightening side effects, like temporary paralysis or liver damage or even death. Of course, the fine black print assures me: "These reactions are statistically rare." But can they promise me that it won't happen? Of course not. And that makes me wonder why has this happened to me in the first place. Why was *I* chosen to get this insidious disease—if I really do have it—and did God have anything to do with that? Did I have to get this disease so that I could hear him and accept the golden key? Or have I only imagined all this?

So far I've only taken two pills, one last night and one this morning, and only because my mother was so insistent. I'm sure I've never seen her so strong willed, so unmovable—like a boulder. She won't budge until she's satisfied that I've swallowed the pill. She even makes me open my mouth wide and stick out my tongue. It's a whole new side of her and not necessarily a bad thing, at least under different circumstances. She certainly wasn't this assertive when my father was alive.

Still I can't see that the pills have made much difference, other than muffling everything. I suddenly feel like I've got a head cold, both inside my head and out, like I'm wrapped in this fluffy gray cocoon. But I haven't begun to shrink yet. And at this rate, I doubt that I'll ever be able to make it through that tiny door. Maybe I am hopeless. But normal seems farther away than ever.

Now I've begun to suspect that the reason I must pass through the tiny door is to reach *the other side.* Sort of like that old chicken-crossing-the-road joke. But even this has me worried. For I have no idea what awaits me on *the other side.* Things could get even worse for me over there in "Normalville." Or what if, like the other Alice, these magic pills make me shrink so small that I cannot be heard or seen—or, worse yet, I cease to exist at all? Or what if I am so minuscule that someone, say Pastor John, comes along and steps on me and crushes me like a bug beneath his boot? What then?

So whether or not to take these pills is not a simple black-and-white question. Like everything else, it's just varying shades of gray. Everything's confusing and frightening, and it seems I have absolutely no control over my life. So I stay in my room, imagining that I might possibly have some control up here.

Being in my little blue bedroom with its fussy eyelet curtains and dust ruffle brought some comfort—at first anyway. I just walked around and around and stared at everything as if seeing it all for the first time, and yet I knew each item, every picture on the wall, my violin case still leaning inside the closet, my stuffed rabbit with the ear that flops down over his eye. It was like a déjà vu. Realistic and familiar but not really real.

Yet it wasn't long before the dimensions of my old room became confining and slightly terrifying. And even now as I sit on my crisp white bed, hands folded neatly in my lap and telling myself just to chill, I still feel that I might totally lose it and that I will scream so loudly the whole neighborhood will step out to the street to see what on earth is going on in the Laxton house. Perhaps the whole town of Warren will be on alert—the KBDX noontime news will warn its citizens to be on the lookout for that crazy girl who went flipping mad on Persimmon Lane.

When I'm not sleeping, I count things—the panes in the windows, the pencils in the cup, the jigsaw puzzles in my closet, even the white flowers on the pale blue wallpaper. Soon my room feels like an itchy wool sweater that shrank three sizes too small. Everything in here is much too tight. The walls press in on me, closer and closer. And those little flowers on the wallpaper are growing to tropical dimensions and suffocating me with their sticky fragrance—just like an old woman's overbearing perfume in a hot, stuffy elevator.

I must have become the other Alice, when she grew bigger and bigger and finally became trapped in the White Rabbit's little house. My arms will soon stick out through the windows, my feet will protrude out the door, and my head will pop right out of the roof or maybe the chimney. I am totally confined and claustrophobic. I cannot breathe. I want to knock down these walls and break free and actually scream. Yes, it seems very clear; I must be going mad.

Like the other Alice, I decide I must take these stupid pills that will shrink me back down to size if I want to survive. Size: normal, medium, regular, average, one-size-fits-all. Oh, I don't really want to become small and shrunken and meaningless again. I would much rather be large and important and special. It frightens me to give in like this. And yet it frightens me not to.

What are my alternatives though? I vaguely wonder if it's possible to break free from here—to escape my boulder mother and this stuffy little room? I imagine lacing up my old track shoes and sprinting right out the front door. I could run and run and run until there's only fluid motion, like a horse across an open pasture. But where would I go? Where would I ever fit in? What if all the doors are just this small? What if I am too big to pass through any? What then? Must I always remain on the other side?

I am so lonely. Exceedingly lonely.

chapter EIGHT

Advice from a Caterpillar

I t's been three days, and I've only managed to fool my mom about not taking my pills twice. She's sharper than I supposed. Sometimes it almost seems like she's on my side too, although I can't really be sure. I'm not sure what I think about these pills either or if I even care. Mostly they just make me sleep a lot, and when I'm not asleep, it's almost as if I'm sleepwalking since I sort of shuffle around in this thick green fog. Sort of like I'm numb, like my whole body's been shot with Novocain. Naturally, my mom acts as though everything's just groovy. She keeps up this positive front and says things like she's "so thankful that God is healing me." What does that mean?

She thinks life is wonderful because I'm finally eating "real food." Of course, I can't taste it and don't feel the least bit hungry. But, hey, if it makes her happy…

Before I got up this morning, I was thinking, or maybe I was dreaming—it's hard to tell—about the old grape arbor that used to grow in our backyard. I remember how I used to sit beneath that sweet smelling green canopy and dream big dreams, back in my childhood, back when I was too little to know any better. I wonder if it's still there—the arbor, I mean.

When I finally make my way downstairs, moving my thick feet in slow motion, it's nearly noon, and I shovel down a bowl of soggy cornflakes. Then as my mom watches, I pop a pill into my mouth and pretend to swallow. She smiles and turns away, and I manage to extract the soggy pill and slip it into the back pocket of my jeans before she even looks back. That makes three times!

After this private little victory I trudge out to the backyard, imagining that I am more myself than usual, but it's probably just an illusion. Still, I am relieved to discover that the grapevine, although somewhat overgrown, remains intact. Not only that, but after a careful search I find that it still has several bunches of fat purple grapes, and they appear to be ripe. I pick a bunch and then just stare at their frosty looking surfaces in wonder. For some reason they seem surprisingly familiar. In fact, they remind me of me. Kind of hazy but with the promise of something good underneath. Or at least I hope so. I wish it were so.

"Whazzup?"

I glance over the cyclone fence that separates our house from the Fosters to see a long-haired, gangly man peering down at me. I squint up at him, trying to figure out why he looks vaguely familiar, then suddenly remember. *Brent Foster,* the pervert who enticed me up into his tree house and then attempted to rape me—well, something like that. I was about five at the time, and he was probably around seven. As I recall, he wanted to "play doctor," and naturally I was supposed to be the patient. But even then I knew what he wanted to do was wrong, and somehow I managed to push him away and run home.

I never did tell my parents about it. I was too embarrassed. Besides, I felt certain they would get mad at me and say it was all my fault. I feel myself flush with embarrassment as I look at Brent now.

Then I wonder why I should even care. It was so long ago, and we were just stupid kids anyway. How small it seems compared to the larger scheme of messed-up grownup lives. I study his shaggy brown hair, leaning toward dreadlocks, and his baggy and raggedy clothes. Not that I should be one to pass a fashion judgment these days. I notice that he's wearing a goofy smile and actually looks fairly harmless today. Plus he's safely on the other side of the fence. Curious for a better look, I stand up and walk over to the fence.

"Been playing doctor lately?" I ask with an air of nonchalance.

He laughs. "Nah, but I wouldn't mind another go-round. Ya interested?"

"Yeah, you bet." I roll my eyes at him with disgust, then return to examining my lovely bunch of grapes.

"Wha'd'ya got there?"

"Grapes." I pluck one off and hold it out temptingly before him. Then he takes it and pops it in his mouth.

"Not bad." He nods his head with satisfaction. "Wanna get high?"

He sits down on an old stump now, carefully rolling out a joint on the knee of his threadbare cords. He expertly twists the ends, then holds it up in triumph. He grins, and I am suddenly reminded of the smoking caterpillar in the Alice book, the one who wanted to give her "advice." Brent pulls out a cheap plastic lighter, and puckering up his face with an almost religious intensity, he ignites his precious reefer. Then his eyes flutter closed, and his face relaxes as he slowly inhales. I watch in fascination as he holds in the smoke, his eyebrows lifting as if he's about to enter a new dimension. Then slowly he exhales, opens his eyes, and holds out the joint.

"Want a puff?"

Now I wonder what effect weed might have if it "interacts with" my "prescribed" drug. At the moment I can't remember the specific warnings that were written in the fine black print. Perhaps it would simply counteract the loathsome pills and completely nullify their effect. And that possibility intrigues me. I am so weary of this dulling sensation. My mind is wrapped in a thick fuzzy blanket, slightly dazed and horribly flat-lined. I know that grass is some sort of hallucinogenic. I remember at least that much from high school health. But I've never actually tried it before. And during my BC life, I never would've considered it at all. But since everything else about my life seems to be messed up and upside down or sideways, I wonder, Well, why not try something new?

"Sure." I hold out my hand. "I'll try a puff."

He hands it over. "Cool."

I imitate him by taking a long, slow drag and hold it in until I finally begin to sputter and cough. I have quite a coughing jag with real tears coming out of my eyes, and I feel rather foolish. But at the same time I feel sort of good, too. It may be an illusion, but it seems this act of defiance has given me a morsel of control again. I wipe my nose on my sleeve, then hand the joint back to him.

Brent is laughing now. "That your first puff?"

I nod as I wipe the sides of my eyes and finally manage to sputter, "But it was"—*cough, cough*—"okay, you know?"

"I know." He takes another slow drag, and I watch as the embers on the end burn bright red. Then he hands it back to me. "Go easy this time."

So, taking it more slowly, I inhale a smaller puff and manage not to make such a fool of myself this time. I hand it back to him feeling pretty cool. "Thanks," I say as I exhale.

"So what're ya doing back home? Thought both you high-performance Laxton kids were in college." He rolls his eyes dramatically. "My mom's always going on about how the neighbor kids got it so together—you about to graduate and Aaron with his scholarship. Man, it makes me wanna puke." He hands me back the joint, and I take another drag.

"Well, if it makes you feel any better,"—I start to giggle now— "I've just been diagnosed with *schizophrenia*." For some reason just saying the word out loud, to someone as whacked out as Brent, totally cracks me up.

Apparently he thinks it's pretty funny too. "You're kidding me? Schizophrenia? Sweet little Alice, the good little church girl next door, is a nut case. *Cool!*"

"Yeah, now I can get my drugs prescribed to me." I extract the little pill from my pocket and hold it up. It's slightly disfigured and gray from being in my pocket. "But today I didn't take it."

"Cool. You can get high with me instead."

I take another drag and nod. "Yeah, let's get high."

"Got any more of those?" He points to my lap.

"These?" I hold up my half-eaten bunch of grapes as if they're a trophy. "These happen to grow right here in our very own backyard."

"No kidding. Can I have some?"

"Sure." I wave my hand in a most congenial fashion. "Come on over. We'll have ourselves a grapefest."

So, like little kids, we sit down under the grapevine and proceed to gorge ourselves with Concord grapes, spitting the slimy seeds at each other until we both look like targets for bird-dropping practice. I find it to all be quite hilarious. I can't remember when I've had this much fun.

"So were you telling the truth?" he asks. "Are you *really* crazy?"

I lower my voice and, imitating the doctor, say, "Well, we don't call it that, son. It's an illness, you see."

He shakes his head. "Too bad."

"Hey, I thought you said it was cool."

He frowns. "Well, yeah, it's kind of cool. I mean I feel sorry for people who are, you know, all ordinary and boring-like. I think life's way more interesting with a few kooks around."

"You think I'm a kook?"

He leans over and appears to study me closely. "Maybe…maybe not. Can't say for sure just yet."

I laugh. "What if I told you that I hear voices and see things?"

"Sounds like you're having your own kind of high."

"Yeah, but some people say it's wrong because I can't tell the difference between what's real and what's not."

"Hey, reality is all in your head anyway."

I nod. "You know what, you're absolutely right." The next thing I know, I'm quoting Brent Foster, high school dropout and doper extraordinaire, as if he is Einstein himself. *"Reality is all in your head."*

"Like *my* reality." He leans back on the damp ground and looks

up at the arbor. "My reality is to live and let live. Just hang loose...
laid back. But my mom thinks I'm totally messed up because,
according to her, I 'don't wanna do nothin' with my life.' But, hey, if
I don't wanna do nothin', then why should I?"

"Why should you?" I echo, then laugh.

"Why should anyone?"

"I haven't the slightest."

"Just get high and be happy." He spews a grape seed in my direction and laughs when it splats me right on the forehead.

Feeling quite profound and intelligent, I say, "In the words of
John Lennon, let it be." Naturally, this leads us both into the old
song. I remember some of the words and hum along with the rest.

Before long, we're both on our backs beneath the grapevine,
holding grapes above our mouths and eating them like the decadent
Romans—or was it the Greeks?—and I am feeling lighter than I've
felt in some time. I think I hear someone calling my name. But it
might be my imagination, and I don't really care. Maybe it's Amelia,
or maybe it's my mom. Maybe it's the White Rabbit wanting me to
go play croquet with the Queen of Hearts. But as Brent says—or was
it John?—just let 'em be.

"Alice!" My mom is standing over me now, looking down on
Brent and me as though she's just discovered us naked. I sit up and
grin stupidly. Then I notice a couple of forms looming behind her. I
peer up to see that it's only the praying church ladies—Mary Cates
and creepy old Mrs. Knolls.

"Back for the next exorcism?" I ask.

Brent starts to snicker.

Mrs. Knoll steps closer and glares down at me. "Alice Laxton! Are you smoking marijuana?" She frowns as she points to the twisted end of the joint still hanging limply between my forefinger and thumb. I'd completely forgotten that I still have it, but it's clearly cold now.

"Not anymore." I giggle as I hand it back to Brent.

She gasps and turns to my mother. "Well, it's plain to see what's wrong with your daughter and why she's so plagued with demons. Why, just look at her!"

"Anybody wanna grape?" I offer the ladies, holding up my slightly picked-over bunch.

"Alice, I want you to come into the house right now." My mother is talking to me as if I'm a preschooler, and I don't particularly care for it.

"Sorry, Mom, but I want to stay out here. I'm playing with my new friend right now." I glance over at Brent and toss him a sloppy grin. He grins back, and I'm thinking he'd probably *really* like to play with me.

"Alice!" Mom's voice is like granite now. I'm sure it's as much for the church ladies as it is for me. "If you are going to live under *my* roof, you are going to abide by *my* rules. *Do you understand?*"

I nod, trying to appear compliant.

"Then get into the house right this minute!"

Now I shake my head in a firm negative. "I do understand. But I guess I won't be living under *your* roof, Mom, because I can't abide by *your* rules. Your rules suck! And the church's rules suck! You all suck!"

"Amen!" yells Brent.

I stand up now, ready for the fight. "I've spent my whole life having you and that stupid Salvation Center telling me what to do, how to act, how to think, how to dress, and, well, I'm just *not* going to do it anymore. Look at you, Mom. You've spent most of your life cleaning up after everyone and acting like you were inferior to a husband who didn't mind taking his fist to you now and then if he got the hankering. You act like it's God's will for people to walk all over—"

I see her gasp as she glances nervously at the church ladies, but I continue anyway, pointing my finger right in her face. "You don't question a single thing the church tells you to do, Mom. Or I should say what they tell you *not* to do. Because that's really what it's all about, isn't it? You can *not* go to movies, you can *not* watch TV, you must *not* read most books, you can *not* wear makeup, you can *not* have a career—if you're a woman, that is—you can *not* think for yourself—"

"Get thee behind me, Satan!" yells Mrs. Knolls, waving her crooked finger in my direction.

Mary Cates doesn't waste a minute either. Now both of them are binding and loosing and casting out the demons. Meanwhile, Brent and I are back on the lawn, rolling and laughing uncontrollably. When I finally recover and manage to look up, I see my mother simply standing there, clasping her hands, with wide, tear-filled eyes. She is clearly horrified by my behavior.

This sobers me slightly, and I almost regret my words. I see the other two women gather around her, probably consoling her for having raised such a wantonly hopeless and evil child. When no one is looking, I sneak the mangled pill from my pocket and slip it into my mouth as if *that's* going to make everything better.

But my futile act of submission makes no difference. Nothing can save me now. Mom straightens her shoulders and announces to

God and everyone else in the neighborhood that she's taking me back to Forest Hills *today.*

She pulls me up by my arm, which seems disconnected from my body. But she and the ladies tug and pull until I am finally on my feet. Then my mother shouts, "Let's go, Alice, now!"

I flap my hand in a pitiful little wave to my caterpillar friend as I am dragged by the church ladies back toward the house. I try to remember his advice about live and let live and just letting it be, but somehow I don't think that's going to work for me at Forest Hills.

"Come visit me at the funny farm," I call over my shoulder.

chapter NINE

The Queen's Prison

It took all three of them to drag me into Forest Hills. Mary Cates, Mrs. Knolls, and my mother. I think Mrs. Knolls put her army nurse skills into action by taking charge of the entire operation. She's pretty tough for an old broad. I even have the bruises to prove it. As I recall, and my memory is still rather blurry thanks to my "stronger and newly improved" meds, she sat on top of me in the back of Mary Cates's minivan. But I think I managed to bite her once. Or maybe I bit myself. I'm not totally sure about the details.

In the end, my resistance proved futile and only managed to get me locked up in the highest security—Level Three, or the Queen's Prison as I have come to think of it. I imagine Mrs. Knolls to be the Red Queen now, the one who always wants to chop off my head, and it seems she is the main reason I am here. Although I suspect there are many players in this game. It's hard to know who is really behind it all, and it doesn't help that I've been heavily sedated for several days—or longer. I'm not even sure how long I've been here. Time is insignificant and something of a blur, since every day looks the same as the one before. But I think it might be November now. The trees have lost most of their leaves, and the sky has that leaden cast of late fall.

What I do remember about the horrible ride is that Amelia finally showed up. And she spoke to me quite urgently. She kept saying, "It's time! It's time!" And somehow I knew what she meant. *Time to kill.* Not the church ladies or my mother. No, it was time to silence myself…before it was too late. I agreed with her to take care of this, but my memory tends to fade after that.

According to Dr. Thornton, I made a feeble attempt to take my own life, but I honestly can't remember such a thing, although I do remember receiving a painful injection into my rump right after I was put into "restraints." But I wonder if the doctor just made up the suicide thing as an excuse to lock me in here at Level Three, where things like padded cells and straitjackets are common. I've been told I can move to Level Two if I become more cooperative, but I'm sure it's just a trick. I'm sure there is only one "level," and it is here. I am not willing to cooperate with people who tell lies.

Although my resistance seems futile because, naturally, they have the upper hand. They have all the restraints and drugs and orderlies and hypodermic needles. If this were a regular sort of prison, I might be able to fight and resist within the freedom of my own mind and soul, but it seems they even control those parts of me now. More and more I feel I have nothing. Am nothing. Why should I want to live? Why do they care whether I kill myself or not? I'm guessing it has to do with my golden key, my notebooks, and the secrets that have been planted into my mind. Sometimes I wish they'd just take everything and simply dispose of me and get this thing over with.

I know they're watching me in the Queen's Prison. Amelia

doesn't visit very often, but when she comes, she always warns me that this place is wired and full of spies. Some of them dress up like staff, and some dress up like patients. However, I do think some of them really are patients—or at least they are here against their will. It's just hard to tell who is which. Therefore, I trust no one. For a while I thought the colors of the blankets provided a code. I noticed right away how some of them are yellow and some are blue. Since mine is yellow, I thought that was for patients. But then they switched my blanket to blue. They are trying to confuse me.

They *say* this is a hospital, but I can tell it's a prison. There are locks on all the doors, and a mesh that looks like chicken wire runs through the glass windows. My food is brought to me on an unbreakable plastic tray (I know it's unbreakable, since I threw it once). I get no utensils to eat with, not even plastic, in case I should decide to hurt myself or someone else. I have been informed by Dr. Thornton that restraints will continue to be used if necessary. So far this has been necessary twice. It is the worst feeling imaginable to be tied up like an animal, completely helpless. You can't even wipe your own nose. Naturally, I want to avoid their contraptions if I can, but I'm not promising anything.

The woman in the room next to mine screams almost constantly. I think she is a patient. I call her the Duchess since she's always in a royally foul mood. She screams so much that I'm sure some of the noise must be coming from the pig baby, and there are times I expect her to blast into my room and throw the squealing swine right at me. But this hasn't happened yet.

The scrawny blond "orderly" with the thin pale mustache is definitely a spy. I can tell by the way he walks, very stiff legged, sort of like a goose. I'm sure he is hiding sound and photography equipment in his baggy pants. He pretends he is cleaning my room, but I know he is gathering information to be used against me.

The stocky red-headed nurse is a spy too. She pretends she's doing medical procedures on me, checking my blood pressure and heart rate and taking blood samples, but I know that she's just trying to get information. I'm afraid she's already inserted implants beneath my skin to monitor me. And every time she sticks a needle in me, which is quite often, I suspect she's filling me full of chemicals to make me forget or else to poison me—or maybe both.

Why else would they need to check these things so often? And why would they need to keep drawing my blood? Do they plan to kill me this way? Slowly so that no one notices? How long does it take to drain the blood from a human before he dies? I'm shorter than average and underweight too, so I'm guessing I could go faster than most.

My mom has been to visit me every day. But so far I've completely ignored her. She is definitely the enemy. This all became painfully clear the day the three of them dragged me in here.

And of course my notebooks are gone. If I were speaking to my mother, I would ask her where they went. Maybe someone here took them. I knew they would fall into the wrong hands sooner or later. I probably should've destroyed them when I had the chance. My mother brought me a sketch pad and pencil, but the pencil was taken away from me when I tried to use it to defend myself. I know the pad and pencil were only a trick—a way for them to extract more information from me. So I'm not talking or writing or anything. I will just stay quietly in my jail cell until I am dead. I'm thinking it shouldn't be long, since I'm barely eating now. It bot

where I'll go when I'm dead. I wish it we

dreamless sleep, but I'm afraid that might r

Sometimes I have nightmares so terrify

I'm awake or asleep. But the experience is

uncontrollably, as if I'm having a seizure ar

burst. I have seen Satan and his demons in these moments. I have smelled their sulfurous smoke. I have even felt their fire melting the flesh from my bones. And I have been horrified by the tortured screams I've heard while there. I am scared beyond words that Pastor John's sermons, the ones I endured as a child and suffered nightmares from, might be true after all. *What if they are true?*

So I wonder sometimes, What if *that's* really what happens when I die? What if the church ladies are right, and I am evil, and I am going to hell? What then? The Queen's Prison might seem hellish to me now, but this is nothing compared to what I've seen in the night. This fear alone almost makes me want to live.

And yet I believe they are slowly killing me here.

chapter TEN

Adventures in Wonderland

It turns out I was wrong. There actually is a Level Two in this place. I suppose this might mean there is also a Level One, but I'm not jumping to any conclusions yet.

After I finally decided to cooperate with Dr. Thornton and his "staff"—this was to determine whether or not they were lying—I was eventually moved to Level Two, or what I now think of as Wonderland.

Many strange creatures inhabit Wonderland. There is this older woman with a shaved head, named Dorothy, who carries around a pink toy telephone and has conversations with God. At first I thought she was telling him about me, but now I'm not so sure. I heard her promising him that she'd be good if he'd come pick her up. So far he hasn't shown.

Then there's Ben. He's pretty old and sweet looking in his plaid flannel shirts. He likes to play checkers and watch sitcoms on TV. He seems pretty quiet and subdued most of the time, but every once in a while he just erupts into a fit of profanity and swearing and has to be given a shot and taken back to his room. I am sorry for him though, because I suspect he doesn't mean to do this. I think I know how he feels.

Then there's this teenage girl with scars all over her arms and legs. She's really sort of pretty with dark brown hair and big eyes like a doe's. When I first saw her, I suspected the scars might be from the implants the nurses are always inserting into the real patients. One day when I was certain we were the only two in the bathroom, I asked her about them.

Without looking directly at me, she simply answered, "No, I did this to myself."

I wasn't sure if I believed her or not. Maybe they told her to say that. Then when I mentioned it to Nurse Kelly, she told me that the girl's name is Lisa and that she's a cutter.

"What's a cutter?" I asked.

"Someone who cuts himself."

Well, this makes absolutely no sense to me, but then not much does anyway.

I've also noticed a guy about my age named Jason, who Nurse Kelly says is schizophrenic too. She keeps telling me that I should talk to him, that I should ask him how he's dealing with his life.

"And you better not wait too long, Alice, since he's about to be moved to Level One," she says.

I eye her suspiciously. "What is Level One, really?" Sometimes I almost think I can trust her, but then again she might just be really good at playing this game.

"Level One is when you're released to go home. You only come in here for outpatient treatment after that."

"What does that mean?"

"You just come in here every week so we can check your blood and make sure your meds are working."

I nod like this makes sense, but I'm not sure if this is true or not.

"Talk to Jason," she urges me with one of her smiles. "He can tell you some of the things he's been through."

But I'm worried that Jason might be a spy, because he looks far too normal to me. Plus he talks with the staff way too much. That in itself looks suspicious.

And the staff people are an odd bunch too. But then what can you expect? I mean they are either spies, and I'm seriously starting to question this theory, or they like bossing around the poor crazy folks. Which one is worse, I'm not sure.

Like this one nurse's aide named Frieda. Talk about weird. She's got orange hair that's styled within an inch of its life. She scurries around like a hyped-up bird, chirping at everyone as if she's in charge of the whole nutty place, and yet she's really just an aide. Her big thing is cleanliness. It's like she's obsessed with it. She's always telling people to wash their hands or clean this up or sweep that. She could drive a sane person crazy. Maybe that's why she's here—to keep us all in our places.

Then there's this male nurse named Henry, a great big black guy who wears a gold chain and looks like he used to play professional football. I was kind of scared of him at first. Turns out he's pretty nice and surprisingly gentle. When he draws my blood samples, I hardly even feel it.

Today I surprised myself by asking Henry if there's a reason for all this bloodletting or if it's simply a form of torture.

He laughs at first but then realizes I am serious. "I'm sorry," he says kindly. "Hasn't anyone ever told you why we do this?"

I shake my head and feel stupid.

"We've got to measure the level of medication in your body. If you get too much it can harm your white blood cells, and that wouldn't be good." He looks me in the eyes now. "The reason you're here is to get better, Alice."

"Really?" I ask.

He nods.

"So I can go home."

"If you get well enough."

"Do very many people get well enough to go home?"

Now Henry glances toward the door as he puts the little rubber cap on the tube of dark red blood. This worries me some.

"Henry," I plead, "I need to know. Do very many people get to go home from here?"

He shrugs and packs up his stuff. "I suppose that's something you should discuss with Dr. Thornton."

So now I'm wondering if they just want to keep people in here forever. After all, this is a way for them to make money. If everyone got well and left, then where would they be? Even my mother tells me, "This place is not cheap, Alice." Then she usually adds, as if it's going to convince me, "I'm doing this for your own good." Another one of her favorite lines these days. I have started talking to her but just barely. I still haven't forgiven her for bringing me—and for the way she did it. I still believe that was very, very wrong. And because of that, I find it hard to completely trust her or believe what she tells me.

Anyway, I'm thinking about talking to Jason and asking him about his "illness." But I'm going to watch him carefully when he answers. After all, I know a little about this whole business myself, and I doubt he can pull one over on me. Then again he may have been carefully trained in how to deceive patients. He might just be a setup—someone they use to get your hopes up so they can keep you subdued while you do your time.

The truth is, I am feeling a tiny bit better these days. Okay, maybe I am a little dopey from the meds, and I don't feel at all human. But I am sleeping a little better, and I eat most of my food— at least the parts that are recognizable. My thinking seems fairly normal, at least to me. If I seem suspicious and skeptical to others, then I'd like to invite them to walk a mile or two in my shoes and see how they like it. There's plenty to be suspicious about around this place.

So if I am better, then why can't I leave? Why can't I get out and get on with my life? Although I'm not entirely sure what kind of life I'll have left. Will I be able to go back to school? Or has the university been informed that Alice Laxton has gone crazy? Have they neatly erased my transcript from their computers, wiped me off their records?

I just wish there were some way out of this place. I've been looking at all the doors and windows and trying to figure how to escape, but so far I haven't come up with anything. But I'm not giving up.

I have this feeling that if I don't take matters into my own hands and get out of here on my own, I'll end up just like my grandma. That I will live inside these walls until I die. Then I remember she did manage to escape every once in a while. Now if an old woman could break out of here, surely I can.

chapter ELEVEN

A Narrow Escape

I'm sitting in Dr. Thornton's office daring to hope that things might finally be changing for me. He's talking all positively to me now, saying how I've made such good progress and how pleased he is with me and how I'm cooperating so well. Then suddenly he switches gears and asks me about my "symptoms," and I stupidly tell him the truth.

He nods with this knowing look, and I suspect this is exactly how he's duped so many other unsuspecting patients before me. "So the hallucinations haven't completely subsided yet." He makes note of this in my file, and I am silently swearing at myself for letting down my guard with him. What was I thinking?

"I didn't really mean that I *heard* something." I attempt to correct things. "I mean that I *thought* I did. Actually, it was more like a daydream."

He nods again, jotting down even more notes. Probably something such as "patient is in denial."

"I just answered you without thinking," I say quickly and try to laugh it off. "I think I was having a flashback at the—" I stop myself now, realizing I am only digging my hole deeper.

"Don't worry, Alice." His voice turns placating as he peers over his half-glasses. "It usually takes time for the psychosis to completely abate. Sometimes one medication works for a while, then for some reason it stops, and we need to switch. We have patients here who take a number of meds to keep their symptoms under control." He smiles. "We call it a 'cocktail.'"

I sigh and slump down in my chair. This is *not* going the way I'd hoped. I imagine the "quiet" patients, the ones who enjoy a little before-breakfast cocktail and then another one before dinner. These are the patients I usually try to ignore. I've never questioned whether they are spies. They most definitely are not. They are the ones that remind me of my grandma. The ones I do *not* wish to become. These are the patients who are so drugged up that they sit like a sack of potatoes and drool on themselves. Occasionally their limbs will jerk or twitch, but other than that there are few signs of life in them

I know this isn't their fault, and I do pity them. Out of respect, I try not to stare at them the way I did as a child. I know I would not want someone standing there and gaping at me. I don't want anyone to assume that just because I look like a vegetable I am a vegetable.

Sometimes, when I'm bored, I try to imagine what these people would be like without their little "cocktails." Would they suddenly burst into life like some weird horror movie called *Awakening the Dead*? Or maybe they would stand up and sing and dance and have a big old welcome-back party.

"Alice?"

I jerk myself back to attention, realizing that I've let my mind run away with me again. Not a good thing to do when you're in Dr. Thornton's office.

"I'm changing your medication to something a little stronger."
He says this as if he's doing me a huge favor.

"But I—"

"Don't worry." He closes my folder and smiles in his usual con-descending way. "Nurse Kelly will walk you back to your room now."

I recognize my cue to stand and exit, but I want to stay there. I want to yell at him. I want to cuss. I want to tell him that he's as crazy as any of his patients. What sane person would abuse the power to prescribe medications? Why does anyone want to turn living people into barely breathing zombies? I want to wail and scream and carry on, but I know what that will get me—a shot in the rump and a free ticket to the Queen's Dungeon. And so, like a good little Alice, I simply nod and move toward the door. He says good-bye in a satis-fied voice, as if he is the king of his crazy kingdom and his rules reign supreme.

When I get into the reception area, I see neither Nurse Kelly nor the receptionist. I can hear a scuffle going on in the hallway. I'm guessing a new and very distraught patient has arrived, and they are now attempting to subdue—

That's when I notice it. The door to the waiting area is propped open with a black rubber doorstop, the way they do when someone is being difficult or in a stretcher or wheelchair. Without even thinking or looking back, I pass through the open door. This time I don't even have to take a pill to make myself fit. I just walk right through like a normal person. Then I simply walk across the vacant waiting room and continue past the main entrance, and suddenly I am outside.

I continue walking, more quickly now, but without looking back. I can hear my grandma speaking to me now. She is saying,

"Go, honey. Just keep on going. Stay to the right. Walk in the shadows of the evergreen trees, and keep on going."

It's getting dusky outside, and I happen to be wearing a charcoal-colored hooded sweatshirt and my dark jeans. Good camouflage for moving through the shadows. I pull the hood over my hair and begin to jog.

I couldn't have planned this whole thing better if I'd tried. It's as if some hand of fate or God or even my dear departed grandma just opened the doors and said, "Go." *Unbelievable!*

As I jog, I think it might've been nice to have my backpack with me, but then it might've slowed me down too. I feel excitement surge through my veins like electricity. It's the first time I've felt this alive since the day they dragged me in and drugged me up. My morning meds are just beginning to wear off now, and I am incredibly free.

And, oh, does it feel good. As I reach the fence by the road, I know I can easily scale it, and climbing like a crazed monkey, I do. I honestly believe I may have escaped. Over my shoulder I hear my grandmother urging me on.

"Go, honey, just keep going."

chapter TWELVE

The Pig Baby

It's the first time I've ever hitchhiked, but I am not a bit afraid. I believe that God or Grandma or maybe even Amelia is watching out for me. I stand close to the interstate entrance with my thumb sticking out and am picked up within minutes. I run toward an old blue VW van with bumper stickers all over the back. One sticker makes me laugh as I see it in the headlights of a semi: Pray for Whirled Peas.

"Where you headed?" asks the chubby guy at the wheel. His hair is a peacock blue and spiky. He has on a leather vest, and numerous tattoos decorate his arms.

I think for a minute, unsure of my final destination, just anyplace away from Warren and Forest Hills. "Portland," I announce as he takes off, reentering the fast-moving traffic with his little engine whirring but barely going forty. A horn blasts behind us, and a set of headlights illuminates the back window.

"Hey, whazzup?" calls a sleepy voice from the back.

"Just picking up a hitcher," says the guy at the wheel.

"Who's that?" I ask.

"That's Phil. I'm Lane."

"Where you guys headed?"

"Salem."

"But I thought we were going north."

"You're turned around, sister."

"H'm." Why should I be surprised?

"What's in Salem?" I ask.

"Peace rally."

"Huh?"

"Want to come?"

I consider this. "Sure. Why not."

He laughs. "All right! A new recruit."

"So what are you guys protesting?"

"We're not protesting. We're advocating peace."

"Cool."

"This whole Middle East thing is getting way out of hand."

I nod, as if I've been paying attention to world events.

"We got to make the Senate understand we're not just playing around here. We're expecting like two, maybe three thousand folks to show up."

"Wow. That should make an impression."

"That's our goal."

"What's going on up here?" asks Phil as he sleepily drapes himself over the back of my seat. "Who are you?"

"I'm Alice."

"Cool. Where you from, Alice?" he asks. I smell the mix of stale cigarette smoke and beer on his breath.

I consider my answer. I'm guessing these guys can be trusted, but then you never know. "Portland," I finally say. "How about you guys?"

"Seattle."

"Cool."

"What're you doing down here?" asks Lane.

"Just visiting." I imagine myself telling them that I escaped from the nut house, and part of me wants to tell them, but a more careful part says don't. And so I keep it to myself.

Then Lane begins to exit the freeway.

"Why are you exiting?" I ask, a tinge of fear creeping down my spine. Suddenly I imagine all sorts of horrible things with these two strange guys I've never met before, things far worse than the Queen's Prison at Forest Hills.

"We got to pick up some others," he says as he pulls off the freeway and turns down a dark side road.

"Others?" I hear a slight tremor in my voice.

"Yeah, don't freak," says Phil. "We're not like going to drag you out into the sticks and hurt you or anything. There's just this commune out here, and we need to give some folks a ride is all."

I am a bit relieved but still shaky, and I'm not sure I can believe him.

"What do you do, Alice?" asks Lane. I get the sense he's trying to calm me, and I wonder how he knows I'm feeling pretty scared. Or maybe he wants me to be scared.

"I'm a student." I consider this, then add, "Or I used to be."

He laughs. "Yeah, we all used to be."

"Right on," says Phil. "The used-to-be's."

"Do you work or anything now?" asks Lane.

"Not really. I'm not really sure what I'm doing, you know."

"Yeah, I hear you." Lane is driving down a bumpy road now. I hold on to the door and consider jumping out. It's pitch-black out here, and I think I can get away if I don't break any bones when I leap.

"Want a beer?"

"No. Actually, I think I'd like to get out."

"Out?" Lane sounds surprised. "You mean you want to get out here? We're still a few miles from the commune. I don't think there's much of anything out here."

"Yeah, but I, uh…"

"Look, Alice," says Phil. "I can see why you're nervous, but we're really not going to hurt you or anything."

"Yeah," adds Lane. "It probably looks weird though. I'm sorry about that."

For some reason I think maybe they're telling the truth. "Well, you guys, I'll be straight with you, okay?"

Lane turns and looks at me as if he thinks maybe I'm going to pull out a gun or something. This almost makes me laugh. Almost. "You see, I just got out of the loony bin, you know, the nut house. I'm really not crazy, but that whole ordeal sort of made me come unglued, you know?"

"Oh, yeah," says Phil. "I can see why you'd be nervous. But really, we're just ordinary guys out trying to change the world, you know?"

"Yeah, I believe you." And mostly I do. However, a small part of me is still suspicious.

Finally Lane turns the van toward what appears to be a run-down farm. I see lights on in the house, and back a ways is a barn. There is a variety of decrepit vehicles parked here and there, and several dogs run up and bark at us as we pull in front of the house.

"Here we are," he announces as he turns off the engine. "Just in time for dinner too."

So we climb out, and feeling relieved, I follow these two guys up the front porch steps. Some pumpkins and cornstalks stand guard in a corner, and I am surprised to remember it's still autumn. It seems as if months have passed since all this started and it should be springtime or summer by now.

Soon we are seated at a big wooden table with a bunch of others eating some kind of bean soup and homemade bread. Even though it's not much, it tastes better than the institutional food I've grown accustomed to lately.

"Are you from Seattle too?" asks the girl next to me. I think her name is Cammie, but I can't remember for sure. I'm guessing she's about my age, but she has a baby balanced on one knee.

"No, Portland." I smile at the baby. "What's his name?"

"It's a she." She grins. "She just doesn't have much hair yet. Her name is Poppy."

The guy across from us grins. "Cammie may have named her Poppy, but we call her Poopy most of the time. She usually needs a diaper change."

"Yeah, yeah," says Cammie as if she's not amused.

The girl with cherry red hair and a ring in her nose refills my soup bowl, and I thank her. The room is warm and noisy, and I'm suddenly very sleepy.

Cammie gently nudges me with her elbow. "So, are you a regular?" she asks in a quiet voice.

"Huh?"

"You know, at the rallies?" She glances around the table, and it seems everyone else is engaged in fairly loud and animated conversations about everything from food labeling to whether terrorists are about to attack.

Cammie lowers her voice and continues. "I'm just not sure if I should go or not. I mean with Poppy. Do you think it's okay for babies?"

"Oh. Well, I don't really know. This is a first for me, too."

She nods, then looks down at her baby and strokes her pale wisps of hair. I can tell she really loves her child. I think I'm going to cry, but that seems silly. Suddenly I want to tell her that she and Poppy should stay home, but I have no idea why I think this, and so I say nothing.

After dinner the whole group piles into the van and another old truck, the only one on the farm that actually works. I think there are a dozen of us in the van, packed in like sardines, but I may be exaggerating. Their plan, I have surmised, is to camp at the capitol tonight so we'll be ready to march first thing in the morning. I sit next to Cammie and her baby. I try to help but don't really know much about babies. I find that I'm useless when Poppy begins to cry. In fact, her crying aggravates me, and I am reminded of the Duchess's crying baby again, and I begin to imagine that Poppy is really a pig baby, and this bothers me a lot.

It's not long before we arrive, but it's getting late, and it appears that most of the campers are settled in. The guys begin to toss out a bunch of tents, sleeping bags, blankets, and other bedding from the back of the pickup.

"You girls and the baby can sleep in the van if you like," offers Lane. As much as I appreciate the offer, I'm not sure I want to sleep with that noisy baby.

"Come on," urges Cammie as she hands me Poppy. "I'll go get us some blankets and stuff."

I jiggle Poppy, and she suddenly quiets down, and I begin to think that perhaps it won't be so bad after all. It is pretty cold outside, as if it might even rain before the night is over. Cammie and I climb into the van and are soon joined by another girl from the commune. Her name is Feather, and she has a squeaky voice. I suspect, from her constant chatter, that she's rather flighty, which seems to fit with her name. Perhaps she's simply excited because she hasn't been off the farm for a few months.

We finally get the bedding arranged, and Poppy is fairly quiet. A mixture of exhaustion and nervousness washes over me. I remember this sensation from before, back when I was just moving into my apartment. It's as if I'm so tired I can't think, and yet I can't stop myself from thinking either. My brain is running about three hundred miles an hour on empty. Amazingly I find myself longing for a sleep med, which just makes me angry.

"I'm going back out there," Feather announces only minutes after we've settled down to sleep. "I need to use the can."

It's a neurotic night of disturbing noises. The van is cramped and damp. The insides of the windows are dripping with humidity, and the air is foul and stinky. I suspect Poppy is being poopy. It seems that Feather comes and goes all night long, and the pig baby is constantly squealing to be fed. Cammie breast-feeds her but actually manages to sleep for what seems like twenty minutes while Poppy wails at the top of her lungs. I begin to suspect Cammie is wearing earplugs.

I can relate to the wild Duchess now, for it's all I can do not to grab the pig baby and toss her right out the window. Finally I reach my limit, and fearing that I might perform such a feat, I get up and go outside.

I can tell by the smoky gray of the sky that morning isn't too far off, but it is cold and damp outside, and I wish I had a heavier coat or had thought to bring a blanket with me. I decide to run around to warm myself. I pretend I am a jogger out for my early morning exercise. For a moment I wonder what it would be like to be that kind of person, one who gets up early with a clear head and jogs just for health's sake. I jog all around the capitol. I am amazed at all the strange vehicles parked about and all the campers. It looks like a refugee camp.

As I'm rounding the east side, the sun begins to come up, glinting off the gold statue on top of the building, and I'm utterly amazed at the beauty. I just stop and stare. It is so spectacular that I am certain I must be looking at God. I believe he is talking to me and gently reassuring me that everything is going to be all right. It only lasts a moment, but it feels real. I think it's going to be a good day.

chapter THIRTEEN

The Mad Hatter's Tea Party

It's clear that I'm in way over my head with these peace demonstrators. First of all, I must admit that I've managed to keep myself pitifully ill informed about world affairs. I fear I've been leading a rather self-centered life, and I don't see that changing anytime soon. Especially since I find this whole protest to be stressful. At first I was somewhat amused, but now I am sick and tired of the continuous noise. People constantly bang on pots and pans or chant and shout. Anything to get attention. This whole business is starting to make my head split, and I'm afraid I might start screaming like the madwoman that people like Dr. Thornton believe me to be. Not that anyone would notice. Perhaps the disturbing part of all this is that I'm beginning to believe Dr. Thornton might have been right about me after all. Not that I plan to go back there. I think I would rather die.

The peace rally started out quietly enough. Early this morning we marched toward the capitol in a peaceful procession. I walked beside Cammie, and we took turns carrying Poppy. We even got filmed by Channel 6 News, which worried me a little at first, but then I reminded myself that my mom and her church friends don't own televisions. During this march we sang some of the old sixties and seventies songs like "What the World Needs Now" and "Give Peace a Chance," and it was all pretty cool. I almost felt like I belonged to something.

After that, we gathered in front of the capitol, and several people gave deeply moving speeches about the atrocities of war and why we need peace so desperately. I clapped and cheered with the best of them. But as the afternoon progressed, it seemed to me that things got increasingly out of hand. It began simply enough. Someone started a fire in a trash barrel, and people were warming their hands over it. Then some guy got all excited and kicked over the flaming barrel, and it rolled into a crowd of people, and everyone started jumping and screaming as if they were being killed. Pretty soon people settled down again and got back to their pounding and shouting, but it seemed to me that the intensity had been ratcheted up a notch or two.

Now I am getting this feeling that something is going to happen before the day is over. Something bad. I can feel it in my skin—this creepy-crawly sensation, and I just want to get out of here. But I don't know where to go. I'm not familiar with Salem, and I'm thinking if I could just get myself back up to Portland, back to my old apartment, everything would be okay. Phil and Lane promised to drop me off on their way back to Seattle, but that won't be until tomorrow afternoon. I don't know if I can wait that long.

So I am pacing, pacing, pacing on the perimeters of the boisterous crowd. I nervously glance at the group of protesters from time to time, trying to figure out what's going on, but it's as if I'm submerged under water. Everything is blurry, and I can barely move—like I'm in slow motion. My arms and legs feel weird, as though they're not attached to the rest of me, and this tingling sensation is buzzing through my brain. I see the policemen, and I know they've been around all day, but suddenly they are growing bigger than life. I notice their helmets and vests have become very imposing, and they appear to be agitated. As if they're impatient for something to happen. Like me, they are pacing too.

"Just go home," I keep telling myself. "Go home." I think I am saying this in my head, but when a woman in a long denim jumper comes up and asks me if I'm okay, I realize I have been speaking out loud.

"I'm just nervous," I tell her. She is looking at me closely now. I think she is suspicious, but I'm not sure why. Then I see the gold cross hanging around her neck, and I am sure that she's been sent here by my mom or Mrs. Knoll or maybe even Pastor John. I begin to move away from her, but it seems she is following me.

"Leave me alone," I tell her.

"Do you need something to eat?" she calls after me.

"No!" I yell as I break into a run. "Just leave me alone." I run until I reach the van and am relieved to find it's unlocked. I climb inside and bury myself in the damp, smelly blankets. I haven't eaten anything besides a sweet roll and several cups of coffee today, and that's only because it was free. Someone from the capitol brought these things out as a "goodwill gesture" this morning. Now I am worried they may have put something into the food. I'm not even sure why I ate it, probably because Cammie did, and I thought she knew what she was doing. Why am I so stupid?

After apparently falling asleep, I open my eyes, and it is dark. I get out of the van and hear the chanting and pot banging going even louder than before. I wonder if they will ever stop. I wander toward the protest area with my hands pressed against my ears. I am curious what's going on, but the noise is splintering my mind. I wonder if they've had their candlelight vigil yet. Feather said that it's usually the last thing on the agenda but that it's very beautiful, and they sing some good songs. I look around, but I don't see any candles, and even with my hands pressed against my ears, I can still hear the noise.

I have just reached the edge of the crowd and feel very much like an outsider. It's as if I have no idea why I'm here or what's going on. I begin to imagine it's a religious gathering of some sort. Several fires are burning in trash barrels now, and they send orange-and-red flames into the darkness. The smoke is illuminated by the street lamps, casting an eerie yellow light on the crowd.

I watch with a mixture of fascination and horror, standing on the edge of hell, just looking on. The crowd quiets down now, and someone is stepping up to the podium. He taps the mike and prepares to speak. He has long dark hair and a full beard, and suddenly I am certain he is Satan. He is talking now, but his words are getting jumbled as they pass over the heads of the crowd. I know without doubt that he is speaking to me, but I can't understand him. I think he is using a foreign language. Hellish perhaps.

He points and gestures, and I am certain he is telling his servants to bring me up there, up to the front where he will humiliate me and have me thrown into the pit of burning flames—the eternal fire that never goes out. I take a step backward, away from him. My heart thunders in my chest. It is even louder than the clanging pots and pans, and I am sure everyone else can hear it too.

Suddenly all is chaos. Things are thrown, and people are running in all directions. I have no idea what has happened, but I am sure I am the cause. I try to run, but my legs won't move. My head is throbbing, and I begin to cry as I'm swept into the crowd. I close my eyes as I sink into the tide of arms and bodies running and jostling around me. I know that when I wake up, I will be burning in the fiery pit. My flesh will be melting away from my bones, and I will be in very serious pain. There seems to be nothing I can do to stop this evil thing. I have no resistance left in me, for I am very, very tired. So I simply give in to it.

chapter FOURTEEN

The Mock Turtle's Story

When I come to, I am stretched out on a paper-covered bed, and I am certain I am back at Forest Hills, probably about to be sent to the Queen's Prison again. But here's what's weird: I am so relieved.

"How are you doing there?" asks a woman with a stethoscope around her neck. Instead of the regular white nurse's uniform, she is wearing a purple sweater and brown corduroy pants.

"Who are you?" I ask.

"I'm a volunteer nurse." She smiles.

"Where am I?"

"This is a free clinic that St. Luke's Hospital set up for the rally."

I frown. "Am I still in Salem?"

She nods. "You took a blow to the head during the riot."

"Riot?"

"Well, things got a little out of hand. No one's totally sure what happened yet, but the peace rally forgot the peace part. It got sort of ugly. A number of more serious injuries have been transported to the hospital. We're trying to handle the less severe ones in here."

"Oh." I struggle to sit up, but my head throbs with the motion.

"How are you feeling?" she asks as she looks into my eyes with a little flashlight. I vaguely wonder what she sees in there.

"Okay, I guess."

"Do you have friends here?"

I consider the proper answer and finally decide on the affirmative. I am guessing that will lead to fewer follow-up questions.

"Do you know what the date is today?"

I frown at her.

"How about your name? Do you know your name?"

"Yes."

"What is it?"

I frown again. No way do I want some nurse writing down my name.

"Okay, a lot of kids don't want to give me their names. Let's see. Can you tell me how many fingers I'm holding up?"

"Four," I answer. "Five if you count your thumb as a finger."

She laughs. "How about the president? Can you name him?"

I comply, and she seems satisfied.

"Make sure you get a good night's rest and drink plenty of fluids."

I tell her I will as I slowly climb down from the examining table. My head hurts, and the lights shine too brightly in here. All I want to do is to get away from all these people. I see a girl throwing up in a wastebasket, and it makes me feel I could do the same. I rush toward the green Exit sign and am relieved to step outside into the damp, chilly evening.

Suddenly the humid interior of the smelly old van sounds comforting to me. I am eager to crawl between the blankets and just sleep. I hope nothing has happened to Cammie and the baby. As much as I disliked Poppy's crying last night, I would feel terrible if she was hurt in the riot.

I walk to the area where I thought the van was parked but am unable to locate it. I wander around and around in search of the blue van with the Whirled Peas bumper sticker, but it seems to have disappeared. Has it fallen into a rabbit hole? Was it ever here at all? Am I simply asleep and dreaming now? I walk and walk, and before long I am desperate. I am so exhausted that I begin to cry. I stand next to the parking lot with my arms wrapped tightly around myself, just rocking back and forth and sobbing.

"You need some help?" asks a guy who's walking by me. He has a cardboard takeout tray of steaming cups. He's wearing a white mock-turtleneck sweater that seems to glow in the lamplight.

I look at him suspiciously, but somehow with his hands balancing the tray, I think he might not be too dangerous.

"I'm lost," I finally tell him.

"What are you looking for?"

"A Volkswagen van."

He laughs. "Well, there are a lot of those here this weekend."

I rub my head and groan. "I know, I know. I got knocked out during the riot, and the van I came in was blue with bumper stickers, and it's not there anymore, and—" Then I start to really blubber. "I just wish I were dead," I sob.

He comes over and puts a hand on my shoulder. This makes me jump, and I eye him with fresh suspicion. "Hey, it'll be okay," he assures me. "You want a hot chocolate?"

I look down at the steaming cups and slowly nod.

"Come on over to our camp, and tell us what's going on."

So I follow him. I know that this could be a trick, or the cocoa could be poisoned, but I am so weary I don't think I care.

I sit down on a canvas campstool and drink the hot chocolate while the guy in the mock-turtleneck sweater proceeds to tell his friends how he found me.

"A lot of people cleared out of here after the riot," explains a girl with mud-brown dreadlocks.

"Yeah, that's probably what happened to your friends," agrees Mock Turtle. He blows on his cocoa. "Some people get a little freaked about being arrested. They're the ones who usually just split when the going gets rough."

"Not me," says Dreadlock Girl. "I'd love to be arrested."

"Really?" I stare at her in wonder. "Why?"

"Just to make a statement." She nods. "I'm not afraid to be persecuted or locked up for something I believe in."

I consider this and wonder what exactly I believe in and if I would be willing to go to jail for it. Then I realize that I was recently locked up. Come to think of it, that was because of my beliefs. "Yeah," I finally say. "That's cool."

"So where are you from?" asks another guy who's been quiet until now. He has long dark hair that hangs down over his shoulders.

"Portland," I answer, trying to sound like one of them and not just an impostor fresh from the loony bin who happened to get picked up by a van going the wrong direction.

"Hey, that's where I'm heading tomorrow," says Mock Turtle. "You can ride with me if you want."

I study his short bleached hair and light-colored sweater. In some ways he looks out of place with this motley crowd, as if he'd be more at home on an Ivy-League campus somewhere. Even so, I'm not sure I want to ride with him. Yet at the same time I'm afraid I won't get any better offers. For some reason the idea of hitchhiking is beginning to unnerve me. I can't believe I did that—was it only yesterday?

I look at Mock Turtle again and try to assure myself he doesn't look too bad. And the mere idea of getting back to Portland, back into my old apartment, suddenly seems well worth the risk. "Sure," I tell him. "I'd appreciate that."

"You need a place to sleep tonight?" asks Dreadlock Girl.

I shrug.

"Well, we've got room in our tent," she offers. "There are three of us already, but it's supposed to be a four-man tent, and you don't look too big, so we could probably squeeze you in." She laughs. "Besides that it might help increase the body heat temperature."

So this is how I find myself wedged between two sleeping bags—complete strangers—with nothing but a spare army blanket to keep me warm. However, Dreadlock Girl was right. Packing the bodies in does manage to create some heat. Somehow I manage to sleep in short spurts throughout the night, but most of the time I'm awake, and once again my mind is racing in all directions at once. I know there are things I must do—a calling on my life. God has started talking to me again. Since leaving the makeshift medical area, I've heard his voice become louder and clearer. There is so much that I must write down. I need to get back to Portland. I try to count myself to sleep and get to 1,782 before I give up.

The following morning Mock Turtle is ready to go as soon as we are up. I am relieved. I can't wait to get away from this place. He asks if I have a bag as we climb into his Subaru.

"No, I like to travel light."

"That's cool."

As he heads down the freeway, I tell myself I am playing a game. The just-be-normal game. I will pretend that I am who I used to be, back in BC, back before everything changed. I hope I can carry it off.

"So are you in school?"

"Yeah." I try not to cringe as I watch the signs and trees and other vehicles whizzing past us at what seems the speed of light. The fluid colors speeding by are making me a little queasy. "How about you?"

"I'm about to get my master's at PSU."

"Me too." I think about this. "Well, not the master's part, but I am at PSU. A senior."

"What's your major?"

I try to remember. I know it has to do with books. "English lit," I finally manage to say. Then as a cover-up, I throw in, "I think getting knocked on the head has scrambled my brain a little." I am clever to have thought of this.

He laughs. "Yeah, you should probably take it easy. I'll try not to ask so many questions. I'd put on some music, but my CD player got ripped off last month."

"Bummer."

"Yeah. I forgot to take it out one night, and the next morning it was history. But at least they didn't get my CD case. I've got this really great collection of jazz and R&B, but it was under the seat, and they didn't see it." He turns on the wipers as it begins to rain, and I amuse myself by watching them go back and forth. The rhythm is hypnotic.

"This was my first peace rally," he confesses as he moves from the fast lane to the center lane. I am slightly relieved that he's slowing down a little.

"Yeah, mine too."

"What did you think of it?" Then he slaps his forehead. "Sorry, I was going to lay off the questions. Okay, I'll tell you what I thought of it. But first I have to confess that I only came out of curiosity. I mean, it's not that I don't want to be socially conscious, because I do. In fact, it bothers me that so many people—like my parents for instance—are materially wealthy when millions of others are literally starving."

He turns the wipers on fast as a huge semi splatters us with greasy spray, but he continues driving at the same speed, as if he can actually see through the streaky window. My fingers dig into the upholstery of the seat as I focus my mind on listening to his words.

"Like my dad is this big executive at Nike and really rakes in the money. Man, he and I have gone around dozens of times about labor practices in China and human rights and all that stuff, but it just never does a bit of good. He and his executive buddies have their own special theories about why it's perfectly fine to force children to labor for just pennies…"

My mind begins to wander, and I can no longer follow his thread of reason. Oh, it's not that I don't care about Mock Turtle's story, because it actually sounds rather interesting, but it's too hard to make my brain focus on his multitude of words, much less digest what they mean. I try to string his words on a cord, like brightly colored beads, but I keep dropping them and mixing them up. Somehow they just don't want to hang right.

Not only that, but the sound of his voice going up and down is giving me a headache, and the swish-swish-swishing of the wind-shield wipers is making me so tired and sleepy. I think Mock Turtle is actually a hypnotist, and for some reason he is telling me, "You are getting sleepy. You are very, very sleepy."

I try to resist, but it's useless. I am going under. I wonder what Mock Turtle will do to me when I'm completely within his hypnotic powers. Maybe he'll whisper the magic words that will make me all better.

It seems more likely that he will transport me back to Forest Hills where Dr. Thornton will reward him for my recovery. Then I will be strapped down, and the nurses will put wires into my brain and extract all the hidden messages that I have collected since escaping from there. Or else give me electrotherapy or perhaps a lobotomy. I'm not sure which would be worse.

I know I should try to fight this thing, to resist. Maybe I could make some sort of plan to leap from his car the next time he slows down, but the wipers have taken control of my brain, and I am so tired I don't even care anymore. I think I can hear Amelia whispering to me. I think she is telling me that it's time to go now. But I'm under the Mock Turtle's spell. I cannot move. I may never wake up again.

chapter FIFTEEN

Neither Here nor There

I feel a gentle nudge on my shoulder and open my eyes, unsure of where I am or why I am here. I feel the motion of a moving vehicle and hear the sound of wet pavement hissing beneath the tires.

"Where do you live?" asks Mock Turtle as he exits from the freeway.

It takes me a moment to remember how I know this guy, or if I even do, but I can tell we're in Portland now, and this is a relief. Finally it comes to me. The peace rally. Salem. I see that we are heading downtown now, toward campus, but I have no desire to tell this person where I live. So I just ask him to drop me at the coffee shop on the next corner. He complies. I think he is relieved to be rid of me. I wonder if perhaps he wasn't the enemy after all. I just wish I were better at telling the difference.

I can't remember if I thanked him or not as I climb out of his car, so I simply duck my head out of the rain and pretend to be going into the coffee shop. I am hungry and would like to get a bagel breakfast sandwich there, no meat of course, but then my pockets are empty. I pull my sweatshirt hood over my head and hurry along toward my apartment building. I long for the dry warmth and safety of my bed even more than I long for food. I think I will sleep all day. As I turn the corner, up ahead I see that Amelia is already there. She is waiting for me by the front entrance.

"It's about time you came back," she says as she leans against the wall by the door, hooking her thumbs into her jeans pockets. "So how do you plan to get in?"

I reach for the door handle, then stop. It suddenly occurs to me that I have no key. I have no purse, no backpack, nothing. I peer at Amelia. "Can I stay at your place?"

She leans her head back and laughs. "Don't be ridiculous, Alice." Then she points over to the brick wall and up to my second-story window. "Why don't you just scale that wall and break in through the window? Don't worry, I'll keep watch for you."

"I'm not much of a climber," I admit to her. "Besides, I'm a little scared of heights."

She looks exasperated by my lack of bravery.

"Maybe Mr. Scoggins will let me into my apartment," I suggest.

She rolls her eyes doubtfully. "You know he can't be trusted, Alice. Have you forgotten the day he let your mother in?"

I consider this. And I must admit that it bothers me to think that this guy can simply pull out his magic key and walk right into a private apartment. There should be a law against that kind of intrusion.

"But I've got to do something," I tell her.

She nods to the wall again. "Just climb, Alice. It's simple."

I shake my head and go into the building and down the hallway toward the apartment that has the Manager sign. I take a deep breath as I knock quietly on the door. When it opens, I can tell that I woke him up. His gray hair is sticking out every which way, and his normally beady eyes look bleary and bloodshot. I forgot that it is still early, and according to the newspaper on his doorstep, it's Sunday. I had no idea.

"Huh?" He scratches his head and looks at me as if he's seen me somewhere before but doesn't quite remember when or where. I politely tell him my name and my apartment number, apologetically explaining that I forgot my key. He begins to chuckle as if this is some kind of a joke.

"Sorry, but you don't have an apartment no more. Your mama settled with me last month when she arranged to have all your stuff put into storage." He begins to close the door, but I keep talking, hoping I can get him to understand my problem, but he just looks through me.

I plead with him. "But I need to get back in there—"

"Look." His voice grows firm now. "You stay away from this building, or I'll call the cops. You understand?" Then he narrows his eyes at me. "Does your mama know where you are right now?"

I step away from his door and move down the hall. Now I hear him calling after me, telling me to wait. But I keep going. When will I ever learn?

Amelia is standing by the front door with a dark scowl. "I told you so," she says.

I chastise myself for being so stupid, then look at Amelia. "What should I do?"

"Why should I tell you? You never listen to me anyway."

I look back to see Mr. Scoggins quickly approaching.

"Run, Alice," urges Amelia.

And so I do as she says, and I run.

I head down Burnside, down to where the homeless people hang out. I know there are missions and places where people can get food and maybe a bed. And yet this frightens me. Everything is so dirty and gross along those streets, and I can't imagine myself sleeping on a cot in a room filled with strangers. Instead I go to the waterfront park, down by the river. The rain has let up and is just a steady drizzle now, and I sit on a damp bench and look out toward the gray river and the maze of bridges that crisscross it. It looks like a giant spider web, and I wonder how anyone can ever find her way across without getting stuck like a fly that's waiting for its predator.

I am cold and tired and hungry now. I ask myself what is the point of existing like this. Why should I even go on? Who needs to live in such desperation? I lean forward and put my head in my hands.

"You're absolutely right," says Amelia. I look up to see her standing in front of me. "You might as well call it quits, Alice. Before things get worse."

"What do you mean?"

She narrows her eyes. "I think you know what I mean."

Her answer surprises me a bit because I always thought she was the one looking out for my best interests.

Then she smiles. "It's easy, Alice."

Perhaps she still cares about me.

"Look over there." She gestures toward the river and the tallest of the bridges. "There's your ticket out of this mess."

"You mean I should walk across that bridge?" I ask. "Is there something on the other side that will help me?"

"There's something *over* the side."

I don't know the name of the bridge, but I think I've heard of people who have jumped to their deaths below. I wonder how long it would take me to walk over there, to make my way across the bridge until I reach the middle and climb over the railing—that's assuming the height wouldn't overwhelm me—and then simply jump off. What would it feel like to fall? Would it be like going down the rabbit hole? Down, down, down? And then what?

"Then, nothing," she answers. "The end of your troubles."

I'm not so sure I can trust Amelia right now. She seems to be acting strangely today. Something about this dismal scenario of leaping from the bridge is quite unsettling. The age-old question that begs for an answer, What will happen next? Once I hit that cold gray water, breaking my neck or plunging to the depths of the tugging icy current until I finally run out of air and drown. But once I'm dead, what comes next? It's the not knowing that stops me.

"Look, Alice, if you're not going to listen to me, I'm not going to keep talking to you." Then she walks away.

So for today I will ignore Amelia's suggestion. We'll see about tomorrow. The truth is, I don't want go to that horrible place where the flesh will melt from my bones. Where the howling and gnashing of teeth never stop. Then I ask myself, Which is worse? To live like this or to die like that? I really don't know. I don't even know if all the things I've heard since childhood are true. Not too long ago I felt certain they weren't. Now I'm not so sure. It's those unknown answers alone that keep me affixed to this cold, damp bench.

It's as if I am stuck, just like that fly in the spider web. I am caught between two confusing worlds, yet belonging to neither. I am neither alive nor dead. Between here and there. Perhaps Amelia is right. Maybe I do need a bridge to take me across.

I am a bridge.

I turn around to see who said that, but no one is there, and I know it's not Amelia's voice. I sigh as I compare this voice to all the other voices in my life. It's not like the voices that are always trying to destroy me. The unnamed voices that spew profanity at me and accuse me of all sorts of horrible, unspeakable things. And it doesn't sound condemning like Pastor John's voice or Dr. Thornton's or even my mother's when she is coming down on me. No, this one feels different. I sense no threatening tone in this voice. I don't think it's trying to harm me or even control me. But I have been tricked before.

chapter SIXTEEN

Tweedle Dweeb
and Tweedle Dumb

I sit on my bench so long that my hindquarters grow numb with cold. I stand up and move around, trying to decide what to do next. My mind seems to be running in circles that get only tighter and tighter, like a ball of yarn being pulled backward. I have no doubts that I am talking to myself as I pace back and forth in front of my bench, but I don't care. I need to solve this problem.

"Hey," calls out a guy who is walking toward me along the path beside the river. I look up to see that there are two of them, or maybe I'm just seeing double. Two round orange blobs. I blink my eyes, then squint, but as they get closer, I realize there are indeed two of them. They are both wearing those puffy down-filled parkas that make them look like the Michelin tire man times two. Both parkas are this obnoxious shade of orange that's a shocking contrast to the gray, watery scene of the Willamette River in November. I imagine that they are chubby twins, like Tweedledee and Tweedledum, but as they approach, I can see that their heights vary, and they look nothing alike. I also notice that their almost neon-colored jackets aren't quite as vivid up close. I can see now that they're streaked with the kind of dirt and grime that suggests a daily life on the streets.

The taller guy's baggy jeans are soaked along the frayed hems, and his dirty blond hair is stringy and wet. But his smile is bright. The shorter guy has a black knit cap that's pulled low on his brow, giving him a rather dark and intimidating appearance. The two of them stop at my bench, and the big guy pulls out a dog-eared box of Camels and asks if I have a match.

I glare at him because for some reason this feels like my last straw. "No!" I shout. I pull out my jeans pockets so that they are hanging inside out like two limp ears. "I *don't* have a match. I *don't* have a penny. I *don't* even have a stinking key to my freaking apartment. I have absolutely nothing. So if you want to mug me, you are totally out of luck!"

The taller guy holds up his hands and steps back as if he thinks I'm about to rush him. "Hey, sorry. I just wondered." He tucks his Camels back into his pocket, then smiles again. "Looks like you could use a friend."

I shrug and glance uncomfortably over my shoulder, then turn back and carefully study these two guys—the Tweedle twins.

The taller guy sticks out a grubby hand. "I'm Martin, and this is my buddy Cal."

I reluctantly shake his hand, but the other guy just stands there without saying a word. I can tell he doesn't like me. I don't tell them my name. I'm not totally stupid. I attempt to act nonchalant as I return my inside-out pockets back to their former state, taking care to wipe any grubby germs from my hands as I do.

"We were just about to go get us some lunch," says the friendly guy as he wipes his damp nose on the already stained sleeve of his parka. "You want to come?"

I narrow my eyes as I try to discern his motives. Why's he being so nice? What's the catch? In my mind I am already calling him Tweedle Dweeb because he looks the part. The other guy I christen as Tweedle Dumb, because he doesn't seem able to speak. Finally I answer. "Look, I already told you that I don't have any money. What do you want from me?"

Tweedle Dweeb nods. "Yeah, I got that. But we're going over to the mission for Sunday dinner. It's free. You want to come?"

I frown and look down at my canvas tennis shoes, which are soaking wet. The idea of a warm meal and a dry place is somewhat appealing. But can I really trust these guys? I study their appearance. The way they look in their matching round parkas almost makes me want to laugh.

"Why do you have the same jackets?" I ask.

" 'Cause they were free."

"Huh?"

"We got them from the homeless shelter. They were donated by L.L.Bean." He shrugs. "I guess 'cause of the color they didn't sell so hot."

I nod. "Yeah, I can believe that."

Tweedle Dumb nudges his friend and nods toward the street.

"Yeah, we better hurry if we want to get the good stuff. Sometimes they run out, and then all you get is a peanut-butter sandwich and a piece of fruit." Tweedle Dweeb starts walking now with Tweedle Dumb right in step. He looks back over his shoulder. "You coming or not?"

I begin to walk, staying a few paces behind them so I can keep my eye on them and watch for any surprises. We go under the bridges and then dash across Burnside and walk toward the Chinese district, stopping at an old brick building where the down-on-their-luck lot are already beginning to line up.

"This is the place," announces Tweedle Dweeb with a grin wide enough to reveal that he's missing a front tooth. "You ever been here before?"

I shake my head as I step into line behind him. Most of the people in line are males. Some very old, but many are my age and even younger. I notice a woman who looks to be about sixty. She has on several layers of clothing and is carrying a garbage bag that's beginning to rip.

"That's Betty," says Tweedle Dweeb. "She's a regular. Sometimes, when she's in a good mood, she'll tell you that she's that old movie star Betty Grable, and if she's feeling really good, she'll even show you her million-dollar legs. That's what she calls 'em, her million-dollar legs." He makes a face. "I wouldn't give two cents to look at them. Most of the time she's a grump though."

Tweedle Dumb frowns at his friend, as if he'd like him to shut up, and I don't think that I disagree with him. I turn to look at the line that is steadily building behind me. I wonder where all these people have come from. Where do they sleep, and what do they do all day? Oh, sure, I've seen the drunken bums curled up on the sidewalk beneath the overpasses, but what about the rest of them? How do they get by? And is this how I'll have to live from now on? The mere thought of this new lifestyle terrifies me beyond words. Suddenly I want to run, sure that if I flee this place and run really fast, I can escape. But where do I go? Where?

"Smells like chipped beef gravy and mashed potatoes," says Tweedle Dweeb as he rubs his grimy hands together. Dumb just rolls his eyes and moves another step forward in the line.

"Come on," urges an old man standing behind me. "Move it." I can smell the saturation of alcohol on him. It's as if it's seeping out through the pores of his skin. His eyes shine milky, and the gray bristles on his chin look like he hasn't shaved in a week or two. His once dark overcoat is faded with weather and hard wear. Reluctantly I move forward, and he steps up right behind me. Too close.

"Want cuts?" offers Tweedle Dweeb.

I sigh and nod in relief. I step in front of him, relieved to be a foot farther from the smelly old coot behind us. Only now I am standing between Dweeb and Dumb, and I can tell that Dumb does not like it. I'm trying to remember their real names, but they are lost in my brain by now, and perhaps it doesn't matter anyway.

Dishes and pans clatter inside the mission, mixing with conversation and the occasional outbursts from those who are disgruntled with either their food or the people they are seated next to, or maybe it's just life in general. I guess that's to be expected. But even so I am a bit surprised at the whining and complaining that goes on. I am reminded of that old saying, "Beggars can't be choosers." But apparently that doesn't apply here.

I wonder how that applies to any of us, or anything else for that matter. I mean, haven't we all made our choices? Haven't all of these choices brought us to the places we are today? Begging. This is exactly what I imagine Pastor John or Mrs. Knoll would say to me right now. I can just see them pointing their fingers and accusing me of being the only one to blame for the sorry state my life is in. According to them, this is all my fault, my reward for being such a sinful person in the first place. But I'm still not convinced they're right. Sometimes I wonder if I'm simply being persecuted for my belief. Because my mind's working differently than everyone else's out there. Because I am God's chosen one. Maybe this is just a form of religious persecution. Although at the moment I am not entirely sure what I believe exactly. Things have been so confusing lately that it's hard to know anymore.

Finally we are seated on a long bench at one of the many butcher paper–covered tables. It is warm and moist in here, almost too warm after being outside all morning, but I tell myself to soak up the heat while I have the opportunity. Voices seem to be coming at me from all directions. So many different smells, like warm green beans and onions mingled with ammonia and body odor, mostly unpleasant. I wish I had some kind of scarf that I could wear across my face, like a bandit or those women from the Middle East. Something to filter the foul air I am forced to breathe. But I will try not to think about that as I scrape the chipped beef gravy away from my potatoes. I will eat everything but that. Red meat still makes my stomach turn.

"You don't want that?" asks Tweedle Dweeb, pointing to my chipped beef with hopefully raised brows.

"Go ahead," I tell him, relieved to get rid of it. I avert my eyes from his dirty hands as he scrapes the mucky mess onto his plate. Then I continue to eat my mushy green beans and white roll and

fruit Jell-O. I like the Jell-O the best and wish I could go back for
more, but I don't want to seem too greedy.

"You want anything else?" asks Dweeb, standing.

"Jell-O?" I venture.

He grins. "You got it."

Suddenly I'm thinking maybe I'm being too hard on this guy.
Maybe he's really okay. I glance over to Tweedle Dumb, and he
appears to be glaring at me with open hostility now. I am sure he
resents my intrusion into their friendship. I vaguely wonder if they
are gay. Not that I care.

Tweedle Dweeb returns with not one but two servings of Jell-O
that he proudly sets in front of me. Then he turns to his buddy and
announces, "They've got chocolate cake for dessert."

Tweedle Dumb frowns and shakes his head.

"He doesn't like staying for the message," Dweeb tells me in a
serious voice.

"The message?" I take a big bite of Jell-O and act interested.

"Yeah." He jerks his thumb over his shoulder toward what
appears to be the staff people standing huddled in a corner. "You
don't get to have coffee and dessert unless you stay to hear them
preach."

"Oh." I nod knowingly, as if this is a bummer. At the same time
I'm thinking it might be worth it, especially since I have so much dif-
ficulty tracking with people's words when they say more than one
sentence in a row anyway. I'm thinking I can just sit here and daydream and then have some chocolate cake and coffee. Plus I might
be completely dried out and warm by then.

At that moment I notice Amelia wedging herself onto the bench next to me. She begins elbowing me and urging me to leave. "Get away from all these dirty, germ-infected people before you catch something," she tells me.

I glance around the room and know she's right. This place is probably infested with all sorts of horrible diseases.

"You gonna stay?" asks Dweeb.

I shrug uneasily.

"You can't trust these guys," says Amelia. "They're going to kill you."

"That cake smells pretty good," says Dweeb, completely oblivious to my friend.

I glance over my shoulder to see Amelia's reaction, but she is leaving. I can tell by the way she stomps out of here that she's mad. Still, I don't go with her.

"The cake's got some really good frosting," he says. "You gonna stay?"

"Yeah. Maybe."

He looks over to Dumb. "Let's stay too."

Tweedle Dumb frowns and looks down at his plate. I can tell he doesn't like this idea any more than Amelia did, but I wonder why he doesn't just speak up and say so.

"Does he ever talk?" I whisper to Dweeb.

He grins. "Yeah. But not much. He's a man of few words, you know."

I nod and begin to eat my third Jell-O.

The crowd shrinks a little after a tall, dark-haired man steps up to a podium. He sets down what appears to be a Bible and then adjusts the microphone and finally clears his throat as if he's trying to get our attention. I watch with interest as his Adam's apple bobs up and down with each swallow. Then he welcomes everyone and makes a joke about a dog and a goat that I don't really get. A few people laugh, but most of us just sit there like the deaf and humorless stones that I am thinking we are. Suddenly Amelia pops in again, and this time she says something nasty to me. I can feel my cheeks flush, and I glance around to see if anyone else was listening. She's furious that I won't go with her. I'm beginning to wish she would just leave me alone.

The man begins to speak, and I attempt to follow his words. I can tell his speech is religious in nature, but it doesn't sound like anything I've heard before.

"Jesus doesn't expect anything of you," he is saying. But I'm thinking that makes no sense. "Only that you open your heart and allow him to love you."

"Get out of here," hisses Amelia.

But I am transfixed by this man's gentle words. I had braced myself for a real sermon—the kind that Pastor John gives—in which this guy would really lay into all of us losers, freeloaders, and sinners. I figured he'd yell and carry on, accusing us of being worthless trash and telling us about hell and then finally urging us toward repentance with an emotional altar call.

But this man is different. He doesn't raise his voice. "God's kingdom is about love and mercy," he says. "That's why Jesus came to earth and why I work at the mission. It's all about love and grace." Amelia curses me and storms off again, but for the moment I don't care. I am starting to get a little blurry now, but I notice this man mentions Jesus a lot, yet not in that old fire and brimstone sort of way. This man's voice is surprisingly kind. Even when my brain is so befuddled that I am unable to process his words, I feel that I am still absorbing his message. I watch his eyes, and it seems he might actually care. Either he is a good actor, or else he is sincere. I know I'm not the sharpest about these things, but I think he really believes what he is saying. I'm not sure if what he's saying is true or not, and I suspect Pastor John would strongly disagree with most of this, but I decide that I like this man's form of religion. If I were into religion, that is.

When he finishes, we have our chocolate cake and coffee, and I notice that some people actually go up and talk to this man. I wonder what I would say if I were brave enough to actually speak to him, but I am not. Finally my cake and coffee are gone, and I'm certain I have thoroughly worn out my welcome here. I head for the door but am stopped by an older woman who has been helping to serve food.

"Do you need a place to stay?" she asks. I notice Amelia is coming back now. She stops right next to this woman and makes a face.

"Doesn't she remind you of someone?" asks Amelia.

"I don't know," I say.

"Are you homeless?" asks the woman.

"She's a friend of your mom," says Amelia. "Pastor John has sent her here to get you. Better watch out, Alice."

I look at the woman with suspicion and realize that she reminds me of Mrs. Knoll, and I begin to fidget nervously.

"Get out of here," hisses Amelia.

"I am," I say to Amelia, but it's the Mrs. Knoll-like woman who answers.

"Well, we have a women's shelter over on Third Street," she says. "I think they have a few open beds. If you go over right now, you could put your name down and—"

"Who told you to talk to me?" I ask her.

She looks surprised. "No one. I just thought that maybe—"

"Did my mother send you?"

She shakes her head. "No, honey, but I'm a mother, and I know how a mother would feel."

I back away, thinking Amelia is right about this woman. I'm sure that Pastor John or my mother or maybe even Dr. Thornton has sent her here to ambush me. I quickly move away from the spy and hurry toward the door. It is cool and damp outside, but at least it's not raining now. Free at last, at least for the moment, I start to walk back down toward the park. Amelia seems happy with my decision.

"Hey, where you going?" calls out Tweedle Dweeb.

I turn to see him and his buddy just a few steps behind me. Tweedle Dweeb must've found some matches because he's smoking a cigarette now. Tweedle Dumb pauses to zip his coat, and I wait for them. I remember how Dweeb got me those two extra Jell-Os, and I'm thinking he can't be too bad.

"What are you doing now?" demands Amelia.

"I don't know."

"So did you like the food?" asks Tweedle Dweeb as we start walking again.

"Lose these two bozos," says Amelia impatiently.

"I guess."

"So where you headed then?"

"Alice!" Amelia shrieks now. "I said lose the bozos!"

I look from Amelia to these two guys and don't know what to do. I don't like it when Amelia yells at me.

"You okay?" asks Dweeb with a concerned look.

"I don't know."

"Why'd you run off from the mission so fast?"

Amelia is cussing now, and I am getting irritated by all this. I turn and stare at Dweeb. Why is he asking me so many questions? "That lady bugged me is all," I tell him, trying to ignore Amelia's temper tantrum.

"They're not so bad," says Dweeb as he takes a puff of his cigarette. "They're just trying to help."

"I don't need *that* kind of help." I pull my hood over my head and begin to walk faster. These two guys are starting to bug me, and Amelia is making me want to scream.

"What kind of help do you need?" he asks as he quickens his pace.

I stop now and glare at him. "Who says I *need* help?"

Now Amelia stamps off, and Tweedle Dumb actually begins to snicker like I've said something pretty funny. It's the first time I've seen him do anything besides frown and scowl at me, and this makes me curious.

"What's *your* problem?" I ask as I peer straight into his face.

He shoves his hands into his pockets and, rolling his eyes, just shrugs as if he couldn't care less.

"What's with him anyway?" I demand from Tweedle Dweeb. "He's so quiet that it's creeping me out."

Then Tweedle Dumb cusses, but his voice is kind of high pitched and strange sounding. Kind of like a little girl's. I try not to laugh.

Now I understand why he doesn't say much. I decide not to mention it as I start walking toward the river. I keep telling myself that maybe these guys are okay, just mixed up, kind of like me. Naturally, Amelia doesn't agree. It looks like she's ditching me at the moment anyway, but maybe that's okay since I don't have to listen to her scream.

We go back down to the park again. There's an interesting mix of people there now. Some look like regular people just out for a Sunday stroll, but many look like us, homeless and sort of lost. I wonder what makes one person fall into one group and another fall into a completely different one. It just doesn't make any sense to me. I notice that Tweedle Dweeb has his arm around Tweedle Dumb, confirming my earlier suspicion about their relationship.

"You guys a couple?" I ask.

"Yeah." Tweedle Dweeb drops his cigarette butt and grinds it into the sidewalk with his heel.

I look Tweedle Dumb in the eyes and say, "Hey, don't worry about me. I had no intention of coming between you two."

He grins, and I think maybe we're all okay now. Weird, but okay.

chapter SEVENTEEN

Tangled Mess

For the next several days—how many I may never know—I stay close to Tweedle Dweeb and Tweedle Dumb. They don't even seem to mind. Well, maybe Dumb does a little, but as usual he keeps his thoughts to himself. I feel moderately safe with these guys and am impressed with their basic understanding of street life in the city. They know how to survive, where to sleep, where to go for handouts, and when. I've discovered that *when* is always important. Just the same, it's not long before Amelia is dogging my heels again, telling me to lose these losers. I wonder who she thinks she is to be talking about losers. I get fed up and even tell her to go away and leave me alone.

After all, Tweedle Dumb even managed to scrounge up a long wool coat for me. That's more than Amelia's ever done. My coat is army green and thick and scratchy. It trails nearly to my feet, but I can wrap it around me like a blanket at night, and it helps keep out the damp and cold. These guys also know the driest and warmest places to sleep, like a covered balcony at an apartment complex or dry spots beneath overpasses. They've even shown me how to pad my body with crunched-up newspapers for insulation.

For a few days it doesn't seem too terribly awful being homeless. That's what I am now, and I'm not ashamed to say it out loud. *Homeless.* Naturally, we stay on the move a lot, but that actually helps us to keep warm. At first I tried to think of it as playing a game, but I have to admit it's getting old. And worse than that, it's getting more and more scary. The danger seems to increase daily. It doesn't help matters that Amelia keeps warning that it's time to go. "Get away from these guys," she keeps telling me, "before it's too late."

"What do you mean?" I've asked.

"They're going to get you," she warns. "They're not really your friends."

So now I'm not sure that I can trust these two guys anymore. I'm not sure which is more frightening—staying with them and taking the risk that they have really turned against me and will take advantage of me, or going out on my own with only Amelia and the other voices I am beginning to hear again for company. I run these confusing thoughts through my mind constantly, but I am a dog chasing its own tail. I can never pin anything down. Nothing makes complete sense.

I am anxious and nervous most of the time now, and my ability to function is as thin as a butterfly wing. Sleeping is becoming more and more difficult. My mind races in all directions at the same time, and sometimes I cannot breathe. Every nighttime noise—each siren or tire skid or slammed-down garbage can lid—makes my heart leap out of my chest.

And lately I am covered with bugs. I awake in the night trying to swat and push them away from me, but they are crawling under my skin now. Amelia told me that the two Tweedles planted them on me when I dozed off for a few minutes the other night. I suspect she is right.

She also said they are both sick and tired of me now and they want to get rid of me. I hear them whispering about me when they think I'm asleep. I think they are planning to drown me in the river this very night. So I lie as stiff as a board next to Tweedle Dweeb. My eyes are shut, and my heart is racing. Amelia says I should get up and run, but I think that maybe it's better to just play possum and slip away when no one is looking. I wonder if I will ever be able to sleep again.

I finally sense that morning is nearly here. I can see the dull gray light through my eyelids. It's the color of raw squid. It seems the Tweedles have not drowned me yet. I am not sure whether I am relieved or disappointed. Maybe I will make my escape today. But when I finally open my eyes, they are nowhere to be seen.

I am surprised and feel slightly betrayed that they have gone like that, even though I had planned to do the same thing. Still, I keep a careful watch, worried that they are hiding behind the trash cans and ready to pounce on me at any moment. I can't believe how I trusted them. I'm sure they knew what they were doing right from the beginning. How easily I am duped.

My limbs are stiff with cold and damp when I get up. I peer at the trash cans to make sure no one is hiding back there, then I remove the layers of wadded-up newspapers from beneath my coat. My hands are black from the newsprint and so many other things. Every day I long to go wash them, to be clean, and sometimes I get the chance but not usually. It's amazing how quickly the working people learn to recognize us so they can shoo us away from their rest rooms. I swat away the bugs that are crawling up my arms, on my face, and I long for a very hot shower.

Sometimes I've been able to sneak into a restaurant during the peak business hours, when people are too busy to notice, and use their rest room. I clean up as best I can in the small sinks, but I know how they hate for me to do that. I've even been thrown out on occasion. If only they knew how it feels to be this dirty and unable to get and stay clean, perhaps they would be a bit kinder.

I decide to trudge down to the public rest room at the other end of the park. The water is icy cold there, and they are usually out of soap and paper towels, but it's better than nothing. But for some reason I am unable to walk on the sidewalk today. I think it's all those cracks. They look like they could split open if there were to be an earthquake. And I know that could happen. Mount Hood is really a volcano and could go off at any time. So I decide to walk through the grass, which is soggy and wet from last night's rain. It isn't long before my thin canvas tennis shoes are soaked clear through to my filthy and threadbare cotton socks. I listen as my shoes make this *squish-squish-squish* sound. I am sure it is loud enough to draw the attention of anyone who happens to be awake right now. But no matter how hard I try, I cannot make my shoes be quiet. It is all very unnerving.

When I reach the public bathrooms, I discover they are locked. I can't remember them being locked before, and I wonder if someone has done this just to aggravate me. I glance around, looking for the culprit, but only see a guy in a navy jogging suit and striped running shoes. Yet as I examine him more closely, I can tell he's suspicious. Amelia tells me that he's really an impostor who's posing as a jogger. The man bends over, pretending to stretch out his calves, but I can see him eyeing me. I see the tiny earplug wire that protrudes from his left ear, and I know for certain that he's wearing some kind of a radio or listening device. So I turn away and walk quickly in the other direction.

Squish, squish, squish. I cannot escape that noise.

"Your shoes are giving you away," Amelia says. "They're making too much noise. You need to get rid of them."

Finally, in desperation, I remove the disruptive shoes and stuff them down into a trash receptacle. Then I run like a cat in my stocking feet. When I finally turn to look back, I don't see the spy anywhere. I am out of breath, and my feet are numb with cold. But at least I lost him. For now anyway.

I go over to a big grate that the Tweedles introduced me to a while back. Thankfully, no one else is there yet. It blows out warm air, and I attempt to thaw my feet on it, but then I notice a couple of businesswomen waiting for the mass transit, or what we call the MAX. They are pointing at me and whispering. I think they must be connected to the jogger somehow, so I move away from the warm air. My socks are still soggy.

I walk over by the fancy hotel with the big green awning. It has a red carpet right out on the sidewalk. You can always count on this to be a dry spot. Not good for sleeping because the fancy doormen will shoo you away—even in the middle of the night when no one is coming or going. But sometimes you can stop here just to stay dry for a minute or two during a bad downpour. Occasionally, the wealthy people staying at this hotel have actually handed me a bit of money, usually just loose change or sometimes a dollar on a good day.

I suppose that was my first experience with panhandling or sp'anging, which is street slang for "spare changing," even though I wasn't actually trying to do so at the time. But after that little success, Tweedle Dweeb encouraged me to go for it. He said that I looked like just the kind of person that people might feel sorry for, and I guess it was true. As it turned out, I could usually make more than both of them put together when we got serious and decided to spend an afternoon sp'anging in the ritzy shopping district. But I never did like doing it. The money always felt dirty, and I worried about getting in trouble with the police and being taken back to Forest Hills.

Fortunately, it's early enough today that the doorman is still inside. I rub my feet on the dry red carpet and hope they will get warm before I am sent away. My arms are folded across my front, and my head is down. I find that if I keep my head low and my eyes downward, kind of like an ostrich, the world is much safer. Only you can't stay that way very long before someone comes along and disrupts your peace.

"Beat it, kid," says the doorman as he pushes out one of those big brass carts piled high with matching luggage of various shapes and sizes. I stare at the luggage in fascination and wonder how one or two people could possibly travel with all of that stuff. I wonder what could be inside—

"Scram!" he yells as he waves at the taxi across the street, and like a little mouse I scurry away.

I head up toward the shopping area, looking over my shoulders as I go. Amelia warns me that someone is watching me now, possibly even trailing me. But every time I look back, the person is out of sight. Finally, I duck into the doorway of a vacant building and just wait.

My heart pounds, and my stomach growls simultaneously, almost like music, but not a happy song. I peek around the corner to see.

There, walking down the street toward me, is old Betty Grable. She has a wobbly-wheeled grocery cart today and is diligently checking out the trash can on the corner. I watch her closely, just to make sure she's not really the one chasing me. But she doesn't even seem to notice me. Still, it could be an act. How can I know for sure?

Finally I step out into full view and just stand there in the middle of the sidewalk. She glances over at me, then frowns when she notices my stocking feet. She shakes her head, walking on past me as if I am some sort of disgusting person, as if she's embarrassed to be seen anywhere near the likes of me. This makes me mad, but I have the good sense to keep my mouth shut. At least I think I do.

More and more these days I assume I am thinking something only to discover that I am actually saying the words out loud. This is especially true when I am telling the other voices to leave me alone. I used to think the other voices were much worse than Amelia's, but I'm not so sure anymore. I don't know the names of the other voices, and I have yet to see them face to face, but I recognize them by the varied tones of their voices. I think there are about three of them, but sometimes it's confusing when they're all yelling at once. It can sound like a dozen or more. They say horrible, unrepeatable things, using profanity I've heard and some I haven't. Sometimes I can hear Amelia yelling and screaming right along with them, and I am certain she wants to kill me. That's when I decide I can't trust her anymore. But then she'll surprise me by acting all nice and friendly. She'll tell me she's been sent to take care of me and that she has a plan for my life— if only I will obey her. But it's hard to do, especially when she's acting so controlling and bossy. Sometimes I just wish she would leave for good. But despite her numerous threats, she always comes back.

I look back down the street again, certain that someone—even if it isn't Betty—is following me. I can feel it in my gut, and Amelia swears that I'm not wrong. Then I see him. He's dressed in a business suit, with a tan raincoat slung over his arm—a clever disguise. I wonder what he's hiding under that raincoat. He sees me see him, and I'm sure he quickens his pace, and that's when Amelia says we must run again. She pushes me into the busy street, and we both dash between cars as horns honk in anger. The morning traffic is beginning to flow, and patience is virtually nonexistent. Then we cut through an alley and down a side street and on and on until I'm sure we have lost him. Finally I stop and hold my aching sides.

Panting with exhaustion, I sit down on the edge of a planter box and try to catch my breath. My feet hurt now, both from being cold and wet and then from running so hard with no shoes. I sit there for a long time, alternately rubbing my feet and wondering what to do.

Finally I remember that I was going to try to panhandle in the shopping district today. Now I am about ten blocks away, and my feet hurt. Still there seems to be no choice other than to walk. Amelia points out the way, and this time I obey. I walk and walk and walk, but it seems I am getting nowhere, just climbing some kind of a hill. Then I realize that I am nowhere near the shopping district. I'm not even sure where I am. It seems to be a residential neighborhood.

This is very upsetting. When I try to place the blame on Amelia, she's not there, and so I begin to think it's all my own fault. It's as if I can't even figure out the simplest things anymore. I used to pride myself on knowing this city like the back of my hand. So I look at the back of my hand to discover that my skin is pale and splotched with grime. It doesn't even look like my hand anymore. I haven't seen my face in the mirror for days, and I wonder if I look like me anymore. Would I even know me if I saw myself on the street? I am completely lost, both inside and outside. I wish I could just cease to exist somehow. Perhaps that would stop all this pain.

Now I'm lost, so I sit down on a rock wall that's surrounding someone's garden area. The garden looks mostly brown and dead right now with dry, spindly things poking out of the ground. I stare at it and think that is exactly how I feel.

"Do you need something?" calls a woman's voice.

I look over to see a woman in a pale gray suit standing next to a silver BMW. Her face looks perplexed, or maybe she's just irked.

I shake my head and stand up, slowly moving away from her rock wall as if it's made of precious stones. I'm afraid she's going to yell at me for sitting there. But she doesn't. She just stands for a moment with her car keys hanging loosely in her hand. She frowns as though she doesn't quite know what to do. I wonder if she's thinking I'm going to break into her house the moment she leaves. I must admit it appears to be quite a nice house with its freshly painted siding and trim, in three different shades of mossy green. The antique hardware on the door and the old-fashioned windows appear to have been completely restored. The place literally gleams with money and care. I wonder how it is some people have it so good. Maybe it's just because they are good people and I am not. Who can understand such mysteries?

It's clear that this is the old section of town where houses are very expensive and real estate is desirable. I'm sure this woman has lots of expensive things in her house that she wouldn't like to have stolen. So I move along, hoping this will reassure her that I'm not a thief who's casing her house. I certainly don't want her to call the authorities on me. And it's likely she has a neat little cell phone in that black designer purse of hers, the fancy kind of phone that flips open and closed. I move more quickly now. I want her to be positive that I am no threat.

After several blocks I sit down again. This time I sit on the curb next to a lamppost. Hopefully, this won't bother anyone. I think that curbs are public property. I watch as a front door opens across the street and a man comes outside with some kind of a terrier. The man picks up the morning paper, then stands and waits as the dog relieves itself on the front lawn. Then the man calls the dog in a childish sounding voice, promising a treat if it will "come to daddy." I think how great it would be if someone would promise me a treat for relieving myself on their lawn. Dogs have it so easy.

Naturally, this reminds me that I could really use a bathroom break. I think it must be nearly time for Pioneer Plaza to open, and their bathrooms are located quite handily next to an entrance, so I decide to make my way over there. If I can remember the way, that is. My sense of direction seems more confused than ever today. Finally I remind myself that it is toward the river, and that means I must go downhill.

I tell myself that if I can just keep moving my feet downhill, I will get there. I imagine myself as one of those cheap plastic walky toys that can wobble down an incline without any batteries. I watch my dirty socks as I go, the soggy toes flopping like dog tongues on the ends of my feet now. Flop-flop-flop. Only the dampness is keeping them on my feet. I trudge, step by step by step, downhill. Just put one foot in front of the other, I tell myself. One foot ahead of the other. After a while I realize that my floppy socks are literally disintegrating right off my feet. I sit down and peel them off to discover that they are nothing more than filthy, shredded rags.

"Who did this?" I ask, looking around for the culprit. Perhaps even Amelia has pulled a fast one. But no one is around to take the blame. So I shove the tattered socks into my giant coat pockets along with the other miscellaneous items I've collected during the past few days. This includes a broken shoestring, a bottle cap, a safety pin, an empty Tic Tac box, a golf pencil, and a brand-new book of matches. I smile to myself to think how Tweedle Dweeb won't like that I got away with his matches.

Now that my feet are completely bare, I can feel the skin on my soles peeling away layer by layer. I wonder if my feet will be shredded up just like my socks, only bloody. Then I suppose I will have to put them into my pockets too. I try to remember where I set my shoes but cannot. I decide that they must've been stolen. Maybe it was Tweedle Dumb. He never did seem to like me.

By the time I reach the bathrooms at Pioneer Plaza, my feet are red and actually bleeding in places. I sit down on the floor in a corner of the bathroom and try to clean them with soap and wet paper towels, but it is useless. The dirt is ground in so deep that I'm certain it will never come out again. And so I decide to wrap them up. I make soles out of folded paper towels, and then I attach these to my aching feet with my shredded up socks and the shoestring, sort of like sandals. But every time I stand up and walk a few steps they start to fall apart. It is hopelessly hopeless. So I just sit there with my head hunched down on my knees, and I cry.

"I want to disappear," I keep saying over and over. "Just disappear." I believe if I chant these magic words enough times, it will actually happen. Finally I sense someone is watching me, but I'm afraid to look up. Afraid that I have finally been caught. I know that I am cornered here in the bathroom, and there will be no escaping because my ruined feet cannot run. Not very far anyway. I refuse to look up.

"Do you need help?" It's a woman's voice, but then this is the ladies' rest room. Finally I look up and just shake my head without speaking. I look back down again, my heart pounding so loud that it echoes off the ceramic tile of the bathroom, *boom-boom-boom.*

Just go away, I think, or maybe I say these words out loud. If I had given it more thought, I might have held out my hand and panhandled. At the moment I just want her to go away and leave me alone, and thankfully she does. But now Amelia is back, and she is telling me that the woman was really a spy and that she has just gone to security or the authorities or whomever, and she is going to tell them I am hiding in the bathroom. Amelia tells me to get up and get myself out of there, and I know I must obey. Despite the stabbing pain that comes with each step, I hobble out.

Tears blur my eyes as I slowly make my way to the park across the street. It seems to take me forever to get there, but finally I do. At last I sit down on a bench and cradle my bleeding right foot in my hands, rocking back and forth as if that might somehow ease my pain. All the voices are yelling at me now, including Amelia's. They are calling me names and telling me how stupid and worthless I am. And it's not that I disagree; I just want them to go away—to leave me alone with my suffering. I am trying to tell them this. I want to explain it and make it perfectly clear, but I can't remember the right words, or perhaps they are just scrambled in my head. I suspect this is Amelia's doing, trying to get back at me. Perhaps it was that woman in the bathroom. Did she do something to my words? Or maybe my words have been encoded so that others won't understand what I'm saying. I'm not sure.

I sit in the middle of the city, removed from everyone and everything, separated, quarantined perhaps. I see people passing by, a blur of winter coats and blank faces, going places I cannot go. I am not welcome there. I am not part of them, and they are not part of me. Maybe they don't even exist. I am utterly helpless, but those busy people cannot help me. They will not. I am encased in Plexiglas, a specimen to be gawked at. It is too late. No one can save me now. I cannot even save myself. I know I can't walk another step. I can't go on. I decide I must simply stay here on this park bench. Forever, I guess.

I imagine myself turning into a bronze statue. There are many artfully placed around this park but mostly animals, I think. I don't recall a human. I particularly like the little otter with the oyster shell on his tummy. And the bear cub. I think humans don't matter so much around here. We are more expendable, disposable, replaceable. Not endangered like the spotted owl or muddy tree toad or whatever it is they're trying to protect here in Oregon these days.

I hold very still now and imagine they will name my statue *The Street Girl.* I see her hunched over on her park bench wearing an overcoat that seems to swallow her whole, with her skinny wrists protruding from sleeves too long, arms wrapped around her middle as if she's trying to hold in all the pain—to contain it so it doesn't spill over and touch or soil or contaminate. Of course, I cannot think these thoughts in real sentences or even in actual words since they are encoded. I can no longer process the events of my life in such a congruent and literary fashion. Instead it's just a long string of jumbled feelings, random thoughts, broken syllables, all coated in layer upon layer of confusion. But who really cares?

I care.

The sky is getting dusky, and I am cold when I feel her standing near me. I cannot see her, but it's as if I can sense her presence. Maybe it's just her body heat, or maybe it's her smell—a mixture of mothballs, old newspapers, and something unfamiliar. Or maybe Amelia has told me she is here, but somehow I know. Even so I am afraid to look up, and yet I'm afraid not to. When I finally force my eyes to focus, I see that it is only Betty Grable, and somehow I don't think she's here to take me away. Not that I would really care. I don't care about much of anything right now.

Betty still has her rusty grocery cart from this morning, but she is holding something out toward me. I try to focus my blurry eyes to see what it is, and for a moment I think it's a gun. Is she going to shoot me? Am I relieved? Then I see it is something wrapped in a gray metallic-looking plastic bag.

"Huh?"

"Here." She nods to the bag.

I take in a deep breath, then reach for the bag.

"Go on, open it." She's frowning at me as if I'm a half-wit.

I untwist the top of the bag and look inside. It is something red.

Two somethings that are red. I take them out. It's a pair of red satin bedroom slippers. The kind with open heels that you slip your foot into. I can see they are slightly used but not badly. And they look clean.

"Put them on."

I study her carefully, wondering if this is some kind of a trick. I remember a story from a lit class about a pair of red shoes, and when the girl puts them on, she can't quit dancing. I think she dies dancing, but I'm not sure at the moment. I imagine myself dancing with my worn-out feet. I can imagine that it would kill me, but I don't know if I would mind.

Carefully I slip them on my raw, aching feet. They are a bit too long in the back but feel comfortable on the cracked, bruised soles of my feet.

"Thanks," I mutter, my eyes still staring in wonder at the shiny red slippers. Then I look up to see that she is smiling. I just stare at her face for a long moment. It looks like a miracle all lit up like that. I've never seen her smile before. Then she grabs hold of her shopping cart and wobbles away. I am amazed. Part of me wants to go with her, to ask her about her million-dollar legs. But then I am not sure if I could keep up or if she would even want me. So I remain on the bench, still pretending to be a work of art, only the title has changed. *Street Girl in Red Slippers.*

chapter EIGHTEEN

In the Mean Time

Days and nights blur into the gray fog of my memory. I am not sure of much of anything anymore. How much time has passed? Who is trustworthy, and who is not? Where will I sleep tonight? I cannot remember when I last ate or where I went yesterday or what I did. Of course I have no idea where I am going. Besides running, that is. My life is all about escape these days. The voices are my constant companions now. So much so that I almost don't even notice them sometimes. Then they start screaming and demanding that I pay attention, and so I do, or I pretend to; I'm not sure anymore.

I do have a few fleeting memories, like the evening Betty Grable gave me these red slippers, which now are stained and threadbare. And I remember the old man in the tweed three-piece suit who bought me a cup of coffee with real cream in it and a whole-wheat bagel. At first I thought he was from the CIA but then maybe not.

I also remember quite vividly the time I was grabbed and then dragged into a dark alley by a big guy in a cologne-soaked leather coat who thought I "wanted some." I tried and tried to scream for help, although I'm not sure that any actual sounds came out of me.

I begged for Amelia to rescue me, but she was nowhere to be seen. The creep had my neck painfully pinned against the cement wall so tightly that I could barely breathe. With his free hand he clumsily unbuckled his belt just as Tweedle Dweeb and Tweedle Dumb turned the corner. When they realized what was going on, they ran over yelling and cussing at the stupid pervert and then pulled him off me. They even threatened to beat him up, and together I think they might've actually been able to do it. More important, the jerk was convinced and took off in the other direction.

I was so shook up that I stuck close to those two for the rest of the night. I would've been content to stay with them all night until Amelia started harping at me to get away from them, telling me I couldn't trust them. Of course the other voices were yammering at me too, and before morning came, I was so freaked that I just got up and quietly sneaked away. Sometimes my head is a really screwed-up radio station that's tuned into everything all at once. Voices, voices, voices—all jabbering at the same time. Sometimes the ones without names almost make sense, but mostly they are cruel and twisted, and violent too. Then there are voices that I think are my grandma's and maybe Pastor John's and a child's voice that makes me very sad. Amelia's is the strongest, but even she can be nasty when she's in a foul mood.

I still see the two Tweedles here and there, and sometimes we talk or get something to eat together, but I am never completely sure if I can trust them or not. And every time I decide to trust them, Amelia assures me that they are truly evil, and somehow she makes me believe her. My life is completely impossible.

Mostly I remember being alone and afraid. I remember hearing the voices and running from the various people who are always after me. That's what my life seems to be about these days. I just don't know how much longer I can take all this. Although some of the voices, including Amelia's, tell me they have the solution. *Destruction.*

But I try not to consider that route. I don't know where it would lead me, ultimately anyway. In the meantime I am trapped in the never-ending nightmare of my pursuers—this is my reality. I know this is how it will continue, and I am so very, very tired, so afraid that I will never be able to rest.

Come to me, and you will find rest.

chapter NINETEEN

The Cheshire Cat

At last I am ready to give up, call it quits, and give in to the demands of the voices, including Amelia's; she is more persistent every day. I accept the fact that I am worthless now—my life is meaningless; I am the refuse of the world. Amelia delights in reminding me that this will never change.

I feel lost and beaten and remember a day long ago. I think I was about ten. I made a kite out of sticks and newspaper. I used poster paint to create an orange-and-yellow sun with a happy face on the front and waited impatiently for the paint to dry. Then I tied it to a ball of string and took it outside. A gusty March wind promised a perfect maiden flight for my beautiful kite. I couldn't wait to see my sun smiling down from the cloudy sky. I didn't really know much about kites and hadn't known to attach a tail. Somehow I managed to launch my kite into the air, but it whipped and zipped wildly about, completely out of control, and quickly snagged on an oak tree, where it instantly broke into a tangled mess. My poor sunny kite became a hopeless wreck as it flapped and fluttered in the branches, beaten by the relentless wind. I am there with it now, I think, battered and abandoned to the elements. It is time to give in.

The early morning fog creeps along the river, and I am creeping toward the bridge. The tall one. The one that keeps calling my name, entreating me to come and admire its heights before I plunge to its depths.

I don't know what day it is, but the city is dressed for Christmas, full of good cheer. Down here by the river it is damp, cold, foggy, and dreary, and I blend in quite well. I am looking for the bridge, but I think I am lost. I can see it, but I cannot see how to get on it. I look at the slate-colored water and wonder if I should just jump from the sidewalk, roll down the steep hill and into the water. Then I could swim to the bridge before jumping off of it and back into the water. This almost makes me smile, but instead I sit down and hold my head between my hands and moan. I need relief.

I feel something warm rubbing against my leg, and this makes me jump. When I look down, I see that it's just a small cat. Not a kitten exactly, but a scrawny tiger-striped cat that isn't fully grown yet. I reach down and stroke its back. I feel all the bones in its spine, and at first I am repulsed, but then I feel sorry for the cat. He looks cold, like me, and I pick him up and move him to my lap. I do this slowly and carefully, afraid that he will become frightened and scratch me. I've heard that cat scratches can be dangerous. He seems grateful for the attention and curls up in my coat and begins to purr.

I continue petting him, and his purring grows louder. I am amazed by this phenomenon. He's like a machine. The more I pet him, the louder he purrs. I wonder if everyone at the river park can hear him. But when I look around, there is no one within sight, so I think perhaps it doesn't matter much.

I spend the day with my cat and call him Cheshire Cat, Cheshire for short, although he does not really say much. I believe that God has sent him to me to save me from the bridge, at least for today. As usual, Amelia tells me that I'm wrong, that he's just a stray and probably full of dreadful feline diseases, but for a change I don't believe her. Cheshire tells me different. He tells me that he has come from afar to be my friend. I believe he will grow up into a human-size cat, and the two of us will stroll along the riverbanks together. He will protect me from my enemies, and we will be friends forever.

For now though he is small enough to fit in my gigantic coat pockets. I move the contents from the pocket on the right into my left pocket, and this becomes his pouch. I am the kangaroo mama keeping my baby safe in my pocket pouch. I will do this until he grows big enough to take care of me. I'm hoping that won't be too long now.

Cheshire and I stay together for a while. Is it only a day? Or a week? I cannot be sure. But when I see the Tweedles, I show them my treasure.

Tweedle Dweeb just frowns. "Your cat looks pretty sick, Alice."

I look down at Cheshire and shake my head. "No, he's just sleepy."

Tweedle Dumb surprises us by speaking. "He looks half-dead to me."

"He is not half-dead," I insist. "Just sleepy." Now, however, I am starting to wonder. He didn't want to drink any water this morning, and that did seem a bit odd.

"You should take him to the Cat Lady," says Tweedle Dweeb as if I should know what that means.

"Huh?"

"This lady who takes in stray cats and knows how to make them well. The Cat Lady. Haven't you ever heard of her?"

I shake my head no and look down at Cheshire. I know in my heart that he's not well. I just don't want to believe it. A gigantic lump, the size of a pumpkin, grows in my throat because I am afraid he might die.

"Where is the Cat Lady?" I demand suddenly. "I must go to her at once."

So the Tweedles lead me to the northeast side of town, where houses are small and run-down. First we ride the MAX, which is free, but then we walk for miles and miles, or so it seems. I am worried that my worn-out red slippers will disintegrate before we reach this place.

It is nearly dusk when we stop in front of a little pink house. It is shaped like a box and has multicolored Christmas lights strung about the windows and a plastic holly wreath hanging on the door.

"This is it," says Tweedle Dweeb with pride. "I told you I could find it."

I stand there and look at the house, wondering what I should do.

"Go on up," urges Dweeb. "Knock on the door."

"But—"

"Go on. She's nice. She can help your cat."

I reach down into my right pocket and touch Cheshire's fur. He is so quiet that I am afraid he might already be dead. I wonder what the Cat Lady would do if I handed her a dead cat.

"Go on, Alice!" Tweedle Dweeb looks mad now. Like he's worked so hard to get me here, and I'm just standing on the sidewalk acting like a complete idiot. Then the two Tweedles begin to walk away, and I am torn. Do I stay with them or take a chance on saving Cheshire's life with a total stranger. I am seriously afraid that they're just playing a mean trick on me. Maybe someone truly evil lives in this house. Maybe someone who eats cats, or people. Or maybe someone who will take me away, lock me up, steal my thoughts, or reprogram my brain. How can I know for sure?

Just then I notice a fat black cat walking up to the tiny porch. He meows for a bit, and after a while the door opens, and an old woman steps out and says, "Why, Oliver, where on earth have you been all day?" And the fat cat strolls into the house as if he owns the joint.

The woman stays on the tiny porch peering out toward me. "Do you need something?" she calls out.

"I, uh, I have a cat."

She nods. "That's nice, dear."

"He's very sick."

Now she frowns as she steps out onto the narrow walkway that leads from the sidewalk to her house. "What's wrong with your cat?"

I take a step toward her, glancing over my shoulder to see if the Tweedles are still nearby in case I need them, but they have vanished into the foggy evening air. Were they even here at all?

The woman is next to me now. She has on a lavender cardigan and red polyester pants, and she smells like onions. I open my coat pocket so she can peer in.

With both hands she reaches into my pocket and removes my lifeless cat. I am certain he is dead now. She sighs deeply and heads back toward her house, then pauses on the porch. "Are you coming, dear?"

I hear Amelia whispering at me, telling me to stay away from this woman, to go back to the bridge and finish what I'd started. But Cheshire seems to be speaking to me too, saying, "Don't leave me alone here."

So I follow the Cat Lady into her box house and watch as she gently lays Cheshire on her plastic-topped kitchen table. She puts on the glasses that are hanging from a rhinestone chain around her neck and stoops over to peer more closely at my cat. Then, looking very much like a doctor, she examines him. I watch in wonder as she carefully checks him out. Then without saying anything, she leaves and goes into another room.

I wonder if this means I've been dismissed. Should I take poor Cheshire and go now? Perhaps he is too far gone and there is nothing she can do. Or maybe she is calling the authorities and accusing me of cat abuse. Worse yet, she may actually be a spy, and this might be a big setup. I am ready to grab my cat and run for my life, but even as I consider this, she returns with a small box and a faded blue towel. She gently lays Cheshire in this box, wrapping him in the towel. I am afraid this is meant to be his coffin, and I begin to cry.

"Is he dead?"

She pats my arm and says, "No, dear, but it's close." She putters over to the refrigerator, and I hear her open the door and then run water in the sink. She hums as she does this, but I keep my eyes on Cheshire. I don't want him to die.

"Have you prayed for him?" she asks as she returns with what looks like a miniature baby bottle filled with something whitish gray.

I shake my head no.

"Well, if you really love him, you should pray for him. God loves all creatures great and small, you know. He cares about the tiny sparrow when it falls from its nest. He cares about sick kitties, too."

I bow my head and close my eyes and honestly try to pray. But I am not sure what kind of words to use. I am afraid that God is still really mad at me for not honoring the golden key. What if I pray for Cheshire, and God decides to smite me by killing my cat—just to show me that I'm evil and that he is still the boss? I sigh deeply, and feeling like a failure, I open my eyes. The Cat Lady is attempting to interest Cheshire in the contents of the bottle, but he is not responding.

"Dear Father in heaven," she says in a soft voice, "we ask you to help our little feline friend here tonight. We know he's not well, and we want you to make him better. We know that you love all your creatures. We know that you are a great healer. Please reach down your loving hands and touch this poor cat. Help him to eat the food he needs to nourish his little body. Help him get better quickly. Amen."

I nod and echo her "amen." And I mean it. I mean it with all my heart.

"He appears to be starving," says the Cat Lady, eyeing me carefully as she holds the bottle in one hand. "You don't look too good either."

I press my lips together and look down at my feet, my shabby red slippers. Suddenly I wonder what I am doing here. Once again it occurs to me to run. But I don't.

"When did you last eat?"

I shrug.

She makes a *tsk tsk* sound between her teeth, then hands me the tiny bottle. It is warm, and the warmth feels comforting in my hand.

"I have an idea." She picks up Cheshire now, still wrapped in the blue towel. "Why don't you sit down and hold your cat like a baby—cradle him, you know?" She leads me to an overstuffed chair that's covered in an old quilt. A large golden cat is curled comfortably in the seat.

"Time for you to move, Juliet," she says as she gently pushes the cat away. I notice that a number of cats are curled up contentedly here and there. Also a lively pair of black-and-white kittens are wrestling together on the large braided rug that covers the linoleum floor.

"Here." She takes my arm and guides me into the chair. "See if you can get him to eat something."

I sit down, and she arranges Cheshire in my lap, and I try to feed him from the little bottle. She returns to the kitchen, and I am able to relax better on my own. I stroke his furry head with one finger as I hold the bottle temptingly near his tiny mouth. "Come on, Cheshire," I say quietly. "Come on and eat something. You'll feel better if you do."

Finally, after what seems like a long time, he begins to lick the milky liquid from the rubber tip, just barely moving his little pink tongue. Soon it seems he likes the taste, and he begins to drink more. It takes a while, but he eventually empties the whole bottle. I want to jump up and down and shout for joy, but I control myself. I simply pet him and praise him for this accomplishment.

"Oh, good for you," says the Cat Lady when she returns to the living room. "I thought he might drink it if it came from you. Cats are like that, you know. They attach themselves to you just like a baby to its mama."

She reaches down and gently removes Cheshire from my lap, and I wonder what she plans to do with him now. I sense that she is kind, that she really loves cats. Why else would her house contain so many?

"Time for you to eat something too," she announces as if that's the most normal thing in the world.

"But I—"

"I will hear no arguments," she insists as she walks back into the kitchen. "It is suppertime, and I expect you to be a good girl and join me."

So I return to the kitchen to find the plastic-topped table, where Cheshire has been recently lying, now set with two places. The Cat Lady carefully arranges Cheshire back into the box that is sitting on a chair in the corner. Then she turns and looks at me.

"Would you like to wash up?"

I look down at my grimy hands and nod.

She points down a hallway from the kitchen. "The first door on your right."

I find an old-fashioned bathroom that is painted a robin's-egg blue. It has a claw-foot tub and several cat boxes. Some that need to be emptied. I scrub and scrub my hands, then worry that I am taking too long, I quickly dry them and return to the kitchen, noticing that the yellowed wallpaper in there has lots of faded cats prancing about on it.

"Would you like me to take your coat?" she offers.

"No." I pull it more tightly around me.

"That's fine." She smiles as she points to a shiny red vinyl-covered chair that looks as if it emerged right out of the fifties. "Have a seat."

Obediently I sit and wait as she carries two white bowls of what appears to be tomato soup to the table. I can tell by the creamy orange color that she made it with milk. For a moment I remember my aversion to animal products, but then I figure if it's good enough for Cheshire, it's good enough for me. My mouth actually begins to water as I remember how much I loved soup like this as a child, and then I think I'm about to cry. She begins to pray, and I listen.

"Dear Father, we thank you for our food and for how much you love us. I thank you for my young guest and her little cat. I pray that you will take precious care of both of them and keep them safe in your ever-loving arms. Amen."

I repeat her "amen" and open my eyes. I want to tell her "thank you," but the words seem lost inside me. Instead I pick up my spoon and hesitantly dip it into my soup. Then, worried that this is just a dream that will suddenly end, I quickly slurp a spoonful of the soup. But it tastes real. I feel the warm creamy fluid wrapping around my tongue, and I hurry for another spoonful.

I am afraid that Amelia is going to show up any minute now, and I know she will chastise me for being here. Or tell me that the soup's been poisoned. However, I honestly believe that drinking delicious poison soup in a warm house might be preferable to diving off the bridge. I wonder what Amelia would say to that. Surprisingly, and to my relief, she doesn't make an appearance.

I realize the Cat Lady is talking to me now, and I fear I have been rude not to answer.

"Pardon?" I am amazed that I still know how to use that word. She smiles. "I asked your name, dear."

I nod. "Alice. My name is Alice. And my cat's name is Cheshire." She laughs. "Just like Alice in Wonderland."

"Yes," I manage to say. "That's right."

"My name is Faye, but lots of people call me the Cat Lady."

"Yes. That's what I heard."

She laughs again, and I think her laughter sounds like tinkling bells. "I don't mind the title," she says. "There are worse things to be called, you know."

I nod again. Yes, I know. There are things like "crazy girl" or "nut case" or "retard" or "loony" or "weirdo" or "whacked-out." Suddenly I wonder if I'm saying this all out loud. But the Cat Lady, or rather Faye, is still smiling and eating her soup as if nothing whatsoever is wrong with me.

Suddenly she stands. "Goodness, I almost forgot our second course."

She returns with two golden brown grilled cheese sandwiches, and I think I have actually died and gone to heaven. Her eyes seem to light up. "You like?"

I nod eagerly as she sets a sandwich on my side plate. "Thank you."

She smiles. "It's nice to see someone with a hearty appetite."

"This is very good." I am proud to have said this much.

"Thank you."

We proceed to eat our meal quietly. This is a relief to me, for I am unsure that I can manage to carry on a conversation and eat at the same time. I am not very good at doing either of those things anymore, and to do them simultaneously in the company of another feels utterly impossible.

I can't remember when I ever felt this stuffed, but I somehow manage to eat all my soup and most of the sandwich.

"I don't have anything for dessert," she says apologetically.

"I am so full," I say, "I couldn't eat anything else anyway."

"Maybe we can have some tea later."

I nod, wondering what "later" means. I wonder if I should offer to help clean up, but I don't quite know how to say this. She stands and begins to pick up the dishes. I follow her and do the same. Then I join her at the sink, and without speaking I try to make myself useful. She seems to appreciate my help, and amazingly I don't break anything. This is a relief, for I suspect her pretty, although mismatched, dishes might be valuable, at least to her.

"I think you should try to feed Cheshire again in about an hour," she tells me after consulting the clock. "We can retire into the living room now."

I walk into the living room and look around. Cats, cats everywhere. And where there are not real living cats, there are statues and pictures of cats. "You must really love cats," I say.

She laughs as she eases herself into the big overstuffed chair, scooping the golden cat into her lap as she does this. "Have a seat, Alice. Feel free to move the cats as needed. They think they own the place, and I suppose in a way they do, but humans get first pick at the furnishings."

I gently lift up the colorful calico that is nestled into the padded seat of a rocking chair. I set her in my lap and slowly begin to stroke her fur. "She's pretty," I say. "What's her name?"

Faye smiles. "I see you know enough about cats to know that calicos are always females. Her name is Constance, but I call her Connie."

"Hi, Connie," I say quietly, shyly, as if the cat might be an uppity sort, the kind that snubs certain types of humans. But she seems to appreciate my fingers as I scratch the top of her head.

"So, tell me, Alice, do you have a home in Portland?"

I sigh and look back down at Connie, thinking it odd that a cat has a home, but I do not.

"I didn't think so." Faye puts her feet on a needlepoint footstool and leans back in her chair. "So many young people out on the streets these days. Such a shame."

"Yes."

"Have you been on your own for long?"

"Sort of." I try to remember time, but the concept of months and days is confusing to me. "I'm not sure exactly. I was still going to school at Portland State during September or maybe October, I think. How long ago was that?"

She appears to be thinking. "Well, this is early December. So it's been a couple of months."

I nod as if this makes perfect sense.

"So you are a student?"

I frown. "I guess so. I mean I was back in BC anyway."

"BC?"

"Before, I mean." I glance away. That old nervousness is coming on me again, like floodwater rising steadily. I'm afraid she's going to figure me out and send me away or else have me locked up.

She just nods, as if she understands. "Oh, I see. We all have a before, don't we?"

"Yes. We do."

We talk some more, but I'm finding it harder to stay on track. And I'm not sure whether I'm speaking or not. When I look at her face, she doesn't seem to mind. She just goes on talking as if I'm really listening and responding in a normal fashion. Finally she looks at her watch and announces it's time to feed Cheshire again. I help her prepare the bottle this time, and she explains that it's soy milk and vitamins, and very good for him. This time he seems to understand what he's supposed to do and quickly downs the bottle. Already he's looking a little bit better. I hold him like a baby and stroke his striped fur.

"Next time we'll see if he can lap it from a saucer," she tells me as she rinses out the bottle. "Then by tomorrow he might be ready for some soft food."

"Oh." Now I am unsure what I should do. Does this mean it's time for me to go? Do I leave Cheshire here? Or take him with me?

As if reading my mind, and this does not surprise me at all, she says, "You and Cheshire can sleep in the spare bedroom. It's a bit cluttered and messy in there, but the sheets on the bed are clean."

"Really?"

I'm sure she sees my astonishment, because she pats my arm and looks me in the eyes and says, *"Really."*

"I need to go tend to some things, and then we can have our tea. Unless you'd prefer cocoa." Her smile reminds me of a little girl's. "I adore cocoa, but I almost never have it by myself. Cocoa seems like something you should share with someone else, don't you think? Do you like cocoa, Alice?"

I nod. "Yes, I love cocoa."

"Oh, good." She shuffles down the hallway, and I carry Cheshire into the living room. I wonder what it is she needs to tend to. I hope she's not on the phone telling the authorities to come pick me up. Somehow I don't think she is. Still I'm not sure. I distract myself by introducing Cheshire to the other cats, but I only know three by name. Oliver, Juliet, and Connie. Then I show Cheshire the elaborate scratching post that dominates one corner of the small living room. It has little carpet-covered boxes of varying colors—green, blue, and yellow—and carpet-covered poles that go clear to the ceiling. Right now the black-and-whites are playing tag on it. "You can play with them when you're feeling better," I promise him.

Finally Faye returns, and she has a plastic shopping bag with her. "Here," she says as she hands me the bag. "Some overnight things for you."

"Thank you." I want to peek in the bag but fear that might be rude. Still, I am amazed at this woman's kindness to me. Part of me believes I am imagining this whole thing or that I'm sleeping beneath an overpass and simply dreaming. But my reality is so blurry that I think perhaps it doesn't matter where I really am.

"There are some bath things, if you'd like to bathe. And some pajamas and, well, whatnot. I see that you don't have anything with you."

I wonder if she thinks I am dirty. I *know* that I am. I know I must be disgusting. I haven't bathed in…so long. And sometimes I feel people looking at me, and it embarrasses me when they scowl at me on the street, turning up their noses as if I smell bad. I probably do, although I can't smell myself very well. I'm far better at detecting bad smells on others than with myself. A "bath." I say the word as if it's something magical.

She smiles. "I have a nice big tub, you know. You can put bubbles in it if you like."

"A bubble bath?" I'm not sure if I've ever had a bubble bath in my entire life.

"I can take care of Cheshire while you bathe," she offers, holding out her hands.

As if in a daze, I nod, then make my way to the blue bathroom. I'm sure this is a dream now. But I hope it will continue long enough for me to see the bubbles filling the tub. I must hurry before everything goes up in a poof and disappears and I am back on the street again.

The weird part is how it feels as though I am at home. Not home like where my mother lives, but home where I belong, like somebody really wants me.

I hope it's not just my mind playing tricks on me.

chapter TWENTY

Bubbles and Bones

It is very strange to remove my clothes. It has been so long that it feels as if I'm peeling off layers of my own skin, but I keep telling myself, no, these are just clothes and dirty clothes at that. I drop them into a sodden heap, then out of respect, I bend down and neatly fold them, stacking one thing on top of another. They are not much, I know, just filthy blue jeans and several various-size T-shirts that I have collected, along with my original sweatshirt and the coat from the Tweedles and my threadbare red slippers that Betty gave me. Still, they are all I have.

The claw-foot tub is full of hot water and bubbles now. Faye had included a box of bubbling bath salts in my plastic bag. The label on the box reads "April Violets," and it's sort of an old lady fragrance, but I think I like it anyway. Besides, it helps to cover up the ammonia smell of dirty cat boxes. I have counted them. There are six. I hope no kitties need to use the facilities while I'm in here because I locked the door.

The steamy bathroom has lots of framed pictures of cats hung haphazardly on the walls. They are the kind of pictures that come from calendars. I begin to imagine that I am going to be swimming with all those cats. Maybe they are catfish and I am a mermaid. The mirror is so foggy that I can see only a blurred image of myself. I am thankful for this.

I try not to look at my bony rib cage as I lower myself into the steaming water. It is so hot that it stings my flesh, and I get goose bumps from the heat. Funny how the body reacts the same way to both hot and cold. I wonder what this means. Although I don't like it, I have become somewhat accustomed to the cold lately. But being hot, now that is something altogether new to me. I'm not even sure I like it at first.

Slowly something comes over me, and I begin to relax a little—another new sensation. I lean my head into the back of the tub and slowly exhale. My tangled hair is trailing down into the water, floating around my shoulders like a fur collar. I try not to think about anything. I try to tune out the voices that are nattering away in the back of my brain. Even though they are quieter than usual right now, it's a real challenge not to listen. But I focus my whole attention on the rhythm of my breathing, watching the luminescent bubbles as they rise and fall like the tide above my chest. My only goal is to absorb the warmth and the smell of violets as I allow myself to melt and meld into the silky water. Is this what it felt like to be in my mother's womb? And what if I could stay like this forever? I think that I would.

I'm not sure how long I have stayed in the water, but my hands and feet are shriveled and pale, and the water has cooled into a dirty lukewarm pool that is about the same shade of gray as the Willamette River on a cloudy December day. For a moment I wonder if I am really in the chilly river, but then I decide that I'm not. I think I should climb out before it's completely cold. I dry myself off with a scratchy yellow towel that feels as if it's been dried on a clothesline. I rub and rub, hoping to remove the last layers of crusty dirt that have become embedded in my body during the past few—what?—days, weeks, months, years? I cannot even remember.

Then I reach back into the plastic bag provided by Faye. Earlier I noticed what appeared to be a nightgown, and I pull it out to discover it is pale pink and flannel. Obviously worn, for it is soft and supple. I slip it over my head and marvel at the texture. It is better than the finest cashmere. I wonder if Faye would like to adopt me and keep me for good.

I pick up my plastic bag and the folded pile of smelly clothes and tiptoe out into the hallway. I hear music playing. It sounds like something old-fashioned, like those big bands that were popular during World War II. I pretend that I have stepped back into time and that I am really someone else. What a luxury that would be.

"Ready for some cocoa, dear?" she calls as I come into the kitchen.

"Where shall I…" I stand there in the yellow light of the kitchen, barefoot and wet headed as I hold my small pile of earthly possessions.

"Your room is down the hallway, first door on the right, beyond the bathroom. I tried to clear it out a little for you. I don't know why I'm such a pack rat."

I tiptoe back down the dimly lit hallway. I'm not sure why I'm tiptoeing, but it feels like the right thing to do. I turn on the light to discover a peach-colored room. An old-fashioned four-poster bed takes up most of the space, with boxes and piles of things all around it. It looks like a storage room with a bed in the center, and yet it reminds me of something. Then I remember how I had used my packing boxes to protect my bed. Yes, I think I will be safe here. I set my clothes bundle on a chair by the door and return to the kitchen.

Faye is standing over the stove now, stirring a saucepan filled with milk that's just starting to steam.

"What's that?" I ask, thinking she is fixing something for her cats.

"This is the milk for our cocoa." She turns off the burner and removes the pan.

"You use real milk?"

She laughs. "Yes, I don't believe that cocoa is really cocoa if you make it out of a package." Then she opens up one of those old-fashioned tins of Hershey's cocoa, the kind that are brown and silver, just like the candy bars. She adds several spoonfuls and then some sugar and a smidgen of vanilla. I watch with amazement as she stirs it with a big wooden spoon.

"I never saw anyone do that before," I tell her.

"Yes, I am often accused of being hopelessly out-of-date. But it's just the way I am." She nods to a cupboard behind me. "Can you get us down some cups?"

I open the cupboard to see an interesting selection of mismatched flowery china. "Which ones?" I ask.

"Pick a cup you like, dear. I'll take the one with the pink roses."

I choose a cup with violets, thinking this goes well with my bath, and I take down another with dainty pink roses. I set these on the counter by the sink and watch as she skillfully pours from the pan, spilling only a few drops.

"There you go, dear." She sets the pan in the sink and fills it with water, then we take our cocoa to the living room where the music is playing.

"Who is that?" I ask. "I mean the music."

She sighs with a happy smile. "That's Glenn Miller."

I nod. I think I've heard of him.

"This was George's favorite song. 'String of Pearls.'" She gets a dreamy look. "I can remember dancing with him in the Twilight Room just before he went off to Korea that winter."

"Was that your husband?"

She shakes her head. "No. My fiancé. We would've married first, but there wasn't time for the kind of wedding we both wanted. I was planning the wedding while he was overseas. But he never made it home."

I frown. "That's too bad."

She nods. "I just couldn't find it in me to marry anyone else after losing my dear George. In my heart we are married, always will be. But I've been happy on my own like this. I had my job at the post office for years and years. Then I have my cats and my pension. The good Lord has been kind to me."

I wonder about this but see no reason to doubt her. She certainly seems content enough to me, and I know I would be happy if I were in her place. I think her life seems just about perfect. Like a fairy tale.

"I like your house," I tell her.

She laughs. "Well, not many people would agree with you there. Most folks think I'm a batty old woman. They come in here and see too many cats. And, of course, the cat hair is everywhere. It's so hard to keep it cleaned up. And, well, I know it smells a little catty, but I am so used to it that I don't even notice."

"I think it's nice."

"I do too. And my cats are good company."

"I appreciate your letting me stay with you tonight." I look down at my cocoa and swallow. "I think you're the kindest person I've ever met."

She smiles now. "Well, you're a sweet little girl. I'm glad you and your Cheshire cat stopped by to visit."

We listen to the music and drink our cocoa, and for the first time in a very long time I am almost normal. I barely remember what normal feels like, but I imagine it is something like this. I just wish that it would stick around for a while.

Finally it is time for bed, and I desperately hope that I'll be able to sleep. Even if I can't, I am determined to stay in the bed and remain quiet. I don't want to walk around the house and frighten Faye. I want to be a good houseguest. I take Cheshire and his little box and say good night.

"Sleep well, dear."

I slip into the bed and breathe in the clean smell of the sheets. Oh, I'm sure anyone else would think they smell catty too, but to me they are nothing but lovely. Once again I wonder if this is real. I wonder if perhaps I really did jump from the bridge and perhaps I am simply dead and in heaven now. This certainly feels like heaven to me. But then I am a bit surprised to think that God would actually let me in. Maybe I missed something.

I try to remember the words Faye used when she prayed to God. It reminded me of some of the things I heard at the mission. I think about how Faye called God "Father." I wonder if God would ever want me to call him that. But then I think of my own father, and I shudder. I am afraid that God is probably just like him.

So I try not to think about God as I tell myself to shut up and go to sleep. I try to block out the voices by counting backward from a thousand. I imagine myself to be sleeping, and, amazingly, I think it is actually working.

chapter TWENTY-ONE

Through the Looking Glass

I am still living in the Cat Lady's house, although I call her Faye. It's been three days now, and I am amazed that she has not thrown me out yet. Not that I've been bad, mind you. I've tried to be on my best behavior, but then there are some things I can't seem to help or control. Like the talking out loud sometimes, especially when I'm telling the voices to go away and leave me alone.

Fortunately, Faye does not seem the least troubled by this. She just smiles and shakes her head as if I'm slightly eccentric, and maybe I am. Still I am worried about having stayed here three whole days. I know it's been that long because she said so herself just this morning. That's when I remembered something my mother used to say about company and fish and how they both become stinky after three days. But then I was stinky when I got here, and I've been keeping myself pretty clean ever since.

Still, I worry that Faye might be thinking I'm crazy, especially like today when I was saying something grumpy to Amelia. I can't recall exactly what it was now, but I know I was pretty irritated with her. I just wish she would leave me alone. Instead she persists in slandering the "Cat Lady"—that's what Amelia calls her. But I think that's disrespectful.

"Get out of here," Amelia demanded as I got out of bed this morning. As usual, she was sitting on the chair, arms folded across her chest and scowling darkly. "You can't trust the Cat Lady. She's onto you, Alice. Get out of here while you still can."

"Leave me alone," I muttered without looking her in the eye. I've thought about pretending that I can't see or hear her. I wonder how she would respond to that.

One time Faye told me that she sometimes talks to herself too. Although I think she was probably trying to make me feel better. I wanted to ask her if she hears voices as well, but I thought better of this. I don't want to frighten her too much. I feel I am a living time bomb, my days here are numbered, and it's just a matter of time before I blow up, shatter into a thousand pieces, and then get tossed out with last week's kitty litter. Sometimes I wish I were a cat because then I could probably stay here forever.

I do try to make myself useful, but I know that my scrambled brain sometimes makes me mess up. Like when I tried to wash the dishes by myself and ended up putting them in the refrigerator instead of the cupboard when I was finished. Now, really, I know better than that.

But Faye is patient with me. Sometimes I think she really likes me, although it could be that she simply feels sorry for Cheshire, and I just happen to be part of that package. But Cheshire is getting better each day. I'm a little worried that he will become so healthy that there'll be no need for the two of us to remain here in the cat house any longer.

This frightens me more than I care to admit, but I know I should face up to the possibility. According to Amelia, it's completely inevitable, and the sooner I make the break, the better it will be for everyone. But I wonder what I will do, where I will go. I wish I could come up with a plan besides the streets. I got so weary of being cold and scared all the time, and I'm sure that it's even worse now since the temperatures have dropped down to freezing the last couple of days.

Cheshire sits in my lap most of the time. I think he knows I saved his life. Well, with Faye's help, of course. I'm afraid I will have to abandon him when I leave this place—for his own good. I am afraid that despite his good progress, he would not be able to survive on the cold winter streets. Will I?

This afternoon I sit in Faye's living room and look out her front window and watch as the world outside grows dusky. It gets dark so early now. I think it's only around four o'clock, and yet it is already a deep foggy blue outside. I wonder if it's always been like this, or if the world is changing. Sort of like global warming, only perhaps this is a global dimming. It seems possible.

Faye is listening to the four o'clock news on her old-fashioned radio (she has no television) as she knits a tiny red sweater for Juliet because Juliet's fur has gotten so thin and patchy lately. Faye is worried that she is cold.

I notice how the glass in her big front window is becoming reflective like a mirror now. I can see everything in the room behind me as if it's really in front of me, as if it's out the window, outside and beyond. It's as though I'm watching something in another world. I see Faye comfortably seated in her overstuffed chair, a red ball of yarn in her lap that Oliver is tapping with one paw. I can see it's just a matter of time before he gets it down on the floor and gives it a good bat. This is a game they like to play, and I am usually the one who must retrieve the ball and roll it neatly back up. But I don't mind. I like to make myself useful.

Still it is strange seeing this tidy little world in front of me, out the window. I see the cats and the pictures on the wall, the braided rug, and the shabby but comfortable furnishings. I see the soft golden glow of the lamp beside Faye's chair. I see her mustard gold sweater and her pastel flowered pants, and I like how the colors clash and collide with each other. At the same time, I think it all seems so very far away, removed from me, like something I can never really belong to or fully participate in. I am cut off and separated from that world by this big sheet of unforgiving hard glass—or something that's just as cold and invisible as that.

I wonder if this is how Alice felt in *Through the Looking Glass*. Oh, I know she claims to have been bored and looking for some kind of adventure, or so the story goes, but perhaps she simply felt out of sorts with the rest of the world. Perhaps, like me, she just didn't fit in. Maybe it seemed that only the looking glass separated her from everything that was real and alive and healthy.

"What are you doing, dear?"

I realize that I am standing right in front of the window now; my breath has made a cloudy splotch right in front of my face. I think I was actually going to walk through the window and try to enter this comforting world. Surprised, I turn around to see that the exact same world is right behind me, only clearer and brighter and probably warmer than the one I've been looking at. Of course everything is backward now, or maybe it's just me. Still, the whole thing confuses me, and for a moment I wonder which side is real.

"Are you all right, Alice?"

I nod and look down at the floor. Oliver has succeeded in getting the yarn ball from her lap, and I stoop to pick it up. It must've been down there for a while, because I can see that he's managed to make quite a twisted mess of it.

"Silly cat," scolds Faye. I can tell she doesn't really mind too much.

I sit down on the footstool next to her and try to untangle this mess, but it only proceeds to get worse, with the knots tightening and the yarn stubbornly snarling the more I tug and pull on it.

"Don't worry, dear." Faye hands me her little brass scissors that look like a stork. "We can just cut that snarl and tie the two ends back together."

I'm not sure what she means by this, so I simply hold the scissors and stare at the wad of twisted red strands. What am I supposed to do? I look at the stork and open his long beak and wonder if he can tell me.

"Here, let me show you." She smiles as she takes the stork and the tangled wad of wool. Then she allows the stork to bite one end of the yarn, *snip,* and then again on the other, *snip.* She hands a snarled bunch of yarn back to me, then ties off the two freshly cut ends and trims them. "See?" She holds up the ball now neatly attached to her knitting project and smiles as if it were the simplest thing in the world.

I am thoroughly impressed. I wish I could fix my life so easily. I wish she could use her stork on me to completely remove the snarled piece of my life and then neatly tie the two ends back together, but I suspect this is impossible with people. And so I sit here with my wad of yarn. I continue my futile attempt to unravel it, thinking I can perhaps salvage it. But it only gets worse.

Finally I hear her calling me to come in the kitchen and help her to set the table. I am relieved as I toss my knotted yarn in the trash beneath the sink. Like me, it is useless. I open the utensil drawer and hope I can remember where the forks and spoons go on the table tonight. So far I haven't been able to get it perfectly straight without her help.

Tonight is no exception. She simply laughs and reminds me that the spoons go on the right and the forks on the left. I wonder if my way would've been correct on the other side of the window since everything is opposite over there.

As we dine on a dinner of homemade chicken noodle soup, I think about the "other" side of the window and wonder if that's really where I belong. The place where everything is backward, like me. I think about this all night long, even after I go to bed. I pet Cheshire as he sleeps in his favorite spot, curled up on my tummy. I wonder if he would want to go with me, if he would like to live on the other side, but I am afraid he wouldn't survive. Besides, he's already at home here; he's comfortable and fits in as if he's lived here forever. He's perfectly happy with Faye and her feline friends. And why not? He is a cat, and this is a cat house. As usual, I am the misfit again.

After a sleepless and worrisome night, I get up just before dawn. Cheshire looks at me like I'm crazy as he continues to lounge in the warm bed. I suspect he is right.

"Are you coming?" Amelia whispers impatiently. "Hurry up!"

I shush her as I quietly dress myself in the semidarkness of the room. Faye has given me some odd pieces of clothing that no longer fit her but that she didn't want to throw away. She doesn't like to throw out anything. Naturally, they are out of style, but I don't mind. They are only a little too big around. Faye and I are about the same height, and she said back in her younger days she was about my size, only bustier. She said this with a smile. Today I just keep on dressing. I put on layer after layer until everything I own, except for my big coat, is on my body. It isn't so much, really, although it does make me look fat, but I don't mind. Then I brush out my hair, something that Faye has been encouraging me to do each day, and I put it into two messy braids that reach just past my shoulders. I don't think to ask myself why I am doing all of this, but I suspect it means I am leaving today. I have held off Amelia as long as possible. Her patience has worn quite thin, and she's even begun to threaten Faye. I wouldn't like to see her harm Faye. I fear it's time to go.

I go outside to test my layers of clothing against the weather. It's cold and icy out there, with bushes and trees covered in a white frosty layer that makes everything look lacy and pretty. I walk around a bit, unsure if I should just leave or go back inside and wait until Faye wakes up so I can say good-bye first. I pace back and forth along the sidewalk and wonder.

"Just leave!" Amelia snaps at me. "The longer you stay, the worse it will be."

"But what about Cheshire?" I plead.

"He's fine. He doesn't need you."

"But what about Faye?"

"Faye doesn't want you around anymore." She says this as if she is the expert on everything. "If you don't leave right now, it might be too late. Faye is thinking about calling the authorities this morning. She thinks you're crazy. You better run while you can, Alice."

I say something in Faye's defense to Amelia, but then I notice a neighbor, Mr. Chutney, is standing on his porch in his bathrobe. He has his newspaper in his hand, but I suspect he is using this as an excuse to stare at me. I know that Faye's neighbors think I am weird. I have felt it in their glances. They look at me intently for a moment, then quickly look away—almost as if they haven't seen me, but I know they have. And it's not as if Faye is on such good terms with her neighbors either. She's told me that they don't approve of her keeping so many cats. Some of them accuse her cats of using their flower beds for cat boxes. Which I seriously doubt since I've seen them use the cat boxes in the bathroom enough. But even if they did, isn't it a free world? Shouldn't a cat be allowed to go where it wants to go? Apparently not.

I turn away from Mr. Chutney and continue pacing and arguing with Amelia. Telling her that the least I can do is to say thank you and good-bye. And what about Cheshire? I should say good-bye to him. Tears fill my eyes now, and I think that my life is not worth living.

"That's right," agrees Amelia. Suddenly I am deluged with suggestions for how to end it all. The voices are yelling at me now, so I press my hands over my ears, but it is useless. They are shouting out every possible idea for how I can end this pain. Everything from Faye's big black butcher knife to the bridge. Finally I let my arms drop to my sides and begin to walk.

"Alice?"

I look back to see Faye standing on her porch, peering down the street at me. She has on her aqua chenille bathrobe, and I can see that she's shivering in the cold. "What on earth are you doing out here, dear?" She has a puzzled expression on her face.

"Just run!" yells Amelia.

Then I notice Cheshire standing beside Faye, and I know what I must do. I must go back into the house and attempt to explain in a civilized way that it's time for me to leave. So I wipe the tears from the corners of my eyes and go back inside and tell Faye the truth. Well, some of the truth. I'm not even sure what all of the truth is.

"But where will you go?" asks Faye as she puts on the teapot. Faye doesn't drink coffee, ever.

I slump down in her kitchen chair and groan. "I don't know."

She presses her lips together as if she's thinking, then says, "Have I done something to offend you, dear?"

I shake my head no. "Oh no, of course not. It's just me, Faye. I am...I just...well, I know that I should leave." Then I point toward Mr. Chutney's house as if that explains everything. "Your neighbors don't like me staying here. I know that they want me to leave. I know they think I'm crazy." Then I look up at her. "Don't you think I am crazy too?"

She smiles. "I think we're all a little crazy. And it's not necessarily a bad thing. And as for my neighbors, well, I do try to be nice to them, but I'm sure they think I'm a little batty too. And I know they don't care for my cats. Still, we manage to get along all right, most of the time. And when we don't, we work together to resolve our little differences."

"But I'll make more problems for you." I sigh. "I am just a great big problem."

"Have you been happy here?"

I nod. "Yes. More than anywhere else. But I'm worried…"

"About what?"

"I don't know. That they're going to find me. Or that they'll tell you lies about me, or that I'm not good enough."

Now she sets two cups of tea on the table and sits down. "Who are you talking about, Alice? Who is going to find you or tell lies?"

I shake my head. "I don't know. That's the problem. I just never know for sure. But it'll happen. It's just a matter of time."

She takes a sip, then gets a thoughtful look in her gray eyes. "I think I'll call Simon," she says decisively.

"Who's that?" The familiar sensation of cold fear climbs up my throat and makes me feel that I'm choking. I am certain that this Simon person is with the CIA or somehow related to my mom or Pastor John or Forest Hills.

"He's my nephew. And he's very wise about all sorts of things. He helps me with my yard in the summertime, and sometimes he gives me rides to the grocery store when it's time to stock up. Like today, for instance. I happen to need some groceries. I'll see if Simon can take us to Fred Myers." She smiles now. "I like Fred Myers. The clerks are so friendly there." Then she proceeds to call him.

I'm not too sure about this plan or Simon for that matter, but I stay long enough to eat some breakfast and then help her with the dishes. And I sweep the floor too. I have discovered that I am quite good at sweeping. Faye says I always do a very thorough job. "Much better than I do," she assures me. This makes me proud.

"Aren't you a bit warm?" she asks as I set the broom back in the laundry room and close the door.

I nod.

"Perhaps you should change into something more suitable for the indoors."

Uncertain about this suggestion, I return to the bedroom and sit down on the bed. Naturally, Amelia is already there, seething. She begins yelling at me, calling me names, threatening all of us, but I pretend that I can't see or hear her. This makes her so angry that she storms out. I sigh in relief, then decide that it won't hurt to remove a few layers of clothing. Just for now. I still have on two pairs of pants, though, and several shirts. After all, I tell myself, it *is* freezing cold outside. I fold the rest of the clothes and set them on the chair. Maybe it will show Amelia that she's not welcome.

"Simon is here," Faye calls from the kitchen.

I am uneasy about leaving the bedroom now. I'm seriously worried about this Simon fellow, afraid that he has come to get rid of me. So I sit on the bed some more and fret. Naturally, Amelia sees this as her opportunity to come back and boss me around again.

"See! I told you this would happen. You should've left when you had the chance." She points to the window laced with feathers of ice. "Maybe you can climb through that." I walk over and examine the window, but before I have a chance to open it, I hear Faye's voice again.

"Come on out, Alice. I've told Simon all about you, and he wants to meet you." She opens the door and takes me by the hand, like a little child, and leads me out to the kitchen where a dark-haired man, probably in his midtwenties, is sitting at the table and consuming one of the ginger spice cookies that I helped Faye bake yesterday morning.

"Hey," he says with a smile as Faye introduces me. I stare at him and respond like a mute woman.

The teakettle begins to whistle again, and Faye tells me to sit down. For some reason I obey, sitting directly across from this stranger who has so suddenly invaded my safe little world. I wonder why I didn't listen to Amelia earlier this morning. It seems she was right after all. I study the stranger. He has shaggy brown hair and dark brown eyes that appear larger than normal behind his tortoiseshell-rimmed glasses. He's wearing a worn navy sweater over a gray T-shirt, going for the shabby preppy look I guess, as if I am the fashion expert. He has on tan cords with worn knees that look like they've been washed a lot. What looks like an authentic old bomber jacket is slung over the back of the chair. All in all I suppose he looks fairly harmless. But how can you ever know for sure?

Faye brings the teapot over to the table, and I scold myself for not jumping up to help her, but it's as if I am frozen. Like the proverbial deer caught in the headlights, I am too terrified to move to the left or the right. I don't know what's going to happen next. Just then Cheshire jumps into my lap. Now this is somewhat comforting, and I calm down ever so slightly as I begin to stroke his soft fur. I think I am breathing now. I like the way he has been filling out these past few days. He has such an appetite that Faye thinks he's going to turn into a roly-poly, but that's hard to imagine.

"Who's that?" asks the stranger, nodding toward my cat.

Still I am speechless. I just stare at him.

"That's Cheshire," explains Faye as she sets three cups on the table. I assume this means I am having tea with them.

"I thought he was a new face." Simon picks up the pot as if he lives here and pours three steaming cups of golden tea. I watch him closely as he does this, worried that he may try to slip something into my cup. While I don't see any hanky-panky, I'm still cautious as I take a sip. I try to see if it tastes bitter or has a chalky aftertaste.

"Faye tells me you're a student at PSU," he says as he dips his cookie into the tea.

I assume he's talking to me again, but I don't know how to answer.

"She *was* a student," adds Faye. "Didn't you say this would be your senior year, dear?"

I glance nervously at him, then over to her, and nod. "It would be," I say in a sober voice that sounds like someone else.

"I graduated from there," says Simon. "Just last spring. Now I'm doing my internship."

"Are you a doctor?" I ask, slightly relieved to break the mute spell. Also to have the questions moving away from me.

"No." He laughs. "I actually considered it until I took a couple of chemistry classes."

"Oh." I want to ask him another question, to keep him off guard, but suspect I've already reached my word limit for this conversation.

"So I decided on psychology instead." He finishes off his cookie.

I nod as if I think that's a good choice, but really I couldn't care less. I wish I could slip out of the kitchen unnoticed. I glance toward the hallway that leads to my room.

"What's your major?" He picks up his second cookie.

I think about this for a minute. Why is it so hard to remember these things? Finally it comes to me. "English lit."

"Now there's a useful degree." He laughs again. "So what do you plan to do with that?"

I shrug and look away, hoping I can simply freeze him out. I wonder what kind of desperate guy would want to pursue a conversation with a crazy loser like me anyway?

"So you ladies want to go to Fred Myers today?" He glances at his watch. "You can have me at your disposal until two o'clock. At that time I've promised to help Julie decorate for the Christmas party."

I wonder who Julie is, a wife perhaps, but then I notice he wears no ring, not that this means anything. Maybe she's a girlfriend. And why should I care anyway? Perhaps the most surprising part of his statement is the bit about the Christmas party. I keep forgetting that it's actually that time of year. It seems we should be way past Christmas by now. Shouldn't it be April or May? But then I remember it's too cold for spring yet.

I notice that Faye has put on a purple felt hat with a long feather attached, and it looks quite becoming on her. She's also wearing her fur coat, which she wears whenever she goes outside, even if it's only to the mailbox. The coat is long and dark brown, beaver I think she said, and it's losing hair in places, but I still think she looks quite glamorous in it. I can almost imagine her wearing it with her beloved George on their way to the Twilight Room in winter. The fact that she has on her floral pants and bright green tennis shoes only seems to add to the dramatic ensemble.

She and Simon begin moving toward the front door now, and I hear Faye telling me it's time to go. I wonder if her nephew thinks I'm retarded or just socially impaired. I decide I don't really care as I climb into the backseat of his old cream-colored Saab. The backseat is draped with a wool army blanket that is covered with light-colored hair. I suspect he has a dog, or his wife or girlfriend has a dog. Anyway, it seems clear that a dog's been back here before. Could be just an enormous cat. I try to imagine a huge, sleek, blond cat sitting back here. I see her with her legs crossed at the knees and lighting up a cigarette in a long cigarette holder and saying words like "dahling" and "fabulous." She probably wears a diamond tennis bracelet.

I hear Simon and Faye conversing like normal people up in the front seat, and I wonder why I can't be like them. I wonder how it was that I got trapped behind the looking glass in the first place. I suspect that everything is backward here in the backseat. Most of all, me. And, not for the first time, I am trapped in my crazy world and I wonder—I rack my brain trying to figure out what I must've done to deserve this kind of life. Pastor John and the church ladies would say it's because I have sinned. But Faye has told me that God doesn't punish us for our sins, that he forgives us for sinning. While I know this can't be true, I do wonder why she would lie to me about it.

chapter TWENTY-TWO

A Christmas Maze

I feel as though I'm five years old and following my parents around the Fred Myers store. Although I must admit we make a rather odd-looking family. Faye slowly strolls along in her molting fur coat, her purple hat with its long feather bobbing up and down at each step, while Simon just keeps pushing the cart and chatting away like we are perfectly normal. I trail reluctantly along behind them like a disgruntled child, wearing scraggly braids and several layers of mismatched clothing. I can sense people looking at us—those quick back-and-forth glances. Or maybe it's just me. Although I suspect we look weird. I'm sure I would've looked at something like this myself, back in BC.

The store is like a giant holiday nightmare. Santas and snowmen and bright lights pop out of every aisle, along with singing reindeer and angels that light up in neon colors. Honestly, it's enough to make you swear off this holiday for good. Talk about sensory overload!

No one else seems to notice the madness. I guess it takes a crazy woman to see that the world has gone completely nuts. Or maybe it's just me.

Finally I am standing in front of this life-size manger scene, the kind with plastic figurines that light up from the inside. I suspect it's expensive and would require a large front lawn to contain it all, but the characters seem almost real to me. I just stand there, slightly awed, as I stare at the baby sleeping so peacefully in the manger, trying to understand this whole thing. I mean if it's really true, if God is for real and he actually sent down his son to be born on this earth…well, *what was he thinking?* If *I* had a baby—which is completely unimaginable—well, I would never send him to a place like this. What kind of father does something as irresponsible as that? I shake my head in disgust and turn away.

"Too much commercialism?" asks Simon. I suspect he might've been watching me while Faye was picking out her holiday paper towels. I notice she finally chooses the ones with the dancing candy canes.

I shrug but say nothing, just continue following the two of them through this maze of row after row of stuff. I wonder where they get all this stuff. Does it come by ship or train or truck? Perhaps all three. I imagine giant ships hauling this stuff across the ocean, then loading it on trains and finally big trucks. Why should people go to so much trouble? I remember how only days ago I was living on the streets without anything. Don't people realize they can survive without all this stuff? What is wrong with this world?

"What?" Simon turns and looks at me as if I said something.

"Huh?"

"Did you just say, 'What's wrong with this world?'"

I shrug again and pretend to study a display for baby diapers that are printed with little green elves that are supposed to turn red when the diaper needs to be changed. Too bad Mary didn't have some of these with her in Bethlehem.

Simon laughs. "Hey, it's okay. I think I know how you feel."

I turn and study him closely. I want to say, "How on earth can you possibly know how I feel? You are normal! Whereas I, the crazy girl, am stuck on the other side of the looking glass!" I hope I did not say this. I really don't think I did because he is still smiling at me and acting as if we two share some private little joke. Oh, if only he knew!

Finally Faye's cart is nearly full, and she announces she is done. I sigh in relief and follow the two of them through the maze, presumably toward the cashiers. As we're passing the life-size nativity again, for some reason this makes me stop, and I can't take my eyes off that baby. I feel so sorry for him. I think I know how he feels because that's how I feel too. I have been tossed into a strange and foreign world, like an orphan, a place where I will never fit in.

Then I look over at his mother, Mary, and I see the look of love in her eyes and think that perhaps it will be okay for him after all. Perhaps Mary will protect him and take care of him. Suddenly I remember how his story ends, and I shudder and step back. Pastor John loves to tell the story of how the cruel soldiers killed Jesus on the cross. How he was brutally beaten and how the nails were pounded through his flesh. I realize that poor little baby's life is as hopeless and futile as my own.

"Go back," I want to tell the baby. "Go back to heaven where you will be safe. Tell your father that earth is a bad place. Tell him that you don't want to live here, that bad men are going to kill you if you stay." I'm crying now. I can see that all is hopeless, and I wonder why people spend so much time and energy and money to celebrate a holiday that is all about death. What is wrong with this world?

"Alice?"

I turn and see Simon standing next to me. I wonder how long he's been there and whether I've uttered these things aloud or simply shouted them within the confines of my troubled mind.

"Are you okay?" He reaches for my arm. "Faye is worried. She thought you were lost."

I look him in the eye and say, "I am lost."

"Hey, join the human race." Then he kind of smiles and begins to guide me toward the front of the store, and I wonder what he means by that.

The human race is not so very human, I am thinking. Or maybe I mean *humane*. But what difference does it make anyway? Hopefully, I didn't say this though. At least, I don't think I said this. I press my lips together and wonder how difficult it would be to contract lockjaw as I allow Simon to lead me over to where Faye is now standing with a cart full of bagged groceries near the exits. She looks relieved to see us, and tired.

"Alice, dear, I thought we'd lost you."

I apologize for dawdling but am really thinking, You have no idea how lost I am. Maybe I say this aloud, maybe not.

Simon pauses by the door as he drops some money in the red Salvation Army pot, and the old bell ringer smiles happily and thanks him. I think I have seen that bell ringer at the mission before, only he wasn't nearly as sober as he appears to be today. I wonder what Simon would think if he knew that I used to hang out with people like that or that I plan to again. It's weird actually, because I almost miss the streets right now. It's almost as if life makes more sense out there than it does in super shopping centers like this.

Simon and I carry all the groceries into the house. Both of us seem to sense that Faye is worn out from her shopping excursion. I urge her to sit down in her comfy chair, assuring her that I can put the groceries away, although I am not sure if I will get them in their proper places. What if I put the eggs in the oven?

Simon offers to help, and I do not reject his assistance. He seems to be neither pushy nor proud as he puts things away, and he certainly doesn't appear to be the least bit controlling as he makes every effort to stay out of my way. I suppose I am almost beginning to trust him, although I must admit this scares me quite a bit. For already I can hear Amelia's familiar warning to "Trust no one!" Fortunately she seems to be lying low at the moment.

Finally we are done, and I think he will leave.

"I noticed some leftover chicken soup in there," he says as he closes the fridge. "Should we heat some up for Faye?"

I suspect it must be well past lunchtime now, and I know that Faye is pretty worn out, so as much as I am ready to have Simon leave, I agree. He seems to be comfortable turning on the stove and setting the pan on it to heat. I try my best to set the table, and I think I get it right, and Simon doesn't tell me otherwise. I even remember to get out some saltine crackers. It seems like soup and crackers go together. How nice for them to be part of a couple.

Finally all is ready, and I go to tell Faye. She looks a little better now and seems delighted that the two of us thought to fix lunch. "There's a jar of peaches in the pantry," she tells me. "I think that would go nicely with the soup, don't you?"

I quickly locate the peaches and manage to open the jar without help. Then we all sit down, and Faye asks Simon if he would like to pray. He agrees, and to my surprise he prays in a way that is surprisingly familiar. I realize that his way of praying is a lot like his aunt's. I wonder if it runs in their family.

Just as we are finishing our lunch, Simon speaks up. "Hey, what are you doing this afternoon, Alice?"

I shrug and look away.

"I thought maybe you'd like to help me decorate for the Christmas party."

I glance nervously at him, wondering what on earth ever gave him this absurd idea, but before I can even make a plausible excuse, Faye jumps in. "What a lovely idea, Simon. I'm sure that Alice would be happy to help you. Wouldn't you, Alice?"

"I, uh, I don't know much about decorating for parties…" This is absolutely true since our church didn't believe in decorating for or celebrating any holiday.

"That's okay. I just need someone who's willing to work hard," says Simon as if it's settled. "You ready?"

"But, I, uh, I should stay and clean up—"

"Nonsense." Faye waves her hand. "You two did such a nice job with lunch. I can easily clean this up myself. You go with Simon, Alice. You two kids will have fun."

"But I—"

Faye stands now. "We won't take no for an answer, will we, Simon?" She looks firmly at me, then smiles. "It's settled."

That is how I find myself sitting in, not the hairy backseat with the sleek blond cat, but the front seat, next to Simon. I have no idea where he is taking me or what he plans to do to me, but I am extremely worried. He's driving up a hill because I can hear his engine whirring, and I know we are just slightly out of town because I can still see the city lights in the gray fog below us. But I also know there could be no place up here that needs to be decorated for Christmas. Why did I ever fall for this? I guess I'm just hopelessly stupid when it comes to these things. I'm dismayed that Faye would betray me like this, but then I should've seen it coming. Three days for company and fish—time to either fry them up or throw them out. It's clear she is throwing me out. I wish I'd left on all my layers of clothes.

So it seems I have made a very big mistake and been duped again. How is it that I am so easily tricked? I am certain I will never see Faye or my dear Cheshire Cat again. Of course, Amelia is sitting in the backseat now and shrieking at me. I am surprised Simon can't hear her, but he seems oblivious as he drives merrily along this twisting road that is engulfed by towering and sinister looking evergreen trees. Amelia is cussing at me, using such vulgar profanity that I am actually blushing.

Each time Simon slows down for a curve, she tells me to open the door and leap from the car. When I don't, because I am too scared and because a part of me doesn't want to, she rewards me by calling me more names. For the most part, I must agree with her. I am a stupid, ignorant moron and then some. Oh, how do I get myself into these messes?

chapter TWENTY-THREE

Simon Says

As Simon drives up the hill, I try to calm myself by pretending that we are just playing a game, convincing myself that none of this is real. I hope this will help shush Amelia's irksome heckling. My game is like Simon says, and this is how it goes. Whatever Simon does or says, I decide that I will simply imitate him. Then perhaps I will appear normal, and it will go well for me. If not, well, maybe I can make a fast break and get away before he notices.

"They say it might snow," Simon says as he slows down for another curve.

I nod. "Looks like it could snow."

"It'd be fun to have a white Christmas. I don't think we've had one in years."

I shake my head. "A white Christmas? Not in years."

He glances at me with what appears to be suspicion, and I wonder if I should think about jumping now.

"Are you nervous?" he asks.

"Nervous?" I echo.

"About being with me?"

I look at him and wonder how I could possibly explain all the various thoughts and feelings and voices that are continually pummeling my mind. Then I remember my game. "Are *you* nervous about being with me?" I stare at him now, wondering if I might actually be able to turn the tables and make him uncomfortable for a change.

He chuckles. "No, you don't make me nervous."

I sit up straighter. "Well, you don't make me nervous either." I notice he's slowed to a stop now, and I turn to see that we're passing some sort of a wrought-iron gate. On closer look, it appears to be some kind of security fence! My heart pounds within my chest like the Saab's engine straining up the last hill we just crossed. Not again!

"What's going on?" I reach for the door handle, but it's too late. He's already inside, and the gates are closing behind us. Why, it's like they were expecting him! I fumble to undo my seat belt and move closer to the door, grabbing the handle, ready to bolt.

"What's wrong?" he asks as he continues to drive toward a tall brick building that looks much too large to be a private home. He's only going about fifteen miles per hour; I'm sure I could easily survive the fall.

"Where are you taking me?" I think I might actually be shrieking now, but I no longer care about games or pretense. He stops the car in the middle of the driveway and turns to look at me.

"This is the Golden Home," he explains in a calm voice. "It's where I work. I intern here with Dr. Golden, and I was supposed to come up here to help his wife decorate for the—"

"But *why* are you bringing me here?" I demand as tears fill my eyes.

"To *help* me." He looks slightly hurt. "Did you think I was bringing you up here for some other reason?"

I glare at him. "I know you're trying to get me away from your aunt. My mother probably called you and told you I'm crazy. Or maybe it was Mrs. Knoll telling you that I'm possessed, or Pastor John or—"

Simon reaches over and puts his hand on my arm. "Look, Alice. I suspected that you might be dealing with some, uh, problems. But that is *not* why I brought you up here. Honest. I work here. And I need to help get the place decorated before the party tonight." He looks me in the eyes now, and I notice that he has long, dark eyelashes behind his thick lenses. "I just thought you might enjoy getting out of Faye's little feline house and doing something different for a change."

I take in a deep breath and tell myself that perhaps I'm over-reacting, that perhaps Simon can be trusted, but even so I don't believe a word of it.

"You fool!" shrieks Amelia, and I cringe and slump down in the seat.

"Are you okay?"

I just shrug, wondering who is really worse, Simon or Amelia? Maybe I should just take my chances. "I guess so."

He puts his car back into Drive and proceeds toward the build-ing. "I promise you, Alice, I'll take you straight home as soon as we're done. With your help it should take only a couple of hours. Julie is going to help too. She's Dr. Golden's wife, and she's really nice. I think you'll like her."

I just roll my eyes and shake my head. I want to say "whatever" but know that will sound childish and immature. Yet a part of me doesn't even care anymore. I figure if I'm so stupid that I don't know who can and cannot be trusted—whether it's Faye or Simon, who both seem to have betrayed me, or even Amelia, who's always yelling at me—well, then maybe I deserve to be locked up.

He parks the car and waits for me to get out. Finally I do, telling myself just to keep playing the stupid game. Simon says, Simon says...if I do as he says, maybe it will go better for me.

We enter some sort of foyer or lobby with marble floors the color of fresh butter and a large circular rug with a geometric pattern in the center. Several comfortable looking chairs are arranged in a corner, next to some large potted plants, and there are windows all around.

"You're here," calls a woman's voice. We are met by a tall brunette who appears to be in her forties, but she's not wearing a uniform. "And you brought help. Great."

"This is Alice, Julie."

She smiles and shakes my hand, and I manage to say something that sounds vaguely like a greeting, although I can't be sure. But the whole time I am looking over her shoulder, expecting a burly orderly to appear—someone who will help to subdue me, perhaps aided by a nurse who will pull out a hypodermic needle and give me a shot in the rump. Then together they will get me safely locked in my padded cell. But no such persons appear.

Instead we are led into a spacious and well-lit room with wooden floors that glow with a warm golden finish. Large, expensive-looking Oriental carpets are placed here and there, and, as in the lobby, a number of potted plants stand guard along the bay of tall windows. At one end of the room is a large rock fireplace with a carved wooden mantel. Next to the fireplace is a huge evergreen tree that goes nearly to the top of the open-beamed ceiling, which I guess to be at least fifteen feet. Next to the tree is a ladder, and it appears that someone has already been putting on a string of lights.

Several chairs and sofas have been nicely arranged into small groupings, sort of like you'd see in a ritzy hotel. Four wooden tables with upholstered chairs wait nearby, as if they're inviting you to sit down and play a game of cards. A couple of these tables have large plastic crates on top.

"I had Jack bring the decorations down earlier this morning," explains Julie. "I don't know why he planned the trip to the zoo today. He knows that we usually decorate the party with everyone here, and—"

"It's my fault," says Simon. "A friend of mine who works at the zoo offered us these free passes, and I took him up on it. I totally forgot about the date of the party."

She smiles. "Well, that's okay. Everyone was so excited about the trip. Did you hear that Andora just had her baby?"

"The elephant?" I ask, amazed that I can remember this bit of trivia, but I think I recall hearing something about it on Faye's radio news the other day.

"Yes." Julie nods as she opens a box. "It's a boy. I can't remember his name, but they say he's healthy and doing fine."

Before long, it is just as Simon has promised, and I am helping him decorate for what appears to be an honest-to-goodness Christmas party. I feel a bit guilty for my overreaction, but I'm still not convinced this isn't just an elaborate setup for my benefit.

"I'm so glad you brought help along," says Julie as she pulls out a long strand of gold tinsel. "I'm already short-handed in the kitchen today, and there's still so much to be done."

"Don't worry. We can handle it out here," Simon says. Then he winks at me as I open a box of shiny red glass balls. "I have a feeling that Alice is pretty good at this decorating business."

"Great. As you can see, I've got the lights pretty much on."

"Cool. We'll take it from here."

She smiles. "Then I'll get back to the kitchen."

Like a little kid on Christmas morning, I open box after box of pretty ornaments and decorations. I actually squeal with delight a couple of times, and I love arranging the glass balls so that they are spaced adequately apart. I find a box that's filled with big red candles and ribbons and artificial greenery and ask Simon if he thinks I should do something on the mantel. I recall an arrangement that I saw in a magazine once.

"Go for it!" he says with a grin. "I'm not really very good at this myself. I'm mostly up here out of guilt because of the zoo trip."

"Who are the people—I mean the ones who went to the zoo?"

"The residents."

"Residents?" I'm playing the game again.

"Yeah. This is a treatment center for the psychologically challenged."

"Psychologically challenged?" I frown as I set a red candle in the center of the mantel, then step back to see how it looks.

"Dr. Golden doesn't use words like *disease* or *illness* or *disorder*. You know what I mean?"

I don't answer him. Instead I pretend that I'm focusing my full attention on setting more candles along the mantel. Still, I wonder what he means. I remember how Dr. Thornton made such a point of telling me I had a sickness. He said I had to accept my illness as a disability in order to get better.

"Dr. Golden feels that we all must play a role in getting ourselves healthy, and he runs this place with the goal of teaching people how to handle their challenges in positive ways. In other words, he gives his patients the tools they need to live independent and successful lives."

Back at the box for greenery now, I hear what Simon is saying, and while I don't understand everything, what I do understand sounds too good to be true. Naturally, this worries me. I try not to let on as I drape the artificial greens around the candles on the mantel. Then I lace the pretty silk ribbon in and out and get completely caught up in my creation. I suspect that Simon is speaking to me again, but I am unable to focus on him or hear his words. I don't want to. Before long he seems to be caught up in hanging his long strands of tinsel around the tree. This is a relief. I go back to the boxes and find a few odd ornaments that I now stick here and there beside the candles. One small porcelain angel really captures my attention, and I place this close to the center, then step back to look.

"Wow, that's really pretty." Simon is standing beside me now. "I had no idea you were so gifted at this."

I shake my head. "Me neither."

"How about doing something like that on those tables?" he suggests, pointing to the game tables and coffee tables throughout the room. "That'd really brighten up the place."

So I go around and put a few greens, candles, ribbons, and ornaments here and there, and finally the room looks festive. I can't help but smile as I look around with a strange sense of pride. I am amazed that I'm doing this. Here I expected to be locked up and drugged by now. I sigh and turn around to see how the tree is coming.

"That looks nice," I say as I walk over and pick up a box of ornaments. "Do you want me to hand you some of these for the top?"

"Yeah, thanks." And so I stand at the foot of the ladder and hand him ornaments, and I wonder how it is that I've never done anything like this before. And I'm surprised that I think this is fun.

"About the residents," I begin as I hand him a brass rocking horse. "Are they locked up against their will?"

"No. Patients are only admitted willingly. You can't just drop someone off here without his consent."

"But what about the gates, the fence?"

"Residents can come and go as they like, although they have to comply with Dr. Golden's rules." He reaches for the red elf I am holding up for him. "The security is only to keep people out."

"To keep people out?"

"Yeah, it probably sounds weird, but sometimes there are family members or friends of the patients who aren't too helpful in the recovery process. That and the occasional curious gapers from the press, you know."

"The press?" I echo, aware of our previous game.

"Well, what Dr. Golden is doing is fairly unusual. Some of his psychiatric peers are suspicious about his methods."

"What are his methods?" I ask as I hand him a flocked reindeer.

"It's not that he doesn't believe in using medication, because there are some cases where it's required. But even then he uses meds along with a lot of therapy and counseling. Mostly he's trying to teach patients to retrain their ways of thinking. In essence to heal themselves, with help. Dr. Golden believes in healing the whole person, not just the brain. His treatment is mental, physical, emotional, and spiritual."

I don't know what to think about all this since it doesn't sound anything like Forest Hills. For a moment I think perhaps I am being tricked again and glance over my shoulder, partially expecting the guys in the white lab coats to bust in here any minute and drag me away.

Simon climbs down from the ladder and looks around. "Wow. I think we're done here. You did a really good job, Alice."

I smile for the second time and wonder if by tomorrow my face will be sore from this unusual activity. "Thanks. It was kind of fun."

Just then we begin to hear strains of Christmas music, and Julie appears with a plate of cookies. "I guess I should've put that music on while you kids were decorating, to get you into the proper Christmas spirit, you know. But better late than never." Then she stops and looks around. "Hey, you guys are really good. That mantel looks spectacular. Did you do that, Simon?"

He shakes his head and points to me. "That was Alice's work."

She holds the cookie dish out toward me. "Then you get first pick here."

I hesitate, glancing over at Simon, then back at her. I wonder if there might be something in the cookies, like poison or a sedative.

"It's okay," she says. "They're made with real butter, but you look like you could afford a few extra calories."

So I take a candy cane–shaped cookie, then wait as Simon takes one just like mine. Playing Simon says again, I follow his lead and take a bite only after he has taken one first. I suspect he knows what I am doing.

"So, Alice, are you coming back to our little party tonight?" asks Julie as she takes a bite of a Santa cookie.

"Yeah," says Simon eagerly. "Why don't you come back with me?"

I don't know what to say now. The room looks so pretty that the idea of a party sounds surprisingly appealing. Yet I'm still not convinced that this isn't just an elaborate trick, a setup to reel me in. However, it does occur to me that this is a whole lot of trouble for someone to go to just to set me up. But you never know. In a twisted way, it seems like the sort of trap that someone like Pastor John might arrange, especially since he's so opposed to Christmas decorations and parties and such. I can just imagine him rubbing his hands together and thinking, "Aha, we've got her now." Pretty tricky really. "I, uh, I don't know," I finally manage to stammer.

"Oh come on," urges Simon. "I think you'll enjoy it. We're all a little nutty around here, but we're a lot of fun. Right, Julie?"

She nods. "You got that right." She leans over and peers at me. "But you better be warned. We don't let the 'normal' people come, if you know what I mean."

"Yes," says Simon. "They are much too boring."

"And ordinary," she adds.

I look from one to the other and wonder if they are pulling something over on me, but despite my misgivings, they seem sincere.

"Say you'll come," says Simon.

"I'll come," I repeat the words, wondering why on earth I did. Then I remember the game. I guess I'm just playing it too well.

"Great!" Julie grins. "Well, I better get back to the kitchen. Guess I'll see you two around seven then."

It's already getting dusky as we drive along the curvy road that leads back down the hill. I want to tell Simon that I've changed my mind, that I've made a huge mistake, but he is talking about his work now. He's telling me how great Dr. Golden is and how he'll probably win the Nobel prize someday. I just sit there like a dummy and listen, wishing that everything he's saying might actually be true.

At the same time I hear Amelia, louder than ever, yelling at me and telling me that I'm a complete fool and that I'm so gullible I'll believe anyone and asking how I got to be so stupid.

"Shut up!" I yell and then realize I have said these words out loud.

Simon looks at me, and I feel my face turning the same color as the glass Christmas balls I hung earlier.

"I, uh, I'm sorry. I didn't mean you," I mutter.

He nods. "Right. I thought maybe you didn't."

We drive in silence through town now. Even Amelia is quiet for a blessed change. Finally, as we're crossing the bridge, Simon speaks. "Look, Alice, I realize that you're going through some hard stuff. Believe me, I understand. I really do. You need to know that I *really* do understand. And I want to help you, if I can. I want to be your friend and help you work your way through this. And just for the record, I don't think you're really crazy, okay? Can you believe me?"

I'm not sure what I believe right now, but I nod and pretend that I do. After all, *Simon says*.

"All right then," he says. "I'll be back here a little before seven." He is parked in front of his aunt's house now. "By the way, just to warn you, this is usually a dress-up kind of affair, but don't worry. I realize you probably don't have anything like that with you. So you can wear anything you want, okay? I don't want you to think you've got to dress up to come tonight."

I nod mutely as I open the car door and let myself out. I feel I might be someone else as I walk into the house, someone who has a chance at whatever normal might be. But then who would I be? For a moment I am terrified that I will become Amelia and start nagging and screaming at everyone I meet. But no, there's someone else, and I try to remember what happened to Alice.

chapter TWENTY-FOUR

A Princess Story

Faye looks up and greets me as soon as I come into the house. "Did you have fun, dear?" she asks eagerly. She looks comfortable in her chair with Juliet and Cheshire both curled in her lap. Her news show on the radio is just ending, and she reaches over to turn it off, looking back at me expectantly. Cheshire jumps from her lap and struts over to me, waving his tail like a flag as he rubs against my leg.

"I guess so." I pick up my cat and sit down in the padded rocker and sigh. This is all I really need—a warm house, a cat, and a rocking chair. I think could live happily ever after just like this. I lean back and try to relax.

"Simon is such a nice boy." She smiles. "Don't you think?"

I nod. "Yes. Nice."

"Did you meet Dr. Golden?"

I eye her curiously, wondering if this might not have been a setup after all. "He wasn't there," I answer.

"Too bad. He's such a good man. I've gone up to his place with Simon before. I hear that his ideas in psychiatry are quite revolutionary."

I study her and wonder what she is getting at, but she simply adjusts her glasses and picks up her knitting.

"Simon wants me to come to the Christmas party." I say the words as if it's a recording on an answering machine. I wait for her reaction.

"That's nice, dear. When is that?"

"Tonight."

"*Tonight?*" Her knitting falls into her lap, and she looks at me as if I've just announced that the president is coming to visit. "Oh dear, you must start getting ready then."

"Why?"

"Because it's a party, dear." As if *that* explains everything.

I shrug.

"Well, you'll have to, you know, *fix yourself up.*" She sets her knitting aside and gently nudges Juliet from her lap as she pushes herself to her feet. "Goodness, what will you wear?"

I look down at my jeans. "This, I guess."

"No, no, no…" She shakes her head, but her expression is thoughtful. "No, I'm sure we can do much better than that." She rubs her chin, then looks at the clock. "First off, we'll have an early dinner. Can't send you off with an empty tummy. Now, do you think you could manage to make us something, Alice?"

"I, uh, I guess so." I'm not entirely sure about this, but after my success at decorating today, my confidence has increased a notch or two.

"Good. I'll go through my closet and see what I can find for you. Then you'll have to bathe, and we'll fix your hair, and…" She claps her hands together now. "Oh this is going to be such fun. I just hope I can find my little camera."

Suddenly I feel like it's prom night, or perhaps I'm Cinderella. But in the next instant I imagine myself wearing old lady clothes, and my illusion pops like a bubble. Why should I care? It's just a nut-house party anyway. I take Cheshire to the kitchen with me and ask him what I should fix for dinner. He suggests sardines, but I'm not sure that's such a good idea. I open the fridge and the cupboards to view the groceries Faye bought today, and I finally decide on tuna fish sandwiches. I know it's not very clever, but I hope that perhaps I can handle something this simple. Besides it was Cheshire's second choice.

I open the can, then drain the juice from the tuna into the sink. So far so good. Then I mix the tuna with some mayonnaise and a little bit of celery that I chopped myself on the cutting board (now that was clever!). Then I spread this onto slices of whole wheat bread and add some fresh lettuce leaves before I cut these into diagonals and set them on a pretty blue plate. All in all, I am quite proud of my accomplishment. I hope that Faye will like it too. I am impressed that I actually used a knife without freaking out or even cutting myself. That is no small thing. I keep thinking I should fix something else to go with this but am not sure what. Finally I decide on bananas. I know this is not very fancy, but I think it makes for a healthy meal, and, besides, the colors look nice together.

Faye smiles when she sits at the table. I don't know if it's because of my culinary skills or whatever she's concocting for me in her bedroom. I have imagined her back there, mysteriously stirring up some sort of magic potion that will make me beautiful, or perhaps she is spinning straw into a golden gown. I must admit she looks rather ordinary just now as she wears her lavender cardigan and bows her head to ask a blessing.

"Dear Father, we are so happy to be with you this evening. We thank you for this fine food that Alice has so lovingly prepared. And we pray that she and Simon will have a delightful evening at the Goldens' Christmas party. Thank you so much for your love and mercy. Amen."

I repeat her amen, and then we eat. I think that my tuna fish sandwich–making skills are first-rate, and Faye appears to agree.

"That was very good," she says as she peels her banana. "You are a fine cook, Alice."

"Thanks."

I start to clean up, but she tells me to leave it. "Come and see what I have for you first."

So I follow her to her bedroom, preparing myself for some bright polyester, floral-print dress, perhaps topped with one of her pastel cardigans and the gaudy costume jewelry she is so fond of wearing every day. I imagine myself going to the party as a colorful clown, and the image doesn't even disturb me very much. It seems almost fitting.

As a result I'm completely unprepared for the magnificent gown lying across her pink chenille bedspread. Images of spinning hay into beautiful cloth suddenly seem quite believable. I stare in amazement at the fairy dress. The fabric is a silvery blue, some kind of satin or taffeta, where you can see two colors at once, kind of sparkly and magical. It has a smooth bodice with soft gathers of fabric around the neckline and off-the-shoulder sleeves. The waist looks tiny with a long full skirt pouring out of it like an iridescent waterfall.

I am speechless at first but then manage to ask, "Where did you get this, Faye?" Right now, she could tell me that she waved her magic wand and pixies flew in and delivered it, and I wouldn't doubt her.

She laughs. "From the back of my closet."

"It's too beautiful," I say, stepping back. "I can't possibly wear something so exquisite and—"

"Nonsense. You *must* wear it. The lonely little dress desperately needs to go to a party tonight." She sighs happily. "And it's full of good memories too. Do you know that the last time I wore it was at the Twilight Room right before George went to Korea? It was in December too. Fifty years ago." She smiles dreamily. "Oh, I just know this is meant to be, Alice."

I think I'm living in a dream as I bathe. The cat boxes are not so smelly tonight since I freshened them all just yesterday. One of my regular chores here is cat-box patrol, and I take my assignment seriously. But as I lie in the warm, violet-scented water, I imagine myself in the lovely room that I helped to decorate today. I pretend I am a fairy princess or Cinderella or even the prom queen, although I never went to a prom in high school or any other dances for that matter. Our conservative church would not condone such immorality. I wonder if I had my life to live over again, making my own choices about these things this time, would I have turned out any differently? Would I still be just as crazy? I remember that Simon thinks I'm not crazy. Of course, Simon doesn't know everything.

I emerge from the tub and put on the flannel robe that Faye has loaned me during my visit. She said it was a Christmas gift from her sister but that she's never been fond of the somber plaid colors. Too manly, she says. But I like it just fine. I tiptoe back to her bedroom where I hear her humming happily, and I decide that I must be Cinderella after all, and Faye is my fairy godmother. I wonder if Simon will show up in a pumpkin coach tonight.

"Sit down right here," she commands when she sees me. "We'll fix your hair first."

I obey, sitting down at her old-fashioned dressing table. It has a glass top and a skirt of faded pink roses. I look into the mirror and pretend that I am not so pale and skinny and plain. I imagine that I am beautiful.

"You have lovely hair, Alice," she comments as she fingers the curls. "With all your natural waves, it'll be easy to make it look pretty. Now my hair was always straight as an arrow, so difficult to pin up nicely."

I glance at her gray hair, curled within an inch of its life. "But it looks so curly now."

She pats her head and smiles. "Perms. I get it done by Margie at Perfect Look every other month." Then she begins to pile my hair on top, curling strands around her fingers and slipping in a hairpin here and there. I'm not sure if she really knows what she's doing or not, but I decide I don't care. Just the feeling of being touched, ever so gently, is so soothing and comforting that I wish she would go on and on for hours. But soon her hands stop moving, and I can tell she is done. I realize that my eyes have been closed, and I open them to see what she has created.

"That's nice," I say as I peer at my strange reflection.

She nods. "Very pretty, if I do say so." Then she frowns. "Do you think we could put a little color on your face, Alice?"

"I, uh, I don't know. What do you mean?"

"I thought just a little lipstick and perhaps a little pink in your cheeks." She looks slightly embarrassed. "It might be nice."

I feel bad for not trusting her. "Sure, Faye, I guess that's okay. I've never been one to use makeup."

She chuckles. "Well, in my day a girl didn't go anywhere without her compact and lipstick."

I close my eyes again, trying to breathe deeply and just relax. Even if Faye makes me look completely silly, who am I to complain? Once again, I notice how the physical attention is very comforting as I feel her applying something to my lips, then dabbing and rubbing my cheeks gently. Next she puts something soft and silky over my nose, cheeks, and chin. It has a gentle fragrance that reminds me of the smell of sheets that have been line dried. I suspect it is powder, but it feels so soft and smooth, I imagine it to be fairy dust.

"Lovely." She seems to exhale the word.

I open my eyes and am relieved to see that I don't look clownish at all. My skin actually looks more healthy, and although my mouth is brighter than usual, it is rather nice and certainly dramatic.

"What do you think?" she looks worried.

"Lovely." I repeat her word just to reassure her.

She smiles. "Oh good." Then she looks at the little clock by her bed. "Goodness, it's nearly seven already. You better hurry and get dressed now." She points out a half-slip and then hands me an exquisite pair of satin high-heel shoes in a matching shade of silver. "I know your feet are about the same size as mine are now," she explains quickly. "But my feet were a bit smaller when I was younger. So these might be a little snug on you, but they went with this dress." Then she nods to another pair of shoes on the floor. They are gold-toned flats and look a bit like old-lady bedroom slippers. "I know those slippers aren't terribly fashionable, but you could go ahead and use them if these don't work."

"Thank you."

"I'll leave you to it then."

I nod and look around me in amazement. I'm not sure I will know how to put this all together. And yet I am not even certain this isn't a dream.

"Call me if you need help, dear."

I get the slip and dress on okay but can't figure out how to do the side zipper and tiny loops. I'm worried that I will tear the delicate fabric or that it will be too small. Finally I call for Faye, and she reappears like magic. I wonder if she might really be my fairy godmother after all, or else she was simply standing by the door.

Soon she has me all fastened up, and I manage to squeeze my feet into the shoes. "They're a little snug," I admit, "but not really uncomfortable."

"They might stretch a bit," she offers hopefully as she adjusts the sleeves below my shoulders. "You need a touch of jewelry. Of course I don't have anything real, but I still have the necklace and earrings I wore with this gown." She goes back to her dressing table and returns with some pale blue rhinestones.

"My ears aren't pierced," I tell her.

"Oh, don't worry. Hardly anyone had pierced ears back in those days," she says as she clips the earrings onto my ears. I arrange the necklace around my neck, and she hooks the clasp in back.

"There you go," she announces, pointing to her mirror.

"I feel like Cinderella," I tell her as I stare at the strange woman in the mirror. "Do you think I look silly?"

She soberly shakes her head. "Not at all."

"I've never done anything like this before," I admit.

"Then I think it's about time."

Just then we hear the doorbell ring, and I jump and let out a little shriek. She laughs. "It's only Simon, dear. I'll go let him in."

I nod nervously, then turn to check my image in the mirror again. I reach up and touch my cheek and am certain that this is someone else, perhaps someone on the other side of the looking glass. Just play the game, I tell myself. Tonight you will be Cinderella. Who knows what or where you'll be tomorrow.

"Simon is here," she calls from the living room, and suddenly I know I cannot possibly walk through that door. My heart is racing, and I cannot breathe. I know this is a big mistake.

"You fool!" Amelia yells at me. "You stupid little fool!" She sounds like one of the ugly stepsisters condemning my hope on the way to the ball.

I press my hands over my ears and tell her to leave me alone, but she continues to rant at me, calling me foul names and accusing me of all sorts of nasty things. I don't hear the door open or see them standing there, but soon they are both beside me, and I feel Faye's hand on my arm, and Simon is looking into my eyes and speaking in a calm tone. "Just relax, Alice. It's going to be okay. Trust me."

I take a deep breath and look at him and then at Faye. Somewhere deep inside I think they don't really want to hurt me, at least I don't believe they do, but even so I realize from experience that they might.

"Doesn't she look beautiful?" Faye speaks softly, and I hear him agree.

I want to be normal, I'm thinking, but maybe I have said this aloud. For then I hear Simon saying, "Normal is highly overrated, Alice. I'd rather you just be yourself. Okay?"

I look into his dark eyes and mumble, "Okay." I will play the Simon says game again.

Now Faye is handing me her beaver fur coat. "I know it's not as nice as it used to be, but it'll keep you warm. The weatherman said it's dropping to the twenties tonight, and it might even snow."

I allow the two of them to help me into the heavy coat. Then Faye puts both her hands on my cheeks and pulls my face toward her. She looks me in the eyes and says, "You *are* a princess, my dear. Your heavenly Father is the King of kings, you know." Then she kisses me on the forehead.

Tears sting my eyes when we step out into the cold, but I try to calm myself as I allow Simon to guide me to the car, which is not a pumpkin. He opens the door and waits as I clumsily crawl in. He even stoops down and helps to push the full skirt inside before he closes the door.

I take a deep breath and count to seven as he walks around and slips into the driver's seat. "You okay?" he asks, peering at me as he fastens his seat belt.

"Okay," I repeat, reaching for my seat belt too. Simon says, I tell myself as I take another deep breath.

"I realize this is really hard for you," he says as he drives away from the security of Faye's little house.

I nod, suddenly noticing that it's dark out here. I am surprised at how many homes have Christmas lights.

"I'm glad you didn't change your mind." He turns on the radio now, a soft jazz station, and I force myself to lean back in my seat and breathe. I remember Faye's words and repeat them to myself. I am a princess. I am a princess.

"Faye helped me to get dressed up tonight," I explain, worried that he might think it's a little over the top.

"You look really beautiful, Alice."

I glance over to him. I haven't even noticed how he looks, and now it's too dark to see anything but his dark pants and what appears to be his old bomber jacket. "You look nice too," I say, still trying to play the game.

He laughs. "Well, if I'd known I was taking a princess to the ball, I'd have rented a tux."

"Did you know that Faye wore this dress fifty years ago?" I hear myself say these words and am surprised. It almost sounds like a normal conversation.

"Really?"

"Yes. She and George went to the Twilight Room before he went off to Korea."

He nods.

"I wonder if they still have the Twilight Room. I know Portland pretty well, but I've never seen it before."

"I've never heard of it. But that was a long time ago."

"Yeah. My mom wasn't even born fifty years ago." The fact that I can do this kind of mental math just now impresses me, and I think I'm actually beginning to relax some. "I'm sorry about how I acted at Faye's. I was just, well, you know, kind of nervous."

"Hey, no problem. We all have panic attacks sometimes."

"Panic attacks?"

"You know, when you suddenly freak out and think that the very worst is going to happen."

"You do that too?" I look at him and wonder if he's pulling my leg.

"Sure. Sometimes it happens when I'm driving, and—well, I won't go there just now. No sense in inviting trouble."

"Really?"

"Yeah. But I've tried to reroute my thinking when I feel an attack coming on. Dr. Golden has helped me to retrain my thoughts not to go down those rocky roads. I'm learning to control my brain."

I consider this with my usual skepticism. Is it really possible to *control* your own brain? What about all those thoughts, feelings, impulses that come raging out of nowhere and assault you from behind? These past few months have felt like a wild carnival ride to me, like I've been strapped in and have absolutely no control as to whether I'm going up or down or sideways. One moment I'm upside down, and then I'm inside out. No control whatsoever.

Oh sure, I'd like to believe it's possible to control your brain, but once again, it sounds too good to be true. Or maybe it's just not for someone like me. It seems pretty obvious that my brain, or the voices, or whatever you want to call these forces that drive me, are extremely controlling. Most of the time I am helpless in their grasp, and on the rare occasions I do have some control, it seems I have very little.

I remember how I started to freak in Faye's room earlier tonight. It's like this thing just came barreling over me, and there was absolutely nothing I could do to stop it. Overwhelming. And, yet, I sternly remind myself, I am here now. I am riding with Simon, in his car, to a Christmas party of all things. Okay, so it's a Christmas party at a nut house. But then who am I to complain? I should fit right in. Right?

chapter TWENTY-FIVE

Another Mad Tea Party

The hill looks dark and foreboding tonight, with a pale blanket of icy fog creeping upward from the river. The towering evergreens look sinister as they hang over the road like gigantic fingers that want to reach down and snatch up Simon's car and then toss it downward, spinning like a toy down the steep incline. My heart is pounding in my throat again, and I'm afraid I'm about to scream. I want to tell him to stop the car, that I can't bear another minute, but somehow I remain silent. I'm sure my hands have made permanent imprints into the seat's upholstery.

My teeth are clenched so tightly that my jaw is beginning to ache. But I am determined to do this thing. I try to focus my mind on the jazz music, but even that sounds jarring and harsh as it grates against my rattled nerves. I wish, oh how I wish I could be normal. I don't care if it's highly overrated or not. I would gladly welcome it right now.

Finally I see the lights of the house as we're passing through the security gates. Now I feel this mixture of increased anxiety that we are here and huge relief that the terrifying car ride is over. Sometimes

I can tell that I'm overwired. Too many impulses hit me all at the same time. I wonder how it is that this mysterious Dr. Golden, whose name even sounds phony, is able to teach his patients to think differently. As if it's possible to control your own brain!

Simon is opening my door now. Reminding myself of Faye's words—that I am a princess—I try to emerge gracefully. Unfortunately the high heel of my left shoe gets stuck in the doorjamb, and I am forced to remove it, tug it out, then shove it back on my bare foot.

Simon is laughing. "You okay, princess?"

I narrow my eyes at him, but then I see that he's smiling in what appears to be a genuine way. I don't think he's actually teasing me, and I tell myself to lighten up. We step through the tall front door and are immediately greeted with the sounds of Christmas music and the chatter of voices. I wait in the foyer as Simon takes both our coats somewhere unseen. Looking around, I realize I should've done a little decorating in here as well, but before I can feel too bad about that, Simon is back. He smiles and takes my arm. "Right this way, princess."

I'm not sure what I think about his calling me princess. I liked it when it came from Faye, but hearing it from Simon makes me slightly uncomfortable. I glance at him as we walk in and think that he seems fairly happy to be with me. Or am I imagining this? I notice now that he has on charcoal gray pants and a black V-neck sweater over a white shirt and thin red tie. Although he's not as formal as I am, he looks quite nice. I wonder if I should tell him again since I really mean it this time.

But it is too late. Julie, dressed in an elegant burgundy gown, is coming our way. I think that if I look like a princess, then she must be the queen. I just hope she's not the Queen of Hearts, for I know the outcome would not be good, and I have no desire to return to the Queen's Prison anytime soon. As she comes closer, I can see that the fabric is velvet, very regal. She is waving to a gentleman over by a refreshment table. He has on a dark suit, very formal. I think it might even be a tuxedo. He is tall with dark curly hair and a beard—strikingly handsome, at least from a distance.

"I'm so glad you came," says Julie, looking directly at me as she grasps my hand. "You look absolutely gorgeous, Alice. I'm not entirely sure I want Jack to meet you." Then she winks at me as if this is our little secret. I like Julie, but the wink makes me even more nervous, like I'm missing something, some private joke. Is it about me?

"Hello, Simon," says the tall bearded man that I assume must be Jack. He has on silver wire-rimmed glasses that seem to blend into his face. "Who have you brought with you tonight?"

"This is Alice," says Julie. "She's the creative genius who helped Simon decorate this afternoon." She turns back to me now. "This is my husband, Dr. Golden, or Jack if you prefer."

He smiles. "A pleasure to meet you, Alice."

I wonder if I should curtsy but somehow keep myself from doing so. I can see that although Dr. Golden is nearly as handsome as I'd thought, he's probably in his late fifties, about the age my father would be if he were still alive. I say something to him but can't even hear myself speak. I hope I haven't embarrassed anyone, mostly myself. Suddenly I'm having an out-of-body experience as a spectator, just watching all this transpire, but I am too far away. I can't quite distinguish the words. Can someone please turn up the volume?

Simon guides me like a Seeing Eye dog throughout the room,

and I am introduced to all sorts of people, of all ages, and from all walks of life. So far I have met an artist, a writer, a physical therapist, a premed student, a musician, and a horse trainer, just to mention a few. I'm having a hard time keeping the names attached to the faces, but everyone seems to know that I am "Alice." I wonder if Dr. Golden made a special announcement before we got here, trying to make me feel completely at home. So that I will fit in. Perhaps they are getting my padded cell ready for me now.

I am mildly surprised to see the "residents" are such a lively bunch. I had assumed they would be subdued and maybe even wearing their bedroom slippers. Perhaps a few, confined to wheelchairs, would sit in a stupor, overly drugged, with their jaws sagging and drooling on themselves, but there are none like that here.

This does make me suspicious, however, and I begin to imagine that all these colorful people are really actors pretending to be the "residents" for my sake. I don't know what makes me think I should be so special that people would orchestrate all this for me, but that's the way life seems sometimes. I realize that not everyone at the party is a resident though. Some are guests. Like me. At least I *think* I'm a guest. Who can know for sure?

There are all kinds of exotic looking foods to eat, like something right out of a Martha Stewart show, but I am afraid to taste anything. What if the brioche is drugged? What if we're all going to go into a deep slumber, and then we'll be carted away to labs where experiments will be performed on our unsuspecting brains, or they'll use our livers and kidneys and hearts to perform organ transplants on people who are wealthy and influential? I believe this could happen, does happen in certain circles. Maybe even here.

"Do you want to dance?" Simon reaches for my hand.

"Dance?" I repeat. I am playing the game again.

He nods. "Do you know how?"

I shake my head no.

"Good, me neither. We'll just have to fake it then."

He leads me to the area where a number of couples are already dancing. Fortunately, other than one couple who are quite dramatic as they dip and dive, everyone else appears to be an amateur too.

"Are you sure?" I nervously ask once we're on the floor.

"Sure, I'm sure." He takes my right hand and begins to guide me to the music. To my surprise, it's not that difficult. We dance a number of times and even exchange partners when a heavyset guy named Brad taps Simon on the shoulder. I guess this is fair in dancing rules. Anyway, Brad is a pretty good dancer, and I think I may be improving myself. But the best part about dancing is that when I concentrate on moving my feet and listening to the music and not stepping on my partner's toes, I don't think about anything else. It's actually rather blissful. I think I could dance like this all night. But after a while the dance floor thins out, and people begin to gravitate toward the food tables. Simon offers me a glass of wine, and surprised that they are serving alcohol, I decline.

"How about punch then?"

"No thank you."

"It really won't hurt you, Alice. It's just plain fruit punch."

I firmly shake my head no.

He goes off to the food table by himself while I stand alone and think about how Faye's shoes are beginning to pinch my toes. I look at the seemingly happy people all around me and wish that I could participate more freely. How I long to have the freedom to be so cavalier, to eat the food or drink the wine, but it just feels too risky to me. Now that I'm no longer dancing, I become increasingly fretful and worried, certain that I've made a huge mistake in coming here. I can feel it deep in my bones. Something bad is going to happen tonight. I know it. Suddenly I wonder what I would discover if I sneaked around this place and looked into all the various rooms, behind the closed, probably locked doors. I imagine hideous torture chambers, electroshock equipment, straitjackets, padded cells. Sure they can make it look pretty good on the outside, but who knows what lies beneath? Too many things just don't seem right about this whole evening. Nothing seems to add up.

"Are you enjoying yourself?"

I jump, then turn to see Dr. Golden. He is drinking a glass of red wine. And that just seems to cinch it for me. What kind of honest-to-goodness psychiatric clinic would actually serve alcohol to patients? I mean, really! Although I do recall overhearing Dr. Golden speaking to a young woman earlier—I believe her name was Maddie—and reminding her to have only one glass since she was on meds. Still, it could all be part of this great big act.

"I guess so," I answer, avoiding his gaze, hoping he'll go away. His attention makes me even more nervous.

"Meaning you're not sure?"

I look him in the eye now, ready to try to discern whether this guy is for real or not. "No, I guess I'm not sure."

"Why is that?"

I glance around the room, then press my lips together as I shake my head. "I find this all a little hard to believe."

"To believe?"

Now I am slightly concerned that I might get Simon into trouble with my suspicions, but then if this guy is really a fake, Simon should find out about it. Or maybe he already knows.

"Okay," I tell Dr. Golden in a conspirator's voice. "I am going to play it straight with you. I've been in a, uh, well, a psychiatric institution before. And let me tell you, it was *nothing* like this."

He nods, his expression intense, as if he's listening closely.

"So all I want to know is, did you set up this whole Christmas party just to trick me?"

He laughs now but not in a mean way. At least I don't think so—and this surprises me. Of course, he's very handsome; he could be an actor too. He puts his hand on my shoulder now, as if to be conciliatory. It feels warm against my bare skin, but I move away from him just the same. I refuse to be pulled in.

"Alice, Alice, Alice," he says, and I wonder if he's condescending to me now. "Do you honestly think we are setting you up for something?"

I point my finger at him. I know this is incredibly rude, but I just can't help myself. I am thinking, See, *this is it*—he *is* the King of Hearts. I was right! It's all beginning to make sense now.

"That's it!" I say triumphantly. "You *are*. You are totally setting me up."

He nods. "And what am I setting you up for?"

I glance over my shoulder now, expecting the white lab coats to come at me any moment. But they are still out of sight. "Well, I'll admit you're really good. And I was sort of fooled at first, what with the decorating and Julie being so nice, and, of course, Simon is quite believable. But now it's clear what your game is."

"And that is?"

"Pastor John." I state this like it's a fact. "He has arranged all this" —I wave my hand—"just to show that it's all my fault. That I am a sinner, and this is what I get. He's using the decorations, the dancing, the wine… Everything is just an elaborate scheme to set me up."

"And why would he do that?"

I think about this for a moment. Suddenly I am unsure. I question myself. Then it hits me. "To prove that he is right. Because Pastor John is *always* right, you know. He has to be right."

The King of Hearts frowns now. "That's too bad."

"What?"

"That anyone would ever feel they always have to be right."

"Don't you?"

"Goodness no." He shakes his head. "Just ask my wife."

"Oh." Somehow his answer rattles me a bit, and suddenly I feel stupid and wonder if I'm just imagining this whole thing. I look down at the silver shoes that are growing tighter by the second. Could they be shrinking? "Do you think anyone would mind if I take off my shoes?" I ask, instantly wishing I hadn't.

He laughs. "Not at all. Make yourself comfortable."

I slip off my shoes and hold them in one hand slightly behind my back. I am confused now and slightly repentant. "I'm sorry if I said anything out of line," I say quickly. "I know I have a problem with that sort of thing. That and imagining things. I might have imagined that you were the King of Hearts."

"The King of Hearts?" He looks amused.

I put my hand over my mouth. "Did I say that?"

He nods but doesn't seem angry. This surprises me.

"See. That's what I mean. I suppose it's true. I suppose I am crazy. Do you have some orderlies that are ready to escort me to the Queen's Prison now?"

This makes him laugh out loud, and I'm afraid we are gathering attention. I must appear childish to him, ridiculous even.

"How's it going, princess?" Simon joins us now, and I think I have some explaining to do.

I glance over at the King of Hearts—I mean Dr. Golden—then back to Simon. "I think I've been insulting your boss."

Simon frowns. "Why?"

"Don't worry," says Dr. Golden. "I think Alice is very amusing and creative." He smiles. "Not to mention perfectly stunning in that gown. She can insult me as much as she likes."

I think I am blushing now.

Simon laughs. "Well, Alice and I have been discussing how being normal is highly overrated."

I turn to Simon and glare. "That's easy enough for you to say. I would give *anything* to be normal!" I want to turn and leave now, stamp away in my bare feet, but I don't know where to go. The bathroom perhaps?

"Really?" says Dr. Golden. "You would give *anything* to be normal?"

I suspect I am being teased now, but I don't think I even care. I can tell I'm in way over my head anyway. It's like I try to cover up who I really am, and that gets me nowhere. Then I try to be honest, and it makes no difference. What does it really matter in the end?

"Yes," I say to Dr. Golden. "I'm sure I would give *anything*. I am tired of being afraid, tired of looking over my shoulder, tired of living on—" I stop myself from saying "the streets" and glance nervously at Simon. I am fairly certain I might be back on the streets after he talks to his aunt about my bizarre behavior tonight. As I recall, though, I was almost back on the streets this morning anyway. At the moment I can't even remember what stopped me from going.

"Okay, Alice, let me guess exactly what's going on with you."

I shrug. Why should I care?

"You were diagnosed with schizophrenia, possibly paranoia, too. You were put into a psychiatric hospital where the staff's main goal was to convince you that you were crazy. And then they medicated you. Probably heavily. Right?"

I nod, now more certain than ever that he *is* connected with Pastor John and Mrs. Knolls and Dr. Thornton and my mother. It's only a matter of time until I will be transported back to Forest Hills and taken to the Queen's Prison, where they will lock me up and throw away the key for good.

"Somehow you escaped that place, but you were afraid to go home, and you wound up living on the streets here in the city. Right?"

I shrug again. Why should I be surprised? He probably has my file sitting on his desk right now.

"Is that true?" asks Simon, his brow creased with concern.

"Didn't you know?"

He shakes his head. "I knew something was wrong. I didn't know it was *that.*"

But the way he says "that" worries me. I feel I've hurt him, betrayed him somehow. And yet at the same time I think he's betrayed me, too. I don't know why I ever trusted him in the first place. I am so incredibly stupid.

"So…" I hold out my wrists as if I expect them to handcuff me and cart me off. "You want to lock me up now?"

Dr. Golden laughs. "That's not how it works here."

I glance over at Simon. "How about you? Did you call my mother and Pastor John? Are they waiting outside with Mrs. Knoll, ready to wrestle me to the ground and tie me up and—"

Simon gently puts his hand over my mouth to shush me, and then he speaks quietly, calmly. "No, Alice. Honestly, we aren't going to do anything like that. We're just having a Christmas party. Nothing more. I promise you. Just trust me."

I frown at him, bewildered by his believability. I turn to Dr. Golden and feel even more confused. "Really?" I ask him. "You guys honestly don't plan to lock me up?"

He chuckles. "No, but I can put you on our waiting list if you like."

"Waiting list?"

"For residency," Simon explains. "Dr. Golden's clinic is becoming so well known that people from all over the country are signing up. I think there's about a year's wait right now." He turns to Dr. Golden. "Right?"

"At least. Julie knows more about that than I do." He leans toward me and peers into my eyes now. "So, Alice, can you trust us that we simply invited you here to eat, drink, and be merry?"

"For tomorrow I shall die?" I ask.

This makes Dr. Golden laugh again. Then he takes me by the hand and leads me over to the dance area. He is a very good dancer, and for a few minutes I forget every stupid word I've said. I notice Simon dancing with Julie and am surprised to feel a small wave of jealousy ripple through me. Then I focus myself on the steps, the music, the moves, and everything else becomes a pleasant blur. When the song ends, I thank Dr. Golden, and we switch partners for the next dance. I am more comfortable dancing with Simon. It's like we move at the same speed.

After a couple more dances, Simon convinces me that the food is neither poisoned nor drugged, and I discover that it's really quite tasty. I visit with Maddie, the artist, and find that she's been to a variety of clinics, but this is the first time she's experienced real success with her treatment.

"It's because I am finally taking control of things *myself*," she explains. "I'm on medication but not so much that I can't think clearly. And then I work to focus my mind on what's true and right and good." She smiles. "You know that's actually a Bible verse?"

I don't think she knows what she's talking about since I was raised on Bible verses, but I know better than to contradict her. Besides, I suspect I've done enough of that for one night anyway.

And so I pass the rest of a surprisingly pleasurable evening by dancing and eating and visiting. I don't feel that I'm at a nut-house party but that I'm with instant friends. I suppose it's possible I'm being duped again, but somehow I don't think so.

When it's finally time to leave, I go over to where Julie and Dr. Golden are standing by the fireplace. "Thank you for a nice evening," I tell them both. Then I turn to Dr. Golden. "And I really am sorry if I sounded rude or terribly suspicious earlier." I shake my head. "I guess it just comes with the territory."

He grins and takes my hand in his, giving it a squeeze. "No problem, Alice. Believe me, we're used to that around here."

Julie laughs. "You have no idea."

I almost ask about getting my name put on their waiting list but think better of this. I'm still not completely convinced. Besides, a year is a long ways off. Anything can happen by then.

I am almost relaxed as Simon drives us home. I lean back in the seat and listen to the jazz music playing softly on the radio. I close my eyes as my fingers caress the silky fur of the beaver coat, and I sigh deeply. Dancing at the Twilight Room was pure magic tonight. I wonder why we don't do this more often. The music, the lights, the laughter. Oh, it's so unfair there's a war going on. I do hope my beloved can return to me unscathed. But how will we ever endure the separation?

And then something happens. At first I think I'm imagining it, but then I sense the car moving sideways across the road. Then we are going backward, fast, and now we are spinning. It's just like my carnival ride fantasy, only this is for real!

I hear myself screaming, and I look to see Simon's face pale and drawn as he tries to control the car on the icy pavement. But it's too late. We leave the road and careen down the steep hillside. I see the foggy city lights spinning in a blurry circle, and I know I'm going to die tonight. I'm sorry to think that Faye's lovely dress will be ruined. Then I remember how she said my Father was the King of kings and that I am a princess. I think I am calling out to him now. I believe I am asking him to help me, to save me! Then all is black and silent.

chapter TWENTY-SIX

Another Rabbit Hole

I am not sure how I got here, but I feel myself falling down, down, down. Another dark rabbit hole seems to have swallowed me again. As usual I have no control over anything. Not a single thing. I see them clearly as I fall. I see my brother, Aaron, except that he is still a child, sitting in the corner with his shoulders hunched forward, his face to the wall. Been naughty again, little bro? Then I see my mother wringing her hands, her blue eyes filled with tears. Are they real, Mother? Are they for me? She does not answer but simply drifts away. I see my father, dressed in white robes, like an angel or a choir-boy. When I get close enough to see his face, it is dark and sad. Why are you crying, Daddy?

I see others, too, flashing by me like kaleidoscope images—the Tweedles in orange parkas and Betty Grable wearing sparkly red slippers. I see Faye in her beautiful silvery blue gown, surrounded by hundreds of cats, each one in a sweater, all the colors of the rainbow.

Then I see Simon, but his face is white and lifeless. His eyes are closed, and there's a dark streak of blood across his forehead. I try to reach out for him, and yet I continue to fall.

Simon says, *I am dead. You are dead. The game is over.*

I see a giant hand, outstretched across a brilliant patch of blue, open and waiting, ready to catch me. It is the hand of the King, and if I am truly a princess, this is where my story will end. Safe in the palm of the King's hand. And there I will rest in peace forever.

Rest in peace. Rest in *peace. Rest in peace.*

Is that where I am now, peacefully at rest? The voices and faces all seem to be gone now, and all I hear is the beating of my heart, or is it the clock?

I wonder if I'm still alive, and yet I cannot move. I'm in a soft white cocoon like a caterpillar. I'm not claustrophobic, not uncomfortable. All is warm and clean and simple. It's as if all the clutter has been cleared away, and I think I shall rest here for a long, long time. I don't have to think about anything. I don't have to do anything or be anything. It's as if my brain is on a much needed vacation.

I believe I shall sleep and sleep and sleep. Please, hang a sign on my forehead that reads, Do Not Disturb.

Why are they trying to wake me up, trying to disturb my rest? I just want to sleep. Why can't they go away? I hear their voices, but they are not mean voices. They don't threaten me or swear at me or demand that I jump from the bridge.

They say things like "Alice? Can you hear me?" Or "Alice, it's time to wake up." But I just tune them out. It's amazing to be able to do this. How long have I waited for this sort of ability?

"Alice?" I recognize this particular voice; it seems like a voice I've known for years. But still I cannot force myself to emerge from my cocoon. Leave me alone.

Then finally I can no longer hold these intruders at bay. There's light in my eyes, and I can see the whiteness, the brightness of it, and I know that the inevitable has finally happened. Like so many things in life, I cannot fight it any longer.

"Alice?"

I blink several times, wishing that it were not so as I see the fluorescent light above me, hear it humming. I'm in a bed with white sheets, covered in a white cotton blanket, the kind with all the tiny holes. It appears to be a hospital bed, and there is a plastic tube taped to my arm and a plastic bag full of what appears to be water hanging on a stainless steel pole above my head. I wonder what is in that water.

"Alice?"

I turn my head, painfully, to my left. There on a chair sits Faye with her knitting. Only the sweater is no longer red. It is yellow.

"Faye?" I think I have said her name, but I am not sure. My voice doesn't seem to be working at the moment.

She stands and comes over, taking my hand in hers. "Oh, dear child." There are tears in her eyes. "I thought I had lost you."

Now it's all coming back to me. The party. The icy road. The swirling city lights blurred by the fog. I want to ask her about Simon, her beloved nephew, but I can't bear to know that he is dead just yet. I don't want to hear her say the dreaded words. My eyes begin filling with tears, and I swallow hard to hold them back.

She pats my hand. "You're going to be okay, Alice. You've been in a coma. You had a head injury…and other things. But you are going to be just fine. I know because I have been speaking to my heavenly Father about you every single day. He has assured me that you are going to be just fine."

I nod, but this hurts my head. I close my eyes and long to return to the quiet place again. I hurt all over, but most of all I hurt deep inside my chest to think that Simon is gone.

Doctors and medical people come and examine me. I pretend I am not here as they prod and poke and listen. I pretend that this is some other Alice, and when they ask me my name and address, I pretend I don't remember, and they seem to accept this. "Just Alice," I tell them as if that should settle it.

"Don't worry," says the woman doctor. "It will come back to you in time."

I hope not, I think. But I don't believe I said this aloud.

Faye has gone home to tend her cats. I lie in the bed feeling more alone than ever before. Finally I give in to my sadness and simply cry. A nurse stops in and asks if she can get me something, but I just shake my head no and continue to cry. I think I shall cry for days and weeks, maybe even years.

I am awake in the middle of the night, at least I think it is, because everything is darker, although the lights are still on and I can still hear people coming and going in the hallway. I can't take it anymore. Just when I thought things were getting better, I am forced to return to this—this so-called life of mine.

I look up at the ceiling above me and imagine that God is really up there somewhere, and I shake my fist at him and demand that he do something about this whole thing. "It's not fair!" I tell him. "If you are really who Faye says you are, then why is my life such a hopeless mess? Why am I here? And why is Simon dead?"

I rant and rave like this for hours it seems, until I am so exhausted I fall asleep. But when I wake up, I feel strangely better. And I begin to speak to God again. But now I don't feel so angry. I just speak to him in a matter-of-fact voice, as I might do with a friend. If I had a friend. It's weird, but I actually think he may be listening. Still, how can I trust my own observations?

So this begins to worry me, and I become obsessed with the fear that I am going right back to where I started this past fall. I suspect that Amelia will be back any minute now, and already I am certain I can hear those voices whispering about me, blaming me, accusing me, and even threatening. But maybe it's really the nurses.

"Why, God?" I demand. "Why did you let me have that reprieve only to bring me back to…to this?" I close my eyes and sigh deeply. "Why do you want to torture me so? What have I ever done to deserve this life?"

I sleep a lot during the next few days. I sense that Faye has been here, but I must've been asleep. The doctor—Dr. Spangler is her name—told me that it's natural to sleep like this. "It's the brain's way of repairing itself."

I think this is interesting, that the brain knows how to repair itself. I wonder if my brain might completely repair itself if I could only sleep for long enough—perhaps a few years. Then perhaps I wouldn't have to return to my old twisted ways of thinking. But I doubt my brain has such superior abilities. At least it hasn't shown these talents in the past. And I am fairly certain that, like my grandmother's, it was defective to start with.

One day I open my eyes to see Faye again. "How are you doing, dear?" she asks.

"Okay, I guess."

"Cheshire sends his regards. He wanted to come visit you, but they have a very strict no-pets policy here."

"Tell him hi for me." I glance out the window to see sheets of rain pelting against the glass.

"Guess we won't have a white Christmas after all," I say.

She smiles and squeezes my hand. "Christmas has come and gone, dear."

"Oh." I think about Simon again. Have they already had his funeral? Is the rest of his family terribly angry at me? Am I in trouble with the police? I want to know the answers to these questions but am afraid to ask.

"Simon is doing much better."

I turn to look at her. "What?"

She nods. "He's doing much better. The doctor says he's healing up quite nicely from his surgery."

"He's *not* dead?"

"Oh no, dear. Did you think he was dead?"

Tears begin to pour from my eyes now. I'm sure they're from relief, but I choke and sob and sputter all the same. "Really?" I gasp. "He's really alive? You're not just saying that to make me feel better?"

She bends down and looks at me. "I wouldn't lie to you, Alice. You were both seriously injured in the accident, but Simon is very much alive. I'm sorry if you didn't know that. Poor thing."

I sigh and lean back into my pillow, surprised that I feel like thanking God. I must've said this aloud because now Faye is joining me.

"Yes," she says. "Thanks be to God. In his great mercy he has spared you both. The doctor in ICU said you both should've been killed in the accident. Apparently the car was flattened, and they had to use the Jaws of Life just to get you both out." She shakes her head. "Just dreadful."

"Was your dress ruined?"

She waves her hand. "Pish-tosh. Who cares about a silly old dress?"

"It was so beautiful."

"And your fur coat?"

"The doctor said that heavy coat probably spared you some other injuries."

I consider this.

"Did you have a nice evening, dear?"

I try to remember, but it's kind of a blur, and I'm not sure where we went. Was it to the Starlight Club? "I think so," I finally say, just to reassure her.

"Dr. Golden and his wife have been by to see you several times. You must've made quite an impression on them that evening."

Then it comes back to me, the Christmas party. "I'm sure I did." I groan as I remember some of my crazy accusations that night.

She pats my hand. "Don't fret so much, Alice."

I wish I could follow her advice, but it seems impossible.

"Do you know what day it is?" she asks.

"No."

"It's New Year's Day."

"Really?"

"And I don't mean to intrude, but I've been concerned, Alice. You're such a lovely young woman, I feel certain there must be a family somewhere who is just sick with worry about you. Would you like me to contact someone?"

I consider this. I do feel bad to think that Christmas has come and gone, and Aaron and my mom still have no idea where I am.

Not that we've ever celebrated Christmas, but I'm sure that Aaron is home from college, and my mother is probably wondering about me.

Suddenly I don't really care if they come and cart me back to Forest Hills. It's not as if I'm having a great time here anyway. I'm fairly sure that when I'm released, I'll be sent to a nut house anyway. And not Dr. Golden's, thanks to his yearlong waiting list. At the moment I have no resistance in me, so I give in and tell Faye my mother's name and phone number, then close my eyes and long to return to that blissful place where all was peace and quiet. Perhaps another blow to the head would help.

chapter TWENTY-SEVEN

Jack and Jill

I am definitely relieved that Simon is alive. Now, though, I feel even more scared and guilty than before. All along I have felt a gnawing certainty that I am the reason we had the wreck that night. I'm not even sure what I did to cause it, but I have no doubt that I'm the responsible party. I thought perhaps I would be able to hide this fact from everyone, but knowing that Simon is alive changes things. As glad as I am and as much as I like him, I am afraid to see him now. I wonder if he has told the police yet. I wonder if I should try to get away from here. They have taken my IV tube out. They said it was only to give me fluids and nutrients, but I noticed the nurse occasionally injected it with a hypodermic needle. At first I was relieved that she was shooting the needle into the tube instead of my skin, but then I realized that it was probably some kind of drug, and that frightened me even more.

Now they bring me my meals on a tray, and because I don't want the IV stuck into me again, I try to eat most of the food. I might as well since I'm also taking the pills they bring. The nurse usually stands over me and watches as I swallow them. She's even worse than my mom. I'm not absolutely positive that she knows I am crazy yet. I wonder how long it takes for these things to leak out.

I try not to think about what will happen when Faye calls my mom. When I gave her the number, I was only thinking about Mom and Aaron and how I really would like to see them again. But I temporarily forgot to consider the whole church package that will probably come with this poorly considered decision. I cringe to think of Pastor John or Mrs. Knoll standing by my bed just now. I will feel so trapped. Just like a caged animal that spectators are allowed to tease and provoke with sticks. And what if they bring Mary Cates as well as some of the other church ladies? Oh, why did I tell Faye about my family?

I have only been out of bed a few times so far and only with a nurse to help me. My head gets too dizzy, and they're afraid I'll fall and injure myself further. A physical therapist comes in every day, exercising my arms and legs, careful not to injure my broken collarbone and cracked ribs, which he assures me are healing nicely even if they do hurt a lot. I try not to complain about the pain since I don't want to risk the doctor increasing my pain medication. The idea of getting all dopey and pathetic again makes me want to scream.

So I decide to try it on my own today. I slowly sit up in bed, the way the therapist has shown me, and slide my legs over the side. I am still amazed and fascinated at the black, yellow, and purple bruises all over my body. I look like a human rainbow. Not only that, but the stitched-up swollen scars on my legs remind me of Frankenstein. I'm really quite a sight. Dr. Spangler said it's miraculous that my legs weren't broken. She said I must be made of some pretty tough stuff. Maybe my body, I was thinking. Unfortunately my brain is not nearly as invincible.

I rest my bare feet on the floor, wincing at the pain this brings. Every part of my body feels as if it's been twisted and smashed. And I suppose that it has. I'm amazed to think that it's been almost two weeks since the wreck and I still feel this awful. You'd think I'd be much better by now. I suppose I should be thankful for my concussion. As a result I will probably never know how much pain I was in. I wonder how Simon feels now.

Slowly I put a little weight on my feet, gasping as I do. My head swims, and I am afraid I will vomit. I did that the first time I tried to stand up. I take slow, shallow breaths and tell myself I can do this. I must get away from here while I can. And for the first time in a long time I think I can hear Amelia again. But this time she's not yelling or cussing at me. Her voice is calm, and she is agreeing with me.

"You need to get out of here before it's too late, Alice."

Without even acknowledging her presence, I slowly stand up, keeping one hand on the bed and the other on the bedside table. I take another slow breath and attempt to steady myself, but the room is spinning around now. I try to adjust myself to the motion, but this only makes it worse. The next thing I know I am lying flat on my face on the cold vinyl floor, and every inch of my body is aching and throbbing from the fall. I am such a fool.

"What is going on here?" demands a loud voice from behind me. I can tell that it's Stacy, my favorite nurse, the one who reminds me of Whoopi Goldberg. I painfully turn my head and look up to see her peering down at me with a concerned scowl. I am ashamed, like a small child who's been caught in an act of disobedience. I feel especially bad since she has been so good to me, and it almost seems that she really cares about me as a person as much as a patient.

"I'm sorry," I mutter as she and another nurse help me to my feet and then back into my bed.

"I know you hate that bedpan, Alice," scolds Stacy, "but you should really buzz us if you need to go potty."

I decide to play along. "I hated to bother you," I say as I lean back into my pillow.

"You want me to get the bedpan?" asks the other nurse.

"No," I say quickly. "I don't need to go now."

"You sure?" Stacy peers down at me with piercing eyes.

"Yeah. Right now everything hurts too much to move. I'll let you know later."

"Okay." She tucks the blanket around me. "I hear you've got a young man down the hallway who wants to come over and visit you."

"Simon?"

She nods. "He's a good-looking one, too. Well, other than all the bruises he's wearing. You two sure must've taken a tumble. Just like Jack and Jill."

"Huh?"

"You know, Jack fell down and broke his crown, and Jill came tumbling after. Only you're the one who broke your crown, and Jack has a broken leg and wrist, and Lord only knows what else."

This is the first I've heard of Simon's specific injuries, and I am sorry for him. "But he's doing okay?" I ask.

"Yeah, he and you both seem to be making a miraculous recovery. Simon says it's because God is looking out for you, and I'm sure he must be right about that."

"I guess that might be true, but doesn't it make you wonder why God let us have the wreck in the first place?"

Stacy laughs at this. "Now, don't you go blaming God for *all* your troubles, Alice. God gave every single one of us a free will, and people make choices that can get them into trouble. Like driving on curvy, hilly streets that are covered in ice. That's pretty dangerous, if you ask me."

I wonder once again just how this is my fault. What is it that makes me so certain of this? But somehow I am. I try to recall if I said or did something that night. Did I act crazy and somehow distract Simon? Did I freak out and cause him to lose control of the car? I just can't remember the details at all.

"Anyway, it looks like the doctor is letting Simon out of traction today, and, boy, is he eager to get himself into a wheelchair and go visiting." Stacy winks at me. "You might want to fix up that hair of yours. After all, it is New Year's Day."

I don't say anything. I'm just thinking, I've got to get myself out of here—and soon! I don't want Simon to come see me, and besides that I don't want my mom showing up with all her church friends in tow. I am more trapped than ever.

"Alice?"

I look back up to see Stacy standing with a brush and a hand mirror. I can tell she was talking to me, but I didn't hear her. "Huh?" I say.

"I said, 'Do you want to spruce up a little?'" She smiles coyly. "In case you get a visitor?"

I shrug but take the mirror and the brush anyway.

"There should be some lip balm in your things here," she says as she busies herself looking through the drawer. "And some lotion, too."

I hold up the mirror and look at my face. But it takes me a moment to focus, and then I think I've made a mistake. I think I am looking at a photo of someone else. A monster or a Halloween mask. Then I realize by my gray blue eyes that it is me. I haven't seen myself since the accident, and I am shocked at what I see now. My hand begins to shake, and I am horrified. I do not recognize this person. She looks like the so-called bride of Frankenstein, only worse. Way worse. My nose is swollen and discolored. There are dark mustard-colored circles around both eyes. One cheek is purple and puffy; the other is yellow and scraped. The worst part is the ugly red scar that runs diagonally across the length of my forehead. Also, part of my hair is shaved on the left side.

Stacy hears me gasp and comes to my side. "Now, don't worry, honey. The black eyes are almost gone now, and that scar on your forehead can be fixed with plastic surgery, or you can wear bangs." She studies my face. "Yeah, I think you'd look cute in bangs. Want me to get the scissors and cut you some?"

I just stare at the mirror in horror. I wonder what else about my life can go wrong. I've lost so much already. I've lost my mind, my apartment, my schooling, my family, and now my face. I wonder what more I can lose. And will I ever find myself again? I set down the mirror and just stare at Stacy. I can feel the tears coming down my multicolored cheeks, but I say nothing.

Gently she begins to brush my hair, speaking to me in a soothing voice, telling me that everything's going to be okay. I wish I could believe her, but I know it's not true. For me it seems there is only one way for things to go. Steadily downhill.

I remember telling Stacy she could cut my bangs, and so I sit and stare blankly at the wall as she begins. For all I care, she can shave my entire head if she wants to. Perhaps she will. Then she gently applies the lip balm to my chapped lips and smoothes some lotion on my hands and face and says, "There now," as if she has made everything better.

I hand her back the mirror. "Here," I say in a flat voice. "I don't need this anymore."

I try to remember who I am as I sit in the hospital bed. I wish I could return to that quiet white place where all was peace and rest. I wonder how I ever found my way there in the first place. Was it a result of the head injury, the coma? Or perhaps the near-death experience brought it on? And I wonder, if that was a sample of what death will be like, well, then why not hurry the whole process along a bit?

I look out the window to a wet gray world of cement buildings. I suspect that I'm in the hospital just down the road from where Simon's car was wrecked, but I don't know this for sure. I've never bothered to ask anyone.

I'm guessing that the river is down there somewhere and that the big bridge, the one that calls me by name, is still waiting for our little appointment. Such a patient old bridge. I wonder how long it would take me to walk down there in my condition. Several days? A week perhaps? A month? I guess the bridge will have to wait awhile longer.

"Don't put it off too long," whispers Amelia. "You've seen what can happen when you delay these things."

I close my eyes and pretend she's not there. I tell myself it's only my imagination again. But as usual I don't believe me.

Take me away, I cry. I'm not sure if I'm thinking or speaking, but I know I am pleading. Perhaps I am even praying. Please, take me away.

I am with you always. Even until the end of time.

chapter TWENTY-EIGHT

Ties that Bind

I must've dozed off, but I sense her presence as soon as I am barely awake. I can actually smell her, something like floral soap and Jergens lotion, but I'm afraid to open my eyes and see her, and even more afraid that she is not alone. I lie as still as a stone and will myself back to sleep, believing I can escape all this. Perhaps she will think I've gone back into a coma, and she will go away, taking her evil friends with her.

Finally I open one eye and peek through my eyelashes. My mother is standing right next to my bed, peering down at me with watery eyes.

"Alice?"

It's too late for my little possum routine. She can tell I'm awake now. Slowly I open the other eye and then peer around the room until I see my brother, Aaron. He fills the entire doorway with his bulky athletic frame but looks uneasy. I think I know how he feels. I continue looking around, but Mom and Aaron appear to be the only ones here. This is something of a relief. Although I realize there could still be others hiding around the corner, lurking in the hallway perhaps. I wouldn't put it past them. It's entirely possible the whole fanatical congregation is out there right now, just waiting to pounce on me and begin their exorcist act all over again. I imagine my head spinning around in circles as Pastor John raises his hands and shouts in a tremulous voice.

I push the button to raise my bed so I can be more upright and hopefully appear more grown-up and even in control of this awkward situation. This rationale is ridiculous, but it's all I have at the moment.

"Hi, Mom," I say in a timid voice. I remind myself of a mouse with its tail in the trap. Then I turn to Aaron and attempt a smile. "Hey, Bro."

He comes over next to Mom now and stands there with his large hands hanging loosely by his sides. He feels big and clumsy and useless. I can see it in his eyes that dart all around the small room, uneasy, unwilling to meet my gaze.

"Thanks for coming," I tell them. Disarm them with the friendly routine, or so I hope. Perhaps I can convince Mom not to send me back to Forest Hills or call in the church troops if I can only act normal enough.

"Why didn't you call us?" my mom begins. I suspect it will go downhill from here on out.

"How are you feeling?" asks Aaron. I wonder if he's trying to help me out by changing the subject.

Ignoring Mom's unanswerable question, I focus my attention on my brother. "I've felt better."

"Yeah, you look—" He stops himself and glances uneasily at

Mom. I know what he was about to say, but somehow this ingrati-
ates him to me. I smile at him again, sincerely this time. My mom
switches her handbag to the other hand and sighs loudly.

"I know," I continue, directing my words toward Aaron. "I try
to avoid mirrors these days."

"I missed you at Christmas," he says. "I even got you a present."

"Really?" Now this fascinates me since no holidays are ever celebrated at our house—it's against the church's rules. We never exchange presents or practice any of the other holiday traditions that
the rest of the civilized world seems to enjoy.

"We even put up a tree," he continues. His eyes seem almost
childlike.

"No way."

He nods, and the glint in his eyes reminds me of the time he
sneaked a frog into his bedroom and swore me to secrecy.

I turn and peer at Mom with open suspicion. "Is that true?"

Mom nods without speaking, and yet she seems slightly frightened as her eyes dart to the door, almost as if she thinks someone
might be listening in. Someone from the church, I suspect. I wonder
if she's telling the truth even now. Perhaps this is a trick to make me
trust them.

"Mom's not going to Salvation Center anymore." Aaron announces this in a way that might almost suggest our mother has just
given up a serious heroin habit. He looks that proud.

"You're kidding!" First I look at Aaron and then back at Mom. A
mixture of doubt and astonishment come over me, and I'm not sure
I can believe either one of them anymore. This is all just too fantas-
tic. I wonder what they're really up to now. I'm certain they're trying

to pull something over on me, an attempt to gain my trust before they whip the rug out from beneath me again.

"Is that really true, Mom? You've honestly quit the church?"

She looks down at the floor and presses her lips together. She looks as if she contains some dark secret. "Yes, it's true, Alice."

"But how?" I study her face, unconvinced. "You've gone there for…forever."

"Not forever, Alice. Your father and I joined when you were a baby."

"That's forever to me. But really, Mom, what's going on?"

"Something happened to me, Alice. It wasn't long after we took you up to Forest Hills." She shakes her head. "I really regret that day. But later in that week, Pastor John had me come to the church, for a session, you know…"

I nod, knowing full well what a Salvation Center *session* is all about. Personally, I would rather be locked up in the Queen's Prison.

"Pastor John and the others just kept telling me that we'd invited this evil into our home by sinning. How it was wrong for you kids to be going to secular schools and how it's all my fault that you'd become demonized. They wanted to do a cleansing on me and the house and you kids as well. It went on and on until something in me just completely snapped. I couldn't take it anymore, Alice." Tears stream down her face now, and my brother steps over and places a protective hand on her shoulder. She looks up at him and smiles with a quivering chin. Then she turns back to me with a look of pure determination in her watery eyes. "It was in that moment that I knew I had to get out. I felt that the church was killing me, probably killing you kids, too. Suddenly it was as if everything about that place seemed twisted and...and evil." She opens her handbag and pulls out a handkerchief and dabs her eyes.

"So you just walked out? Just like that? You didn't let them do the cleansing?" I struggle to imagine my soft-spoken mother standing up to the church leadership like that.

She shakes her head no. "I told them I'd had enough and to leave me alone. Then I went home. I was so scared that I locked the doors and took the phone off the hook. I didn't know what to do. It's not as if I wanted to turn my back on God. *Just those people.*"

I'm not sure what to say. It's not that I don't believe her, but it's just so incredible. I glance over at Aaron and can tell by his expression that he's buying all this. I wonder what makes me such a skeptic. "So then what happened?" I ask.

"I didn't know what to do. I was so scared and distraught that I got down on my knees, and I prayed, but I didn't pray a church prayer. Instead I just said how I honestly felt—about the church and what had happened to you and just everything. I guess you could say I poured my heart out to God. When I finally finished, it seemed crystal clear that everything at Salvation Center is all wrong—well, for me anyway. I guess I can't really judge for anyone else. But it's as if a little light bulb went on in my head, and I knew beyond a shadow of doubt that I needed to leave Salvation Center for good." She sighs now, and her speech does sound believable.

But I'm still not completely convinced. She's gone to that church for more than twenty years, and it seems almost inconceivable that she could walk away like that. I'm still not sure this isn't a clever trick to get me to trust her again. Just the same, I definitely want to hear more.

"Then what happened?" I ask again.

"Well, just a couple of days after I decided I was done with Salvation Center, I had to go to the grocery store. Naturally, I was worried that I'd run into someone from church if I went to Grocery Outlet, and so I made a change and went to Safeway."

Aaron lets out a low whistle as if this is some hugely daring move on Mom's part. And I suppose it is since Salvation Center considers spending money unnecessarily to be sinful. Paying full price for groceries must be right at the top of the wasteful list.

"I ran into an old friend at the Safeway store, Sheila Bennett, and right out of the blue, she started telling me about this Bible study that she leads and how I'd be welcome to come if I liked. Well, something about her seemed so warm and genuine. So I actually called her that very same evening. She was so nice on the phone that I felt as if someone had popped a cork out of me, and I just poured out the whole story. And I mean everything!"

I am worried now. Has my mother jumped out of the frying pan and right into another kind of fire? "Uh, what kind of church is this Sheila lady involved in?"

Mom smiles like she knows where I'm going with this. She pats my hand. "Don't worry, Alice. I checked it out. It's just a regular church where they sing old-fashioned hymns and have ladies' teas once a month. They even put up decorations and had a Christmas program where the children dressed up like elves and snowmen and put on a play about the real meaning of Christmas."

"Elves?" I feel my eyes open wide. "Pastor John would have a conniption."

She actually giggles about this. "I know. I think that's the best part."

She takes my hand in hers now, a surprisingly warm gesture for someone like my mom. "I'm so sorry, honey. I wish I had seen all this sooner. It's as if I was blind. I can't believe we stayed in that church for so long. I guess I felt trapped. I think your father was beginning to see that just before he died. You know he had stopped going to church and kept saying that Pastor John was wrong about a lot of things. And he started questioning everything. At the time I thought he was being sinful, and Pastor John actually told church members to have nothing to do with him. But now I can see he was just trying to find the truth. I hope he did." She begins to cry again, and I am confused. I remember my father being controlling and mean—head of the household, and he wanted everyone to know it. He demanded our respect and punished us, even Mom, when we refused to give it. It is hard to feel too sorry for this man now.

And yet I could recall how my dad seemed to change just as I was getting ready to leave for college. He'd been so against it from the start, and I suspect that Pastor John had been riding him for being a bad leader in our family.

"No one from Salvation Center goes to a secular college!" he'd yelled at me when I'd first announced getting a scholarship from Portland State. Somewhere over the summer he had softened up, and by the time fall came, he even offered to drive me to school. We didn't speak much during the ride; I was afraid to open my mouth, afraid that he'd launch into some kind of religious lecture. But amazingly, he didn't. He even hugged me before he left to go home. I remember thinking how undadlike that had been, how totally out of character. Then he died from a heart attack early that winter, before I ever saw him again.

I look at Mom now. Studying her saddened face, I try to determine if this is really true or just another trick. My mind spins, remembering so many unhappy things all at once, yet at the same time hoping that somehow it's all about to change. I'm not sure what to think, and my head is about to explode. I wonder how much contradictory information the human brain can contain.

"They hounded me for a while," my mother continues. I wonder if she's been talking the whole time and if I've been distracted, lost in my own thoughts. "Leaders from the church began calling constantly. I even considered changing the phone number, but by then you'd run away from Forest Hills, and I was afraid that you might try to call home and not get me."

"I even suggested she get a restraining order for them," says Aaron. "Get those creeps put in jail for harassment."

I consider this as I stare at them both in wonder. If it's an act, it's a pretty good one. They should both get Oscars for their performances. And yet something about my mother seems genuinely different to me. I consider telling her about how I started talking to God yesterday, how it seemed more real than ever before, but decide to keep this to myself. I'm not totally sure she would understand. I don't know if I even understand it myself. It could be just my imagination. But then so could my mother's experience. How do we know what is really real and what's our imagination? Especially when it comes to religion. Could that be what faith is, deciding the difference and then acting on it?

"So, Mom, are you honestly telling me that you really believe that Salvation Center is wrong? That Pastor John is a fake and a hypocrite?"

"Something like that." She nods. "I don't really want to judge them, but I know they were wrong when it came to us. And I'm so sorry you got hurt. I feel like it's my fault that you've been so…so sick, you know. I keep thinking that if your father and I hadn't forced you to go to that horrible church…well, all this might never have happened to you." She glances over at Aaron with a worried look. "I keep telling Aaron that I don't want to see this happen to him."

He just shrugs. "Don't worry, Mom. I don't plan on going crazy anytime soon."

"Thanks." I try to look like a big sister now.

"Sorry, I didn't mean to say—"

"It's okay. I probably am crazy." I sigh and look down at my bruised arms, tracing the stitched-up marks along a dark red scar with my finger. Frankenstein's bride.

"So maybe you will begin to get better now." My mom looks hopefully at me. As if she thinks her decision to leave Salvation Center will make a real difference with my troubles. As if she honestly believes she has some sort of control over my life or even my brain. Thinking this almost makes me want to laugh.

"Yeah, maybe," I say.

"And as soon as you're well enough, you can come home," she offers. "I can take care of you now, and you'll get better in no time."

A part of me really wants to believe this. I even tell myself that what she's saying is true, that I can go home with my mother and she will make everything better. But at the same time, something more convincing keeps telling me it just doesn't work that way—that if I go home, things will only get worse. And the mere thought of disappointing my mother frightens me. As if she is in a fragile state and needs to be protected, which really seems ridiculous if I think about it too hard.

So I decide to play her game. I nod and agree, and this makes her face relax a little. Suddenly I know how she feels. I understand her guilt. It's terrible to blame yourself for someone else's troubles. I feel like that about Simon right now. I know it's my fault that he nearly died and his car got wrecked and he's all messed up. I bet he wishes he'd never met me. I wonder if he will file some sort of lawsuit against me or if the police will come here and arrest me soon.

"Faye seems very nice." My mother is talking, and once again I'm afraid I haven't been listening. "I'm so glad that you were able to stay with her."

I nod.

"I must admit that I was a little surprised at how many cats she keeps. You'd think the city would have a health ordinance against such things. Goodness, I never saw so much cat hair in one place."

Aaron makes a face. "Yeah, and her house smelled like a giant litter box."

I am defensive now. "That's because it was my job to keep them cleaned," I say quickly.

"Well, even if it's not the most sanitary place," my mother continues, "it was kind of her to take you in."

"Faye is a *kind* person." I hold my head up. "She's more like a real Christian than anyone else I've ever known." I realize that I risk hurting my mother's feelings by saying this, but it's the truth. Besides, I don't like hearing my family faulting Faye for her love of cats.

"She seemed kind of crazy to me," says Aaron.

I bristle at the word but then remind myself that Aaron probably doesn't mean to sound malicious.

"I'm curious about something, Alice," says my mother.

I wait a bit and then finally ask her what.

"Well, after you disappeared from Forest Hills, where did you go? Where did you stay before you went to live with Faye? I was so worried about you. I filed a missing-person report, and my new church even donated money to have posters made with your photograph on it."

This horrifies me. I can't bear the idea of having my face plastered on telephone poles across the state with the word MISSING in bold caps, as if I'm a lost dog. No wonder I am so lost most of the time if they have proclaimed it like that. Fortunately, I don't voice this since I'm sure she wouldn't understand.

"Yeah," chimes in Aaron. "Where were you?"

I sigh and wonder why it matters now. "On the streets mostly."

My mother gasps, but Aaron looks slightly impressed. "No kidding?" He pulls up a chair now, as if he wants to hear more.

"Yeah. It's not much fun out there."

He leans forward. "Were you scared?"

I want to tell him that I'm *still* scared, that everything about life scares me, and that most of all I scare myself. But instead I just nod and try to act cool. "Yeah. It can be pretty scary sometimes."

He shakes his head. "Man, that is so weird. I can't imagine my sister making it on the street."

I can tell that my mom is getting more and more horrified with all this, and I actually feel sorry for her. What with the church and everything, I think she's been through a lot.

"How's school?" I ask Aaron, hoping to change the subject.

"Cool. We had a great football season. Almost made it to the playoffs."

"Congratulations."

"Yeah. Then I pulled a stupid hamstring." He rubs his thigh.

"That's too bad."

"Yeah, I missed the last two games, but the doc says I should be back in shape in time for next season."

"Cool."

So we sit and talk like a happy little family, but the whole time I am thinking I should stay away from both of them. I know I am more than they can handle right now. And I am certain I will only bring them more heartache and misery should I decide to go home. It's sweet that my mom thinks she can make me better if I go home, but talk about delusions! Even though I can imagine her bringing me soup and sympathy, she has no idea what she's up against. I'm not even sure myself.

Finally, and mercifully, visiting hours come to an end. Nurse Stacy comes in and tells Mom and Aaron that I need my rest now, and even though I feel guilty, I am relieved to see my family go. For a moment I think maybe I can just stay here forever, suspended between my crazy world and normal life, if there is such a thing. I don't even mind taking my pain pills so much anymore.

"I'll be back tomorrow," Mom promises.

Aaron reaches over and pats me gently on the head. "I'd come too, Sis, but I gotta get back to class and work on getting the old GPA back up."

"Yeah." I remember those days like a previous life on another planet, remember how something as insignificant as a less-than-glowing midterm grade could obsess me. Oh, if only life could be that simple again.

Mom leans over and kisses me on the cheek. I am unable to remember her doing this since I was very, very little. It's a sweet gesture, and I try to smile even though I want to sob.

At last they are gone, and Stacy hands me a pain pill, which I take quite willingly. I want to just drift away into fantasyland; it hurts too much to be real. I wonder how addictive these pain pills are. I wonder how hard they are to get on the outside. For the first time in my life I think I understand how addiction begins, and I think I am ready to give it a whirl. I mean, really, what do I possibly have to lose?

chapter TWENTY-NINE

A Golden Moment

Apparently the doctor decided that Simon must remain in traction for a few more days. Stacy gave me a note written by him on hospital stationery, and I now know which facility I am in. But the handwriting is childish and shaky. She explains that this is because he's left-handed.

"Huh?"

"He had to use his right hand to write this since his left one is still in a cast. He broke his left arm and left leg."

"Oh." I read the note as she takes my blood pressure.

Hi, Alice. Hope you feel better now. Glad you are out of your coma. I'll try to come by as soon as I'm free of this confounded traction contraption. Best, Simon.

"We could get you into a wheelchair and take you to see him," she suggests. "Dr. Spangler says you should be getting up more now."

I consider this. I'd like to be getting around some, but I definitely do not want to see Simon. Despite his polite note, I'm certain he is angry at me. Why shouldn't he be? It's obvious I've ruined his life.

"So what do you think?" Stacy is brushing my hair now.

"Yes, I'd like to move around and get some exercise," I say carefully. "But I'm not sure about visiting…"

She sets down the brush. "I think I understand, Alice. You probably don't want Simon to see you like this. Well, that's okay. Give it a day or two. In the meantime, we'll get you moving around some. That'll make you feel better."

She helps me to get out of bed, and together we shuffle down the hallway. I grow dizzy, and each step is painful, but I am determined to become mobile. I ask Stacy to make sure that I don't walk past his room, explaining that I would be too embarrassed to have him see me like this. We walk in the other direction, down to a waiting area and back again. I'm exhausted when I get back into my bed and feel as though I've run a marathon.

"Good job," she tells me. "You should do that again this afternoon. And again later this evening. You'll be surprised at how much easier it will be each time."

I find this hard to believe, but I nod as if I do before I close my eyes and try to find one part of my body that isn't racked with pain. Then it occurs to me, when I am in this much physical pain, my brain seems to function better. I wonder how this can be. But it reminds me of when I was dancing at the Christmas party, how it helped me not to worry so much. I find this interesting. I also find it interesting that I am still talking to God. I'm not entirely sure this is a good thing, but I finally told Faye about it, and she encouraged me to keep it up.

"He wants us to talk to him, Alice. He wants to be our best friend. He's always listening, and he knows how to fix things."

I hope she's right. And it does seem to make me feel better. Yet at the same time I am getting this eerie feeling that I am special again—*chosen*. I have been remembering the golden key and all the things I wrote down. I wanted to ask my mother about my notebooks when she was here yesterday, but I didn't want to make her suspicious. I must keep these things under wraps for now. It's weird, but even the accident seems to play a part in this, like God has done something miraculous with me, allowing me to face death and yet survive.

But here's the weirdest part. I really tried not to think anything of it at first, but it seems to be getting clearer with each day. When I first came out of my coma a few days ago, Dr. Spangler asked me a bunch of questions for her medical form. One of the questions was "When did you have your last period?" Well, I had to really think about that, and the honest truth was that I couldn't remember. It seemed like it had been months ago. So then she asked if I was on the pill, but I told her no.

"Is this normal for you?" she asked, glancing over her clipboard.

"Normal?" I echoed, wondering how that word applied to my life.

"Do you normally skip a month here and there?"

I shrugged, unsure as to what the correct answer might be.

"Could you possibly be pregnant?" she asked without even blinking.

I think I laughed at this and said something about "immaculate conception." But since then I have been seriously wondering. Is it possible that God has given me a baby? Maybe it happened during that peaceful time during my coma. I'm just not sure. I must admit this idea seemed completely ridiculous at first, but not so much now. How would I possibly explain something like this to my mother? Or even Faye? I'm afraid they would think one of two things—that I am crazy or that I am promiscuous. Neither scenario appeals much to me. So for the time being I will keep my mouth shut.

I wake up this afternoon to discover Dr. Golden standing by my bed. I blink in surprise, thinking he's simply an apparition that will disappear if I'm patient, but he is still here. Now I wonder if this is a social or professional visit.

"Hi, Alice," he says. "I was just visiting with Simon and thought I'd stop in and say hello. Last time I saw you, you were pretty out of it."

"Yeah. I guess so." I remind myself that this is Simon's boss and good friend and that it's highly possibly he is here to try to uncover what I did to cause that wreck.

"How are you feeling?"

"Fine," I say quickly.

He smiles, it seems to himself, as he sits in the chair by my bed. "In the psychiatry world we say that *fine* is an acronym for something not so fine."

It takes me a moment to remember what an acronym is, but then I say, "What do the letters stand for?"

"Foolish. Insecure. Neurotic. Egotistical."

I feel my brows lift. "That sounds fairly accurate."

This makes him laugh. "I figured as much."

For some reason his demeanor makes me want to relax, to let down my guard, but this disturbs me, and I try even harder to stay on my toes. "How's Simon?" I ask, hoping to deflect the attention from myself. So much for egotistical.

"He's much better. But he really wants to get out of traction, poor guy. And his leg is itching something fierce."

"I'm sorry." I look down at the corner of blanket that I am steadily wadding into my hand.

"Yes, so am I." Then he pauses, and I feel his eyes on me. "You know it's not your fault, don't you?"

I look up and stare at him without saying anything. I wonder what he's getting at. Does he know something I don't know?

"I'm guessing that you are blaming yourself for the accident."

"Why?" I ask, but even *I* can hear the defensiveness in my voice. "Why would I do that?"

"I guess that would be the egotistical part."

"Huh?"

"You think you have control over things like that. Perhaps you get scared or think something bad will happen. And then when it does, you take responsibility for it. As if you have some supernatural powers."

I stare at him and wonder if *he* has some supernatural powers. How else would he be able to read my mind like this?

"But you need to know, Alice, the accident was *not* your fault. Simon has told me he was going a bit fast down the hill that night. He said he'd had such a good time at the party that he'd forgotten about the icy conditions. He'd had only one glass of wine, but he places some responsibility on that, too. Poor Simon swears that he will never drink again." Dr. Golden shakes his head. "I don't really think that had anything to do with it, but just the same it makes me feel a little guilty for being the host that night."

I can't believe that Simon is blaming himself or even that Dr. Golden feels somewhat responsible. But somehow this comforts me.

"I really believed it was my fault," I confess. "I couldn't remember why exactly, but I felt certain that I must've said or done something to cause it."

He nods. "I understand. But you need to keep telling yourself that it's not so, Alice. You have some control in the way that you think."

I shake my head now. "I've heard Simon say that, but I find it pretty hard to believe. I mean you haven't been inside my head, Dr. Golden. You have no idea the kind of stuff that goes on in there." I glance around the room now. "Or out here, for that matter. My reality is different from other people's. I think I just have to accept that."

He rubs his beard. "Some of that is true. You're right. We all have our own realities. But sometimes there are interfering factors—things that skew your reality. And you need to deal with those factors in order to live a functional and productive life."

"Deal with them?" I remember Pastor John's way of dealing with them through exorcism. Or Dr. Thornton's prescriptions to dull my perceptions into a stupor. "How exactly do you suggest I deal with them?"

"I think you've already made some good progress, Alice."

"What do you mean?"

"I mean the way that you are able and willing to talk about your psychosis with a fair amount of clarity."

"My psychosis?"

"Yes, the things that are happening to you that aren't real. The voices and whatnot. You are able to talk about these things, and you can sometimes differentiate between what is real and what is not. Am I correct?"

"I'm not sure." I consider telling him my latest, my immaculate-conception theory, but think better of it.

"I'm not saying that you've got this thing beat." He sighs. Is it in exasperation? "The truth is, I am concerned for you, Alice. I feel you need some serious treatment."

"Serious treatment?" Now I am imagining electroshock, strait-jackets, restraints, hypodermic needles, perhaps even brain surgery.

He smiles. "I mean *good* treatment, Alice. Some good counsel-ing, group therapy, and, yes, perhaps some meds if needed but only to get you stabilized."

"You think I'm unstable?"

"What do you think?"

I look away.

"Alice, I know that I told you we have a yearlong waiting list, and it's true; we most certainly do. But I've been discussing this with Simon, and I'd like to see if we can make an opening in the treatment center for you. If you're interested, that is. Remember, we only take residents who *want* to be there. The Golden Home is only for people who truly want to get well, people who are willing to take an active part in the healing process."

I'm not sure what to think about this. Before the accident, an offer like this would've made me run fast—in the opposite direc-tion—but so much has happened since then. I just don't know how to respond. But I know I won't commit to anything. If anything, I will try to appear cooperative and interested. Anything to get him off my case and out of here. I can see Amelia lurking like a shadow over by the bathroom. Has she come to protect me, to warn me? I think I've actually missed her a little. Then I notice the dark, skeptical expression on her face. She doesn't need to say a word. I know what she's thinking.

"I realize you'll need to give this some thought, Alice. Perhaps you'll want to discuss it with your family. I just wanted to let you know that we would consider making this exception."

"I appreciate it," I manage to say, diverting my eyes from Amelia. He is standing now. "Well, give it some thought. Talk to Simon about it. He can tell you more about our program. You might even want to come up and look around. See what happens on a daily basis."

"Oh, sure," says Amelia. "Do go in and see, Alice." Then she laughs in her harsh, sarcastic way. "And see if you ever walk out of there again."

My heart begins to race as I imagine myself in captivity again. I want to tell Amelia that this place might be different. If the patients—rather residents—are allowed to come and go at free will.

"Don't be a fool, Alice. Can't you see this is just an elaborate hoax?" She rolls her eyes, then turns abruptly away.

Now, I realize that Dr. Golden is speaking to me again, but I've totally missed it. "I'm sorry," I say.

He smiles. "I was just saying that Julie sends her best. She said to tell you that she's been praying for you."

"Praying?"

He nods. "Yes, we believe prayer is an integral part of the healing process. Connecting with God is vital to good mental health. But I know it's not always easy."

"God can be pretty confusing."

"I realize this. But it's just one of the many things we try to work through at our facility. I think you'll find we have quite a unique approach," he says. "I hope you'll give us a chance to help you, Alice. We think you'd fit in well."

I thank him again and watch in relief as he leaves. Why is he so persistent? What's in it for him? He must know I have no money. Does he run a prostitution ring? Or sell body parts on the black market? Oh, I know those thoughts are preposterous, at least part of me does, and I hate being so suspicious, but it's just the way I am. What can I do?

"He wants your baby," whispers Amelia. I didn't realize she was still in the room. "You're absolutely right to suspect him, Alice. He has ulterior motives. Dr. Golden knows that you are carrying God's child. And he wants to keep you in his prison until the baby is born. Then he will steal your baby and kill you."

I try to convince myself that this is totally absurd. That Amelia is crazier than I am or simply part of my "psychosis," as Dr. Golden might say. Despite my arguments, her words seem to have the ring of truth. After all, she's been right before, and like the seed that is planted in my womb, her words are planted in my mind.

chapter THIRTY

The White Knight

I am mostly convinced now that I am not to blame for the car accident. As a result I finally persuade myself to pay Simon a visit. I know that I still look pretty awful, but I wonder why I should even care. I brush my hair, apply some lip balm, and slowly make my way to his room.

"Alice," he says when he sees me, "I thought you'd never come."

"I'm sorry." I shuffle over to his bed and look at him. We look amazingly alike in our colorful patchwork covering of bruises and lumps. Only he doesn't have a long scar across his forehead like I do. He looks like he's wearing a partial coat of armor with his long casts on one arm and one leg. Like half of a white knight.

"No, I'm the one who should apologize," he tells me. I see tears form in his eyes, and I notice he's not wearing his glasses. "I am so very sorry, Alice. I can't believe that I almost killed you that night. Will you ever forgive me?"

"Of course, I forgive you. It wasn't your fault, Simon."

He closes his eyes and sighs deeply. "I think it was. I wasn't being very careful, and I'd had that glass of wine, and—"

"But one glass, Simon. I just don't see how…"

He opens his eyes and looks into mine. "I don't know why it happened, Alice, but I know that I wasn't driving carefully enough. Let's not talk about it anymore. I'm just so relieved that you forgive me. You have no idea how worried I was that you'd be angry or hold this against me. Who would blame you?"

I consider telling him how I thought it was all my fault, but somehow I'm not sure I can even begin to explain this. It makes so little sense to me now. And yet it seemed so real just a few days ago. I wonder how that can be.

"I hear they are going to release you," he says.

"Yeah. Tomorrow."

"Where are you going?"

"I'm not sure yet."

"I know Faye would be glad to have you back."

"Yeah. She's probably my first choice."

"What about the Golden Home?" I can sense the hesitation in his voice, as if he is afraid he will offend me.

"I've been thinking about that."

He smiles. "Good. Dr. Golden and I talked about it some. He said he was going to mention the idea to you. It's such a great place, Alice. You'd really like it there."

"Maybe." I look away. For some reason I don't want to hurt his feelings. Maybe it's because he looks so vulnerable with his leg strung up like that. I'm not sure.

"Do you have some reservations?" he asks. "I can understand if you're worried. I remember how you kind of freaked at the Christmas party." He laughs.

"Yeah, I was acting pretty weird that night." I try to pretend like that was something out of the ordinary, as if I never act weird. Who am I fooling here?

"But I'm guessing you've had some bad experiences," he continues. "I know that some psychiatric hospitals can be pretty awful."

"Yeah." I wonder how he knows. "Have you ever been locked up, Simon?"

He shakes his head. "But I know what it's like. And I've visited some real sorry places while doing research for a paper. It can be pretty pitiful."

"Yeah. Pretty pitiful."

"But the Golden Home is nothing like that, Alice. You should go up there and visit. Julie said she'd be happy to give you the complete tour."

I want to ask why they are being so nice to me, but instead I pretend this interests me. I tell him that I will give her a call.

"It's amazing that Dr. Golden is willing to bump you up on the waiting list," he continues. "I don't think I've ever seen him do that before. But I could tell he liked you that night."

Yeah, I'm thinking, I'm sure he likes the fact that I am carrying God's baby too. But even as these words flash through my mind, I am thinking the whole idea sounds completely outrageous —totally absurd. I almost come clean with Simon just then; I nearly pour out my crazy story to see if he can straighten me out. But I don't.

"You should take him up on the offer, Alice. Just go right in there as soon as you get released from here. You won't be sorry. I promise."

"How can you make that kind of promise, Simon?"

"Because I work up there. I know that place inside and out. It's the best facility in the entire—"

"Okay, Simon, if it's the best facility, then how can I possibly afford it?" I demand. Suddenly I am eager to expose these people for who I honestly believe them to be. "Look, I'm not even sure if my mom still has insurance on me. And I am basically penniless."

Simon laughs now. "Don't worry, Alice, it's not about the money. Dr. Golden's wife, Julie, inherited millions about ten years ago. She's invested most of it in the clinic. They use a sliding scale for residents."

I narrow my eyes at him. "But *why* are they so eager to get me in there, Simon? Don't you think that's a little suspicious in itself? I mean, first they tell me about this yearlong waiting list, and the next thing you know they say I can come right in."

"It's only because they really like you, Alice. I think it was Julie's idea."

I shake my head. "Something about this just really bugs me."

He looks me in the eyes and says, "Okay, tell me then, what exactly do you think their motives are? Do you honestly think they're after your money? You say you don't have any."

"There are things beside money."

"Maybe they want to knock you out and steal your liver? You mentioned something like that at the Christmas party." He laughs now. "And, no offense, but that's not a terribly unique form of paranoia. We get that a lot. And the guinea-pig thing. A lot of patients are afraid they will become human guinea pigs."

I nod, as if he is helping to make my point. "See? How can we know these things don't happen?"

"By going up there and taking the tour, Alice. Just look around. See if you find anything questionable going on."

"Well, maybe I will!" I stand up and move toward the door. I am fed up with Simon, and I'm almost ready to take back my forgiveness for the car wreck. But then I see him lying there all strapped up, and I can't do it.

He is smiling though. "Well, I'm going to be really praying for you, Alice. I'm going to specifically ask God to break through all the nonsense in your head long enough for you to figure out that the Goldens are perfectly legit. I'm praying that you'll know they only want to help people."

Sometimes I wonder who's really delusional in this world. I just smile and tell Simon to take it easy.

"Will you come back and visit me?" he asks in a little boy voice.

I consider this. I don't want to lie, but I don't really want to come back either. It's one thing when I'm stuck here as a patient, but I'm not sure I could return of my own free will. It's beginning to feel much too confining, almost like a Forest Hills sort of place. "I'll try," I tell him. At least this is honest.

He frowns. "Then I probably won't see you again until I get out of here."

I shrug. "It's hard to say, Simon. The truth is, I don't know what will happen with me. I mean, I'd like to tell you that I'm going straight up to the Goldens', that I'm going to sign myself in, and that everything will be hunky-dory by the time you get out of here. But I just can't do that."

"I know. I appreciate your honesty. I hope you believe I'm being honest with you. Why would I lie?"

"I don't know. But then there's so much I don't know. Sometimes I wonder what difference it makes whether something is the truth or not. Reality is sort of in the eyes of the beholder, don't you think?"

"Only when you live in a world all by yourself."

All by myself. I think about this. I wonder if I can even find such a place. I wonder if I would be happy there. I'm standing at the door now, feeling as if I'm seeing Simon for the last time. To my surprise, this makes me sad. I think I am about to cry.

"Alice," he says in a quiet and serious voice, "I hope you know how much I care about you."

"I care about you, too." Playing Simon says again?

"No, I mean I *really* care about you." He taps himself on the chest. "It's like you're inside of me, you know?"

I just stare at him and wonder how I could possibly be inside of him. Sometimes I'm not even inside of me. I shake my head and walk slowly back to my room, wiping the tears as I go.

I sit on my bed and try to imagine what it feels like to really love someone. I thought I loved Shay last fall. Now I can barely remember what he looked like. If I saw him on the street today, I would just keep going. That's not love.

I think about the feeling I experienced just now as I was leaving Simon's room. It felt like a blade was twisting in my heart. But if that's love, it sure doesn't feel very good. I have enough pain in my life without willingly inviting more. Besides, how can I possibly love anyone when I don't even love myself? I wouldn't know where to begin.

Begin with me.

chapter THIRTY-ONE

A Disagreeable Agreement

Apparently the hospital had communicated with my mother about my impending release. I know I didn't tell her. When she showed up here this morning, she also proceeded to tell me that she'd had a long conversation with Dr. Spangler about me. This has me seriously worried.

"Is there anything you need to take with you?" she asks as she hands me a bag that has some of my clothes from home in it.

I shake my head and go into the bathroom. I really hadn't expected her to come today. I had hoped to return to Faye's and just quietly fade into the woodwork for a few days or until I figure things out.

"I spoke to your friend Faye on the phone last night," she calls to me through the metal door. "I told her I was coming to get you today, to take you home. She asked if you wanted to pick up your cat, but I told her it might be better if she just kept it for the time being."

I step out now, still buttoning my shirt as I stare at her in disbelief. Who does she think she is to butt into my life like this? I'm a grown woman. Well, sort of. "But that is *my* cat, Mom. I can't just leave him behind."

"But Faye seemed perfectly happy to keep him—"

"Of course she would keep him. She's a sweet lady, and she *loves* cats."

"But don't you think it would be better—"

"No, Mom, I *don't* think it would be better. I'm beginning to think it might be better if you didn't interfere so much. This is my life, and like it or not, you're going to have to let me live it."

She starts to cry now, and I feel absolutely rotten. I'm a perfectly horrible person. A despicable daughter. Maybe Pastor John is right. Maybe I do have demons in me.

"I'm sorry, Mom. It's just that I'm so frustrated and confused right now. I think I need to have some kind of control over my life."

She slumps down into the chair, setting her purse on her lap. This is when I notice that she has on pants. Navy blue wool pants with creases down the front. I am amazed. I have never seen my mother wear anything but skirts, dresses, jumpers—mostly home-made by her.

"Mom!" I exclaim. "You're wearing pants!"

She looks up and faintly smiles. "Yes. I don't think God minds. Do you?"

"No, of course not."

Now for some unexplainable reason, seeing Mom in pants makes me willing to take the risk of going home with her, but I ask her if we can stop by and pick up my cat first.

"Of course, dear," she says. "If you think that's best."

I nod firmly. "I do."

It seems that Faye is expecting us because her teakettle is just beginning to whistle as she opens the door to let us in. Of course, I know it's just her normal routine to have midmorning tea, but I tell myself she is doing it for us. It feels so good to be back in her cozy little house. I can tell my mother is uncomfortable with all the cats and the hair and the smell. She stands like a soldier at attention, as if she's afraid to touch anything or get hair on her nice new pants, but Faye's cats and house don't bother me in the least. I take time to greet each cat by name, lavishly petting them and laughing as their hair floats in the air and causes my uptight mother to sneeze. More than ever I wish I could just stay right here in the cat house.

Faye has made a loaf of banana bread and announces that it's cool enough to cut now. My mother looks as if she's afraid to eat it, as if she thinks the cats may have contaminated it somehow. This idea had never occurred to me before, and I'm not even sure that I would care. For some reason the cats seem much safer to me than most humans. I eat a slice of banana bread without reservation.

"Have you told your mother about the Goldens?" asks Faye as she refills my cup with amber tea. I think it is jasmine today.

"The Goldens?" repeats my mother. She glances at me with what feels like suspicion.

"Dr. Golden is Simon's boss," I say as if that explains everything.

"But what about them?" asks my mother.

I wonder how much Faye actually knows. She seems oblivious and just smiles and takes another piece of banana bread.

"Dr. Golden runs a home," I say quickly. "Kind of a psychiatric hospital, you know. Only they say it's different from other places. Simon works up there."

"It's a beautiful place," says Faye.

"You've been there?" I ask. Is she involved somehow?

283

"Oh yes, lots of times. I teach knitting classes up there some-times. When there's a resident or two who wants to learn how. Knit-ting is very soothing," she says this to my mother as if she should give it a try, and I'm thinking perhaps Faye is onto something here. "But it's a lovely place. I wish I could live up there myself sometimes."

"You could *pretend* to be crazy," I suggest, thinking I'm being funny.

"Oh, lots of people think that I am." She laughs. "And I don't mind really."

"I think you're one of the sanest people I know," I tell her. Then I wonder how much that can mean coming from someone like me.

"Would you want to go there?" my mother asks me, very tenta-tively, as if she thinks she's treading on a minefield, which is proba-bly not too far from the truth.

"I don't really want to *go* anywhere." I turn and glare at her.

"Oh, I know, honey. I just mean would you want to—"

"In fact, if I could have my way, and if Faye didn't mind, I would prefer to stay right here." Even as the words are out of my mouth, I know that I have hurt my mother's feelings again. I sit there like an idiot and just watch as fresh tears spill down her cheeks. I am such a stupid and evil person!

"There, there," soothes Faye as she pats my mother's hand. "Alice has been through a very difficult time. I'm sure she didn't mean to hurt you."

"It's true, Mom. I didn't mean to hurt you," I plead. "But I just don't feel right about going home to Warren right now. Something about being stuck in that town, with the old church nearby, well, just really upsets me. I don't know if I can take—" I realize that I am on my feet now, pacing back and forth across Faye's tiny kitchen and wringing my hands. I must appear totally crazy to them. Not exactly the look I was going for. I sit back down and take my mom's hands in mine. I saw this on television once, back when I had a life and a roommate who liked to watch old movies with me. It seems just the sort of pose you'd take when you want to communicate something true and hard and honest with someone you care about.

"Mom, I really do love you, and I appreciate what you're trying to do—both for me and for yourself. I mean it's so cool that you're wearing pants now." I glance at Faye, and for some odd reason she seems to understand. "But I just don't think it's a good idea for me to come home with you right now."

"But what will you do, Alice?" She shakes her head. "You can't just stay with Faye forever."

I look at Faye. "I'm not even sure I can stay with her at—"

"Of course you can stay, dear. I love having you here. You're a good helper and fine companion, no trouble at all."

"But what about school and…" I can tell my mom wants to say something about my "illness" or the "diagnosis" or even the word itself, "schizophrenia," but she can't make herself do it. For that matter, neither can I.

"I just need to figure things out," I assure her. "I don't really know what I should do next. I mean I'd like to go back to school, finish my degree, but I don't think I can handle that yet."

"Perhaps you just need to rest a bit," suggests Faye. "Recover from your injuries and see what happens next. The good Lord has ways of leading us when we keep our eyes on him. I'm sure he is leading you now, Alice, even as we speak."

Just then Cheshire jumps in my lap, and I begin to relax as I stroke his soft coat. "Yes, I think you're right, Faye."

My mom nods now, as if she has resigned herself to this sudden change of plans. "But what about these Goldens, Alice? They sound like good people."

I nod. "They seem nice."

I'm afraid to say too much or to voice any concerns. I'm certainly not going to lay all my cards on the table just now. I can't imagine what my mother, or Faye for that matter, would think if I suddenly announced that I'm pregnant, possibly with God's baby, and that I'm afraid the Goldens are planning to lock me up until the child is born and then to dispose of me as quickly and neatly as possible. Without a trace, I am sure. I admit that it sounds slightly bizarre even to me right now. But there are times when I am absolute certain about such things.

"How about if we make a deal?" suggests my mom.

"What kind of deal?" Another wave of suspicion washes over me. What if the Goldens have been in contact with her too? What if they are working with everyone I know and almost trust. Like Simon and my mom now. Why, even Faye seems to think they're wonderful.

"If I let you stay with Faye, will you promise me that you'll look into the Goldens' hospital or clinic or whatever it is they call it?"

My chest grows tighter, as if I'm losing control of everything all over again. But I take in a deep breath and tell myself just to chill. *Play the game.* Then I sense Amelia leaning over my shoulder, and I hear her whispering to me. "Say whatever it takes to get your mom off your back and out of here. You can sort it all out later."

"Can you do that for me, Alice?" My mom is looking directly into my eyes, like she used to do when she thought I was lying. "Dr.

Spangler mentioned that you could use some additional treatment. I promised her I'd try to find you something. Maybe this is the answer, Alice. Will you at least check them out?"

I lock eyes with her, thinking that I'd better follow Amelia's advice this time. Just agree and get this over with as quickly as possible. "You mean just go up and look around?" I say.

"Yes, just look around and talk to them."

I nod. "Sure, I can do that."

My mom smiles, and I can tell she thinks she is victorious. I smile too, playing along, as I stroke Cheshire's fur. The warm, smoothing motion helps to calm my churning insides. I know without a doubt that I must come up with another plan now, and soon. Somewhere I can go and be safe—just until the baby is born. Hopefully Faye won't push too hard on me to keep my promise to my mom.

Finally my mom announces she should go. I pretend to be sad as I stand and give her a hug. Mostly I am tired and worried and scared. As soon as Mom is gone, I turn to Faye and excuse myself to my room.

"I'm sure you must be exhausted, dear. You go and sleep as long as you like."

As long as I like? I wonder how long that would be. Forever perhaps? As I lie on the bed, I can barely remember that sweet sense of peace I experienced during what I'm now sure must've been my coma era. But I can faintly recall that warm white cocoon that seemed to envelop me—safe, secure, peaceful. I look up at the stained ceiling tiles and long for that kind of peace again.

My peace I give you.

chapter THIRTY-TWO

I'm Late, I'm Late

The next morning I overhear Faye speaking on the telephone. She probably thinks I'm still asleep in bed, but I am wide awake and standing in the hallway, listening.

"She seems better," she says. "Yes, she told her mother that she is willing to go up there and look around."

I tiptoe closer to the kitchen, straining my ears to hear each word.

"That is very kind of you, Julie. You know I don't drive. Yes, I think around noon would be just fine. Yes, I'll tell her."

I slink back down the hallway to my room. I know what they are doing. They are arranging to have me transported to the Golden Home.

"It's time to go, kiddo," says Amelia as she steps behind the door to my bedroom. "I'm warning you, they're onto you. They want that baby."

Without answering her, I close the door and begin to dress in layer after layer of clothes. Three pairs of socks make Faye's old rubber boots a bit tight, but I know I won't be sorry once I hit the streets.

The city is cold in January. I top all this with my army-green coat and a hat that Faye knitted for me herself. It's made from all her leftover yarn and looks like a rainbow. Worried that he might try to follow me, I scoot Cheshire out of the bedroom and close the door. Then I open the window and climb out.

I double over with pain as I hit the ground. My ribs ache as if they've cracked all over again. I realize I can't reach up to close the window again, and I feel a little guilty, letting all that cold air into Faye's warm little house.

"Don't worry about that," says Amelia. "Don't forget that Faye is betraying you right now. She's in there plotting with Julie and Dr. Golden. Even your mom's in on it."

I nod as I hold on to my middle, trying to contain the pain. Hunched over I make my way through the wet grass in Faye's backyard.

"Hurry," she urges me on. "Get far away from this evil place, and never come back."

I cut through the alley that passes between the backyards of the houses and slowly make my way down toward the MAX stop. After a few blocks the pain seems to subside a little, and I can stand up straighter as I try to walk faster. I used to worry about using public transportation, afraid that I'd be spotted by a pursuer, but my body isn't up to a long walk today. Besides, I think it may be all right this time since it's possible no one knows I've escaped just yet.

Amelia warns me not to look at anyone, so I keep my eyes down, avoiding onlookers' glances as I wait for the train to arrive. Then I climb on quickly, taking a seat next to the door just in case I have to get off fast. I haven't had time to formulate any sort of plan yet, but at least I have a destination. I know that I lasted a few weeks down by the river park before. I can probably do it again, but I must remember to be very careful.

My face is wet as I step off of the MAX in the city center. I didn't even know I'd been crying. Was it for Cheshire? Or Faye? Or maybe for myself. I think about going up to the hospital to see Simon. I'm not even sure why. I guess there's a tiny part of me that hopes I can trust him, and yet I don't know why I hold on to this. Maybe it's because he is so helpless with his casts and traction devices. Perhaps that makes him safer, makes me believe that he can't really hurt me. Then again, I'm not so sure. There are all sorts of pain.

I make my way through the shopping district, imagining that I am blending into the crowd of fast-walking shoppers. It's too bad I don't have a bag to carry. It seems that everyone has bags today. Then I realize they are probably still returning their unwanted Christmas gifts. I remember when I worked at Nordstrom last Christmas season—was that only a year ago?—that the first business day after Christmas was such a killer. By the end of my shift, the cash register was more than seventeen thousand dollars in the hole. At the time I thought it was rather ironic and pitiful. Today I wish I were one of those people who actually had a gift to return. I remember that Aaron said he'd gotten me something. I guess it's still at my mom's house. If it's really true. Aaron may be in on this.

"Trust no one," says Amelia.

I walk over to a tram stop and sit down like I know what I am doing. I guess I have decided to visit Simon after all.

"What are you doing?" demands Amelia.

"I need to see Simon." I try to keep my voice calm. "Just one last time."

"No!" she screams. I look around to see if she frightened anyone, but no one seems to care if she throws a fit. "No, you are not going up there, Alice!"

"I have to," I tell her in a firm voice.

"You are a complete fool!" she yells, along with another string of profanity.

"Leave me alone," I tell her. I notice the man with the newspaper moving away from me now, glancing nervously from the corner of his eye.

Amelia stamps off, and I wait for the right train to come, and with shaking hands I climb on. If only Amelia could understand that this is a one-time event. It's not like I'm stupid. I know it's only a matter of time before they sound the alarms and announce to everyone that Alice is on the run again. And maybe it is foolish, but I need to see Simon, and it's as if the risk is driving me now.

It's almost ten o'clock when I walk through the big double doors of the hospital. Without speaking or looking at anyone, I ride the elevator up to the fourth floor and head straight to Simon's room. But when I get there, I hear people talking, and for a moment I am certain that Dr. Golden is already here, on the alert and looking for me. I wonder how he found out about me so soon. And how did he know I'd come here? I stand out of sight behind the door and listen intently. But soon I realize that it's only Simon's doctor talking to him about his progress. I decide to hang out in the rest room for a while until he leaves.

"Alice!" exclaims Stacy as I enter the rest room. "What are you doing back here?"

I frown and search my scattered mind for an appropriate answer. "I have an appointment," I say quickly.

She nods, but I can tell by her eyes that she doesn't completely believe me.

"And I wanted to say hi to Simon," I add.

This seems to satisfy her as she rubs her hands beneath the blow dryer. "That's nice," she says. "I heard he's finally getting out of traction today. I'll bet he can't wait."

"Yeah." I go into a stall and close the door, hoping she will go.

Then I hear Amelia's voice. I can tell she is very, very angry. "Why did you come here, you stupid little fool? Don't you know this is the first place they will look for you? What is wrong with you, Alice? Why don't you listen to me? You are such a fool!"

Leave me alone, I am thinking. Just go away! I press my hands to my mouth, afraid that Stacy might still be there listening, that she might alert security. I listen and hear the door open and close. I wait a few minutes and hear only the sound of a dripping toilet. Finally I emerge. No one is there. Now I'm not sure whether to listen to Amelia and get out of here or to stop by and speak to Simon. I slip out into the hallway, and avoiding a particularly unfriendly nurse, I turn left and head directly toward Simon's room. I pause by the door, and when I am certain he is alone, I stick in my head and am immediately spotted.

"Alice!" he calls out in what sounds like a happy voice. "Come in."

I walk in and glance around. I am afraid they will be here shortly. That I will have to make a run for it, bolt out the door, and use an emergency exit to get away. But so far I see no one.

"How are you feeling?" he asks.

"Okay."

His smile seems to fade as he peers at me more closely. "Are you really okay?"

I shrug and move a step closer to his bed.

"You don't look okay."

"Thanks a lot." I glance over my shoulder now. Feeling jumpy. Very jumpy.

"Get out of here, you fool!" Amelia is standing in the corner of the room just yelling at me. "Run while you've got the chance."

I want to press my hands over my ears, but I control myself.

"Look, Alice," Simon says. "I know this is hard for you. But you've got to listen to me, okay?"

I don't know what to do. Something in me really wants to listen to him. But at the same time Amelia sounds like she's going to go berserk if I don't make a move—and fast.

"I know what you're experiencing feels real, Alice. And I understand that you find it difficult to trust anyone. To believe that anyone—" He stops abruptly. "You're hearing the voices right now, aren't you, Alice?"

I look over my shoulder again, ready to run.

"Listen to me, Alice. I am real. They are not. Do you know that?"

I use all my energy to focus my attention on him, and at the moment I can believe him. I slowly nod. "I think so. Right now anyway."

"Okay. I know what you're up against—"

"How can you know, Simon?" I shake my head, suddenly afraid

that he's stringing me along too. "How on earth can you possibly know?"

"Alice." His voice is calm. "I want you to listen to me, okay? Really tune into my voice. I know what you're going through because my mother had schizophrenia too. Do you understand me?"

I stare at him now, unsure that he's being truthful with me. "Honestly?" I ask him, trying to see into his eyes, to detect the signs if he's not telling the truth.

"Honestly." He shakes his head now, and his eyes get sad. "I don't like telling people about this, but I want to tell you. Are you listening?"

I slowly move my chin up, then down. I think that I am listening.

"Okay." He takes a breath. "According to my grandma, my mom started displaying symptoms not long after I was born. I even used to think that having me was what made her go crazy. At first the doctors thought it was postpartum depression, but instead of getting better, she got worse and worse. Finally I was taken away from her, and she was hospitalized. In a pretty bad place too."

"Like Forest Hills?"

He nods. "Yes, very similar. Anyway, when I was little, I would go visit her with my grandma, but she never seemed like a real person to me. And she never acted like a mother. She didn't really seem to know who I was."

This sounds like my grandma.

He leans his head back now and sighs loudly, as if this next part is hard to tell. But I am listening. I even take another step forward, not wanting to miss a word.

"When I started junior high school, I refused to go see her

anymore. I told my grandma I was too busy, but it was really because, as an ignorant teenager, I was embarrassed to have a mom in the nut house. Besides, I figured if she didn't know whether I was there or not, how would she notice if I didn't come? And, honestly, she was so doped up that she probably didn't. But then when I was just starting high school, she killed herself. Slit her wrists right there in the hospital. Used a pocketknife that she'd somehow gotten from an orderly. And just like that she was gone."

I take another step toward his bed and put my hand on his cast. "I'm sorry," I say. Tears pool in his eyes, and I have no reason to doubt his story.

"At the time I blamed myself. I told myself that if I'd only gone to see her, she wouldn't have done it. That's when I started reading books about mental illnesses, trying to figure this whole thing out. Then I learned about heredity and got freaked that I was going to end up just like her."

"But you're not," I tell him, sadly thinking that I am.

His brows lift slightly. "Not yet anyway."

I frown. "Do you really think that…"

"There's no guarantee." Now he looks at me closely. "But I'll tell you what, Alice, if I started getting symptoms, I wouldn't freak."

I shake my head. Easy for him to say.

"Honestly. I've watched Dr. Golden work with people. He uses good therapy and counseling and a minimum of medication, and people are living normal lives."

"*Normal?*"

He rolls his eyes. "As I've said, normal *is* highly overrated."

"Yeah." But I'm still not convinced.

"Alice, did you know that most people with schizophrenia have an above-average IQ? Many are borderline geniuses, artists, writers, musicians, scientists. I can give you a whole list of famous people as diversely gifted as Vincent van Gogh, John Nash, Virginia Woolf, and Friedrich Nietzsche, who all probably suffered from some form of schizophrenia."

"Why are you telling me this?" I am tired now. Exhausted from my morning travels, I ease myself into the chair next to his bed and lean forward, shoulders slumped as I stare hopelessly at the floor. It feels hot and stuffy in here, but then I realize I am dressed quite warmly.

"Because I want you to get the help you deserve, Alice. And you are being handed an amazing opportunity with Dr. Golden."

I look at him from the corner of my eye. "Did someone already call you and tell you I ran away?"

He just laughs. "No, Alice. But it doesn't take a genius to guess where you're headed."

"Where?"

"I'm guessing the streets. If you let the voices bully you, you'll most likely be hiding around the corners, sleeping in Dumpsters or under the bridges, jumping at every noise."

I stand up again and study him closely. How does he know about this?

"It's just the way it goes when people give in to their symptoms and refuse to get good help. You become everyone's victim, and you run and run and run, but you never get away."

"What then, Simon? Are you telling me to go to the Goldens? To allow them to lock me—"

He reaches out with his good hand and grabs my arm as if to get my attention. It works. "*They do not lock anyone up, Alice. Why would I lie to you?*" He releases my arm and leans back again.

"I don't know." I reach down and touch my stomach, wondering if God's baby is really in there after all. Or is this just another delusion? It all seemed so real and believable this morning. How can that be?

"I really care about you, Alice. I have no reason to lie to you. I just want to see you get help and get better. I want to see you finish college and enjoy a functional life where you're not running from the shadows all the time."

"I want that too."

"Well, it's up to you then."

"Are you telling me to go up there, Simon?"

"I can only tell you that I think it would be the best thing for you. But you're the one who must make the final decision. No one is going to force you into this. And if Dr. Golden isn't convinced you're there of your own free will, he won't even let you in."

I sit back down again. *My own free will.* It seems like nothing in my life is about my own free will anymore. It's not my will for Amelia to scream at me or to be confused all the time. And it's not my will to be homeless and hungry.

"What if I don't have a free will anymore?" I ask.

"You do, Alice. It's in there. I've seen it. But all that other stuff is confusing you. Think about what you really want in your life, then ask yourself how you're going to get there."

I think about things like peace and safety and rest. I think about being warm and loved and fulfilled. For the moment I know I won't find these things on the streets, running from shadows as Simon put it. I suspect he is probably right.

"Julie was going to pick me up at Faye's at noon," I tell him. "I don't know if I can get back there in time." I stand up and move toward the door. "I've got to go, Simon. I don't want to miss her."

He grins and waves, and I take off. I am tempted to use the emergency exit but don't want to look too crazy. Instead I go the longer way, walking as fast as I am able down the hall, ignoring the glances tossed my way. Once outside, I move quickly toward the train stop, ignoring the jolt of pain with each jarring step. I wish I had taken a pain pill this morning. Somehow I reach the stop at the same time as the tram. I climb inside, sitting close to the door, clutching my midsection with my hands, preparing myself to jump out and catch the downtown connection that will take me back across the river again.

Time is usually inconsequential to me, but now I am worried about each minute as the tram rumbles across the bridge. I fret that I am too late, that Julie has already come and gone without me, that I've missed my chance. I want to ask the woman with the little boy if she knows what time it is but am afraid she already thinks I'm dangerous. I noticed how she looked at me and then quickly turned away as if she thought I might harm her or her child. I turn and stare out the window. Why is this train moving so slowly?

There, directly across from me, is the big bridge, the one that used to call my name. I stare at it, wishing I could overpower its evil draw, somehow prove to it that I am stronger. But I fear I am not. I fear that left to its own devices, the bridge would easily win over me. I turn and look away. If only I'm not too late.

I begin to pray, whether it's aloud or in my heart I'm not quite sure. I don't think I even care anymore. *Dear God, please help me to get there on time. Please don't let me arrive too late. Amen.*

chapter THIRTY-THREE

The Garden of Live Flowers

A melia is verbally assaulting me as I step off the tram at the last stop. Trying to ignore her, I pause to glance at the clock in the waiting area. It is nearly noon. I know it will take at least twenty minutes to make it back to Faye's, and that's only if I walk fast. I'm not even sure that I can.

"Go ahead, you stupid little fool," she yells as she stamps along beside me. "It's not going to do any good. You'll never make it on time, and even if you do, it won't matter. They don't want to help you—"

"Leave me alone! Leave me alone!" I yell to block out her harping as I hurry along. I am breathless when I finally reach Faye's street. My ribs burn like twigs in a fire, and my heart is about to burst through my throbbing chest. I ache all over and would trade my rubber boots for a pain pill right now. But I keep on trudging. I cut through the alley again and finally find her backyard and make my way across the still wet grass. I slip in the back door and prepare myself for Faye's questions. Where was I? What was I doing? Not that she's ever been that intrusive before. But I am ready.

"Hello, dear," she calls from the kitchen as I remove my coat in the laundry room. "I just told Julie that you should be here any minute."

I step into the kitchen and see Julie sitting at the little table, drinking a cup of tea and petting Oliver.

"Hi, Alice." She smiles. "I was hoping I hadn't missed you."

"I just, uh, went for a walk," I tell her as I unbutton the first layer beneath my coat, one of Faye's old cardigans, a hot pink color that always makes my face look paler than normal.

"Would you like some tea?" asks Faye.

"Sure." I sit down and attempt to catch my breath.

"Faye thought that you might like to come out and see our place," says Julie as she helps herself to a slice of banana bread left over from yesterday.

I nod. "Yes, I'd like to do that." I peer at her. "Just to look around, right?"

"Just to look around," mocks Amelia. "Right!"

"Definitely, it's just to see the place. We don't even have a space available until the end of the week. But you can certainly check it all out."

Faye sets a cup of tea before me, then cuts a generous slice of banana bread and even spreads it with butter before she sets it on a napkin in front of me. "You need to eat something so you can take one of your pain pills, dear."

"Oh sure," says Amelia as she leans against the refrigerator with narrowed eyes. "Go ahead and take a pill, Alice. See where that gets you, you stupid moron!"

I avert my eyes and hungrily devour the bread before I *willingly* take a pill. Amelia could be right, but somehow I just don't believe her. Or maybe I don't care. My body aches so badly that all I can think about is getting a little relief.

"Don't eat too much," warns Julie with a smile. "I thought you and I could have some lunch along the way and just chat a little."

"A little lunch?" Amelia shakes her head. "Don't fall for it, Alice. That's how she'll start the poison in your system."

I study Julie for a moment, thinking Amelia could be right; this could be a trick. Then I force myself to replay Simon's words. I make myself remember what it is I really want. And what I don't. I think Julie and Faye are talking again, but I'm not catching their words.

Faye places her hand on my arm, as if to get my attention. "Do you want to change your clothes, Alice? You seem awfully bundled up."

I nod and return to my room. The window has been closed, and I suspect that Faye knows exactly what I've been up to. Despite Amelia's threats and warnings, I remove most of my layers. Not all, since you never can tell. I brush my hair and then go back out and say that I am ready. Part of me agrees with Amelia. I might be handing myself over to the executioner. The rest of me is too tired to resist or even care. And so I go.

Julie has a nice silver car. I'm not sure what kind, maybe a Beemer, but it's pretty and smells like leather and expensive perfume. I remember what Simon said about her inheritance. I think how lovely it would be to have someone give you a bunch of money and wonder what I would do if that happened to me.

She takes me to a downtown restaurant where they greet you at the door and offer to take your coats. I hang on to mine and get very flustered. Then I am even more confused when I try to read the menu. It's as if everything is in a different language.

Julie sets down her menu and looks at me. "I'm getting the Asian salad, Alice. It's very good."

I nod. "I'll have that too."

Then the waiter comes, and she orders for both of us. At first I am relieved, but then I get worried. I haven't seen Amelia since we left Faye's house, but what if she is right? What if Julie planned this whole thing? What if the waiter has been instructed to slip something into my food?

"I think I know how you feel," she says as the waiter leaves.

"What do you mean?" I look at her curiously.

"Are you worried about the food?" She glances over her shoulder. "That someone is going to put something into it?"

I shrug.

"Would you be surprised if I told you that I used to feel the exact same way?" She laughs. "Sometimes I still do. But then I tell myself to shape up."

"Huh?" I'm really confused now. Is this a trick? I look over my shoulder thinking Amelia must be nearby.

"The reason I brought you here first was so I could tell you a little about myself, Alice. Because you remind me of myself about twenty years ago."

I study her carefully and wonder how I could possibly remind her of her gorgeous self. She is tall and beautiful, dressed stylishly, confident, and completely in control of her life. We are as different as night and day. I felt the stares we got as we walked into this upscale restaurant. I may be crazy, but I'm not stupid. The host probably assumed that Julie had picked me up off the street. Like she was doing her good deed for the day by giving a poor homeless girl a free meal.

"I know you feel very skeptical right now, Alice. You may even suspect that I want to hurt you. I have felt those same exact feelings. You see, I've lived with schizophrenia for more than twenty years now. It's only in the last twelve years that I've experienced anything close to a normal life—if you want to call it that. But that is thanks to Jack."

"Dr. Golden?"

She nods. "He was working as a psychiatrist in the hospital that I'd been stuck in. But he saw something in me that no one else did. He spent time with me and drew me out of myself." She pauses to take a sip of water, then sets down her glass. "And I was pretty far gone too. I wasn't functioning nearly as well as you are."

"You think I'm functioning well?" This makes me want to laugh...or cry.

"Comparatively speaking. So was I to start out with. But things got progressively worse, and it wasn't long before I was entrenched in my way of thinking, afraid of everyone and everything. I became unable to function."

I'm trying to process her words, but some of them seem to bounce off my brain like a superball. And she speaks so effortlessly that I begin to worry it's all just a rehearsed speech, to convince me to trust her. I don't think I believe her. Yet I nod my head and pretend that I do.

"That's why my parents put me in the hospital," she continues. "Naturally, they thought it was only going to be for a short time. The doctor assured them that I might improve with rest and medication. Only I never did. Not until Jack came along." She smiles now. "He's not perfect, Alice, but he helped rescue me. And he's helped hundreds of others since then. He can help you."

When our salads come, Julie bows her head to say a prayer. I follow her lead, but my heart is beginning to pound with fear. I am certain that my salad is poisoned, but some of the words in her prayer remind me of Faye, and I am able to breathe again. Like a parrot, I echo her *amen* and then stare at my salad. I am unable to pick up my fork.

"Do you want to switch?"

"Huh?" I look up.

"Salads." She smiles. "We could switch if it makes you feel better."

Now I feel silly and force myself to pick up my fork, and she does the same. But then I hesitate. Why is this so hard?

"Here, Alice." She reaches over and picks up my plate and exchanges it with hers. "Does that make you feel better?"

I nod and take a tentative bite. To my surprise the salad tastes pretty good. Much better than hospital food. I really don't think it's tainted, but only time will tell. I look up at Julie and think she looks like a person you can trust. But how do you know? I almost consider telling her about my pregnancy fear but cannot force these words to my mouth. Instead I ask whether she and Dr. Golden have children.

"No, I always wanted to have children, but some of the procedures during my hospitalization made me sterile." She shakes her head. "It's sad the way some mental institutions used to treat their patients. Actually some still do. There should be laws to protect patients."

"You mean there aren't?"

"Not very good ones. That's something that Jack and I are always lobbying for too." She laughs now. "We're considered pretty radical in some circles."

That should probably console me some, but it doesn't. My mind seems stuck on four specific things. One, there are dangerous procedures in mental institutions; two, there are no laws to protect mental patients; three, the Goldens are considered radical in some circles; and, four, they are childless, and Julie wishes she had children. I tell myself not to dwell on all these things, but no matter how you look at it, this all seems to add up to trouble for me. I glance toward the closest exit and tell myself to make a fast break.

"That's right," says Amelia, although I don't see her. The other voices chime in, telling me to run and that I deserve to die and that I'm worthless. I keep myself from putting my hands over my ears, but I'm not sure whether I speak or not.

"Are you okay?" I see Julie's lips moving to form these words, but I'm not sure whether I heard her or not. I do all I can to focus my attention back on her, but my head is pounding, and my ribs hurt, and I am suddenly very tired. I think the pain pill is making me sleepy, or maybe there really was something in my salad after all. Maybe she had planned the whole switching thing with the waiter.

"That's right," says Amelia as we're leaving the restaurant. "She's got you now, you stupid idiot. I don't even know why I waste my time with you."

I offer no resistance to either Amelia or Julie as I get back into the pretty car. It makes no difference. Whether it's Julie who destroys me or Amelia—what does it matter? I lean my head back and focus my attention on counting trees as Julie drives up the hill.

I try not to remember the last time I was on that hill. That icy night when Simon's car went spinning out of control. Control. I have no control.

God, help me! I'm not sure if it's a prayer or a curse or whether I have spoken it aloud or screamed it inside my head. But I think I hear that voice again.

I am with you always.

Julie slowly passes through the security gates, but instead of parking in the front as Simon did both times before, she continues around to the back. This worries me a bit. She parks and gets out, and finally I decide I might as well too.

"I came back here so I could show you the greenhouse first." She points to a large glass building ahead of us. "For some reason I think you might like it."

I'm glad I still have on my rubber boots as we trudge through the wet grass. I notice that her smooth leather boots are getting soaked, but she doesn't seem to mind. I guess when you're rich, these things don't trouble you so much.

"Here it is," she announces as she opens a door.

I walk in and am surprised at the warmth and humidity inside. I wonder if this is what a tropical island might be like. And the colors and the smells are unlike anything I've experienced before. I am stunned to see all sorts of blooming flowers—pink, yellow, purple, red, white. It's as if we've stepped out of gray January right into spring. The smell is almost intoxicating—a mixture of floral sweetness and earth and water, I think. I just walk around and stare at everything in wonder. There are lilies and tulips and orchids as well as all sorts of flowers that I don't even recognize. I feel as if I am in paradise. But I carefully keep my thoughts and feelings to myself. I still have a faint concern that this is all just a beautiful trap.

Julie walks me around and introduces me to several people who are working in here. Some look familiar, but their names go right through me. At the moment, I am more interested in plants than people. She shows me the water garden area where there is a large pond with flowering plants and colorful fish and a fountain that pours over a large sculpture of rocks.

Finally she shows me a section where they grow food for the kitchen. There are familiar things like tomatoes, lettuce, herbs, peppers, cucumbers, onions, and eggplants, as well as some tropical plants I've never seen before. My mother used to have a garden, but it wasn't nearly as amazing as this. She grew standard things like carrots and green beans, and then she would can them. My job was to weed the garden, but I was never allowed to choose what we grew or even to plant the seeds. Still, I've always had a secret fascination for gardens and dreamed of having one of my very own someday.

"Do you like it?" I can tell by Julie's bright smile that she's hoping for a positive response. And so far I've barely mumbled a few words.

"It's nice," I mutter.

"It was my own special project," she explains. "Growing things has been so therapeutic for me. It still is. I can't wait for spring when we can move a lot of these things outside. You should see the gardens then. Really beautiful."

I nod. "I'll bet."

"Ready for the rest of the tour?"

I shrug. I am not eager to go inside.

She takes my arm. "Don't worry, Alice. We have no intention of locking you up. I promise you are only here to look around."

And so we begin the tour. I must admit that this place is pretty impressive, if not convincing. Julie tells me that it took two years to complete the construction. "And the whole time I was so impatient," she says as she pets a dog that's just run up to greet us. "Now I realize that it's remarkable we finished it so quickly."

"Simon said that you inherited money to build it." I lean down and pat the head of the friendly dog. I think it's a yellow Lab, and he seems happy to meet me.

"Yes, it's no secret. Although it wasn't exactly an inheritance. No one has died yet. My family has always had lots of money, and I think my parents felt so bad about the years I was locked away that they wanted to make it up to me." She laughs, and I wonder why she thinks it is funny. "When they learned about Jack's dream to create a place like this, they offered to help."

"You allow pets here?" I ask.

"This is Simon's dog. His name is Peter. We're watching him while Simon's in the hospital. But you're right, we do have pets. Animals help people get better. We have three other dogs: Herman, Pinky, and Joyce. Then we have a couple of cockatiels that can actually talk. Several fish aquariums. Five cats. And various hamsters, mice, and gerbils. And I'm probably forgetting someone."

The first room we visit is an enormous kitchen and dining area. We are greeted by several people who seem to be working in here, but somehow it seems more like they're playing than working. I notice there's a lot of laughter, teasing, and tasting going on.

"Everyone helps out with the meals," says Julie, pausing to

sample a bite of cookie dough. "We have a roster, so everyone gets a turn."

Then we go down a hallway and peek into a music room where two men and a woman are playing piano, flute, and cello to a small audience. It's classical and sounds pretty good to me. I think I recognize a couple of the faces from the Christmas party but can't be sure. Then we go through an art room, where about a dozen people are working on all sorts of projects. I notice the heavyset dancer who cut in on me at the party—was his name Brad? He's working with a large lump of brown clay, creating something that looks like a grizzly bear.

Julie shows me the library with its walls and walls of books, a computer room where I recognize Maddie, the woman from the party, and a crafts room with sewing machines and big tables. The people in there are working on some sort of quilt. I think it's interesting that there are more men than women in that group.

Now we go up a flight of stairs, and Julie points out a couple of counseling rooms. They have windows, and I notice that Dr. Golden is talking to a young man in one room. And in the room next to this, I see a woman talking to a middle-aged man.

"These are the group session rooms," says Julie as she points to a couple of conference rooms. "We really believe in group therapy. It's one of our most effective tools toward healing."

Then she shows me where the "residents" live. There is a woman's floor and a men's floor. "We have full-time medical personnel on hand," she explains. "But if anyone has a real emergency, we have them transported to OHS. Fortunately, that's only happened a couple of times." She lets me peek into a room on the women's floor. It looks fairly typical, like a nice hotel room. "We have single and double rooms. We leave it up to the residents to decide. Some people enjoy the company of another, some don't."

I notice there is a phone, TV, and computer, and I wonder if these are for real or, like in furniture stores, just mock-ups. I ask about this.

"We want people to be completely comfortable here. These are optional. Some people want a phone or TV; some don't. The whole idea is to make this place as much like the outside world as possible. Well, perhaps with a little less stress." She laughs. "Not that there isn't any stress here. With this many people, you can't avoid an occasional conflict. But we consider them opportunities—learning experiences."

We then go down to the basement where I am shown an exercise room, weightroom, complete spa, sauna, indoor swimming pool, large home theater, and game room. And then we go up some stairs and down a hallway until we reach what appears to be a small chapel.

"This is one of my favorite places," she whispers from the doorway since several people are in there with bowed heads. "I come here a lot."

I peer in to see a large stained-glass window that portrays Jesus with some children. The people in the chapel seem to be sincere, and I'm thinking if this is all just a show, well, it's pretty amazing. But I am beginning to think that it's not. More and more I am beginning to suspect that this place is the real thing. Just as Simon said. A place of healing. And surprisingly, I haven't heard a peep out of Amelia since we got here. I hope she's so mad at me that she's left me for good. But I doubt this. I seriously doubt this.

I am quite apprehensive now, like I'm standing at the edge of a precipice, or maybe it's the bridge, and I am getting ready to leap. My heart is fluttering and pounding, and I think I might implode or explode or just totally lose it and make a complete fool of myself. But I am thinking, *If this is the real thing and if they really will let me come here, is it possible for me to hold on to this moment of clarity long enough to get myself officially booked in, signed up, whatever it is they do to seal the deal?* And suddenly I am terrified that something will go wrong—that just like the child pressing her nose up to the toyshop window as the shopkeeper pulls down the shade and turns off the lights, I, too, will not be allowed to enter. Dr. Golden will change his mind.

We're in the big room now, the one I helped to decorate for the Christmas party. Naturally, the decorations are all removed and put away, and everything looks just as it did when I first arrived that day. Except a number of people are milling about, sitting, talking. I guess there may be a dozen or more. Many of them wave to Julie, calling out greetings or invitations to join them in a game or conversation.

"So, what do you think?"

"I think it's fairly amazing," I say honestly.

"Not a hoax then?"

I shrug. "I don't really think so. But if it is a hoax, it's a good one."

She smiles. "Ready to go now?"

I look around once more. And that fear is clutching at my chest again. What if I mess up somehow? What if they decide I'm not good enough? Then I shake my head. "Not really. I'm not sure I want to go."

This makes her laugh. "Oh, I can't wait to tell Jack." She turns and grins at me. "*And* Simon!"

We go back through the kitchen now. The cookies are just coming out of the oven. Julie reaches over and snatches one, and the guy with the bright yellow oven mitts playfully slaps her hand.

"Don't you want one?" she asks me as she takes a big bite.

I look longingly at the chocolate chip cookies. *Of course I want one.* The question is, can I force my hand to reach out and pick one up? And if I do, can I make myself eat it?

"Aw, come on," says the guy in the oven mitts. He holds the plate of cookies in front of me, waving them back and forth temptingly. Finally, when I don't respond, he frowns and sets the plate back down on the big butcher-block island.

"Wait!" I say, grabbing for a cookie. "I *want* that."

This makes several of them chuckle. But not in a mean way. Almost like they know exactly how I feel, understand my inner struggles, my longing for some kind of normalcy. Then I wonder if I'm simply imagining this, wishing it to be true.

I glance around the spacious kitchen as I nibble my cookie, which is still warm and chewy. I study the varied faces as they go about their culinary chores. Most of them appear to be about my age. But I am confused to see how they appear to be so normal and healthy. And then I am suspicious. Perhaps they are just actors, pretending to be residents? It's possible.

Then I notice a guy who's peeling potatoes at the sink. Despite the fact that there are others around, he seems cut off or isolated somehow. He keeps glancing over his shoulder with this furtive expression. I can tell he's uncomfortable, or he doesn't trust the others, or maybe he's just watching his back. But he is clearly troubled about something. He reminds me of someone, and I think it's me. Somehow just seeing him like this gives me a faint glimmer of hope. Perhaps I would fit in here after all.

chapter THIRTY-FOUR

Another Golden Key

I know it sounds cliché, but I literally feel like a cat trapped on a hot tin roof as I stay with Faye in her cat house, waiting for my "appointment" with Dr. Golden. I pace and worry and can't seem to relax. I'm sure I even make the cats nervous, and I know Cheshire doesn't appreciate it. Naturally, Amelia has been coming around a lot, haunting and taunting and insulting me. I try to block her out with "self-talk," a tool that Julie explained to me. She told me to talk to myself but only saying things that are encouraging and kind and good and true.

"How am I supposed to know the difference between what's true and what isn't?" I asked her the day that she dropped me back here after my visit to the Golden Home.

"It's hard. Especially at first. But it helps to talk to others too. If you feel confused by the voices, just talk to Faye. I know she'll understand." Then she handed me a Walkman and a small case of CDs. "Try to avoid being alone too much, Alice. That's not good. And don't allow yourself to have long periods of silence."

"Silence?" I rolled my eyes. "I wish."

"Yeah, I know. But try listening to these CDs. That'll help. Some are soothing music, and some are positive thinking exercises. Hang in there. It won't be long now."

Even so, I am still afraid that I will blow it when I go in to see Dr. Golden. Or that I'll mess up before I even get the chance to go in. I'm afraid I'll give in to the voices, the threats, the pressure, and hit the road before I can get help. But at least I am finally willing to admit I need help. When I spoke to Simon on the phone, he said that's the first step. And I can admit that, at least for the moment. And I still believe that the Golden Home is legitimate. Or so I keep telling myself—more self-talk. But who knows what I'll believe by tomorrow? It's unsettling.

It's been three days since I went to visit. Three very long days. My mother came to visit yesterday. She said it was to drop off some of my things, but I could tell by her eyes that she's still very worried about me, and I'm sure she was just using this as an excuse to check on me. I don't know if I reassured her or not, but I did my best to appear confident that everything was going to be okey-dokey. Perhaps I shall become an actress someday. It seems I get a lot of practice pretending to be what I am not.

My mother told me that her new church has a prayer chain, and they are praying for me. I thanked her for this, but quite honestly, I'm not sure if that makes me feel better or worse. I am still trying to realign my thinking in regard to religion. Trying to separate God from the negative church experiences of my childhood. But it is so difficult to differentiate. And sometimes I think my poor little brain is going to explode. I usually put in one of Julie's CDs about that time. I wish I were able to think about these things more clearly, but everything gets so meshed together in my brain. I suffer from Vege-matic of the mind; my thoughts and beliefs get chopped and whirled and puréed until they're a pile of mush that makes absolutely no sense.

But at least I've stayed on speaking terms with God. I even talk to him when I'm angry, which seems to be a lot lately. Faye says that's okay. She says he likes us to be honest and open with him. I hope she's right because sometimes I am pretty certain he's going to shoot down a lightning bolt and zap me right off the face of the planet. This hasn't happened yet, although we did have a pretty good thun-derstorm last night, and I wondered if God was trying to tell me something. I'd feel terrible for Faye and the cats if he actually destroyed her house. I even considered leaving, but Faye enticed me to have cocoa, so I stayed.

Even though I've tried to be honest with God—and what is hon-esty anyway?—I still haven't mentioned anything about my baby to him. For one thing, I don't want to appear ungrateful, and besides that, it might be considered a lack of faith on my part. What if I am his chosen one but I wimp out on him? How would that make him feel? What would it do to his plans? Sure there are times when I am fairly certain that this whole pregnancy thing is just another trick of my imagination. But even then I'm not sure. Naturally, Amelia still tells me it's not. But I've really been trying to ignore her.

Today is the day that I get my "interview" with Dr. Golden. I am so nervous I couldn't even eat breakfast. I feel like I'm applying for a job, only it's not just a job, it's my whole life. I am so worried that I will say or do the wrong thing or offend Dr. Golden or freak out and run. I try not to remember all the stupid things I said to him the night of the Christmas party or in the hospital. I wonder if he's forgotten them yet.

Julie is trying to be helpful. She even offered to pick me up and take me there. Just the idea of this made me uneasy. Instead, I have hired a taxi with some of the money my mom gave Faye for me. (I'm sure Mom thinks I'm too irresponsible to have my own money right now.) Just the same, this gives me some control over my situation, but even that scares me. If I have control, I might tell the driver to stop in the middle of town and drop me off on a corner. Or on top of the bridge, where I will leap out of the taxi, scale the guardrail, and then jump. Or I could chicken out altogether. So I crank up my Walkman as Miguel Hernando drives through the city traffic. I was careful to read his ID on the dash when I got in, just in case he was a fraud. But I don't think he is. The CD I'm listening to is about positive thinking, and I'm surprised I don't have it memorized by now. For all I know, I'm probably answering the questions out loud, but Miguel doesn't seem to mind. I'm guessing he's used to driving kooks around in his taxi. He probably figures it's safer that crazy people don't drive their own cars anyway.

We're passing through the security gates now, and I remove my headphones, coil up the wires, and tuck the Walkman into my new backpack. This is what Aaron got me for Christmas. I wonder if it was my mom's suggestion since I am pretty certain she disposed of my old one. But what did she do with the journals and the secrets they contained? I still think about this from time to time, but I've been afraid to ask her. Afraid it will worry her that I still care about such things. But I do. I still think some of the words I wrote have important messages—things I didn't completely understand at the time but things I may still need to know about.

The taxi stops at the big front doors, and Miguel tells me how much I owe him. I take what I think is the right amount of money from my jacket pocket, although I'm afraid I'm confused. I hand the wad of bills to him, then immediately suspect I've given him too much. I wonder if I should wait for him to give me change or just let him keep it. Are you supposed to tip taxi drivers? This is all so foreign to me. Finally I decide to just get out and let it go. It's only money.

I walk up to the big double doors, push one open, and step into the foyer. No uniforms, nurses, orderlies, or stained lab coats to meet me. Dr. Golden's secretary told me just to go up the stairs and right to his office, but even so, I feel like an intruder. I think I need someone to sign me in and take me by the hand. I hear voices in the big front room, but no one comes to help me. So I walk up the stairs, counting each step as I go. I find that counting is a good way to keep my mind occupied sometimes. But I need to be careful about this. I don't want to turn into one of those freaks who can't stop counting lampposts, parking meters, whatever happens to come in multiples. I remember this homeless man downtown who everyone calls "the CPA" and how he counts everything he sees. Once I heard him on 7,435. He was counting sidewalk cracks. I felt sorry for him at first, but then I realized there are worse problems.

I see the door to Dr. Golden's office. I wonder if I'm supposed to knock or just walk right in. I know that he has a secretary, since she's the one who called me. But I'm not sure which door leads to her office. Finally I knock on Dr. Golden's door, peeking through the window as I do. He is on the phone, but he waves me in anyway. I slink in and sit down in the chair he points out to me. I glance around the paneled room with lots of full bookshelves and observe that there is no leather couch anywhere in sight. I'm not sure whether to be relieved or disappointed.

"That sounds just great," he's saying into the receiver. "I'm looking forward to it, Hal. Thanks for everything." Then he hangs up the phone and smiles at me. "How's it going, Alice?"

"Okay." Already I'm second-guessing my answer. Should I have said "not so good"? Or put on a positive front and said "great"? Or simply have been honest and told him I'm really scared? Which is the right answer? At least I didn't say "fine."

He starts going over what sound like fairly typical questions. Personal perhaps, but then he is a doctor. He asks me things about family history, relationships, general health, and then the hardest question, When did I first begin experiencing my symptoms?

"You mean the actual voices and things like that?" I ask, hoping for clarification. Or perhaps I'm just stalling.

"Yes, voices, feelings, smells, hallucinations…or just anything that you might consider out of the ordinary. The first events that began to lead you away from your normal life."

I frown. "The truth is, I've never considered myself to be all that normal. I mean, how would I know what normal is? But even as a kid I thought something was weird about me. It's like my imagination would take over sometimes. And then I was always uncomfortable around people—kind of anxious, you know?"

I see that he's making notes, and this worries me a bit. I'm afraid

I am saying too much or all the wrong things. "It's not that I was neurotic exactly," I say quickly. "Just different. Sort of. I don't think I fit in very well."

He smiles now. "Don't worry, Alice. There are no right or wrong answers here. I just want to get to know you better so I can help you through this."

"Does this mean I'm getting in?"

He looks up and smiles. "Yes. Of course. Didn't you know that?"

"Not for sure. I thought today was kind of like a test."

He chuckles and sets down his pen. "No. It's just some preliminary stuff. I've got most of your medical records already, and even some of your charts from Forest Hills, but I wanted to hear your own perceptions. That really means more to me than the observations of others."

He's going over some papers now. "Usually I require a physical for all new residents, but Dr. Spangler at OHS has provided me with everything I need for now." He peers at a yellow paper in the pile.

Suddenly I am uneasy. I wonder if Dr. Spangler wrote down the part about me missing my period. Does Dr. Golden believe that I'm pregnant?

"Of course, you little imbecile!"

Surprised, I look to my left to see Amelia sitting on a side table, one blue-jean leg crossed over the other with her cowboy boot swinging back and forth. "Why do you think he's so interested in you?"

Panic rises inside me, like a cold reptilian creature crawling from my stomach to my throat. I try to take a deep breath, one of the relaxing techniques I've been trying to use, but it's not working, so I begin to fidget in my chair. Suddenly the room is hot and stuffy, and

I am desperate to get out of here. I imagine myself bursting from this office, running down the stairs, out the door, and down the driveway to the gates. Would they let me out? I wonder if this might be a good test. Find out if what they've been telling me is really true.

"Alice?"

I look up and suspect by his expression that he's been talking and I've been lost in my own mind again. "Yes?" I sit up straighter, at attention.

"Are you feeling uncomfortable?"

"No."

He smiles. "I don't think you're being honest."

"Okay, I *am* feeling uncomfortable. I think I want to go now."

"That's a good girl, Alice," urges Amelia. "Stand up and leave—before it's too late!"

"No one is stopping you." He leans back in his chair and waits.

"Are we done?"

"If you're done, then I'm done. I don't want to keep you here against your will, Alice. But I do need to know something."

I am afraid he's going to ask me about the pregnancy thing. I look down at my backpack and try to think of a good answer.

"I need to know if you really want to join us here, Alice. Do you really want to work on getting well?"

I look up.

"Because it takes real self-discipline to get better. Are you willing to give this your full effort?"

I swallow, then nod. "Yes. I really do want to get well."

"Don't be a fool, Alice!" screams Amelia. "Don't fall for his lies!"

I close my eyes and try to block her words.

"Is there anything else you'd like to tell me?"

With my eyes still closed, I press my lips together and firmly shake my head. Then I stop. I know I must tell the truth. I open my eyes and speak. "Just one thing, Dr. Golden."

"Go ahead."

"Well, I'm not sure. Sometimes I don't even think I am. But then so many things are so confusing, how can I know for sure..." I look intently at him, then blurt, "Do you think I could be pregnant?"

He studies me for a moment. "What do you think?"

"Okay, I know this might sound crazy. But then what do you expect from a..." I try to laugh, but it probably sounds more like a weak cackle. "I mean I haven't *done* anything, you know, that could make me get pregnant. But I keep thinking that perhaps God might've, well, somehow might've *made* me pregnant." I shake my head. "That does sound crazy, doesn't it?"

He leans forward. "Would it surprise you if I told you that you're not the first woman who's come in here and said something just like that?"

"Really?"

"I don't want to make you feel insignificant, Alice, but imagining that you've been chosen by God for some sort of immaculate conception is not all that unusual with schizophrenia."

"It's not?" Although I'm relieved, I still find this hard to believe.

"I'd estimate I've worked with at least twenty women who believed that exact same thing. Maybe even more."

"You're kidding."

"No. For some reason we get a lot of religious connections in schizophrenia. Probably half the residents here have had some sort of a religious experience. We've had quite a few who believed they were the Antichrist, many who thought they were prophets—"

"I thought I was a prophet."

He nods. "You're going to find that it's not really so mysterious once you start to understand the condition better. You begin to see there are patterns and reasons for certain types of experiences. And the more you know about schizophrenia, the easier it is to deal with it. Of course, there's still so much we don't know. But we've really made some good progress in the past couple of decades."

I sigh. "So I'm probably not carrying God's baby."

He shakes his head. "You can have a pregnancy test if you like."

I shrug.

He glances at the papers again. "Dr. Spangler notes here that you're underweight and malnourished. Probably the reason you've missed your periods."

"I started eating again after I went to live with Faye," I explain. "But I guess I hadn't been eating too well before that."

He nods. "That's not unusual either. Many of our residents have dealt with the fear that their food has been tampered with or poisoned. That's why we get you immediately involved in the nutrition program here. One thing you'll hear a lot around here is that *knowledge is freedom.*"

"Yes, I've already been listening to some CDs."

"Good for you." He closes the folder now. "So when do you want to check in?"

I take in a sharp breath. "Now?"

He smiles. "Are you worried that you're going to freak out on us and run off if you don't do this today?"

"Sort of."

"Again, I don't mean to make it sound as if you're not unique, but that's pretty typical too." He writes something down. "You can move in whenever you like. Your room is all ready for you. It's a private room. But you can have a roommate if you like. We have a woman who's been sharing a room but is open to switching to a private room."

"What do you think is best?"

"It's hard to say. Some people feel they can relax better on their own. It's easier because they're not so concerned about what's going on with the other person. Some find a comfort in the companionship. I'm guessing you've led a more solitary life. You might prefer the private room to start with."

"Yeah. I think so."

"My secretary, Candice, will help get you set up. Then once you're settled, you can meet with Julie to arrange your schedule. We have classes and group therapy and counseling sessions. Well, it's all in the packet."

I thank him, and I think I really mean it. Then I go and speak to his secretary. She's an older, gray-haired woman with a kind smile.

"Oh, you're Simon's friend, aren't you?" she says as she hands me a packet and a notebook.

I nod.

"I remember you from the Christmas party. How is Simon doing?"

"I haven't been over to visit for a couple of days, but the last time I saw him he'd just gotten out of traction and was able to use a wheelchair. He thinks he'll be walking with a cane in another week."

"Oh good. We miss him around here."

Candice takes me down to see my room. It's painted a buttery yellow and faces the south side where the sun washes across the wooden floor in a puddle of gold. "It's lovely," I tell her. "I wish I could move in right now."

"No reason you can't." She hands me the key. "It's all yours, Alice."

I stare at the brass key in my hand and realize that I've just been given the golden key. Only this one is for real.

Candice leaves, and I remain in the room. It seems too good to be true, but I keep telling myself that it is. Even so I am hearing the voices again. They are yelling obscenities, and Amelia is telling me that I've been duped again.

"You are stupid and useless and sinful!" she shrieks. "Not to mention completely deluded. You think these people are going to help you? Ha! Don't you realize that you don't deserve to be helped, you spineless wimp!"

"God loves me," I say aloud, practicing my self-talk. "These people are good. They're going to help my life to get better—"

"It's all a trick, you ignorant fool," she shouts. "Your life will never get better. Never!" Then she lowers her voice, "Get away from here while you can, Alice, before they start doping you up again. Don't be an idiot!"

"No," I tell her. "You are wrong. I am going to get better. You're a big fat liar, Amelia."

Then just to prove to her, or maybe to prove to myself, I pick up the phone in my room—and to my pleased surprise it really works— and I call for a taxi and wait in the foyer until it comes. Then I climb in and actually smirk as the taxi passes through the security gates without the slightest glitch. Now if only I can get back in as easily.

chapter THIRTY-FIVE

My Own Invention

I am barely out of sight of Golden Home when I begin to feel that something is very wrong. My heart begins to pound, and I cannot breathe. Suddenly I'm certain that I'm making a huge mistake. I remember incidents from my stay at Forest Hills—some incidents I had completely blocked out. As various scenes flash through my memory, I am certain that these strange things actually happened, and now I am horrified that the whole nightmare will begin again at Golden Home. Oh, why am I so gullible?

Amelia is in the backseat of the taxi with me, reinforcing all my fears and contributing her own recollections. I know I should pull out the CD player and listen to the recordings on positive thinking, but I am paralyzed.

I want to leap from the taxi, certain that this driver is in on the whole thing, but instead I lean over the seat and tell him to drop me at the hospital. I think my voice sounds calm, but I might be screaming. It's hard to tell. I know that I'm screaming on the inside.

I *must* see Simon. For whatever reason—maybe it's still the safety of his temporary disability—but somehow I believe I can trust him.

I may be delusional, but I want to talk to him about my concerns, or rather my unspeakable terrors. I hope he can straighten me out.

Yet even as I walk up to the hospital entrance, Amelia shrieks at me. "What are you doing, you little fool?"

I tell her, "Shut up!" as I walk through the doorway, but she continues harping at me during the entire ride up the elevator.

"You're such a pitiful sucker, Alice. Don't you know that Simon is part of their little scheme? You should understand by now that they are all against you. You stupid imbecile! You'll never learn!"

I try to cover my ears and block out her words, but it's useless. Several others glance my way in the elevator. I try not to look at them, even though I think the woman in the leopard-print coat is asking me if I'm okay, but I ignore her. I feel that her coat is really a large leopard in the process of devouring her and will come after me next, but I rush from the elevator before it has the chance. With pulse pounding, I hurry to Simon's room. He's not there.

I fall across his bed and sob, unsure what to do now. My reserves are empty, and I have nowhere to turn. More and more I have been convincing myself that Amelia is my enemy, but she is so persistent and controlling—and sometimes she really seems to care. Oh, what am I thinking? I know that she hates me, wants to destroy me. And what about the others? They're even worse. Oh, why won't they leave me alone? If I could run and run, I might possibly escape them, but when could I stop? My chest feels as if it will burst. I wonder if I'm having a heart attack.

"Alice?"

I stand up to see Simon in a wheelchair, rolling himself into his room, the cast on his leg sticking out like a prow in front of him. I am totally surprised to see him. I honestly thought he was gone for good. Suddenly I feel silly for my theatrics. What is wrong with me? I try to wipe away the tears and regain some sense of decorum, although it seems quite hopeless.

"What's wrong, Alice?" He wheels closer and reaches for my hand.

"I don't know." I shake my head. "I think it's…it's just me…and my hallucinations…running away with me."

He sort of laughs and then gives my hand a warm squeeze. "Have you had your interview with Dr. Golden yet?"

I nod.

"And you're still planning to move up there?"

I sigh.

He pats the chair next to him. "Alice, I want you to sit down, take a deep breath, and just try to relax."

I attempt to follow his instructions as I ease myself into the padded chair.

"You need to know it's no big deal that you're feeling this sort of apprehension. Really, it's perfectly normal."

"*Normal?*" I glare at him now. "Nothing about me is normal."

"You know what I mean, Alice." He sighs and looks down at his leg, then sadly shakes his head. "Who's *really* normal anyway?"

I study him more closely and realize that he seems a bit somber. I wonder if something has been going on, and it bothers me that I may have overlooked this before. I am so neurotically self-centered. "How are *you* feeling, Simon?" I ask.

"I'm feeling like I can understand why certain situations can drive a person, even a relatively *normal* person, stark raving mad."

"What do you mean?"

"I mean being trapped in this hospital, stuck in these stupid casts, unable to do much of anything for myself. Then you layer on all the noises, being awakened over and over throughout the night. Dr. Golden always says that it's possible to drive anyone over the edge if you use the right recipe. I think I know what he's talking about now."

I am sorry for him, and for some reason this makes me feel better. I realize how I have become completely unaccustomed to feeling empathy for someone else during these past months. "I'm sorry, Simon." I squeeze his hand. "Sometimes I think I'm the only one with problems."

He smiles now. "Yeah, I guess that's just part of the human condition. We tend to think our own troubles are always the worst."

"I hate to admit it, but I think maybe I do need some sort of medication." My unexpected confession surprises me.

He nods. "I know. But not like what you were given at Forest Hills."

"No, I don't want anything like that. But maybe just enough to calm things down a bit, you know what I mean?" I shudder to think of how close I am to the edge at this moment.

"Yeah, I know exactly what you mean. So what are you going to do right now, Alice?"

"I'm not sure. I thought I was going back to Faye's to get my stuff. I thought I might even pay for the taxi to bring her back with me to visit you again before I checked myself in."

"That sounds like a good plan."

"Yeah, but what if I freak again?" I press my lips together, trying to suppress the anxiety that is clawing just below the surface. Oh sure, the voices are quieter right now, but they could erupt with wild screaming and yelling at any moment.

"Hey, why don't we call Faye and invite her to come over here? Maybe she could bring your stuff with her. We can all visit a while, maybe have some lunch down in the cafeteria. Then you can go back to the Goldens' afterward."

And so it is done. Simon calls his aunt, and within the hour she arrives, and we all visit a bit, have some bland cafeteria food, and behave almost like normal people. She even offers to ride in the taxi with me back up to the Goldens'. At first I almost refuse, but then I think it might be nice to have her there, to sort of hold my hand. I guess I'm not above needing someone to hold my hand from time to time.

Faye thinks my room is absolutely wonderful. She goes around and carefully examines everything, making comments like, "Such soft towels…and sweet-smelling lavender soap…a pretty view… lovely bedspread." Things I hadn't even noticed before.

Then someone knocks on my door. I jump at the sound, then look at Faye for direction. She nods to me to go ahead and open it, so I do, and there stands Julie holding a basket filled with goodies.

"Welcome," she says with a big smile.

She hands me the lovely basket, and I just stare at it in wonder.

"Everyone gets a welcome basket," she tells me. "I'm the official welcome person today, but the basket was put together by a number of the residents. I already took a peek, and it looks quite nice."

I nod and set the basket by the window.

"Simon called Dr. Golden a bit ago," she continues. "He said you thought you might need some meds."

Suddenly I'm not so sure about this idea anymore. When I mentioned meds to Simon, I felt so unsettled, but I feel a little better now.

"Well, don't worry about it, Alice." She hands me a small amber bottle. "No one will force you to take anything here. Just so you know, Dr. Golden had already decided to recommend that you try a low dosage of this new antipsychotic. It has very few side effects and is really quite helpful. Honestly, though, it's up to you."

I look at the plastic bottle and sigh. "I'm just not sure."

"They're not magic pills, Alice, but they might help you gain some control and suppress those hallucinations. And combined with everything else, they might increase your ability to manage your thoughts better. Dr. Golden believes that the path to healing is found when *you* take that kind of control over your life. You do understand that, don't you?"

I nod slowly. "Yeah, I think it's starting to sink in."

"Good." She pats me on the shoulder. "It's always roughest right at the beginning."

Faye comes over now and puts an arm around my waist. "You're in such good hands, dear. I won't be the least bit worried about you." She turns to Julie now. "What about her cat, Julie? Can she have little Cheshire here with her?"

"Of course. All we ask is that residents take full responsibility for their pets' behaviors and needs, but we've got a number of cats that do just fine."

Faye smiles. "Oh good. Cats are such a comfort. I have a cat carrying case. I'll bring him up here tomorrow—and some kitty litter things." She looks at me. "Will that be all right, dear?"

"That'd be great." I look at the bottle of pills again, then back to Julie. I have made up my mind. "Should I take one of these right now?"

"It's up to you, Alice. Read the instructions first. I think you need to have a little food in your tummy with those."

"We just ate lunch a little while ago," says Faye hopefully.

"Okay." I nod my head firmly. "I am going to do this. I want to get better." Mostly I'm thinking I don't want to hear Amelia or the others ragging at me anymore. It has just occurred to me that the voices of people like Faye and Julie and Simon are much preferable to Amelia and her bossy cohorts. I wonder how I have been so deluded, but the fact is, I was. I am. And any form of denial won't help me get better. I already know this from listening to one of my CDs.

So I take my pill, and both women seem pleased for me. Then Faye announces that she should go, so I hug her good-bye and thank her, once again, for everything. She promises to return tomorrow with Cheshire, and Julie mentions she has a few people interested in knitting classes again.

"I'd like to learn to knit too," I say.

"And so you shall." Faye nods. "You can make Cheshire a sweater. I think he would look splendid in blue."

Now they are both gone, and I am alone in my new room, playing a classical CD and putting my clothes into the drawers and closet. I really don't have much to put away, but I am taking my time and doing a careful job. Waves of anxiety flood me, that old feeling that I've made a huge mistake. Amelia peers out from the bathroom, haunting me with her sharp words of criticism.

Julie explained that it will take a while before the meds begin to kick in—from a few days to a couple of weeks. I'm determined to continue taking them unless I begin to feel like I felt at Forest Hills—dead and zombie-like. Then I will stop immediately. But it is a consolation that I am the one making the choice here. It's good to have this kind of control. It feels right. Maybe Dr. Golden really knows his stuff after all.

Julie said that I'm not expected to help out on my first day here but that she will have a schedule for me by dinnertime. "We like to keep you busy," she said with a wink. I think that sounds wise since I really don't need too much time on my hands. I don't want to dwell on things.

Finally there is nothing left to do in my room, and I tell myself to go out to the common area and make some sort of an attempt at being "social." But I must admit the mere idea of this new step frightens me beyond words. I just know I will say or do something totally stupid, and I am so inferior, like I'm a crazy person among a bunch who are already well on the road to recovery. I tell myself this probably isn't the case, and I remember the guy peeling potatoes in the kitchen, yet I am not convinced. Finally I force myself to leave my room. I lock the door, slip the golden key into my pocket, put one foot in front of the other, and walk toward the big room.

I sit in an armchair next to a window and just look out over the grounds. The view is so peaceful and pretty with grass and trees and a long pond that meanders around the property. I even spy a few large orange-colored fish swimming happily along. I wonder what it would be like to be as carefree as a fish.

It's not long before a young woman, about my age, comes over and leans against the chair next to me.

"New here?" she asks.

I nod and swallow.

"Scared?"

Somehow I manage to say yes.

"Yeah, so was I at first. But believe me, you'll get over it." She sticks out her hand. "I'm Margot."

"Alice."

"Nice to meet you." Then she glances outside and back at me. "You smoke, Alice?"

I shake my head no.

"*Really?* Almost everyone smokes—at least when they first get here—but the Goldens only let us smoke outside." She acts as though she's shivering. "And it's so blasted cold out there."

"Guess that might make it easier to quit."

"Nah. I'm not quitting. A few do, but I'll bet they go straight back to it once they're out of here and on their own again."

"Why?"

"I don't know really, but I read somewhere that something like ninety percent of people with schizophrenia are smokers."

"Seriously?"

"Yeah. Weird, huh? You must be in that lucky ten percentile."

"I guess." I'm thinking I should be thankful for small favors.

"Well, I think I'll go out for a smoke. You wanna come along?"

I decide to join her. Not that I want to take up smoking, but she seems nice—or at least friendly. We walk around the gardens and along the pond, and mostly she talks. She tells me she's been here for a month and plans to stay for another. She says that despite her "attitude," it has helped her a lot.

"I'm not, like, totally well," she tells me as she blows out a puff of smoke. "But I'm way better than I used to be. I feel like I can actually return to my job now."

"What do you do?"

"I'm a chef." She stands up straighter, as if merely saying this gives her a sense of pride or purpose.

"That's cool. Have you done a lot of cooking here?"

"Yeah, I've been teaching some cooking classes too." She takes a long drag.

"Maybe I'll learn to cook while I'm here. I'm pretty hopeless in the kitchen."

"Yeah, and watch out. When Julie finds out whatever you're good at, she'll really put you to work too."

I shake my head. "Well, I'm not really good at much of anything."

Margot laughs. "Then she'll probably help you find something totally new that you didn't even know you were good at. She's just like that."

"But you *do* like Julie, right?" I am a little worried now. Margot's cynical attitude is hard to read.

"Oh yeah." Then she snuffs out her cigarette. "But to be honest, I couldn't stand her at first. She reminded me of my mom, and I thought she was acting superior. But after a while I decided I was totally wrong. I think I've been wrong about a lot of things."

We head back inside, and Margot announces that she needs to go help in the kitchen. I am glad to stand by the fireplace and warm up a bit. I consider what Margot said about being wrong and hope that I've been wrong too. Not about this place, but about believing Amelia and the others. The more I think about it, the more I believe that they have been entirely my own invention and not real. Not that this is new to me. I think parts of me have known this all along. But the problem was my inability to distinguish. I still can't. I guess that just comes with the whole crazy territory. And I suppose it's true that it is all in your head. But even so, it doesn't make it any less real.

After I am warm, I decide to find the little chapel. I head in what I think is the right direction and, surprisingly, walk straight to it. No one is there, and I slip in and sit somewhere near the middle. I bow my head and just sit there for a bit, thinking I should be praying. Isn't that what people do in a chapel?

But I am distracted with uncomfortable memories of my previous experiences in a church sanctuary. I hear Pastor John's raised voice and see his brow furrowing deeper and deeper as he chastises his listeners about *sin*. I hear his fist pounding on the pulpit, and I cower down in my seat, wishing I could just disappear in a puff of sinful smoke.

I tell myself that this chapel is different and that Pastor John is not here, but I'm still not sure what to do with myself right now. I think that something must be expected of me, and yet I know I am unable to do it. My life is a shambles, and I have nothing to give.

Finally I look up and see the stained-glass window in front. I study Jesus and the children, and I read the words inscribed below: "Unless you become as a little child, you will never enter the Kingdom of Heaven."

It sounds so simple, and yet it's so foreign to all that I learned as a child. As a child I was taught that I needed to "grow up" and "become mature" and "do good works" and "be a disciple" and most of all "to sin not." That was always the hardest part because it seemed like everything I naturally wanted to do was considered sinful.

So trying to grasp something like this—that it's not only good to *be* a child, but that it might actually be required—is fairly confusing to me. I'd like to believe in something that sounds this simple and good, but it goes against everything in me. Or almost.

Once again I try to pray. Now I am unable to form any actual words in my head. I tell myself that it's just talking to God, like I've been doing the past few weeks. But something about being in a church setting brings back all the old prayers that I learned as a child. It's as if all these prayer words are mixed up together—like every one is a piece of a jigsaw puzzle that's been shaken in a box.

So I just sit here and wonder what I am supposed to do. Surely I should *do* something. I become anxious again, then remember the CD that instructs on the practice of controlled breathing—an exercise that's supposed to reduce anxiety. I take myself through the steps, inhaling slowly, deeply, filling my lungs to capacity, then slowly exhaling, emptying all the stale air out. I do this again and again. And as the recording suggests, I imagine that I am breathing in God's truth and God's love. I imagine they are becoming a part of me and that I am exhaling old lies and confusion, blowing them away from me.

I continue this exercise, feeling more and more relaxed. And it's not long before a strange sensation begins to wash over me. Warm and unexpected, it's unlike anything I've ever felt before, and yet familiar somehow, like something I experienced without really knowing it. Yet how can that be?

Then it occurs to me; I am experiencing *peace*. A quiet yet substantial peace. And I believe it's coming from God. Part of me wants to grab hold of it and cling tightly, but I have a feeling it will vanish like a vapor if I do. And so I just sit there and breathe it in, hoping it will simply become a part of me.

I sit there for a long while, as if I'm on the edge. But it's not the bad sort of edge where I'm afraid I will fall or leap to my demise. This is the edge of something new and good. It's a beginning, a door, an entrance. I want to walk through it, but I'm not sure I can. Already I hear the voices again, mumbling and grumbling as they threaten and scold me, warning me to avoid this dangerous passageway at all costs.

When Alice stepped through the looking glass into a different world, it turned out to be a twisted and crazy world, not unlike the place I have wandered these last few months. If only I could pass through this new entrance, I believe I would find myself in a better place where life makes sense. For the first time I sense a wave of real hope washing over me, and I want to hold on to it, savor it, even if only to remember this moment. I slowly inhale and exhale—breathing in the good clean air of change, blowing away the bad smog of my disease. A small sense of control returns to me. And it feels good.

Then I hear a bell and suspect it is for dinnertime. I slowly rise to my feet, reluctant to leave. But as I stand, I tell myself that even if this feeling, this experience, is gone in the next instant, *I will remember what it felt like.* And perhaps more important, I will expect to experience it again.

chapter THIRTY-SIX

Waking

A full month has passed since I entered the Golden Home. It hasn't all been easy and wonderful, but I will never regret coming here. Never. As Dr. Golden likes to remind us, we have to work out our sanity as much as we have to work out our salvation. For the first time, I believe the two go hand in hand.

I've found the greenhouse to be my favorite place. Sometimes I think I could live in there. Maybe it's all the oxygen the plants put out, but I always feel more alive and energized after spending time among the green growing things. I love the smell of fresh dirt and have become especially attached to the orchids. They're so strange and mysterious, so fragile and delicate, yet it seems to take so little to keep them alive—as long as you keep their environment perfectly balanced.

Margot says it's like making bread, which I've been learning to do this week.

"You need the right balance of flour, water, sugar, and yeast," she explained as she watched me sift the flour. "Remove or mess up any one of these vital ingredients, and the bread ceases to be bread."

I nodded, remembering the pasty glop I had thrown out the previous day.

"It's quite philosophical, really," she continued in a serious tone. "Don't you think?"

I considered this as I carefully measured the salt. "I guess so."

"It's like our lives. When one part of us, like our body or mind or spirit, isn't right, it knocks us completely out of whack."

I eyed my yeast-and-water solution, worried that I might've gotten the water too hot, and I know this can ruin the yeast and consequently spoil the bread. "You're right," I told her. "It's all about balance, isn't it?"

"That's right." Margot looked at my yeast mixture and smiled with satisfaction. "Mess up your ingredients, and you cease to be who you were meant to be."

As it turned out, the water wasn't too hot, and my bread came out just fine. Now if only I can keep my life ingredients as well balanced. I feel more hopeful with each passing day.

It took more than two weeks for Amelia and the others finally to depart from my life. For the most part I think they are gone, although I can sometimes still hear them nattering away in the back of my mind—especially if I am overly tired or stressed. But I try to tune them out. I am still taking the meds, but Dr. Golden says I probably won't need to take them indefinitely. However, I am not so sure, and the idea of quitting frightens me. I don't want to go back to my "old ways." It's ironic, considering how opposed I was to medication at one point. Now I fully appreciate that it's more important to function than to fret over taking a little pill each day. The only side effect I've experienced is a little dry mouth. Small price when you consider the large picture.

Medication is one of the many areas where Dr. Golden departs from some of the "old school" psychiatrists who still believe that "once on meds, always on meds." He is quick to admit that a few of his patients are still on meds and may always be, but he and his staff continue to monitor them carefully, and he stays up to date on the latest advancements in medications.

"I never give up hope, and neither should any of you," he says fairly regularly. "The science of medicine is constantly changing. We must all be willing to change with it."

Dr. Golden makes it clear he's not afraid to try new methods, but his greatest interest is in therapy. Most of all, he wants what's best for his patients, and he wants his patients to be actively involved in their treatment and healing. "You're in control," he's always telling us. "It's your life. How do you want to live it?"

Regaining control over my life has probably been more healing to me than almost anything. Or at least an important first step. I remember how helpless I felt at Forest Hills. I felt like a complete victim, totally at their mercy. I had no control over anything. I couldn't even use the bathroom without permission. This only reinforced my belief that everyone there was plotting against me. It's no wonder so many institutionalized patients grow paranoid. Who wouldn't under those circumstances? I love knowing that I can walk out of here anytime I please. The funny thing is, other than visiting Simon in the hospital during the first couple of weeks, I rarely want to go anywhere now, but at least I know I can. I don't understand why medical professionals would think that removing a patient's right to think and choose would help that person to get healthy again. It certainly didn't help me a bit.

I'm so thankful that I found Golden Home and wish that everyone experiencing schizophrenia could come here. I realize it's nothing less than a miracle that I got to come. And as I look back on the string of events that led me here, I've come to believe that God was watching out for me the whole time. Oh I'm sure there are those who wouldn't agree with me, especially during the hard times when I was on the streets. I'm sure they would think I was in great danger, and maybe I was, but I can't help but think something or someone was protecting me.

Naturally, my mother claims this has to do with the prayer chain in her new church. And I have no reason to doubt her, although I think there's more to it than that. Just the same, I do appreciate those little old ladies taking the time out of their day to pray for me. My mother continues to be involved in her new church, and she seems to be getting stronger all the time. I derive this from her letters since she's only been to Golden Home once, but that has more to do with me than her.

At first I was excited that she was coming to visit. I'd been here about two weeks and felt eager to show her my progress and take her on a full tour of this amazing place. But shortly after her arrival, I realized that I wasn't quite ready to be around her yet. Like it or not, I guess my mother and I have a history that will take some time to heal. It's not that I blame her for my childhood, exactly, but I think a lot of her decisions, particularly in relation to the church, affected my life in some negative ways. She's a good-hearted woman, and as much as I love her, I realize that some of her attitudes aren't conducive to my recovery. And, as Dr. Golden says, my recovery is my top priority, and I must take responsibility for anything that's not helping. My mother was *not* helping. Whether she can see it or not, I think she's still affected by her church-controlled past. Or maybe I'm just overly sensitive.

After I finished giving her the tour, she got this funny expression and said, "Goodness, this place is certainly into New Age."

The way she said "New Age" sounded like it was a contagious disease. "What do you mean?" I asked her.

"Well, all this focus on art and music and growing things…" Her brows lifted as she shrugged. "I just expected there would be more Bible studies and such."

"Dr. Golden has a Bible study group," I said defensively. "And Julie has a prayer group." Even as I spoke these words, I wished I hadn't. Not that those things aren't important, but they are just one piece of the package.

She nodded and smiled. "Well, that's something then, isn't it?"

Her tone sounded condescending, and I didn't feel the need for that right now. I told Dr. Golden about it during our session the following day.

"Don't worry about it, Alice," he assured me. "Eventually you'll get strong enough to be around your mother without being adversely affected. In the meantime, give yourself some time and space."

"But I don't want to shut her out," I said. "I mean, she's been through so much too."

"No, don't shut her out. But perhaps for the time being you might communicate through letters. Writing can be quite therapeutic. Your mother might enjoy it too."

I'm pleased to say this is working well. My mother is opening up more and more, and I've discovered I can more adequately explain my feelings and progress through the pen.

Now Aaron is a whole different story. He's been here numerous times, and I have no problem visiting with him. We both laugh and joke a lot, and that feels pretty good. He asks some thought-provoking questions too. I can tell he's dealing with some of the same things that I am—things like negative childhood memories, false beliefs, old wounds, and weird family traditions. I had suspected that he was carrying a lot of baggage of his own, but now I think he might actually be recovering vicariously through my treatment. I think that's great. And I certainly hope that Aaron never goes through anything like I've experienced. But if he does, I will be the first one to leap to his aid and get him good help.

Simon returned to work last week. He still walks with a cane and a limp, but he says that he should be free of both in a month or so. Everyone was so glad to have him back that we decided to throw a big surprise party. He didn't expect that at all. I was so excited to see him again that I even helped Margot bake and decorate the cake! A real first for me.

But having him here hasn't been as wonderful as I'd imagined. I know this is my own fault, and it's a little embarrassing to admit, even to myself. But before I came to Golden Home, and even during my early days here, I liked to imagine that my relationship with Simon was special somehow. We talked on the phone almost daily, and I went to see him at the hospital a lot, and I suppose I developed something of a crush on him.

Now that he's here, I can see that he's closely involved with most of the residents, and everyone seems to love him. As a result I don't feel nearly so special anymore. At first I was pretty bummed, but I am trying to accept that he simply has this amazing rapport with almost everyone. I think he's gifted that way. It's probably just as well I don't have any individualized counseling sessions with Simon. Fortunately, I still meet with Dr. Golden. Simon leads my therapy group, though, and I think he's much better than the previous leader, Dr. Schlatz. Not that she wasn't good, but Simon has this easygoing' manner and a really sweet way of drawing people out.

After I recovered from my disappointment over my dashed romantic expectations with Simon, I realized that I should be thankful for the whole thing. Naturally, this realization only hit me after I confessed my feelings to Dr. Golden yesterday.

"Can you see how this was a good problem, Alice?" he asked me.

I shrugged. "Not really."

"Do you think you would've come here if Simon hadn't been involved?"

I considered this. "Probably not."

"I don't mean to sound trite, Alice, but perhaps God really does work in mysterious ways."

So now I believe that the whole thing with Simon was no mistake. Oh, my heart may still ache a bit. But even so, I will always care deeply for Simon. And I'm grateful that we're such good friends.

Last night we stayed in the common room just talking for several hours. I'm amazed at how we have similar interests in literature and movies and all sorts of things. He loves Emily Dickinson almost as much as I do, and he's seen *Casablanca* more times than I have. He's even an *Alice in Wonderland* fan, although he admits to preferring

C. S. Lewis to Lewis Carroll. It makes me appreciate the value of being able to carry on a "normal" conversation that isn't twisted by my paranoia or psychotic delusions. I'm so glad that Simon is getting to know me as I really am, especially since he's been through so much and seen me at my very worst. I've done a decent job of hiding my heartache from him, I hope. At the very least, my relationship with Simon has shown me the kinds of qualities I might look for in a husband someday. Not that I'm looking or even should be right now. I still can't believe that I actually thought I was in love with a guy like Shay Reynolds last fall. But I was on the verge of losing my mind back then too. Guess it all just figures.

I preregistered for spring term yesterday after Dr. Golden assured me that I'm ready, even though I'm not totally convinced.

"What's the worst thing that can happen?" he asked.

"I suppose I could drop a class or two or perhaps even fail them all."

"Would that be the end of the world?"

I smiled and shook my head. He likes to say this a lot. And so far he's been right. Besides, I'm only taking nine hours. I think I can handle it. And I get to continue living here. That will help a lot.

Faye has been coming on Tuesday afternoons and teaching five of us how to knit. Already I've completed a mohair scarf for my mother's birthday next week and am now attempting to make Cheshire a sweater, but I doubt he'll need it by the time I'm finished. I guess I'll just save it for next winter.

Right now we're getting ready to move the hardier plants from the greenhouse to the gardens. Julie says I have a green thumb. I have decided that when I leave—and I hate to even think about leaving—

I must have a place where I can keep my own little garden. Even if it's nothing more than a few terra-cotta pots of herbs and flowers. I agree with Julie that there's no activity as therapeutic as helping plants to grow. But that might just be me. Brad says that's how he feels about painting. I am a lousy painter, and yet I absolutely love the feel of soil between my fingers, not to mention that clean earthy smell and the warmth of sunshine on my face!

However, Julie has helped me see there's something else I love doing too. I guess Margot was right after all. It's funny I didn't figure this out sooner, but Julie said that's usually the way it goes when you're gifted in a certain area.

"Think about the things you do and totally lose track of time," she told me one day when I was frustrated about not being good at anything.

"Working in the greenhouse," I said.

She nodded. "And that's great, but I suspect there's something more, Alice. You're a very intelligent woman."

I thought about it long and hard. "I've always loved books," I finally told her. "And writing."

"Bingo!" she pointed her finger victoriously in the air.

I realize now that I *love* to write. Perhaps I was experiencing this to some degree when I was keeping my crazy journals, which seem to have disappeared off the face of the planet. But it's just as Julie said; every time I sit down to write, the time just seems to vanish. That's a good sign.

I suppose my English lit major wasn't too far off the mark from this goal, and Julie assures me that any good writer is usually a good reader, too, but I've decided to try out some journalism classes. And who knows? I may even change my major, but I'm not sure yet. Right now I'd be happy to have a degree of any kind. Dr. Golden keeps reminding me that I don't need to have all the answers to all my questions at once. It's enough that I simply keep moving forward, one step at a time.

So that's what I'm doing. Sometimes I imagine myself as a little kid who's learning to walk again, just putting one foot in front of the other. And if it's rocky or rough, I envision God walking alongside me and holding my hand. It's amazing how this simple mental image frees me up and helps dissolve my anxiety. I'm not saying I never get scared or worried, because I still do sometimes. But I get stronger every day, and I'm not so afraid of what lies ahead anymore.

chapter THIRTY-SEVEN

Finding Alice

I t's been nearly ten months since my first experience with psychosis and schizophrenia. As the other Alice once said, "I could tell you my adventures…but it's no use going back to yesterday, because I was a different person then."

Part of me can echo her sentiments completely because I *was* a different person then. Most of the time I would just as soon forget or even suppress those dark and confusing memories when I was experiencing psychosis and paranoia on a daily basis. And yet, unlike the other Alice, I believe there *is* some use in going back to yesterday. As long as you don't choose to dwell there too long or put down permanent roots, I think the willingness to open your eyes and look back can be helpful sometimes. If nothing more, it can ensure that you never pass that way again. And I certainly don't plan to go back there, at least not willingly.

I'm midway through my summer term, and it's because of my journalism class that I've chosen to retrace my steps. For my term project, I want to create a documentary of my own experiences in crazyland. So I have decided to go back and examine a few things about my life. My hope is to document my strange experiences, and perhaps this will prove helpful to someone else who is moving through those same dark passages. Sort of like *Alice's Adventures in Wonderland* with a schizophrenic twist.

In this documentary I will interview a number of the key characters, the ones I can find anyway. Dr. Golden approved of the idea but warned me to take it carefully and to gauge the amount of stress it might create for me.

"You must remain balanced and in control," he said finally. "But I think you're ready for this."

I decided to start at the beginning or as close as I can tell. So last week I made an appointment with Pastor John. Naturally Mary Cates wanted to know the exact nature of this appointment, but I managed to keep my answers vague. Today I return via stuffy Greyhound bus to my hometown, Warren. I go home first, where I plan to spend the night—the first time I've been home since last fall. My mother's pleased that I am visiting, but I see the look of alarm in her eyes when she hears that I'm going to see Pastor John.

"Oh, Alice!" she exclaims, clasping her hand over her mouth. "What are you thinking?"

"That I need to do this," I calmly tell her. "It's part of my documentary."

"But Pastor John!" She shakes her head. "He is so, so domineering."

"Only when we let him." I smile as I pick up my backpack. "Don't worry, Mom. I'll be just fine."

"Well, I'm calling my prayer group right this minute," she says as she rushes for the phone.

I nod and head toward the door. I can understand or at least respect her fear. Even though she has physically escaped the grasp of that controlling church, I sometimes think they still have a hold on her.

I begin to grow nervous as I wait in the dimly lit church foyer. Mary Cates, as usual, is sitting behind her gray metal desk, sneaking bites of some hidden, probably forbidden, pastry when she assumes I'm not looking. She appears to have put on even more weight. Or maybe I just hadn't noticed before. She glances anxiously at me, probably preparing herself for the likely event that I might need serious exorcising again. But I remain perfectly calm. My questions are written down in plain black and white, and my goal is to keep this interview as professional as possible.

Of course, that turns out to be impossible. Instead of answering my questions, Pastor John persists in hammering me with his own.

"You are a lost lamb, Alice," he tells me with a serious face. "You have wandered from the flock and been deceived by the wolf in sheep's clothing."

"I just want to ask you a few questions," I persist, wondering if I've come on a fool's mission.

"We're very worried about your eternal welfare," he continues, ignoring me. "You and your mother must return to the flock immediately, Alice. It's your only hope for salvation. You must repent of your sins—"

"I just wanted to ask about—"

"No, it is I who must ask you. Are you contrite for your sins? Are you ready to perform an act of penitence?"

I look down at my neatly printed questions. They are primarily about his ability to recognize the signs of mental illness in church members and how the clergy might be able to help them find adequate care. But he is going on and on, launching into a complete sermon about sin and repentance. I can see that he won't play according to my rules.

"Please, John," I try one more time, purposely deleting the title of "pastor," which I feel is undeserved. "I need to know if you understand anything about mental illness."

"Mental illness"—he stands now, puffing out his chest—"is nothing more than a New Age word for demonization, Alice." Now he leans forward and peers at me. "I think you and I both know that."

"You are wrong. Mental illness is very real and treatable—"

"Enough!" he shouts as he moves toward the door. "I will not listen to such blasphemy in God's holy house. You must leave, Alice. Unless you repent of your sin and rebuke Satan from your life, you are not welcome here."

I take a deep breath and stand, recalling an old Bible verse from my childhood, probably one learned in this very church. "Fine," I tell him. "And I will shake the dust from my feet as I go."

To my complete and utter relief, he has no response to this, but Mary Cates sputters as I catch her listening at the door.

"Have a good day," I tell her as I leave. Despite his lack of cooperation, I think I got the answers to my questions. Still, I find I must breathe deeply to calm myself as I walk toward my mother's house. I admire the neat lawns and colorful flower beds as I go. I hear the birds singing in the lush green canopy of trees overhead. I think how God has made a spectacularly beautiful world and am sorry that people like John Campbell go through life focusing on demons and shadows and just totally miss it.

My mother is anxiously waiting for me, and I confess that my mission was basically fruitless. Then I tell her I'd like to ask her a few questions. This naturally makes her even more nervous and anxious. So I try to keep my questions simple, direct, and somewhat clinical. My intent is not to lay blame, but merely to enlighten.

"Do you recall anything unusual during my early childhood?" I ask.

"No, you were perfectly normal."

"Did I ever receive a blow to the head?"

"No, never."

"Did I ever do anything different or—"

"I don't know why you're persisting in this, Alice. You were perfectly normal. Oh, perhaps a bit precocious at times and a little too smart. But perfectly normal."

"What about your birthing experience with me—anything unusual?"

She shakes her head now. "Normal, normal, normal."

Then just as I close my notebook, she says, "Wait a minute, Alice. I guess there's something that wasn't completely normal about your birth. It's funny how mothers forget these things once they're over with. But now that I think about it, you were turned around backward during your birth. Not that it's so unusual."

"Do you mean backward as in breech or backward as in facing the wrong way in the birth canal?" I ask quickly. I'd spent some time reading up on these things in Dr. Golden's library last winter. Various forms of birth trauma can mean something.

"Not breech, but facing the wrong way. Several church ladies came to the hospital and fervently prayed that you would turn around. But time just kept going by, and you didn't. Finally the doctor insisted on using forceps to turn you."

"I was a forceps delivery?" I ask, slightly amazed.

She nods. "But that's not such a big deal. Why is that important?"

I sigh. "Well, it might not mean anything, but one of the connections to schizophrenia, along with genetics, is head trauma during the birthing process."

"Oh."

I think she's about to cry now. "But don't feel bad, Mom. You couldn't help it. It's just good to know these things. Knowledge is like power, you know."

She nods, but I'm afraid she's not convinced. So I go over and hug her and tell her not to worry, that I'm just fine. I think she believes me. It occurs to me, not for the first time, that she is an extremely fragile woman. For a pleasant change, I'm so relieved that she's in a better church now, with some really nice friends who seem to love and support her. They may not be my cup of tea, but they seem to be good for her. Besides that, she's still wearing pants!

I return to the city feeling slightly disheartened. Other than the bit about the forceps delivery, I wonder if my trip home was a waste of time. Then I think about the time spent with my mother and figure that was worth something. Perhaps I needed to be reminded of John Campbell's true colors. In case I'd forgotten, which seems highly unlikely. However, part of my healing process at the Golden Home is to forgive anyone who has hurt me in the past. This is so they can't continue to hurt me in the future. Naturally, John would top this list, as well as many of the church members, particularly the leadership.

As I go over my encounters during my crazy era, I write about my brief visit to the commune and the anarchist rally. I think about the girl with the baby. I can't recall their names, some kinds of flowers I think, but I do remember thinking the baby was the Duchess's pig baby. It makes me laugh to realize that I honestly believed that! I wonder if I could find the commune but finally decide it's not that important to my documentary. Still I hope for the best for that girl and her baby; I hope she finds what she's looking for. I also remember the guy who gave me the ride back to Portland. The Mock Turtle. Poor guy, he probably had no idea he was transporting a crazy person. Still, I am thankful for his kindness.

I return to my old apartment and look for Mr. Scoggins. It's weird to be there, and I almost expect Amelia to pop in, but, thankfully, she doesn't. I can tell the old manager doesn't recognize me when he opens his door. When I tell him why I'm here, he looks a little uneasy; perhaps he thinks the crazy girl has returned to harm him in some way. I try to appear sane and businesslike as I explain that I'm working on a documentary and I want to get his perceptions.

"You mean I'll be on TV?" He opens his door wider now, stepping out into full view, glancing around as if he thinks I might actually have a camera crew with me.

"Well, it's just a written documentary right now." I pause. "But it's possible that it might be filmed someday. You never know." I don't think this is untrue because our professor mentioned this is how many television documentaries begin.

So I get out my minirecorder and ask him a few questions, and

Mr. Scoggins turns out to be a pretty interesting witness, although I'm not entirely sure if he's telling me real facts as he remembers them or just getting dramatic in case the cameras actually show up someday. He tells how Linda next-door was terrified of me, how she complained and wanted him to give her a new apartment. "She gave her notice right before you left. She said she didn't want to live in no nut house."

I tell him I'm sorry about all that and thank him for cooperating.

"No problem, little lady. Looks like you got things all worked out." He smiles now, and I notice he's got a gold front tooth. "Fact is, I think we're all a little crazy sometimes. It's all in how you look at things."

I tell him that I agree and then leave. I'm not sure how helpful his observations will be, but at least they're colorful.

Next I decide to head down to the river-front park, to the area where the homeless folks hang out, the corners and pockets that "normal" people tend to avoid. I notice how these spots seem a lot more crowded than last winter. I guess there are more homeless people in the summertime, or maybe they just come out of their hiding holes when the sun's out. I walk along for a bit, scoping out the riverbank in search of a pair of bright orange parkas, before it occurs to me that the Tweedles wouldn't be wearing winter coats on a warm, sunny day like this. Still, I figure they might be around here somewhere, or maybe I'll see someone who knows their whereabouts. I wish I could spot Betty Grable rambling along with a grocery cart. She'd be an easy one to recognize, and I'd really like to thank her for the red slippers. I still wonder what made her do that; it meant a lot to me at the time.

Finally I notice a guy who looks a lot like the bigger Tweedle, but he's sitting by himself on a park bench, and I'm not too sure. If I could remember his real name, I'd call out to him. I decide to walk over and get a better look, although I doubt it's really him. I can't imagine him without his quiet buddy at his side. But suddenly the guy glances up and actually seems to recognize me.

I can tell by the slightly goofy smile that it's him. I wave as I approach. "Do you remember me?"

He nods. "Alice."

"Yeah. I remember your face, but I forgot your name…"

"Martin."

"And your friend?"

"Cal?"

"Yeah. Where's Cal?" I glance around.

Martin looks down at his dirty feet, now clad in cheap rubber flip-flops, and frowns. "Cal's gone."

"Where'd he go?"

He looks up at me with damp eyes. "Cal died about a month ago."

Now I sit down on the bench next to him. "Oh, I'm so sorry, Martin." I shake my head wishing for something better to say.

"That stupid AIDS virus!" He leans over and pries a stone from the dirt, then chucks it into the river.

I put my hand on his arm. "But what about you, Martin? Have you been checked for the virus?"

He shrugs. "Who cares?"

I look into his eyes. "I care, Martin. You were a good friend to me when I needed it. Really, have you been tested?"

"Nah, what's the use?"

I'm not so sure myself, but somehow it seems important. "Can I help you in any way?"

Now he seems to peer at me as if he's really seeing me. "You're not homeless no more, are you, Alice?"

"No, I got some help. I was pretty crazy, huh?"

"Yeah. We kind of thought so. At first we thought you was just high. Then we figured you was pretty whacked. But you made us laugh a lot."

I'm not so sure about that, but I suppose I did provide some comic relief with my delusions. "You guys were good to me."

"Hey, what happened to your cat?"

"He's fine." I smile now. "Thanks to you guys and the cat, I stayed on with the Cat Lady. Her name's Faye, and she's really nice."

He nods. "Yeah, we thought maybe she was."

"But what about you, Martin? I'd like to help you—if you want help, that is. I realize it would have to be your choice."

That's when Martin starts pouring out his whole story about how his mom ran off with some guy when he was fourteen and how he lived with his dad for a while, but when his dad found out that he was gay, he threw him out of the house, and he'd been on the streets ever since.

"How old are you now?" I ask. It's hard to tell beneath the layers of grime.

"Seventeen."

"*Seventeen?*" I am shocked. "I thought you were about my age."

"Yeah, I was always big; people always took me for older." Then he tells me how he met Cal, who actually was older, twenty-five, and how Cal taught him to fend for himself and survive on the streets. "I would've died out here without Cal."

"But what about now, Martin? How are you going to take care of yourself now?"

"I been trying to get a job, but it's kind of hard when you look like crud." He holds out his filthy hands, and I can see his point.

"What about the mission?"

He firmly shakes his head. "No way. Cal always said they don't help people like us there."

"Like you?"

"You know. Gay."

"Oh."

He smiles again, revealing the missing tooth. But his smile doesn't look convincing. "Hey, don't worry about me, Alice. I'll be just fine."

I'm not so sure. I think about his situation for a moment before I speak. "Okay, Martin, this is what we're going to do. I'll give you some cash today. Use it for whatever you need. And then I'm going to speak to a friend of mine and see if he knows anyone who can help you. Okay?"

"Well, yeah, okay, I guess."

"Will you be down here tomorrow?"

He laughs now. "Don't know where else I'll be."

"Okay then. I'll find you tomorrow."

So I return to the Golden Home and immediately track down Simon and wait as he finishes a counseling session. After hearing my story, he gets right on the phone, and by the end of the day we have a men's halfway house that's willing to help Martin. The next day I return to the river park and find Martin. I tell him the news, but, naturally, he's a little skeptical at first. Then I tell him some of my own story and how it was hard for me to admit I needed help but how glad I am that I did. Finally he agrees to give it a try. First we go to a secondhand store, where we buy him some clothes, and then we ride the tram to the address and meet Richard, who runs the place.

"Hey, man," says Richard. "Come on in."

We go inside an old Victorian house that's a little run-down but feels friendly. Richard gives us the tour and shows Martin a room that he'll be sharing with three other guys. "Everybody helps out around the place," says Richard as he shows him a work chart.

I notice that Martin has tears in his eyes when I tell him I should go. I'm not sure if he's sad to see me leave, scared to be left behind, or just plain happy to have someone care. I guess it doesn't really matter.

When I check back a few days later, Martin seems to be doing just fine. He tells me he's had two interviews, one for a janitorial job and one for unloading freight at a discount store. Not only that, but Richard is helping him to study for his GED. I hug Martin and promise to stay in touch.

When I sit down to write my documentary, I wonder if all my work will produce much of anything as far as an actual term paper, but when I'm done, I think it has. If nothing else, I am more certain than ever that God had his hand on me during my whole bizarre experience. Of course, I may never know why he allows people to have mental illnesses. But if you think about it, nobody's life is perfect. Or, as Julie likes to say, "God doesn't give us perfect lives down here so that we can all look forward to heaven someday."

I turn in my paper and am pleasantly surprised to get an A+. The professor even asks if he can keep a copy as a sample for future students. Of course I agree. Then he invites me to work on the school's newspaper next fall. I know this is quite an honor and gladly accept his generous offer, and after thinking about it, I decide to officially change my major from English lit to journalism.

I used to resist change, back in BC. I think I had an intuitive fear that any drastic change might prove my undoing. In a way, I was right. But on the other hand, my "undoing" was inevitable. Now I can accept that some changes are good—in moderation anyway. I respect the need to keep my life in balance, and I realize I must make the changes that are improvements and avoid the rest. It's just part of being in control. I think about the other Alice and how her biggest problem was that she had absolutely no control. She was jerked and tossed about by a crazy world where she never knew what lurked around the next corner. Not so unlike schizophrenia. What a relief to be standing on this side now, looking back and hoping that I never have to go there again.

chapter THIRTY-EIGHT

Further Adventures

It's been a full year since that day last fall when Amelia showed up and turned my life inside out. It's fall term, and I am a completely different person than I was back then. And yet I am the same, only more so. I finally moved out of Golden Home. Selfishly, I didn't want to leave, but I know their waiting list is long, and there are people who need it more than I do at the moment. Besides that, I believe I am ready. I've been off all meds for nearly three months now. Ironically, after I had fought taking any meds so hard at one time, it was difficult to quit because I was worried the voices would return. Dr. Golden assured me it was completely my choice and I could go back on them if needed, but so far I haven't needed them. The big test, according to Julie, is moving out on my own.

"It's going to be stressful at first," she warns as she drives me to my new apartment. She continues her little lecture as we carry the second load of my stuff up the stairs. "Give yourself time to adjust to the new surroundings, and don't expect too much from yourself at first."

She sets a pretty planter of lavender and rosemary, a house-warming gift from her, on the small kitchen counter. "And don't be surprised if you don't sleep very well at first." She digs in her purse until she locates a small bottle, then holds it out to me. "There's only a week's worth of sleeping pills in here, and you may not need them at all, but Jack told me to give them to you just in case. Be sure to use them if you have any trouble sleeping. It's better than allowing yourself to get exhausted and stressed, which can really set you back. And try to keep all your basic habits the same; continue sleeping and eating right." She laughs at herself. "Oh well, I'm sure you know my little spiel by heart now." Then she hugs me. "I'm really going to miss you, Alice."

"But I'll see you when I come in for my appointments and group sessions," I remind her. "And I want to have you and Dr. Golden over for dinner once I get more settled."

"Yes, but it's still hard to see you leave." Then she smiles. "Just the same, I'm so happy for you. It's like graduation day."

And so it is, I tell myself as I wave to her from the top of the stairs. Even so I feel a little uncertain. Not to mention alone. It's amazing how quickly I became accustomed to group living and the comfort that came from being around friends.

After a full week, I think I am slowly adjusting to being alone. Julie was right about not sleeping at first, and I found I did need help for the first couple of nights, but after that I began to relax. I slowly got back to my old routines and now feel fine. I'm taking a full load of classes this term, and I'm beginning to appreciate the ability to come and go as I please, keeping my own schedule and studying for uninterrupted hours if needed. I can see now that this was exactly the right thing for me. And although I'm still a bit lonely sometimes, I do enjoy the sense of being independent again.

I went in for my counseling and therapy as usual this week, and it was reassuring to see my old friends again. I realize more than ever how they are like family to me, and I plan to maintain those relationships indefinitely. After my group therapy session, Simon took me aside and asked how it was going. I told him that I'm getting used to it and that I like being on my own. He seemed pleased. Then he surprised me by asking if he could drop by and see my place sometime. Of course I assured him he was always welcome.

Three days have passed since then, and he hasn't stopped by yet. I know I shouldn't have gotten my hopes up like that, because I'm sure Simon was only trying to be friendly and encouraging. But I suppose I actually thought that he planned to show up the very next day. And, naturally, I'm disappointed that he hasn't. I need to remember to be more realistic about life.

Now it's Saturday, and with no classes I am trying to get this place a little better organized. Aaron and a couple of his football buddies came by last night and helped me get some of my old things out of storage. So now I have all these strange and slightly bedraggled boxes piled all over the place. It's the stuff my mom put into storage from my last apartment, back when my madness first set in and I was, in essence, evicted. But I must admit the presence of these old things is a bit unsettling. They remind me of an era I'd just as soon forget or at least not think about too much. Sometimes it's a little depressing to consider what was lost during the past year, although I realize it's a natural part of the grief process and a step in my ongoing healing.

I know my brother and his friends were trying to be helpful, and there's no reason I shouldn't simply plunge in and sort through this stuff, but just seeing these cardboard boxes heaped around my apartment is disturbing. It's not that I plan to pile the boxes into walls and use them to barricade my bed. And I've had no visits from my old "friend" Amelia. Still it's a bit unnerving, and I'm not quite sure how to proceed.

Consequently, it seems perfectly natural that I nearly jump out of my shoes to hear a knock at my door. With a pounding heart, I go to open it, peeking out the peephole first, to discover it is only Simon. He has a potted plant in his hand.

"Come in," I tell him with relief as I fling open the door. "And please excuse the mess. I'm still getting settled in."

He smiles and looks around. "You need a hand?"

I consider this, unsure that I want Simon to see all my weird junk. Who knows what we'll find in those old boxes? So feeling a bit silly, I explain the peculiar circumstances and how I'm uneasy, but he just laughs and says, "Hey, let's just roll up our sleeves and get it over with."

It turns out that Simon is a whiz at unpacking and organizing. He seems to have an innate sense for what is and is not junk. He doesn't even seem terribly surprised when he opens up a taped box that contains the smashed components of what used to be my perfectly good computer. However, I want to cry when I consider the waste.

"It's just a *thing,* Alice," he reassures me. "Things are replaceable. You, on the other hand, are not."

I appreciate his sensibilities, and when it's all said and done, I really don't know what I would've done without him today.

"How can I begin to thank you?" I ask as we haul the final remnants of the packing materials out of my apartment.

He seems to seriously consider my question as we walk toward the recycling area. But his face is grim, and he doesn't say a word. Consequently I grow fairly uncomfortable. It suddenly occurs to me that Simon didn't have to spend his free day doing this, and I'm sure he could've found something or someone else much more interesting to occupy his time. Now I begin to feel seriously guilty.

"Really," I continue in earnest. "You have been a godsend today. I owe you big time. I hope you'll let me repay the favor someday." I even consider offering to cook him a meal but am well aware that my culinary abilities aren't much of a reward for anyone just yet.

"Well, there is something you can do." He turns around after stuffing the last of the cardboard in the receptacle.

"Sure, just tell me." I wait.

He removes his dust-coated glasses, then takes his time to carefully clean the lenses on the tail of his denim shirt.

I continue waiting, shamelessly staring at those dark eyes and thick lashes while he's too occupied to notice.

He replaces his glasses, then looks at me and grins in what seems a truly sheepish fashion, like a little boy who's been caught sneaking candy. "Well, Alice," he begins slowly, "you could go out with me."

I stare at him in shock. I wonder if I heard him correctly. Is he actually asking me to date him, or did I just imagine it? It takes me a moment to get my bearings, and I can tell my hesitation is making him uncomfortable.

"I'm sorry," he says with a quick shake of his head. "I shouldn't have said that, Alice." He waves a hand and smiles. "Just forget it."

"Wait a minute." I put my hand on his arm. "Did you just ask me to go out with you?"

He shrugs. "Well, I shouldn't pressure you—"

"Pressure me?"

"Well, we're not allowed to date residents and—"

"But I'm not a resident." My hopes rise.

He nods. "I know."

"So are you serious then?"

He glances away, and now I'm worried he's having second thoughts. Just the same, I do not plan to let this opportunity slip away without a good fight. I step forward and peer up into his face. "Look, Simon, if you're really asking me to go out with you—I mean I don't want to pressure you either—but my answer would definitely be yes."

His eyes light up. "Really? You'd go out with me?"

"Of course, Simon. I'd like to go out with you." I want to tell him that I've longed to go out with him, that I've dreamed of going out with him. But at the same time I don't want to overwhelm him and scare him off.

"Well, all right then." He sighs, then surprises me by taking my hand and giving it a squeeze. "I've been waiting a long time for this, Alice."

"Really?" I study him curiously. "Just how long?"

"Since the Christmas party last year."

"Are you serious?" I am doubtful. "But I was a real nut case back then."

He grins. "A totally lovable nut case."

I laugh and hug him and look forward to the day when I can tell him how much I love him. But not today. If I have learned anything this past year, it's to take things more slowly, more carefully, intentionally. Avoid too many ups and downs. It's not that I suppress my emotions exactly or deny their existence—certainly they are just as alive and real as ever—but I do try to mange them better. I make an effort to keep my thoughts and feelings under control. I know that if I control them, they have less control over me, and as a result my life will flow more smoothly and evenly. And that is a good thing.

It's like that kite I made so many years ago. I had the right idea, and it was a beautifully constructed kite with such a lovely sunny face, but without a tail to control its flight, it was destined for failure. God is the tail to my kite now. His influence balances me, holds me steady in my flight, and allows me to reach new heights without the constant threat of wrecking.

Does that mean I have no worries or concerns for my future? That I don't wake up in the middle of the night frightened by memories of things unseen, unheard by others? Of course not; I am only human. But like the kite that takes to the sky, pitched against a blustery wind with the power to shred it to pieces, I welcome each new day with the hopeful expectancy that I, too, will rise above the ordinary. For I am not content to live a merely "normal" life or settle for an average existence. No, I am destined for more—much, much more.

Traditional Book Resources

Rachel Miller and Susan E. Mason, eds., *Diagnosis: Schizophrenia* (New York: Columbia University Press, 2002).

E. Fuller Torrey, *Surviving Schizophrenia: A Manual for Families, Consumers, and Providers* (New York: Quill, 2001).

Progressive Resources

Richard Gosden, *Punishing the Patient: How Psychiatrists Misunderstand and Mistreat Schizophrenia* (Carlton North, Victoria, Australia: Scribe Publications, 2001).

Sylvia Nasar, *A Beautiful Mind: The Life of Mathematical Genius and Nobel Laureate John Nash* (Waterville, Maine: Thorndike Press, 2002).

Robert Whitaker, *Mad in America: Bad Science, Bad Medicine, and the Enduring Mistreatment of the Mentally Ill* (Cambridge, Mass.: Perseus Publications, 2003).

Web Sites and Telephone Numbers:

successfulschizophrenia.com

National Mental Health Association (NMHA)
1-800-969-NMHA

www.nmha.org
www.nmha.org/infoctr/factsheets/51.cfm

National Alliance for the Mentally Ill (NAMI)
1-800-950-NAMI; for EMERGENCY call: 1-800-784-2433
www.nami.org

National Alliance for Research on Schizophrenia and Depression
    (NARSAD)
1-800-829-8289
www.narsad.org

National Institute of Mental Health
301-443-4513
www.nimh.nih.gov

A Word from the Author

One of my goals as a writer is to make readers *think*. I love books that stretch me as a person, and I like being transported to places I might not normally have the opportunity to experience. Sometimes those are difficult places, places where life doesn't flow in a straight line. And much of my recent writing reflects this. I like to tell stories about some of the less traveled roads. Or at least those that often go unspoken of and unseen, particularly within the church culture that exists in our country today.

I truly believe that God wants us to use the various trials from our own life journeys. Why else would we be faced with so many unfortunate situations? I'm amazed at how many trials and tribulations I've personally witnessed. Challenges like watching loved ones struggle to find their way through mental illness, addiction, or disorders. It's not easy to watch your own children contending against such fierce foes, but in the end I feel that I'm a better person for it. Or at least I hope so. And I hope that I've been more than just a spectator along the way. I pray that I've shared whatever portion of comfort and encouragement I have to offer and that my tears have not been in vain.

My prayer for my readers and myself is that we will learn to embrace life and all its disappointments and upsets and surprises. That we will begin to see God never meant it to be perfect or normal or, worse, ordinary. But he meant it to be *lived*. Lived to the fullest—with him by our side—celebrating the adventure of love and mercy and grace!